Hold Me TODAY

MARIA LUIS

HOLD ME TODAY

PUT A RING ON IT

MARIA LUIS

ALKMINI BOOKS, LLC

Rock bottom has never felt so good.

At least, that's what I tell myself when I bargain with the enemy and score a renovation for my hair salon.

The enemy? Nick Stamos, my best friend's older brother.

He's got a body and face the Greek gods would envy but his personality needs a major overhaul.

He's surly.
A rule-follower.
Did I mention he's seen me *naked*?

I may have crushed on him for years, but the only place I want Nick swinging his hammer nowadays is at my salon.

Except, he needs something in return. . .

A fake girlfriend.

And I'm just reckless enough to say *yes.*

Hold Me Today (Put A Ring On It, Book 1)
Maria Luis

Cover Photographer: Wander Book Club Photography

Cover Models: Zack Salaun and Dina A.

Cover Designer: Najla Qamber, Najla Qamber Designs

Editing: Kathy Bosman, Indie Editing Chick

Proofreading: Dawn Black; Tandy Proofreads

❀ Created with Vellum

To Theia Mina, the original Ermione "Mina."' Life is not as bright without you in it. I miss you daily, and I hope - that if you were to ever have had the chance to read this book - you would have done so with a laugh and a few of your favorite four-letter words. S'agapo.

Good job, honey.

AUTHOR'S NOTE

Culture plays a big role in *Hold Me Today,* and it was important to me that we hear our hero and heroine speak the Greek language. As a Greek-American raised in Boston, much like Nick and Mina themselves, I have made sure that all words used in the book are explained within the context of the story. To note, Mina's full name "Ermione" is pronounced: *Er-me-o-nee.*

1

NICK

ON A BEACH SOMEWHERE IN BALI

Breaking hearts isn't in my DNA.

Call me a pussy, a romantic, a believer in the unicorn of all emotions—true love—but I want the real deal. I crave what my parents have shared for thirty-something years; what my younger sister Effie has with her wife; what I *almost* had six years ago before my ex-fiancée dumped me at the altar with a half-hiccupped, "I'm in love with someone else."

That *someone else* turned out to be her I-wear-pocket-protectors-like-a-douchebag boss, the bastard.

So, yeah, I'm talking about the white-picket-fence, make-love-even-when-you-haven't-showered happily-ever-after. The kind that sinks into your bones and accelerates your heart rate and turns your hands into a clammy mess.

My hands aren't clammy now. They're ice cold despite the balmy weather and the fact that I'm wearing a Hawaiian T-shirt the color of puke and a pair of too-tight board shorts that hug my crotch the same incessant way my grandmother anxiously squeezes her stress-relief balls.

"Women will *love* that bulge," the wardrobe crew assured me with a pat on the shoulder.

The women might, but there's a good chance my ability to reproduce will die today.

"Gamóto."

The Greek curse for "fuck" flies off my tongue, as it has since my teenage years when my Greek mother warned me and Effie against using English profanity in public. I've never been more grateful for speaking two languages than when I showed up on set for *Put A Ring On It,* a reality show that might as well be the budget-cut edition of the infamous *The Bachelor* franchise.

See: the Hawaiian T-shirt and board-shorts bit.

I shift my hips and pray for relief.

The small, velvet box burns in the front pocket of my shorts as I face down the production crew. Louder, in perfectly clear English, I grind out, "I can't do this."

"Buck up, Stamos," rumbles Joe, the show's director. He side-eyes me like I'm a caged animal clawing for escape, then casually claps me on the back like we're best buds. I'd have to be tone-deaf to miss his hearty, *fuck-you* laugh. *Prick.* If I wasn't determined to leave this island uncuffed, I'd throw a fist right at his pretty-boy, Hollywood face. "It's only pre-engagement jitters. You love her, dontcha?"

It was easy to think so in the midst of orchestrated dinner dates and cameras being shoved into my face and producers pointedly asking, "How do you feel? You love her yet?"

I haven't answered "yes" once. And now that it's down to me and one other contestant, the questions have narrowed down to the most vital: "How are you gonna propose?" It's all I can do not to ditch the wannabe-surfer outfit and make a break for it, away from the white, sandy beach where Savannah Rose is waiting.

She deserves better than what I can offer: nothing but a

gut-deep awareness that marrying her would be the equivalent of getting hitched to myself. I like me—hell, I even enjoy my own company most days—but there's a reason why my mom thanked the Good Lord that I didn't turn out to be a twin, like the doctor first predicted. Thirty-two years later, she's still pinching my cheek and praising her lucky stars like she won the MegaBucks.

So, yeah, me and Savannah? Despite the high hopes I had coming onto the show, we turned out to be the same blend of black and white, equally balanced in temperament, opinions, and our shared preference for the introverted, hermit life.

Savannah Rose is lovely, but I just don't *love* her.

I open my mouth, ready to flay Joe alive with the reminder that, according to the contract I signed before embarking on this shit show of a journey, I can leave whenever the hell I want. Including on the last day of production, when I and the other runner-up are expected to get down on bended knee and propose.

Joe beats me to the punch. "Listen, Nick. Fact is, you gotta do it now, 'kay?" He thrusts a finger at the narrow cobblestoned pathway that leads from the cottage I've been sharing with my fellow contestant, Dominic DaSilva, to the beach. "Right there. She's waiting for you *right down there*. You gonna disappoint her? You gonna let insecurities cloud your judgment? You said you loved her only last night!"

The hell I did.

"Joe," I grunt, shoving one hand into my pocket to grab the engagement-ring box, "I'm not doing it. Not for you, not for TV, and definitely not for Savannah Rose. She came here lookin' for love and I'm not going to be that asshole who lies to her for the sake of good ratings, you hear me?"

I slam the velvet box down on the entryway table to my right.

And, because the gravitational pull of the universe is a

conniving son of a gun, the box skids as I let go, turning over onto its side and falling from the table.

Crashing to the floor.

Cracking wide open.

The diamond ring, which probably costs more than my restoration business is worth back in Boston, pops out from the box. It circles on the tile floor, once, twice, before teetering flat on its side. Sardonically, I lift a brow. "If that isn't an ironic show of how this is about to go down, then I don't know what is."

Joe's knees pop as he snatches the ring off the floor and shoves it back into the box. With a speed I don't anticipate, he crams the whole thing into the pocket of my shorts and comes mighty damn close to fondling the family jewels.

Full confessional: there's not much wriggle room in these things.

I arc my ass backward, away from his wandering hands. *"Jesus!* What the hell are you doing, man?"

"Earning myself a damn paycheck." He jabs an accusatory finger in my face. "You're going out there with this fuckin' ring, Stamos, you hear me? You're gonna get down on one knee and we'll let Savannah know before filming rolls that you want out. She'll do the dumping, not you."

My jaw drops without ceremony. "You've got to be kidding me. I told you yesterday that I wanted to talk to her without the cameras. I don't want to hurt her. She's a great girl—"

"But she's not the one for you." Joe rolls his eyes and twiddles his fingers in the air like a complete asshat. "Yada, yada, yada. I've heard this shit before when I was working with Chris-fuckin'-Harrison on *The Bachelor*. You think this is my first rodeo? No, Mr. Adonis, it's not. We're doing this my way since it's my goddamn show. And *my* way is letting Savannah land the proverbial kick to your balls. *Capiche*?"

"No fucking *capiche*."

Savannah isn't any more in love with me than I am with her, if the few lackluster kisses we've shared are anything to go by. And that was all before we unanimously agreed to skip the overnight date last week. The way I look at it, that decision hammered the final nail in our coffin. I'm no virgin, and she isn't either, which leads to only one conclusion: neither of us are feeling the chemistry.

It's disappointing, yeah, considering I showed up at the *Put A Ring On It* house with big hopes of leaving with the love of my life. Sure, I only ended up *on* the show because Effie was convinced that I was failing—epically—in the dating department on my own. She wasn't wrong, much as it grates me to admit it. I have a bad habit of choosing women who, in the end, don't choose me back. And maybe there's something to be said for letting someone else play matchmaker for once. Clearly, I haven't been doing myself any favors since Brynn stormed out of that church.

After I pulled my head out of my ass (and my sister chewed me out for being a stick in the mud), I gradually warmed up to the idea of meeting a woman I never would have crossed paths with in my routine, day-to-day life in New England.

Hello, my name is Nick Stamos and I'm a closet romantic.

Sue me.

End of the day: it didn't work out. But that doesn't mean I'm keen on ending the relationship with lies tripping off the tongue. My mom taught me better. My dad taught me better.

And, yet, ten minutes later I find myself being led, like a lamb to the slaughter, down to the beach. I spot Savannah Rose immediately—it's hard not to. With her caramel skin, thanks to her Creole heritage, and her rich, dark hair, Savannah is a show-stopper. Tall and willowy, she dropped jaws throughout filming, whether it was when she stepped out in a dress for a night out on the town or put on a bikini while relaxing on the beach. She's serenity personified, rarely raising her voice, though I'd have to be an idiot not to notice that her spine is laced with steel.

Like I said, the two of us are peas in a pod. Reserved. Sometimes shy. But with unwavering backbone—being taken advantage of isn't a concern.

My molars grind together as Joe waves me forward from where he sits beside the camera crew. They're camped out between two sky-high palm trees, as though the rotund barks are wide enough to provide some sort of coverage and conceal them from sight.

To provide us with the illusion of privacy.

My hands clench at my sides.

Do the right thing, I shout at myself. *Get down there and do the right thing.*

I'm not a bad guy. Hell, I've always been the *good guy,* if I'm being real honest about it. The guy mothers love. The one they have no qualms about their daughters spending time with because, "that Nick, he's just *such* a nice person."

I don't feel all that nice right now.

Don't feel all that good either.

My bare feet sink into the warm sand as I come to a stop before Savannah. She peers up at me through long, spiky lashes. I hold onto her dark gaze, trying to get a read on her. Has Joe told her a damn thing? Has he relayed the message that I need to tell her myself—that I don't love her the way she deserves to be loved?

That I can't propose forever with her, let alone the rest of today?

Her pink, glossy lips curl in greeting, offering a shy smile that sucker punches me in the gut.

She doesn't know. No way in hell would she smile at me like that—or at *all*—if she knew how I really feel.

Ah, *fuck*.

I slide a quick glance over to Joe, who keeps his attention locked on the monitor set up before him.

He wants his good TV. It's his job, and I get that too.

But that doesn't mean I'll willingly ruin mine and Savannah Rose's lives to pacify the public's demand for cheap shots and trashy entertainment.

"Nick," Savannah Rose murmurs, her gentle New Orleans accent barely audible over the crashing of the ocean waves behind her, "I just want to say how—"

"*Óxi*."

She blinks. Then blinks again. "I'm sorry, what—"

"Do you remember what I taught you when we were in Australia?" If Joe wants to publicly humiliate me, I'll go along —but only if Savannah catches on, and he's clearly passed along nothing of what I told him. *So much for letting her hold the reins.* The asshole obviously didn't plan to tell her anything, preferring to send her into today's proposal as blind as a damn bat. "The Greek words?" I prompt when she says nothing.

"Well, yeah, I think—" She scrunches her nose, clearly trying to recall our exact conversation from a few weeks back. "*Óxi, óxi* that means . . ."

I refuse to look away until the word registers in her head.

No. It means *no*.

And I'm banking on her understanding everything that I'm not saying, so she can keep her pride and hold her chin up high when it's obvious that Joe the Prick wants nothing more than to see her fall—and watch the show's ratings skyrocket in contrast.

"Oh."

The word emerges from her mouth, small, hesitant, and then she's blinking away, running a hand through her dark hair and nodding, nodding, nodding, like she's trying to get her brain back into the game plan.

Tell me no, I mouth slowly, *tell me no*.

I drop to one knee, just as she fixes her gaze on my face.

Her eyes are clear, her mouth relaxed and un-pinched. My guilty conscience kicks in, and, dammit, but I'm seriously hoping that she was prepared to accept Dom's ring today. That'll make this easier for the both of us when we go our separate ways.

I'm sorry, Savannah Rose.

I never break hearts.

Until today.

2

MINA

BOSTON, MASSACHUSETTS

"My heart feels like it's going to give out."

The words leave me on a rough exhale, and my best friend does nothing but shove a glass of vodka-on-the-rocks into my hand like it's the cure to end all shit-tastic days. "It's called anxiety," Effie Stamos tells me, all no-nonsense attitude and calm-in-the-middle-of-my-storm as she sips from her own glass. If she thinks it's weird that we're camped out in my unfinished hair salon, guzzling booze like it's our job, she doesn't say so out loud.

Her dark eyes flit over me, though, no doubt cataloguing my very obvious lack of fucks to give. I haven't showered in days. Haven't shaved in days either. If I cared to look in the mirror, which I don't—the scent clinging to my skin and clothes are all I need to know that I look like hell—I'm very certain I'd come face-to-face with the modern-day Yeti. It's not a look I'd ever suggest to one of my clients when they come in to get their hair cut.

Then again, I don't have clients anymore either.

My heart seizes again, lungs clamping tightly, and I briefly contemplate ditching the dainty glass Effie's given me for the entire bottle instead. Nothing says *Yay For Hitting Your New Low* than drinking to excess on a weeknight.

"Alcohol always helps," Effie says from her perch on the far side of the sofa. There's at least three feet separating us, which I'm sure is her way of trying to avoid the stink that is currently me. *Smart lady.* "Stub your toe," Effie continues, lifting her glass in a toast, "drink Tito's. Flat tire, drink Tito's." Her dark eyes light with a forced, let's-laugh-this-one-out-together humor. "Find out that your handyman ran out on you with your check for ten-thousand dollars—"

I'm lunging for the bottle off the coffee table before she even finishes her sentence. The vodka tickles and warms its way down the back of my throat, a reminder that I rarely drink anything heavier than wine or a fruity cocktail weighted with more calories than a burger from McDonald's. I've never been one for the Skinny Girl menu.

Effie's mouth twitches.

"Just say it," I mutter morosely, waving the bottle in her direction. "I'm an idiot. A screw-up. A—"

"I was actually thinking about the fact that he took your lucky penny."

"*Bastard.*" I down another mouthful of Tito's and pray to the alcohol gods that I won't be tossing up my cookies tomorrow morning. A hangover is not in the plans—then again, neither was trusting a scammer.

"Who *does* that?" I point Tito to the far side of my newly purchased hair salon, which is empty save for the sofa we're sitting on and the cute receptionist's desk I picked up at an antiques sale a few weekends back. "It wasn't enough that he took the ten-K? The jerk went through *my* desk and took *my* lucky penny. I've had that thing since your mom gave it to me on prom night."

Aleka Stamos, the hairdresser who gave me my first pair of shears, promised that if I kept the lucky penny on me, one day I'd have the chance to see it in my very own register at my very own hair salon. *Envision your dreams,* she said, *manifest them into reality*. The penny's copper was worn down, smoothed thrice over, and had survived over a decade of being almost handed over to cashiers time and again. Well-earned battle scars, only to be swiped from my register before I even opened *Agape*'s front doors.

"I'm telling you," I mutter darkly, "that crossed a line." Another pull from Tito the Great. "*Bastard.*"

"You're starting to sound repetitive."

My brows lower. "I'm drunk."

"You've had one shot and approximately three gulps of vodka, half of which is drenching your shirt."

I glance down, and sure enough, not only am I pulling a Yeti in terms of hair growth, I look like I've taken a dunk in a pool of D-grade vodka.

What a good look, Miss New CEO.

I can't even find it in myself to crack a smile at my poor attempt at sarcasm.

Since my teenage years, I've worked toward only one dream: running my own hair salon. I've never wanted anything else, never deviated from the path I set into motion after the first time I watched Tyra Banks on *America's Next Top Model*. Call me crazy, but the show—dramatic as each season was—gave me hope.

I was never the smart girl in school. A *C* was as good as an *A* in my book—considering all the work and sweat and tears that the *C* cost me. My inability to keep up with my peers in class was then matched by my very Greek and *very* traditional father, who thought sports were a waste of time, as were other extracurriculars like drama and singing. I was, effectively, particularly good at doing nothing. Unless you included my expert skills at babysitting. As the eldest of the three Pappas siblings, I was tasked with taking care of Katya and Dimitri every day after school.

For *years*.

And that included helping with their homework, which, no surprise there, was more hellish than burning off my eyebrows for just the fun of it.

Back then, I craved the confidence I saw in those women on the show. I craved their vitality and their uncontained excitement and the way they stood proudly as though to publicly declare, *This is who I am, and you can either love it or kiss my butt.*

I wanted their swagger.

And it may have taken some time, but I learned to cultivate that same swagger for myself until—

"I need a plan."

Effie eyes me warily. "How about we wait till tomorrow when you aren't on the verge of a meltdown?" She casts a quick glance about the empty salon. Before I bought the space, and the small apartment above it, the building had housed a floral shop. A few potted plants still linger here and there, their soil dry and leaves bronzing, even though I've done my best to keep them alive.

Turns out that a hairdresser and a horticulturalist are not synonymous occupations, despite the fact that shears are used for both.

My best friend takes another sip of Tito. "How long are you going to make us sit down here in the dark? It's creepy."

Ambient light filters in through the bare windows, basking the concrete floors in shadowy figures. Instead of a building meant to kickstart my hopes and dreams, the eerie vibe tonight gives the space more of a haunted-house-attraction appeal. "You own a ghost tour company," I say, cupping the vodka bottle to my damp chest like a babe about to suck on a nipple, "creepy may as well be your middle name."

Rolling her eyes, Effie points a finger at me. "You need a lawyer."

"I need money for a lawyer." Feeling the all-too-familiar punch to my gut, I strangle the neck of the vodka bottle and try to stem the well of tears burning at the backs of my eyes. I don't cry—haven't for years—and I have no plans to start now. But, jeez, learning that Jake Rhodan disappeared with money intended to cover a third of the renovation costs is crippling. Like a kick to a blistering wound when I'm already down and bleeding. "I've already reported him to the cops but nailing his ass to a wall isn't possible until they find him." My vision swims like I've put on a pair of drunk goggles. Oh, right—I *am* drunk. The room is positively *swaying.* And when did Effie get a twin? I close one eye. Stare a little harder with my other. Plant a flat palm on the cushion beside me and curse Tito while trying not to slur my words. "What money is left has to go to finding a new reno company or I'm *totally* screwed."

Confession: Effie and I both know that I'm already screwed.

Though I once worked for Effie's mom, I've spent the last few years at Twisted, a high-end spa and salon situated in Boston's ritzy Beacon Hill neighborhood. I cut the hair of congresswomen and celebrities, all while scraping together every penny until I could open my own salon.

Agape, my salon, is the pinnacle of my career.

Unfortunately, I must be on the universe's naughty list because I've been slapped back down more times than I can count in these last few months.

First, my former boss pulled out the contract I signed years earlier without paying much attention to the finer details. It stated, in no uncertain terms, that while I could open a salon within close proximity to Twisted, I was legally bound to one stipulation: I couldn't bring my clients with me.

Yay to starting from scratch.

And then, of course, I committed the ultimate error in trusting a recommendation for the renovation itself. Seeing as how the reference came from a friend of a friend, from back in high school, I see now that I should have treaded more carefully.

As in, I should have gone with the glaringly obvious choice.

Nick Stamos.

CEO/Head Honcho/He-Who-Does-Not-Smile of Stamos Restorations and Co.

Effie's older brother.

Also, the bane of my existence . . . and my teenage crush.

But Nick was off galivanting around the world for his thirties-life-crisis, the sober part of my brain offers up, as though reminding me that, *Hey, this is why you didn't ask him in the first place.*

I don't actually know *why* Nick skipped town—for once, Effie didn't spill the beans—but Drunk Me nevertheless shushes Sober Me, and baldly announces, "I need your brother."

My best friend chokes on her vodka. "You hate him."

"I'm desperate."

"If he heard you say that, you'd never live it down."

"I never live anything down when it comes to him," I grumble, not even bothering to hide the exasperation lacing my tone. This is why no one should ever be judged for youthful infatuations. All those hormones brewing—it messes with the brain and causes severe lapses in judgment, like that time I convinced myself that Chris was the hottest *NSYNC member. Two decades later and I don't even remember what Chris looks like. "I swear to God that man has a memory like an elephant. Nothing ever gets past him. It's annoying. *He's* annoying."

"Like an *elephant*?" Effie's brows lift with curiosity.

"Elephants never forget." When she stares at me blankly, I roll my eyes and help myself to more vodka. "I saw it on *Jeopardy*. Anyway, that doesn't matter. What *does* matter is that I have a plan."

"A plan for my brother to overhaul this sad, empty shell of a space into something beautiful?"

I nod sharply and feel the corresponding roll of nausea crawl through my belly. *Motion-sickness and I'm not even driving*. The back of my skull collides with the sofa's armrest, the sole of my foot crashing down to the floor like dead weight.

This must be what rock bottom feels like: cradled Tito's bottle, unshaven armpits and an unwaxed upper lip, and the single prayer that the one man who I'd prefer to avoid for the rest of my life is now my only hope.

Rock bottom sucks, big time.

"He doesn't come cheap."

I sigh, resignation settling heavily over my chest like the set of dumbbells I purchased years ago and have never used. Cutting hair all day means my biceps and arms are perfectly lean. The same, however, cannot be said for my butt and thighs, both of which fight my jeans on the regular. J.Lo has nothing on the Pappas butt, as the women in my family like to say.

"No, Effie," I tell my best friend, "he doesn't come cheap."

It's a good thing he owes me—and I'm finally ready to collect.

3

MINA

"Holy shit, this is going to be the best damn pee of my life, I'm telling you right now."

Tulle and lace and pearl beading fill my hands to overflow as I keep my gaze locked on the bride's upturned face—not that I can see anything below the belt.

Effie's cousin Toula hovers ass over toilet, her wedding dress hiked up to her shoulders, as she manhandles the metal handicap railing with one hand and clutches my forearm with the other to keep from toppling over. One wrong knee bend and she'll be face down . . . or ass up, depending on which direction gravity pulls.

Her stiletto heel skids across the linoleum with a whine as she tries to redistribute her weight. She wobbles, eyes flicking up to meet mine in panic, and then sinks her pointy, coffin-shaped fingernails into my forearm.

"You owe me," I tell her as her shoe connects with mine. When Toula asked that I come with her to the bathroom to check her hair before the wedding reception, there'd been no mention of "bathroom" duties. *This is what happens when you play nice with everyone—you risk the possibility of being peed on.* I inch my shoes back a solid two inches in self-preservation. "I don't care if you saved me way back when after I got stuck in a bathroom stall and couldn't get out. We're talking—"

"Don't Rose and Jack me, Mina," Toula pleads with all the drama of an actress, which is, to the surprise of no one, her day job. "I'm too young to go out like this."

The urge to roll my eyes has never been more potent. "The toilet isn't the damn Atlantic Ocean, Tou—" A stray layer of tulle sticks to my mouth, my glossy lipstick acting like suction, and I spit out the fabric, batting it away before *I'm* the one succumbing to Death by Wedding Dress.

"Eep, don't let go!" Toula cries out.

With nimble hands, I grab the dress before any bits of tulle can take a dip in the toilet water. A relieved sigh stabs me in the chest when I catch it all. No doubt I look like Easter threw up all over me—so much tulle, so much lace. All I need are the bunny ears and a carrot. "All right, you're good. Go forth with the mission."

"I can't tell if I'm over the toilet."

Oh, for the love of—

I yank the dress skirt higher, out of the way of impending disaster. "Squat and pray. Just squat and pray."

And please don't pee on my shoes.

Toula screws her eyes shut, her mouth pursing in overt concentration. Good Lord, she might actually be praying. Laughter climbs my throat, just as the trickling, telltale sound of urine hitting water echoes in the linoleum-covered bathroom.

Effie's cousin drops her head back, moaning with pure, unfiltered relief.

"Didn't the bridal shop prepare you for this?" I ask, stepping to the side when Toula gives her butt a firm wiggle. If I even dare try to give her some toilet paper, I'll probably lose my hand in the countless layers of fabric. Instead of opting for a sleek, modern cut, she's gone for Cinderella-impersonator, tiara included. Family friend or not, she's on her own from here on out. Mark my words, my duties are hereafter *complete*.

I'm in desperate need of a cocktail.

And then, if I'm lucky enough, Nick Stamos will appear like the white knight he isn't, and I'll have the chance to plead my case. I'm already dreading the moment when his pewter-gray eyes land on me, shrewdly giving me a once-over that has always—*always*—left me feeling lacking. Wanting. Like I'm forever disappointing him, even though I don't care one bit about what he thinks of me. I don't care *anymore*, at any rate. I used to, back when I was a disillusioned youth.

If there was ever a chance of me knowing what exactly goes on behind those uniquely colored eyes of his, I've long since given up figuring it out. Nick's as stone-cold as an ancient Greek statue. If there's any luck in the world, he's the opposite of an Adonis and has a dick small enough to fit behind the requisite leaf coverage.

You know that's not even remotely true.

With an imaginary needle, I pop the very *vivid* memory of a teenage Nick straight from my head.

At any rate, the likelihood of him agreeing to my proposition is close to nil, but I haven't gotten this far in life by going belly-up and accepting fate's bad hand.

Vini, vidi, vici, right?

I came, I saw, I conquered.

I'm working on the conquering bit, but I have no doubt that some magic can be spun to maneuver things into my favor. Not that Nick has ever allowed himself to be maneuvered into anything. Not that time when we were kids and I begged him to sneak Effie and me out of Greek school or that horribly awkward moment on prom night when I thought for one crazy second that he might actually—

Nope, don't even go there.

I suck in my bottom lip and focus on the situation at hand.

"How about putting a warning label—No Solo Bathroom Trips—on the dress tag?" I tell Toula when she flushes the toilet. "Or, maybe, I don't know, go eighteenth-century and cut a slit in your underwear for easy access?"

"Bad news, I'm not wearing any underwear."

I'm not even surprised. When we were kids, Toula spent an entire summer stripping naked. She flashed everyone from the mailman to the family dog to unassuming passersby outside her front yard. When we turned eighteen, she opted out of college for a career in burlesque.

Unless it glitters and shimmers, Toula can't be bothered.

As for me, I like clothes. Hell, I *love* them. There isn't a skirt I won't wear or a top I won't try at least once, but my love for clothes can't compare to how much I obsess over getting my hands into someone's hair. Un-creepily, of course.

"Let me make sure the bobby pins are holding up." I motion to Toula after she's washed her hands in the sink and I've done the same. "Once you're announced into the reception, I'll be lucky if I get another chance to fix you."

Dutifully, Effie's cousin drops her chin to let me survey my handiwork from earlier this morning. I've arranged her black hair—the same charcoal hue as mine now that I've removed my usual hot pink—in an elegant up-do with sweeps of locks here and loose braids strategically placed there. I straighten the bobby pins, sticking the butt of a pin between my molars while I tug and rewrap a braid. Once Toula hits the dance floor in an hour, I'll let nature do as it wants but until then . . .

"You sure you don't mind me posting the picture on Instagram?" I ask, slipping the pin from my mouth and into the thick, intricately styled bun at the nape of her neck. "I don't want you to feel—"

Toula flashes me a quick grin. "I told you earlier, it's all good. How else are you going to build clientele for your new salon?"

Not for the first time, I feel the sting of my current reality. It zaps me right in the heart before burrowing deep in my gut. It'd be all too easy to sink into the black blanket already clinging to my legs, all while subjugating myself to endless nights of Tito's, cryfests, and more hours of reality TV than my brain can possibly digest. Crying isn't a solution to my problem, though, and neither is alcohol.

I'm an entrepreneur, something I never once imagined might be possible years ago. A *CEO*, for heck's sake. Me, Ermione Pappas, Cambridge's Most Likely to End Up Flunking Out of College. Okay, so that wasn't a *real* vote in the ballot senior year, but some asshole had scrawled it across the final printed sheet in the cafeteria for all to gawk at like lemmings tripping over each other to all rush off the cliff together.

If I'm a hot mess, I'll own it. But the hot-mess express is about to embark on its grand finale voyage, if I have anything to say about it.

C.E.O.

I may need the three letters stamped across my forehead as a constant reminder to myself that I'm as kickass and well-deserving of success as anyone else.

"I'm scrappy," I say to Toula now, refusing to let my voice quiver with nerves. "I'll figure it out. And then my old boss can eat her damn words when *Agape* becomes *the* go-to hair salon in the Boston-metro area."

"Is your construction guy back from vacation yet?"

My smile freezes like I'm the one caught squatting, naked, over the toilet.

Don't panic. Don't cry. And, no matter what you do, don't *laugh hysterically because you can't handle the stress.*

"We're right on schedule," I lie through a tight smile.

If by schedule I mean "we're on track for the biggest shit show this city has ever witnessed," then there's never been a truer statement uttered in my life. Aside from Effie, who was with me when I first realized Jake took off with the money, no one else knows my ass isn't just heated by the fire, it's roasting in it. I can only imagine what my father might say—and all that he *wouldn't* say.

"Your place is in the home with a husband, Ermione," he'd rumble, crushing me with the disapproval in his voice, "not owning a business."

Embarrassment for being so naïve and trusting has kept my mouth shut thus far, but dogged determination to prove them all wrong is what drives me. What's always driven me.

When Toula eyes me skeptically, I wave away her concern. "I'm *good,* I promise. And enough about me—your husband is waiting for you."

It's the perfect distraction.

With a shimmy and a grin, Toula twiddles her fingers at me and throws the bathroom door wide open with enough force that it thwacks the wall with a dull *thud*. "Oh, *husband!*" she calls out, and I wince even as I laugh because Toula is just Toula. Crazy, outgoing, and so insanely kind.

Hooking my hand through the purse I abandoned on the bathroom counter during #PeeGate, I hold the door open with the heel of my stiletto and then head for the elevator that'll take me up to the fifth floor of the Omni Parker House Hotel, where the wedding reception is being held.

The hotel itself is beyond exquisite. Oak-paneled walls. Gold-leaf accents. Bellmen dressed in smart, navy-blue suits. Men in tuxedos wander along the halls, crystal tumblers in one hand and fawning women tucked in close with the other.

Their smug, masculine smirks are shadowed by the flickering of old-fashioned lamps, which offer an ethereal glow that even has my unromantic heart sighing.

Figures that the lamps would get to me while the men don't inspire so much as a quickening of my breath. I prefer to keep my relationships simple, uncomplicated, and out of sight and out of mind. *Agape* is where my head's at, and where it has to remain if I want to drag myself out of my current hellhole.

With a *ping!* the elevator doors open and I step in.

I knuckle the fifth-floor button, then lean against the outer wall of the elevator.

"You're fine," I mutter to myself, the base of my skull connecting with gold-embossed wallpaper as I release a heavy breath. "If anyone else asks about the salon, just—"

Just, *what*?

Lie and then lie some more? How long can I really expect to get away with the lying game? My mother watches us kids like a hawk, no matter the fact that we're all grown and adulting to our very best abilities. My dad . . . Well, after the Nick-Brynn wedding incident from a few years back, I've managed to stay off his radar for the most part. When it comes to money and business, however, nothing escapes his notice—and I have no doubt he's already standing by and waiting to announce each and every mistake I make.

No doubt about it, I'm *fuc*—

A masculine hand sticks through the closing elevator doors, cutting off my train of thought as I lurch forward to jab the KEEP OPEN button. I smack it once with a heavy, don't-fail-me-now finger, then again, my gaze flitting to the doors that are inching closed like the gates of Mordor.

That hand balls into a fist and then a suit-encased forearm appears, followed by a long leg and a brown, leather dress shoe. The leather is so soft, so visibly supple, I wouldn't doubt that they cost more than my mortgage.

"Gamóto."

At the Greek curse, and the more than familiar gravel-pitched voice, my back snaps straight, and I yank my gaze up. Up past the lean waist not even a suit jacket can hide. Up past the barrel chest and the bulging, I-swing-hammers-for-a-living arms. Up to a face that's as unforgiving in its aristocratic, angular bone structure as his hair is a wild, dark mop on his head.

Only that curly hair and a pair of full, pillow-soft lips —*not* that I've ever tasted them, of course—make him seem more human than rigid statue.

Bingo.

Has there ever been more appropriate timing? I don't think so.

She who asketh shall receive—or however the saying goes.

For possibly the first time in six years, I smile at the man standing just inches away.

Nick Stamos stares down at me, his pewter eyes hard and narrowed with suspicion. "Trying to amputate my arm, Ermione?"

My smile slips, hackles twitching like a cat's fur standing on end when stalked by a predator. *Er-me-o-ne.* His tongue rolls over the *R* in my given name, his Greek accent perfect and sultry despite the condescension dripping heavy and thick with every purred syllable.

Don't let him get to you.

Only, he's gotten to me for years now.

"If by amputate you mean save," I murmur with practiced flippancy, "then sure. It's not my fault if technology doesn't want to work for you."

Those slate-gray eyes, unlike any pair I've ever seen, drop to where I'm still pressing the KEEP OPEN button. When his dark brows rise, taunting me with their perfect arches, I follow his lead and glance down at the illuminated button.

CLOSE DOORS.

Oh. *Oh.*

Air puffs up my chest indignantly as I inhale swiftly. "You didn't really need that arm, did you?"

Nick snorts derisively. Without sparing me another look, his big hand circles my wrist. His touch is bold, his skin hot. A shiver of *something*—revulsion, I hope—rolls down my spine, unwinding and unfurling until even my gold-painted toes curl in my heels. And, as though he fears I'm *completely* incompetent, he angles my still-pointed finger at the button to close the doors.

Pushes down and lingers, as though to taunt, *see? This is how a contraption called an elevator works. Welcome to the twenty-first century, Ermione.*

Ermione. Even in my head I can hear him slinging around the name I inherited from my maternal grandmother, knowing that it makes my mouth pinch and my hands clench.

My smile has, as it always does around him, completely evaporated.

The elevator pings shut.

Locking me in with Satan's mortal sidekick, my best friend's older brother.

4

NICK

Ermione "Mina" Pappas looks exactly the same.

Releasing her wrist, I shove my hands into the pockets of my slacks and lean back, shoulders to the wall, and ease my gaze over her familiar features. Thanks to my stint on *Put A Ring On It,* and life before that, it's been a solid seven or eight months since I've seen her last.

But Mina is nothing if not predictable in her unpredictability.

She's been Effie's best friend since the two of them were in grade school and amputating their Barbies instead of dressing them up. I've had twenty-four years with Mina existing in the periphery of my life, darting in and out whenever the occasion called for it.

Like on the night of my almost-wedding to Brynn Whitehead, my college sweetheart.

My heart barely gives an extra thump in grievance for what could have been, all those hopes and dreams that were once tied up with Brynn now unmoored and wasting away in the waters of Never-Gonna-Happen-Again.

For a moment, Mina does nothing but stare openly at me. Her honey eyes, rimmed with the warmest amber I've ever seen, dodge downward and skate over my frame. They stop momentarily along the way, like she's yielding at a four-way intersection, pausing at my shoulders and my stomach and my hips and my feet.

Her unconcealed perusal is an instant reminder that Mina, although I've known her since I was eight years old, has a reputation for flaying men alive with her tart tongue, even as she lures him into bed with her curves.

I've never been lured, and have no plans to be, thanks to her status as Effie's best friend, and so I end her little intimidation tactic with a cough into my fist and a dismissive murmur that I know will goad her into the Ermione I've preferred for years: awkward and just a little off-kilter.

It's the unofficial, dog-eat-dog game we always play: who can outwit the other?

I've worn the victor's hat more often than not. Mina's unpredictable, reckless, even, but she shows her cards before she plays them. Those amber-rimmed eyes of hers hold no secrets. At least, they never did when we were younger.

And I can't deny that I've always enjoyed watching her scramble for things to say that might, finally, shock me.

Settling in, I cock my head and steadily meet her gaze. *Round one, here we go.* "What're my chances that my *yiayia* is gonna take one look at you tonight and declare you as the next bride-to-be?"

She visibly stumbles on nothing but air, her hand going to the metal balustrade that lines the walls of the elevator. "She's out of luck." Mina's voice comes out raspy, like she's swallowed a bundle of surprised nerves. "I'm already taken."

I might as well be ass-over-head, landing right into a pile of sawdust at a jobsite. Disbelief suctions my feet to the ground like magnets to a refrigerator. *No way*. Hell would *actually* freeze over if Mina did anything more than casually see a guy.

Like I said, she's been on my periphery since forever. I spent most of my junior and senior years of high school watching out for her, at my sister's urging. *"She gets bullied a lot, Nick. Just make sure everything is gravy, would you?"*

Even if things aren't gravy, Mina never lets down her walls.

Except that one time on the night of her prom—which, even then, lasted no more than the seconds required to shore up my reserve and step away from the danger zone. Crossing *that* forbidden boundary with my sister's best friend just isn't gonna happen.

I squint down at her and try to read her expression. For once, her honey eyes tell me nothing, leaving me to stand out in the cold. Well, damn. Is she . . . *bluffing* me? "Effie didn't mention you were seeing anyone."

Mina's vampy, dark-painted lips twitch into a dreamy smile as she sways back and links her arms over her chest. "He's amazing. So giving."

I cock a brow and opt to wait out whatever ace she thinks she's got up her sleeve.

I'll give her that. Mina's always been particularly good at planting the seed and letting the tangled web she weaves give her the upper hand. *Trouble,* my grandmother always said, *That one is trouble*. Most of the Greek community here in Boston agrees, for one reason or another. It's not an opinion that I share. She may be reckless, but Mina is also one of the most selfless people I've ever met.

Not that I'd give her any ammunition by telling her that.

"Austere, really," she goes on, her tone light as a feather and with her eyes still fluttered shut. Her makeup today is smoky, bronze highlighted with gold, and it's in that moment when I realize her crazy pink hair is long gone. Strands as black as a cloudy night sky curl over her collarbones, the tips brushing the upper swells of her breasts.

I jerk my gaze up, just in time to hear her add, "He's so cold, but sometimes, in the early mornings when the light filters in through the windows, I can tell he'll be something a little more one day. Not just a money-hogging jerk that's like a noose around my neck."

Like a noose around—

Game over.

My lips compress into a flat line. "Ermione"—her name rips from my chest in warning—"if he so much as touches you, I'll—"

Her honey eyes pop open, and the flare of humor that I see there has my chest deflating with relief. The relief is short-lived. She's busting my balls. Again. *Round two goes to you—bravo.*

"You'll what?" she pushes, as the elevator dings our arrival on the fifth floor. The doors crack open, but before I can even think to escape, Mina hops around me and smacks one of the buttons.

The elevator hiccups, doors jerking back shut, and the pressure beneath my feet increases as we ascend to the next floor.

"Ermione."

With her back to the row of buttons, she kicks one foot up on the wall behind her, the heel of her shoe clinking as it meets metal. "Oops." Her mouth purses as her brows go hairline high. "Wrong button."

I'm going to kill her.

I haven't even been back in Massachusetts for more than two weeks and already I'm going to find myself trading in my work boots for an orange jumpsuit and a cell mate named Bend Over.

My voice sounds like gravel-infused-with-nails when I finally find the words past the sudden frustration swirling in my brain. The idea of her dating a man who might put his hands on her—*Jesus*. I scrub a hand over my jaw, then shoot her a pointed glare. "No more games."

"Not a game," she replies, all honeyed, cajoling tone, "I need to talk with you . . . in private." She gestures toward the elevator like she's found us the perfect location for a little rendezvous.

The last time we "talked" we ended up sharing a hotel bed for the night, drunk off our asses, while my grandmother busted in the door and promptly told the entire family that Ermione Pappas had seduced me.

There'd been no seduction of any kind.

Only too much booze, hours' worth of *I Love Lucy* re-runs, and—on my part—a reluctance to face the music: that I was dumped at the altar. I slept in my tux, fully clothed, with my bow tie still locked around my throat like a noose.

Like a noose.

Dammit.

I rub the back of my neck, then try to smother the urge to demand answers. *She is not my business,* I remind myself. But the damn words worm their way out anyway when I blurt, "Are you seeing anyone whose ass I need to beat down for treating you wrong?"

Her nostrils flare, a little tell that infuses curiosity through my veins, before she's shaking her head. "It's sweet that you care, but no. It was just a joke, a stupid metaphor for my professional life. I'm not seeing anyone—" *Ping*. She reaches behind her and presses another button without looking to see which one.

Impulsive.

If someone were to ask me one word to describe my sister's best friend, it would be that: impulsive. Her spontaneous nature would be admirable if it also weren't so ridiculously frustrating.

"You want to talk?" I wave one hand toward her. "Then talk."

She sniffs at my command, dimpled chin tipping up in defiance. "Being polite wouldn't kill you, you know. A girl likes a bit of sugar when she's spoken to." Honey eyes narrow pointedly, and I already know her brain is spinning, chugging round and round like a hamster on a wheel. "Then again, sugar isn't exactly your . . . speed."

I'm going to regret asking what she means.

Hell, I tend to regret a lot of things when it comes to Mina—the woman gets under my skin like no one else, needling me, endlessly frustrating me—but this . . . I already know I'm not going to like her answer.

"What exactly *is* my speed?"

She nibbles on her bottom lip, her white teeth a sharp contrast to the plum-colored lipstick. *Ping!* Her fingers find another button, giving us more time for our private "talk," and my heart feels suspended in mid-air as we change directions and zoom down, down, down.

"Romantic strolls on the beach."

Guilty as charged, thanks to a week spent visiting the Australian coast for *Put A Ring On It*. In my pocket, I crack my knuckles, one by one, buying myself time to think out the best way to answer.

I'm not given the opportunity.

"Getting individual bags of popcorn for a date at the theater," Mina throws out a heartbeat later, like the prospect alone is offensive and a complete turn-off.

My jaw clenches. "There's nothing wrong with two bags of popcorn. It's easier that way."

"It's safe. And predictable, like the romantic strolls, which means both options feel very *you.* Plus, the point of sharing a bag is to battle it out for the last kernel and let your fingers brush and your hands tango it up."

I shift my weight, sneaking one hand up to tug at my tie. Unless she cornered me in this elevator to list out all my faults, in which we'll be here all night until security kicks us out, I've got a feeling she's deflecting. Even knowing Mina as I do, and *knowing* that she's scrambling to keep a hold on whatever nerves are eating her alive, I can't help but think back to Savannah Rose.

We were too similar to work.

Too set in our ways.

Predictable. *Safe*. Rigid. All things the woman in front of me snubs her nose at, preferring adventure and new experiences to stability and the familiar. Mina has me all riled up, so much so that I'm aware of the short rise and fall of my chest, and the low ringing in my ears. *Maybe it's because she's telling you the truth—you're* uninteresting.

Instead of doing the smart thing, the *mature* thing, and calling her out for procrastinating with this private talk of hers, I cave. Hard.

"I don't like to dance," I mutter, hands back in my pockets.

Mina leans forward, her dark hair falling forward in big ringlets, caressing the tops of her breasts again, and taps me on the chest. "It's called foreplay, Nick. Not all women are in it for the pump-once-and-quit-it bedtime activities."

Gamóto, I feel like I'm choking.

Does she think . . . There's no way she could possibly think that I . . .

"I pump more than—"

I cut off the second Mina folds over at the waist, laughter creasing her cheeks and screwing her eyes shut. "Oh, Nick," she whispers out between gusts of laughter, "your face when you . . . oh, my God, I can't. I'm dying."

Heat warms my cheeks and the tops of my ears.

When faced with Mina's enthusiasm and crazy sense of humor, I almost regret walking away from the calm that is Savannah Rose. Almost, but not quite.

Pushing off the wall, I bump Mina out of the way with a hip-check and jab the button for the closest floor. The elevator skids to a stop, and I'm half expecting hotel security to be waiting to cart the two of us away when the doors swing open.

Thankfully, the third floor is blessedly empty.

"Nick?" comes Mina's inquisitive voice behind me. "Wedding is on the fifth floor."

The sole of my shoe connects with the maroon carpet, and I swallow a sigh of relief to be back on solid ground. Glancing at my sister's best friend over my shoulder, I meet her hopeful gaze. *Don't fall for it, man.* She had her chance to talk. It's not my problem if she wasted it by playing verbal volleyball. "I'm taking the stairs."

Another step that leads me away from the only person I've ever met who can send my temper from zero to a hundred in the span of minutes. I never lose my cool. Never raise my voice or say things I'll regret later on. But Mina . . . she's the black to my white, the heavy rock to my classical, the bungee-jumping-crazy to my downward-dog-yoga.

She drives me fucking insane.

"But—"

"Foreplay's over, Ermione." Against my iron-clad will, my gaze sweeps lower than her cleavage. Her black dress hugs her curvy frame, its slinky material glittering under the soft lighting as she darts out a hand to keep the elevator from closing on her face. She's not classically beautiful—her nose is just a little too big, her jaw a little too sharp, her eyes a little too luminous. But she wears confidence like a second skin, and there's never been a man I've met in the last decade who can turn Mina down. "Find someone else to tango with."

The elevator whines with its urge to get a move on, and Mina claps her right hand over her left, prolonging our staring contest.

"I actually do really need to talk to you," she says, that always-there confidence of hers visibly waning. "I got carried away with trying to prove a point. I-I don't even remember the point, though that's always the way with us, don't you think? We each always want the last word. It's our thing—if we had a thing. Which we don't." She laughs awkwardly. "But I wasn't kidding when I said that I'm having trouble, but . . . I, uh, I bought a place. A hair salon. I'd love to maybe know—if you have the time, obviously—if we could talk about a renovation contract. In private. Maybe. If you have the time."

I've never heard Mina ramble before. Or, at least, not since our school-day years when she sat quietly in the back of the Greek school classroom and stammered whenever the teacher—*Kyria* Yiannoglou—called on her to answer a question or conjugate a verb.

Learning Greek came easily to me, probably because my parents spoke nothing else in our house while I was growing up. But Mina . . . she'd struggled, and the more she panicked, the more she rambled, and the more she rambled, the more she liked to tap her fingers.

My gaze cuts to her hands now, which are still locked over the elevator.

Her slender fingers curl in and stretch out, as though fighting the urge to tap away to their heart's content.

My heart gives an erratic thump that might as well be synonymous for, *Oh, c'mon, man. Let her squirm a little before you concede the battle.* It'd be in my best interest to show that

Mina can't push me to react. For one, she will, and always will be, an annoying pain in my ass. And, second—

"Meet me at my office on Monday. 8 a.m. Don't be late."

I don't wait around to see if she has a comeback.

I'm not a bad guy, but I'd be lying if I said that Mina doesn't pluck at all my good-guy feathers and make me want to go rogue.

5

MINA

At seven-forty on Monday morning, I'm loitering outside Nick's office and contemplating my life decisions.

Life decisions that will not be remedied with Tito's, thank you very much.

Instead, I've opted for two cups of coffee—one for me and one for Nick—that I picked up from Dunkin's on my train ride into Watertown. Only the little cardboard cutouts keep my palms from scorching as I pace the cracked sidewalk and crane my neck back to stare at the white-painted sign hanging over the front window.

Stamos Restoration and Co. is located in the heart of downtown Watertown, a suburb not even ten minutes outside of Boston. Unlike *Agape,* which takes up the first floor of a nineteenth-century brownstone, Nick's office is located in a contemporary building with gray-stucco walls. He's sandwiched between a dance studio and a hair salon, and it takes every bit of self-control not to peek into the salon's windows and scope out their setup like a peeping Tom.

With the hum of cars rushing down the Massachusetts Turnpike behind me, I juggle the coffees into one hand and ring the doorbell.

Thanks to nerves and a bad habit of losing my mind around Nick, I missed my window of opportunity to talk to him about *Agape* at the wedding. I could blame my scatter-brain for my inability to close the deal with him—or *initiate* the deal in the first place, if we're getting into the details—but I'm not one for pretense.

Nope, I straight up cornered that man in an elevator and proceeded to bust his balls like I was back in kindergarten—when kicking a guy you like in the nuts was the surefire way to announce the two of you were destined for marriage.

Yeah, not my brightest moment.

I'm hoping to make up for it today.

The door swings open a heartbeat later, and I open my mouth to greet Nick—only to realize that the person standing there isn't Nick at all but rather a guy around my age. His blond hair is a rumpled mess, which is in no way outdone by his wrinkled clothing, the scruff on his jaw (though his upper lip is as smooth as a baby's bottom), and half-tied shoelaces.

If I'm the Hot Mess Express, then this man is the conductor leading us all to our inevitable doom.

His eyes widen at the sight of the coffee. "You must be Ermion*ehh*," he says, greedy hands reaching for the Dunkin's. He plucks one out of my grasp and brings the plastic lid to his nose, inhaling like an addict. "Damn, now that smells like heaven."

Actually, it smells like *my* heaven.

I look from the cup now clutched in his big paws to the one still in my possession. This morning I'd hobbled out of bed, ignored my Keurig, and tumbled into the shower and then into clothes. I'm half-awake, in desperate need of caffeine and—

I'm not looking for a reason for Nick to throw me out on my rear end. Pissing off his employee won't earn me any brownie points, so I offer the coffee thief a big ol' grin, ignoring the screech of my heart that's shouting *give it to us!* like Gollum himself has taken up residence in my chest, and mutter, "There's milk and sugar in that one."

Angling my body past him, I step inside Nick's place of work for the very first time. Call me crazy but it feels like I'm about to see him in an all new light. I've known him for my entire life: as my best friend's older brother, as my teenage crush, as the man who drives me up a wall with his sly wit and quiet reserve.

But I've never seen him in a professional setting, and something about that has me . . . eager.

With the sole coffee-left-standing pressed to my diaphragm, I take in the room before me. It looks more like an architectural exhibit at a museum than an office. Miniature wooden structures stand on short, ankle-high tables. I spot a Victorian mansion painted in eggshell blue and trimmed with lavender over to my right, and then, on the far side of the room, what looks to be a church with a half-built spire. More pieces are littered throughout the space, each as intricate and intriguing as the one before it.

Did Nick make these?

For a moment, I let that image settle in, visually projecting him sitting behind the incomplete church. His rough hands molding the wood, his face a mask of concentration as he toils away the daylight until the afternoon sun kisses his olive skin and he breathes out a sigh of contentment. I can only imagine the hours needed to complete each structure, miniature or not. If patience is a virtue, then Nick is the most virtuous one of us all.

Feeling more rattled than I'd like to admit, I spin on my heel to face the coffee thief. "You can call me Mina, by the way. It's easier."

"*Mina*." The guy's face sags with relief. He takes a swig of coffee and doesn't even flinch at the heat. "Thank God. You know how many times I practiced Ermion*ehh* in the mirror this morning? Had to have the boss-man audio record it for me over the weekend 'cuz it was either that or, well, ya know."

Compared to Nick's fluent Greek tongue, this guy pronounces my name like his mouth has been stuffed with cotton. Each syllable is all wrong, but I give him a big smile anyway. "I appreciate the effort."

"I'm *all* about the effort, Mina."

He doesn't wink, but I get the feeling he's doing it in his head but trying to stick to whatever rulebook has been shoved up his butt from day one. Nick's a stickler for certain things.

Like buying two bags of popcorn and never letting a woman notice that he's checking out her cleavage.

"Anyway," Coffee Thief goes on, "Boss-man's just wrapping up a meeting, so I'll bring you in there. As a head's up, his office looks like my grandma's after a *Family Feud* marathon." At my side-eye, he shrugs, all nonchalant. "Steve Harvey really gets her worked up. Point is, Nick's office is a disaster since he's playing catch-up now that he's back from that dating show or whatever."

Hold up.

Pause.

Rewind.

My stride careens to a stop as I shoot a wild glance over at CT. "I'm sorry, did you say that Nick was on a *dating* show?" I refuse to believe it. Nick—my predictable, safe Nick—would rather walk into a room full of clowns than subject himself to TV. And reality television at that. "Was it *The Bachelor?*"

Oh. My. God.

Is Nick engaged? *Married?*

My head swirls with the endless possibilities and I'm suddenly grateful to CT for taking hold of at least one coffee because I'm seconds away from pulling a Tower of Pisa and going down, face-first. I talked about foreplay with him. *Nick*. And hand-tangoing! And I may or may not have prayed for his penis to be leaf-coverage tiny.

No wife deserves that sort of discovery, and I instantly regret the insult, even though it never left my head. And even though I know it's not true.

I'm going to be sick.

"You okay, Ermiona?"

I don't even bother to correct CT.

Though I hate black coffee, I bring Nick's cup up to my mouth and take a hearty swig of the java. For self-preservation. Fortitude. And because I need to do something with my hands besides stand here with my mouth agape and my eyes the size of saucers. The coffee burns on the way down, like a bitter truth bomb that I'd rather not be forced to swallow.

My red lipstick stains the white-plastic lid.

Evidence of my freak-out. Just wonderful.

"Carl!" bellows a husky voice. "Any day now!"

CT—*Carl*—flashes me a conspiratorial wink, followed by a quick pull of the Dunkin's blend. "He's a new man these days. Probably all that sand and sun and sex—"

The door to my right flies open, and this time the body that greets me is all too familiar. Though I'll admit that I've never quite seen Nick so . . . dressed *down* before. Jeans and T-shirts have been his go-to outfit of choice for years now.

Today, he's decked out in clothes that look like they've been worn to the brink of extinction. A threadbare, black T-shirt clings to the flat planes of his big chest. The logo for Stamos Restoration and Co. is emblazoned in faded white over his left pectoral muscle, and maybe it's my imagination, but I swear I can see the hard ridges of his abs through the thin fabric. *Wishful thinking, maybe.* The front of the T is stuffed haphazardly into a pair of paint-splattered cargo shorts. They hang low on his hips, suspended in place by an old leather belt that matches the same dark brown of his scuffed work boots.

The latter look heavy enough, and *big* enough, to send ants everywhere scurrying to the hills or risk being stomped into oblivion.

My stomach seesaws at the thought, and, by reflex alone, I draw another sip from the coffee as I meet Nick's gaze. The stained portion of the lid faces him like an illuminated beacon of my mistakes, and I slowly lower the Dunkin's.

I shift my weight from foot to foot. Lift my arm and carefully wiggle the Styrofoam cup. "Black, right?"

It's a miracle I sound so calm and collected.

Married. *Nick.*

I should have grabbed the Tito's before leaving my apartment.

My fingers dig into the sides of the coffee cup, and it releases that awful squeaking sound only Styrofoam can produce.

Nick's gray eyes flit from the coffee to me to Carl and then back again. In a voice as smooth as velvet, he rumbles, "I can never say no to Dunkin's." Then, without another word, he takes the cup from my hand, lifts it to his mouth, and promptly drinks from the same, lipstick-stained spot that I boldly marked like a dog peeing on a hydrant.

With a defiant tilt to his chin, Nick's attention remains fixed on my face.

It's entirely unfair that a man so good-looking can be

both the reason I want to learn how to pack a punch *and* the reason I once slipped my fingers under my panties at night.

As though he's aware of the R-rated direction of my thoughts, a masculine groan reverberates in his chest.

The sound echoes in my ears, delicious and unforgettable. My gaze latches onto his Adam's apple as it bobs down the length of his throat with each swallow.

When he pulls the cup away, he does so with purpose—and cuts the distance between us. He touches the coffee to the center of my chest, his fingers careful not to get all touchy-feely with my breasts, and then leans down. Full, pillow-soft lips to the shell of my ear. Pure gravel in his voice when he murmurs, "For future record, I take two spoonfuls of sugar in my coffee. A guy likes a little sugar when it's being offered."

Jerk.

Unwanted laughter at his unexpected arrogance threatens to escape, before I shove it back down into non-existence.

"Ah, you need me, boss?" Carl asks, reminding me that Nick and I aren't alone. Over the years, we've rarely been alone. Except for my prom night and his wedding night, both of which ended not at all as my favorite romance books would have led me to believe.

Nick Stamos is a good guy. The *best* sort of guy, if you're to believe all the Greek mamas here in Boston, but to me, Nick will always be an enigma I want nothing more to crack and dishevel.

He speaks to me like I'll never understand even a fifth of what he says.

Watches me like he has a secret I'll never know.

Judges me with his mercurial, pewter eyes and his perfectly perfect self.

Now, he steps back and gives me breathing room again. "You're all good, Carl. Thanks for letting in Ermione."

Ermione.

Not Ermion*ehh*.

A shiver curls down my spine.

I do my best to curtail the urge to let my mind wander and think about the *what-ifs*.

The realities are this: I need Nick's expertise for *Agape*. Nothing more.

That's it.

As I enter his office behind him and hear the *click* of the door shut behind me, I remind myself that this is business. Only business. By the time I sit down at the desk across from my best friend's brother, I do what I've done for the last decade and counting: shove any youthful hopes and dreams hung on the shoulders of one Nick Stamos back into the black abyss of Only-In-Your-Dreams.

6

NICK

I recline in my leather chair, hoping that Mina won't notice the strain in my expression as I set my computer to sleep mode. My unease this morning has got nothing to do with her and everything to do with the phone call I just received from one of *Put A Ring On It's* marketing people.

Savannah Rose rejected Dominic DaSilva's proposal.

Their breakup wouldn't be an issue—it *isn't* an issue, not for me—except that production is speeding up now, all thanks to someone on staff spilling the beans.

"Someone leaked footage of Savannah turning you down, man," Taylor said over the phone, "and Dom's already been outed too. I'm telling you right now, heads are gonna fucking roll over at the studio for this. Lucky for me, that's not my problem—I'm in PR, so what I'm gonna need you to do is lay low until *TMZ* remembers you're not as exciting as you look and stops replaying that botched proposal of yours."

Six months ago, the thought of *TMZ* even knowing who I am would be laughable. Stamos Restoration and Co. has a wildly successful reputation in the Boston metro area. We did work for the Boston Public Library a few years back, and the company name landed on every newspaper in the state after I single-handedly won the bid at an auction for a house that once belonged to Nathaniel Hawthorne's family. Yes, *that* Nathanial Hawthorne. Restoring the property earned the company recognition in ways I never fathomed, but those successes belong to Stamos Restoration and Co.

Not me, *Nick* Stamos.

I hate the public eye, hate even more the idea of being center stage. The only reason I went on the show in the first place is because I truly hoped it might be crazy enough to work.

That by the end of it all, I'd be crazy in love.

Dammit, why couldn't Savannah see that Dom was her perfect match? If she had, the press wouldn't give a rat's ass about me. Wedding planning. Honeymoons. Speculation about future children. Every reporter in the goddamn country would be interested in *them*, not me. That's the way this was supposed to go.

You need to keep your head in the game and focus on the matter at hand.

With stiff shoulders, I glance up and find Mina watching me with those luminous honey eyes of hers. She looks like the quintessential professional today, like she thought I might take her to task for her usual dark lipstick or showing off her cleavage or wearing her hair down in loose waves.

"You look stressed," she says, reaching up with two fingers to tug at the high-neck collar of her sleeveless shirt. A bow with long, flapping wings cinches the material closed like those old-fashioned pins Victorian women used to wear.

If she can tell I look on edge, there's no point in denying it.

Briefly, I debate whether 8 a.m. is too damn early to break out the scotch I keep in my office. On a morning like today, when my head feels close to exploding, I don't think there's such a thing as too early. It's always five o' clock somewhere. Plus, if Mina has some with me then there's no reason to feel like a total schmuck.

Right?

Right.

"Want something a little stronger than coffee?" I ask.

Her teeth sink down into her bottom lip. "Really, I shouldn't."

I should make a funny quip and tease the light back to her eyes, but if there's one bonus to having known Mina my entire life, it's that I don't have to pretend. She may not know all that resides in my soul, but she still knows *me*. Just as I know her. Though I guess we only really know what Effie's told us both.

Still, I make a last-ditch effort, more for her sake than mine. "I'll even get you your own glass. You don't have to worry about catching cooties." I nod to the Dunkin's cup on the desk. "Then again, if that was a concern, you shouldn't have offered me your coffee."

A slight laugh escapes her. "If it helps, this one was meant to be yours." She pokes the cup with a gold-painted finger. "A peace offering, if you will, for me behaving . . . out of turn on Friday night."

"Out of turn" implies that Mina hasn't always loved to bust my chops, and we both know that isn't true.

As though nervous about my contemplative silence, she hastily adds, "I'm sorry about the elevator incident, by the way. Sometimes I . . . sometimes I just—"

"Like to fuck with me."

Her fingers drum a nearly silent beat on the desk. "I

wouldn't phrase it *quite* like that. It sounds so aggressive." She smiles at me, wide and full like she's innocence personified and not full of shit. "And I'm not an aggressive person. I'm all about the hugs and unicorns and kumbaya moments—"

"Admit it, Mina," I murmur, barely leashing in a laugh as I struggle to maintain a straight face, "you love to mess with my head. Nothing makes you happier than seeing me thrown off balance."

Funny how only five minutes of back-and-forth ribbing with this woman has pushed my own problems to the periphery. And that's all before I have the satisfaction of watching her squirm in her chair. That dainty, ultra-feminine bow, black and lined with red seams, stands a direct contrast to her olive complexion. She plays with the end of one wing, rubbing the silky fabric against the pad of her thumb.

"But you make it so easy for me to . . ." She drops her hold on the bow and lifts both hands, palms facing out. "No, no, I will *not* let you distract me from the mission at hand."

I lean forward, elbows dropping to the desk. "Which is?"

She swallows and sends a quick, searching glance up to the ceiling like the heavens will answer her prayers. If she wanted the angels doing her a solid, she should have gone to a priest. Instead, she's here, in my office and seated on my chair.

In all the years I've known Mina, she's never asked me for anything.

Independent may as well be her middle name, and my interest spikes as she drums her slender fingers and gathers her thoughts. Her mouth pulls to the side as she taps, taps, taps. "I came here planning to tell you the short and sweet version of recent events."

Call my curiosity solidly piqued. I spread my arm wide with a flourish. "Floor's all yours."

A groan escapes her mouth, and the sound loops around me like a soundtrack of defeat. "I can't." She tugs at the bow again, and it comes a little undone. Against my will, my gaze zeroes in on the smallest hint of bare skin that she's exposed with her fidgeting. "You're going to think I'm a complete *maláka*. A naïve little idiot, and I'm telling you right now, you aren't wrong. In my defense, I'm new at this."

New at *what*?

"Ermione, I've known you since you were six. We've got history"—some, admittedly, that has been more than a little exaggerated by all the Greek mamas and grandmothers to something it never was in the first place—"and I'm telling you right now, there's nothing you can say that'll make me think you've got a loose screw under all that hairspray."

"I hired a guy to renovate my hair salon and he took off with my money."

Well, damn.

The words haven't even left her mouth completely before I'm jumping up from my chair to grab the scotch. She looks likes she needs it—I know *I'd* welcome the burn, so I untwist the plastic cap and toss it onto the desk.

Looks like we're both in a rough spot.

Knocking the Dunkin's cup out of the way with my knuckles, I set the scotch down in front of Mina. "You sound stressed," I tell her, using her own words, and she offers a pained grimace before wrapping her hand around the bottle's neck. Rings decorate each of her fingers, some stacked one on top of the other. They *clink* against the glass as she lets out a short, defeated sigh.

"Stressed doesn't even cover it." Her eyes flutter shut as she takes a hearty swig, then comes up spluttering, swiping her lips with the back of her hand, smearing red lipstick like a lover might and I—

My cock twitches in my pants.

Oh, hell to the fucking no.

Not Mina. Not here. And most definitely not now.

Completely oblivious to the activity happening south of my belt, she tilts her head, bottle poised inches away from her mouth. From that smeared lipstick. *God help me.* "Are you okay?" she asks.

I want to point at my dick and demand, *do I* look *okay?* Because there's got to be a rule somewhere about getting it up for your sister's best friend. As in, *it's not done.* Since I'd rather be castrated than confess to how far I've fallen, I gesture at my mouth. "You got a little something right"—I brush my bottom lip with the pad of my thumb—"here."

"*Oh.*" Putting the scotch down, she angles her body in the chair for a little privacy. Then goes rummaging in her purse for what looks to be a small mirror. Good, that lipstick smear has got to go. Too erotic. Too dangerous. Too damn tempting.

Clearly you're in a dry spell if lipstick *is where you cross the line nowadays.*

Desperate to erase the evidence that Ermione Pappas of all people just *turned me on,* I yank the hem of my T-shirt out of my shorts and drag it over the growing tent in my pants. I retreat back to my side of the desk and sit down.

I've never—not once—allowed myself to look at Mina as anything other than my sister's best friend. Not during my teenage years when my parents sent Effie and I along with the Pappas family to Greece when they visited Mina's uncle, her father's brother, each summer. My parents were unable to afford to go themselves, but for their kids, they wanted us to be as Greek as possible. That meant three days a week quarantined to a classroom with other Greek-Americans learning the mother tongue; volunteering at the local *ecclesia,* or church, including at every festival known to mankind until we reeked of *gyros* and *souvlaki* for days after; and speaking the language as fluidly as my parents and their parents did before them.

We might have been American on paper, but we were Greek in blood and heart.

I spent my summers lounging on beach chairs next to Mina. Hours of time pretending that all her little verbal jabs at my "rigid" disposition never scraped at my youthful insecurities and made me retreat.

Because if there's one thing I've always known, it's that if I'm the moon, sullen in the darkness and content in my solitude, then she's the sun, setting fire to everything in her path. Sister's best friend or not, a girl like Mina would regret dating a "safe" guy like me. She lives for spontaneity, adventure, and if she'd been on *Put A Ring On It*, she would have been the Dominic DaSilva of her season.

Larger than life, and totally out of my reach.

Forcing a light note to my voice, I attempt to ease her strung-out nerves. "Are you sure he took the money?"

Mina's fingers erupt into another tapping sprint. "He took my lucky penny—the one your mom gave me."

I lift a brow. "*And?*"

She plants her hands on the chair's armrests and maneuvers her weight around. The bow at her neck teases open, revealing another notch of skin that tantalizes more than it satisfies. "*And*," she grinds out, as though revealing this is beyond painful, "he left an IOU."

A pin dropping would carry more sound than my office does right now.

I lift a hand to drag through my hair, the strands catching on my blunt, short fingernails. "That's . . . courteous of him."

"Courteous?" Mina's normally husky voice grows to an uneven pitch. "An IOU, Nick. Who *does* that? Even my *Thieo*

Marko, who we *both* know might as well have every loan broker in New England on speed dial, has never left an IOU. And my mom's brother isn't one for classy escapes when it comes to owing people some Benjamins."

Understatement of the year, right there.

"You reported the guy?"

"Yes."

I stare at her and begin to feel the weight of dread seep into my limbs. She's watching me like I carry all the answers to her questions, like I may be her very last hope, and if I'm being honest—I'm not in the right mindset to have someone else place their hope on my shoulders.

Not when I've been away from my company for months and I'm up to my elbows in menial admin work that Carl did but not to my specifications, and then there's the whole *TMZ* thing to consider . . . and whatever fallout comes with the news of Savannah Rose dumping *both* suitors on prime TV.

My phone vibrates on my desk, and I drag it close to see the sender. *Dom.* The pit of my stomach drops. If former NFL player Dominic DaSilva is texting me, then shit has officially hit the fan.

"Mina," I drag out slowly, buying myself time, "it's not that I don't want to help." My phone lights up with another text, this one also from Dom. Snatching it up from the desk, I drop it in the top drawer. I can only deal with one imploding catastrophe at a time. "But maybe, if you're needing some cash to borrow, you could ask your dad?"

Yianni Pappas is a stick-up-the-ass prick, something I well remember from all those summer vacations years ago, but I've never known him to turn his daughters or son away. His children have always come first—his one, and only, redeemable feature.

Mina's cheeks hollow on a rough exhale. "*Óxi.*"

Her accent isn't smooth, more than a little rough around

the edges, and I grunt out, in Greek, "What do you mean *no*? Aren't you here to ask for money?" It's not as though she can ask Effie or Sarah. They're trying to have a baby, and even Sarah's six-figure salary, working for an investment firm, hasn't made the process any cheaper. "A loan so you can finish off the work that needs to be done?"

With a shake of her head, Mina lowers her gaze to the abandoned Dunkin' Donuts coffee cup. She reaches for it with both hands, and, *aw, shit,* but there she goes. *Tap. Tap-tap-tap.*

"*Ermione.*" I growl her name, a four-syllable warning that has her bringing the cup up to her mouth and draining whatever's left. A thought springs up, dangerous and tempting—a way to solve both of our problems. It's risky. And there's a good chance she'll tell me no, but it'd be . . . perfect. For now, obviously. Just a temporary thing.

A way to keep the press off my back while I help her with whatever she needs.

Assuming what she needs doesn't require my firstborn, a kidney, and my 401k, I'll have the better end of the deal, but I doubt she'll complain.

"Why are you looking at me like that?"

Her voice, weighted with suspicion, breaks through my thoughts, and I jerk my attention back to her face. She's studying me the way a scientist might a new discovery, like she's not all sure that I won't leap from my cage and sprout horns and a set of fangs.

No horns in the foreseeable future. Just a fleeting distraction that'll keep the paps off my back and give them a reason to look elsewhere—like set up a stakeout in front of Dom's house, not mine. *Sorry buddy, ol' pal.*

Coughing into a closed fist, I clear my throat. Then ask, "If you don't need the money from me, then what do you need?"

Tap.

Tap-tap-tap.

The silver rings on her fingers glisten under the florescent lighting overhead, and then she says the words I never anticipated:

"Nick, I just need *you.*"

7

MINA

Unreadable as his expressions often are, Nick's an open book right now.

Oh, those pewter eyes of his seem to say to my blunt admission: *oh shit.*

Unfortunately, "oh shit" isn't a viable option—and I'm prepared to push a hard bargain.

Before he can protest, I dig into my shoulder bag and pull out a manila folder with my budget plan. A budget plan that took me longer than it should have to draw up. Maybe if I had more *in* the budget, I could hire a financial analyst to help me move all the puzzle pieces into place.

But I don't have money to spare, so it's as good as it'll ever get.

One by one, I move the papers around on Nick's desk, angling them so the writing is upside down for me but clear as day for him.

I need this to work.

I can't—*can't*—fail. I won't let that happen to me, to my dream.

"I have enough money to cover the remaining material

costs. Maybe not as many of the high-end features I've been eyeing but *Agape* will look beautiful no matter what." I'll cry over my lack of slate floors another day. *And the hydrotherapy room I've been dying to put in.* Ugh. Floors can be replaced. Fixtures can be updated. Rooms can be altered later on. But I'll never have another opportunity to get the ball rolling like I do now. "I can purchase the necessities—the sinks and the laminate flooring and mirrors and all that."

And if my personal finances squeeze a little too tight over the next few months, then that's just fine.

The dream makes it all worth it.

My chest tightens, heart skedaddling into an uncoordinated two-step, and I risk a glance up at Nick.

He's as rigid as stone.

Keep talking!

The heel of my hand lightly taps on the desk, and I focus on my research. On my plans. And pointedly ignore the fact that Effie's older brother looks like he's planning to expedite my death just so I'll get out of his hair.

His curly hair.

Hair I've cut only once—the day before his wedding.

Ruthlessly, I shove the thought aside and take a deep, steadying breath. "I was told the renovations wouldn't last any longer than a month. Maybe less if longer hours are put in." The expected timeline I printed out over the weekend mocks me with its set-in-stone punctuality. I'm already behind schedule. *Yay.* "I don't know how to say this exactly, but I . . . I wouldn't be here if there was an alternative."

There isn't one.

No other options that I can foresee except for Nick, a man I've known for decades, coming in to save the day.

It wouldn't be the first time he's gone out of his way to help me, but overhauling *Agape* is a heck of a lot more time-consuming than a single dance spun around his mother's living room on prom night. No one asked me to the dance, and he . . . well, Nick had made me feel special. That one dance spurred fantasies of the two of us for months after, each one rawer and more sexual than the last. Or as sexually explicit as any virgin eighteen-year-old knows how to get, at any rate.

"What's in it for me?"

My chin jerks up, tongue pressing flat to the roof of my mouth to keep myself from asking what he means. *Think before you speak,* my tutor in school reminded me whenever I grew flustered in class, *allow yourself the moment to truly think about what's been said.*

I do that now, acutely aware of the fact that sweat beads on my brow and my spine has never been straighter in my life. *What does he mean? What does he* mean? Logic tells me that the romance novels I always listen to are misleading—he's not asking for me, the woman, but something else.

I just don't know what.

I drum my fingers on the desk and summon vague words to my tongue. "I have enough cash in the bank to buy anything we might need." Leaning forward, I tap on the upper corner of one sheet, and wait for Nick's gaze to drop to where I point. "I took out a bank loan to buy the place. The chances of them giving me another so soon is unlikely." A hard swallow that feels like I've downed a sharp-edged boulder. God, it rankles to have to come crawling, metaphorically on my hands and knees, and ask this of him. Especially because . . . "I can't pay you, Nick."

I'd planned to bust in here with the reminder that he owes me for letting my reputation swirl down the drain of misrepresentation. After his wedding night, everyone assumed I slept with an almost-married man—and I let them believe what they wanted.

Because Nick needed me that night. He needed a friend,

someone to sit beside him and offer comfort while he grieved the loss of the woman of his dreams . . .

And I'd hoped, in the deepest, most secret parts of my soul, that moment would be the one when he realized Mina Pappas—that *I*—was the girl he'd been searching for all along.

We didn't kiss. Didn't hold hands.

He slept atop the covers in his wedding tux. I burrowed beneath the sheets in my pajamas, pretending the warmth that surrounded me wasn't 100% Egyptian cotton but the heavy weight of his muscular arms tugging me in close.

Hope dwindled to resigned acceptance as the little and big hands on the hotel's grandfather clock mixed and mingled, signaling the passage of time.

When his *yiayia* burst into the room the next morning to check on her poor, heartbroken grandson, everything went straight to the shitter.

Did you hear how Mina Pappas snuck into his bed? the elderly women at church whispered the following Sunday. *She's so bad. Poor Nick, having to suffer through all that.*

He'd suffered the nightmare experience of bad, naughty Mina, and I lived and breathed the afterlife of seducing good, nice guy Nick.

The damage was done, no matter what he or I said to anyone. And, boy, did Nick throw a fuss. Good, old Saint Nick, martyring himself to the fight of proving to all that I did nothing wrong. If he could have posted a bulletin that announced, WE DID NOT HAVE SEX, he would have. It wasn't the first time (and certainly won't be the last) that a woman felt the brunt of the fall.

I don't blame Nick, especially knowing how much it bothered him that no one paid him any mind. I don't blame him, no, but that doesn't mean I've forgotten the one get-out-of-jail-free card I've carried with me all these years.

Except here I am, desperate for his help, and I can't even bring myself to rake him over the coals and bring up the old hurt. His hurt at being left at the altar; my hurt at realizing that my youthful fascination for my best friend's older brother would never amount to anything more. At the end of the day, I'm nothing but big talk. Nick could backstab me tomorrow and I'd never do anything to make him feel the same pain inflicted on me.

That's how friendships, how family *should* be, even if it's a lesson not yet learned by all in the Pappas household.

I let out one long exhale that rattles in my chest.

Rock bottom, how we meet again.

Instead of answering, Nick rouses his sleeping desktop with a shake of the mouse, then adjusts the monitor so I can see the screen too. Curiosity has me literally sitting on the edge of my seat as he opens a new internet tab and taps away on the keyboard.

I wait, heart in my throat, for him to make the next move.

Or at least clue me in to whatever it is he's thinking.

Like that's ever going to happen.

When the page finally loads, I find my voice. "*TMZ*, Nick?" I try not to laugh at the thought of him scouring celebrity tabloid sites late at night before bed. "I never would have pictured you as—*holy* crap."

I blink.

Then blink again.

Lift my butt clear off the chair and lean across the wide desk to grip the computer monitor and twist it so that I can get a better look.

"Oh, my God, CT wasn't high."

Yup, that right there is one-hundred percent Nick Stamos down on one knee. He's dressed in the most godawful Hawaiian T-shirt I've ever seen, and the shorts he's wearing aren't much better. All he needs is a frat-boy visor on his head and he'd look like every other American tourist who used to crowd the Greek beaches in my family's village.

I feel a swift kick of *something* right in the gut when I fix my attention on the woman he's kneeling before. She's stunning. The sort of stunning I used to see, and stare at in awe, while bingeing *America's Next Top Model* episodes.

Back when the dream hadn't taken form quite yet.

But this girl . . . she looks as though she knows her place in the world.

I envy her that.

"CT?" says Nick in a tone that suggests it's not the first time he's asked.

I don't bother elaborating. Not when there's more important matters to discuss, like, "Are you *engaged*?"

"No."

I can't look away from the very obvious proposal that's going down in the picture *TMZ* uploaded. "She turned you down?" Emotion I'd rather not name blooms in my chest. *Don't ask, don't ask, don't ask.* I ask because, clearly, I'm a glutton for punishment. "Do you love her?"

Silence.

It steals into the room like an unwanted visitor and turns my skin to ice.

"What do you think?"

The words aren't voiced in English, and it takes me a solid ten seconds to work through his flawless Greek and translate it all in my head. I jerk my gaze from the screen to Nick's face. He looks as surly, as unapproachable, as always.

I hate that it's such a good look on him.

"Ermione?"

At his quiet, but adamant push for me to answer, I plop back down in my abandoned chair with a swallowed sigh. "You look about as thrilled as the time I stole your swimming trunks and replaced them with a flamingo-pink speedo."

He'd been sixteen to my fourteen, and I'm only a little ashamed to admit that that day, of all days, is when I learned the definition of a "dick print." Thank you, horrible hotel Wi-Fi. Thank you, Google. Thank you, sixteen-year-old Nick who was already hung like a horse.

The last bit of gratitude has me shifting in my seat and crossing my legs at my ankles.

Nick chokes out a rough laugh. "It was a bikini bottom, not a speedo."

I give a little *what-can-you-do* shrug. "I'm resourceful, what can I say?"

A mischievous smile curls his full lips. "Were they Effie's?"

It's not hard to imagine him in that moment. Still growing, still half a foot taller than me, he'd barged out of his room in a pair of boxers, waving the bikini bottoms like a flag of truce. Or war, more likely. Then he'd demanded, in no uncertain terms, to know where his swimming trunks were.

I'd bet that he didn't have the balls to strip down to what essentially were tighty-whities.

He proved that he did.

In epic, hot-pink, dick-cupping fashion.

Going forward after that, my dreams were a little more vibrant, a little *fuller*, if you get my drift.

I lick my lips, then meet his inquisitive stare. "Mine," I say just above a whisper, "trust me when I say how surprised I was to see that they fit you."

It's a throw down, I know. One of my old, customary barbs just to get a rise out of him. *Will Good Guy Nick take the Bait? TMZ* missed out on an epic headliner, if I do say so myself, although perhaps not. Nick proves that he's all mature adult and leaves me hanging.

How disappointing.

"Read the article title."

With a little grumble at his command, I nevertheless do what he says.

Nick Stamos—Brokenhearted and Alone: How One Man found Himself Dumped Twice By Women He Loved.

Uh oh.

"Brynn?" I ask slowly. Had his ex spilled the beans about their almost-wedding?

He doesn't mistake my meaning. "Hell if I know. Effie got me on the show. She knows how . . . well, she knows how much I've been wanting to meet someone new." With a single click, he closes out the tab and once again reaches for the scotch. He lifts it to his mouth, as though prepared to guzzle it all and blot out his troubles, but instead balances it on his thigh. "And she may have convinced me that I must not want love badly enough if I wasn't willing to take a major risk."

"She *convinced* you?"

Nick smiles sheepishly. "More like she sat me down for a come-to-Jesus moment and told me to stop being a pussy. There's no better motivation to do something you're hesitant about than having a younger sibling goad you into doing it."

For over twenty years, Effie and I have told each other everything. I was the first one to know about her being into women; she was the first and only person I told when I lost my virginity at the age of twenty to a guy in his early thirties.

Secrets don't exist between us . . . except, I guess, they do when it comes to Nick.

I push aside the sting of hurt that's not mine to feel. Her relationship with her brother has nothing to do with me, and it's not as though Nick has been a well-versed topic of discussion for us, well, ever.

Needing something to do with my hands, I fiddle with the empty coffee cup. "I didn't realize you were having trouble with—" I cut myself off. Is it any of my business that he was failing in the L-O-V-E department? No, it's not. Just like it's not his business that I've watched every episode of *The Bachelor* from season one. And though I find it odd that *Nick* of all people went on a dating show, I can't help but ask, "Did you meet Chris Harrison?"

"Not even close," he mutters, bouncing the scotch gently on his knee. "Calling *Put A Ring On It*—that's the name—the budget-cut version of *The Bachelor* would be giving it too much credit. It was a shit show." Nick grimaces, jaw clenching. "Not that it matters anymore."

"Then what does matter?" I gesture to the papers spread out across his desk. "You agree to fix up my salon, and I . . . what? Find you a new girl to date?" I gesture toward the computer. "Hire a hit man to kill off whoever wrote that article about you? I'm creative, as we both know, but I need to know what I'm working with here."

I say it flippantly but Nick's response is anything but:

"I need you to pretend to date me."

If I thought Mr. IOU had me suffering heart palpitations, then there's no comparison to the way my lungs clamp tight and air comes slow and reedy through my nose now. Of all the times I've imagined him asking me out, I never once cooked up *this* particular scenario. "I'm sorry, can you repeat that? I thought you said—"

Nick has the good grace to look embarrassed. Maybe even a little flustered. The tips of his ears flush, and if it weren't for his Mediterranean skin, I know they'd be fire-engine red. "Date me," he mutters, voice low and rough, "I need you to date me."

Yup, that settles it. I'm dreaming.

Or being pranked on the comeback season of *Punk'd* with Ashton Kutcher.

Nick pushes his chair back like an animal on the prowl. "I need you." He sets the scotch on the table, twists the cap back on to secure it tightly, and begins to pace the length of his office. It's jampacked with random woodwork, most of which he steps around or nudges to the side with his boot. "Trust me, I never thought I'd say that either, but the truth is . . . the last thing I want is the press digging into my life. Even if I've got nothing to hide, that doesn't mean I'm interested in having everything dissected."

This makes me snort out loud, and when Nick side-eyes me, I only shrug. "Nick, what are they gonna dissect? That time you ratted me out to our Greek school teacher that *I* was the one to steal her whiteboard markers? You confessed for *me.*" I jab my thumb to my chest.

"She paid for them out of her own paycheck."

I roll my eyes at his justification. "Jesus, do you know how *good* you are? Saint Nick—the old nickname still rings true, doesn't it?"

Something in his expression tightens and he spins away before I can look too close.

"I'm oh-for-two in the wedding bell department, Ermione."

"Third time's always the charm. Don't lose hope just yet. Pretty much *every* female will be begging for you to look their way soon."

His shrewd gaze finds me over his left shoulder. "I need a break from relationships." He grumbles something under his breath and then says, louder, "I'm done with dating."

My mouth falls open, and I don't have the good manners to clamp it shut when he blows out a breath of heavy frustration. "Don't look at me like that."

Like what? Like he's having a mid-life crisis at the age of thirty-two? Because that's the vibe I'm getting right now. Good Guy Nick is trying to remove his gilded crown and I have no idea what to make of it.

"You've never even had a one-night-stand," I say, because *someone* needs to knock some common sense into him.

Because, honestly, *who is this man standing in front of me?* With my gaze glued to his broad back, I go on, "There are two types of people in this world: people who have no qualms about jumping into the sack with a stranger, and those who need to know a person's blood type, direct lineage, and whether or not they recycle their trash every week. You, Saint Nick, fall into the latter camp."

From the way his back muscles twitch under his T-shirt, I've got a feeling he doesn't appreciate the comparison. Well, tough. It's true. Nick is the relationship guy. The full-on-love type of guy. And to see him want something else is weird, mind-boggling, and, yes, more than a little uncomfortable for me, seeing as how I've known him for two decades and counting.

I don't like the idea of him breaking out of the box I've put him in—the pedestal he's sat on for years—and, yes, I know that makes me sound hypocritical. But there's something comforting in knowing that what I see is what I get with Nick, and this revelation is throwing *all* of that out of whack.

Stiffly, Nick turns to face me, then rests the curve of his ass against a waist-high bookshelf. His arms cross over his chest and those gray eyes of his home in on me, unwavering in their intensity.

"I didn't say anything about a fling," he grinds out, so low that I strain my ears to hear every word. "Savannah turned down Dom, which means I'm publicly single in a way I've never been before. It'd be one thing if she and I were together—at least that's how I reasoned it when I agreed to the show. We'd be together. We'd be in love. Everything else would be nothing but background noise."

"But that's not what went down."

"Exactly." Nick nods sharply. "She voted me off, and that was fine too. Because then the focus was gonna be on her and Dom and their new engagement, and I was gonna get off with a pass to fade back into obscurity just the way I like it. No harm, no foul. Except that's not on the table anymore. So, you want me to overhaul your salon for free—"

"Free sounds so cheap," I cut in, trying to infuse humor back in the conversation. "Pro bono sounds better. More professional."

Nick talks right over me. "And I want the chance to work in peace without magazines and single women hounding me left and right. It's a win-win."

"What will Effie think?" Effie, who knows all about my stupid crush from yesteryear. Effie, who was right there with me when all the Greek mamas and grandmothers at church couldn't keep my name out of the rumor mill for months. Even now, years later, they still whisper about that time *Kyria* Stamos found her grandson in bed with Bad Girl Mina Pappas. "What about your mom?"

"They'll know the truth," he tells me simply. "They'd never believe we were dating anyway."

"Because we aggravate each other." My voice is small, a sentence more than a question only because I deliberately keep every word succinct.

Nick spares me a quick, searching glance. The onceover is done before I can savor it—no, *not* savor anything. Slowly, he shakes his head, and his wild curls fall across his forehead deliciously. "A girl like you would be bored by me, Ermione. And a guy like me . . . you'd burn me without thought."

You'd burn me without thought.

Growing up, I was called dumb, stupid, slow. I know now that I had a severe case of undiagnosed dyslexia. It made learning hard, reading harder. But in my adult life, I've been called worse: reckless, bad, slut.

I don't sleep around, but when I do choose to let a man in my bed, it's with the understanding that there's nothing more to it than uncomplicated sex. One and done. I've always preferred to work toward my dreams of opening my own salon than be caught up in guy drama.

You'd burn me without thought.

I'm not so dumb that I can't read between the lines: Nick thinks I'd hit it and quit it. Quit *him*. That I'd do to him what I've done to the other six men who have ever shared my bed.

Six.

Not sixteen or sixty or six-hundred.

It takes every ounce of control not to let my voice shake when I finally gather the strength to speak. "I've never burned anyone." Those aren't the words I wanted to say, but they're the words that come out regardless. "Just because you love being in a relationship doesn't give you any right to judge how I live my life. Not everyone wants to settle down."

His head jerks back, full lips parting. "What the hell are you talking about?" The question comes in Greek, and it's almost ironic to me that it's his default language. When he's excited. When he's angry. And, apparently, when he's completely flummoxed too.

My shoulders hitch up. "You make it sound like I'm . . . flighty, like I jump from bed to bed."

Awareness enters his expression, turning his pewter eyes a deeper hue, the color of a stormy sky just before the winds wreak havoc. "Mina, I didn't—" He cuts his hand through his hair, pulling at the curly strands. "That's definitely *not* what I meant. I'm not judging you. Fuck, I've *never* judged you."

Nick plays favorites with Greek obscenities, and, at the very English four-letter curse, steam rolls off my back. "Thank you." I pause. "So, we'd date in name only."

Nick's nod is short and clipped. He meets my gaze, and I see hesitation lingering there. "You're Effie's best friend, Mina. You can tell me no and I'll still work on your salon." Again he spears a hand through his wild hair. "*Gamóto,*" he grunts, "I shouldn't have even asked you. It's crossing so many boundaries."

He's a rule-follower. Nice guy, Saint Nick.

And I'm reckless, at least according to all our family and friends.

"I'll do it."

His body snaps in my direction. "What?"

Old crushes stay dead, right? I swallow, hard, and pray I'm not putting myself in the flames. "We have a deal. You work on my salon and I'll . . . I'll date you." I try to crack a grin. "For the record, I wouldn't sleep with you anyway. I don't mess around with Greek guys."

Dark brows arch high. "Any reason for the aversion?"

There are so many reasons, starting and ending with the fact that nothing else would bring my father more joy than a Greek son-in-law for his Greek daughter. So perfect, so completely nauseating. *And what if he turned out to be just like your dad? Controlling, stifling.* A shiver slithers down my spine.

Instead of telling Nick the truth, I flash him a wide smile. "It all goes back to one teeny-tiny, pink bikini bottom." When his jaw snaps closed, I saunter to the desk and grab all the papers I set out earlier. "There I was, a young, impressionable teenage girl, and I thought . . . Greek men are legendary in bed. That's what *everyone* says, or, you know, at least *Cosmo* does. It has to be because they're packing something extra-large down *there*." I shove the manila folder in my bag, then hang the strap over my shoulder. The coffee cup I pick up and tuck close to my chest before moving toward the door. "Imagine my surprise when I caught sight of the reality after we all went swimming."

My hand closes over the doorknob just as Nick emits a growl of warning. "It's called shrinkage. I can promise that—"

"No promises required." I look back over my shoulder. "I'll email you all the details for the renovation."

The last thing I hear is Nick shouting my name.

And I'd be lying if I said it doesn't put a smile on my face for the rest of the day.

8

To: Nick Stamos <nstamos@stamosrestoration.com>
From: Mina Pappas <mina@agapehairsalon.com>
Subject Line: Renovation Details + Your Dating Show

Hey! You know, in all these years I don't think I've ever emailed you? Not that email is a thing anymore but (confession: please scope out my email addy. How cool, right!?) you're officially the FIRST person whose ever recieved an email from me. Count yourself as blessed.

Also, excuse all typos. Sending this while I'm on the way into the salon on the T. Trains + keyboard typing are not a match-made in heaven.

Speaking of match-making in heaven . . . I saw you're face on TV last night. You looked—well, I'm hoping that you smiled at least ONCE when you were trying to woo the bachelorette? (Say yes). Am I not supposed to call her the bachelorette if it's a different show? Did you get roses? Those delicious candy ring-pops from the vending machines?

GASPS Chastity belts in case someone was feeling frisky while you traveled the world? (I'm a little jealous of the last one. I haven't left the country since the last time we went to Greece together. Oh, what a trip.)

I've attached all the materials that were chosen for Agape to this email. Can we set up a time for you to come by so we can look at the space together? Decide on how much I need of everything before I buy it and cry into my empty bank account?

Not-a-hug,

Mina

P.S., I know how much hugs don't do it for you. Hope this works instead.

To: Mina Pappas <mina@agapehairsalon.com>
From: Nick Stamos <nstamos@stamosrestoration.com>
Re: Subject Line: Renovations Details + Your Dating Show

First email recipient ever, huh? I'm not sure if I'd count myself as blessed but I've tagged this message so it'll always be remembered. When you're old and graying and thinking about your youth, feel free to let me know and I'll pull this baby right out for you, typos and all.

Please don't tell me you're a secret *The Bachelor* fangirl. I thought so highly of you, Ermione, and you're crushing all my expectations. No, we didn't get roses. And hell no to the chastity belts. There was *one* virgin on the show though. Man's gonna have a field day when the episodes start airing.

How about I come by tomorrow? Got a meeting early in the morning, but I'm free around noon. Let me know if that works for your schedule—and hold off on the tears until I get a look at the space. I'll bring tissues in case you start leaking.

P.S., What gave you the impression that I don't like hugs?

P.P.S., For the record, not all Greek men are tiny down under.

P.P.P.S., Care to cut my hair tomorrow while we're at it? Pro bono, and all.

To: Nick Stamos <nstamos@stamosrestoration.com>
From: Mina Pappas <mina@agapehairsalon.com>
Re: Re: Subject Line: Renovation Details + Your Dating Show

OMG, you are just so *kind.* Not that I'm trying to inflate your ego or anything because let's face it, it's already rivaling Mercury, at least, in terms of girth. *rolls eyes* Old and gray. You really know how to throw that sugar around, Saint Nick. I'm tasting the sweetness through every period and comma you're throwing at me.

ANYWAY, I'll admit to nothing. Pleading the fifth. Although I'm very curious about this virgin. Was their a sacrifice? A de-virgining ceremony with whips and chains and at least one condom? If not, *my* expectations are clearly not low enough.

Noon works for me.

P.S., In over twenty years, you've hugged me exactly two times. I suppose I'll have to wait till the end of my thirties to earn another. Although I remember them being rather . . . limp. I'm sure they've improved since then . . .

P.P.S., If you say so.

P.P.P.S., YES. How do you feel about going bald? Wanna pull off the Vin Diesel look? You could rock it.

To: Mina Pappas <mina@agapehairsalon.com>
From: Nick Stamos <nstamos@stamosrestoration.com>
Re: Re: Re: Subject Line: Renovation Details + Your Dating Show

I swear you get mouthier with every year.

P.S., Girth. De-virgining (de-virginizing?). Limp. If I didn't know any better, I'd think you were sending subliminal messages about my dick.

P.P.S., For the record, I've had no cause for complaint where the latter's concerned.

P.P.P.S., Shave my head and I'll put in the worst glitter wallpaper you've ever seen in your life. That's a promise.

To: Nick Stamos <nstamos@stamosrestoration.com>
From: Mina Pappas <mina@agapehairsalon.com>
Re: Re: Re: Re: Subject Line: Renovation Details + Your Dating Show

Glitter wallpaper? Now you're talking the stuff of fantasies.

Bring it on.

P.S., I know there's a secret part of you that loves my mouth.

9

MINA

I know there's a secret part of you that loves my mouth.

Sweet Baby Jesus, has there ever been a more awkward moment in the history of awkward moments? I don't think so—particularly since Nick never answered.

Not even that time when my bathing suit top came undone can trump this.

Okay, maybe it can.

At fifteen, my breasts were flat and practically non-existent but my nipples—God, my nipples—met the salty ocean breeze, the heat from the sun, and Nick's wide-eyed stare as a wave crashed down on his head and took him under the water in one clean pull.

Good news: he survived, and my bikini top was recovered by an elderly woman with skin that could rival the world's finest leather. Bad news: the ocean didn't take pity and swallow me whole.

My breasts might be cupped and propped up now by a pretty nude bra, but I feel just as vulnerable and exposed as my younger self.

A groan rumbles to life in my chest as I thumb off my cell

phone and toss it on the pleather loveseat. It bounces once, then falls flat in acceptance. Yup, totally *not* re-reading that email thread for yet another time in the last twenty-four hours. Once was acceptable. Twice could be forgiven. But thirty times is obsessive, and I'm dangerously closing in.

Silent steps on my Craigslist-find rug bring me to the floor-length mirror that's propped up beside the front door. Digging into the nearby bowl of makeup, I pluck out my favorite red lipstick and swipe it on.

I know there's a secret part of you that loves my mouth.

"You are *not* dolling up for Nick Stamos," I warn my reflection. I suck my thumb between my lips and let it out with a *pop!* Red stains my thumb, and I smile at the mirror for a teeth check. *All clear.* "Professional. You're a business-woman and he's, well, he's *him. Agape* comes first."

I drop the lipstick back in the bowl, take one last glance at my simple boyfriend jeans and cable-knit, white sweater, and head downstairs to wait for my new handyman to arrive. It's quarter to noon, and knowing Nick, he'll be early.

Sure enough, by the time I'm entering the empty salon less than a minute later, he's standing outside the large windows and peering in, one hand level at his brow. Even from my vantage point, there's no missing the way his work clothes fit him to perfection. Jeans encase his long, lean legs, and instead of a T-shirt, he's decked out in a navy, Boston Blades sweatshirt with the sleeves pushed up to his elbows.

He looks rugged and masculine and even a little dangerous, which is insane to think about because Nick earned his nickname the old-fashioned way: by being so nice, so kind, to everyone he meets.

It wouldn't surprise me to learn that he brings his bed-partners tea after sex, but not until after he's gathered a warm washcloth like some Victorian-era gentleman and gently cleaned her up.

I bet he doesn't even make a sound when he comes.

Catching sight of me, Nick knocks on the glass window and mouths something I can't make out.

Deep breath, girl. You can do this.

My lungs contract, and I catch the scent of dreams and must and dead flowers.

It's official, the potted plants have to go.

Crossing the distance to the front door, I unlatch the key and slip the door open wide, poking my head out. "Did you bring the tissues?"

His full lips tug upward. "Something better, actually."

My focus changes trajectory and darts down the length of him, to the plastic Walgreens bag he's gripping in his left hand. "Forewarning, if you kill me and try to dispose of my body, I will *never* forget that you failed to uphold your end of the bargain." I step back as he turns his big body to edge past me. His jean-clad ass grazes my stomach—our heights are so varied, and I suck in my belly to eliminate contact.

Damn all those cookies I ate last night, waiting for him to hit REPLY and make me feel less pathetic.

"I'm not going to kill you," Nick says, coming to a stop as he hits the center of the room. The plastic bag hangs at his side, its contents hidden by the red logo, as he plants his free hand on his hip and slowly spins on his heel to survey the space. "Those plants look mutilated."

I look to the pots in question. Remorse stings my throat as I cringe. "I tried to keep them alive."

Nick's throaty chuckle curls my toes in my shoes. "With what?" he deadpans without looking in my direction. *"Bleach?"*

"Water," I mutter quickly, half under my breath. He's not wrong. The poor plants look like they've attempted to mosey on through the Sahara Desert and haven't come out the other side to tell the tale. "I hope you realize I'm not paying you for the chit chat." The words are matter-of-fact, my tone teasing.

It catches his attention, and he swings around to look at me. "Keep talking about payment, and I'll start collecting." He winks—*winks*—and then stalks over to the old sinks that line the far back wall and sit cattycorner to the hallway leading to a few back rooms.

"What were you thinking for this area?" he calls out. Light invades the space when he flicks a switch, and I scramble to hurry over and meet him. "A bathroom? Maybe a separate room to wash hair instead of having it all out in the open? The salon next door to me, they've done a great job utilizing the square footage they've got." Nick knocks a balled fist on the wall to his left. "We can do the same thing here. Play with the room size, the layouts."

I think back to the initial sketches Jake the IOU Man himself drew up. Sketches that I feel do the job, even if they aren't incredibly unique. "Did you get the plans I sent you? The ones attached to the email?"

Nick spares me a quick glance. "I trashed them."

My mouth falls open. "I'm sorry, I thought you just said that you *trashed* our entire email thread?"

He sets the Walgreens bag down by his feet. Then, from the back pocket of his jeans, he pulls out his phone and swipes it open with a flick of his thumb across the screen. One tap, two taps, and then he's turning the phone toward me and I'm staring at the layout of the salon Jake created before bailing with my money.

"This," Nick murmurs, wiggling the phone in my face, "is the work of a man who doesn't give a shit. He's got a bathroom next to the kitchenette, and nobody, Mina, wants to shit where they eat."

"I thought the saying was 'shit where they sleep'?"

"Yeah, you're probably right." Head cocking to the side

and lips curving in a sly grin, he pockets his cell phone. "I told my mom once that I wanted to write a book with all the sayings I get wrong because she never understood them in the first place." With a low chuckle, he teases, "First-generation problems, am I right?"

His self-deprecating tone pulls a laugh from me. It's definitely true. My mom and dad certainly haven't cornered the market on American colloquialisms, even after thirty years of living in Boston. "It'd be an instant bestseller," I tell Nick, "something they'll pick up right after they've watched *My Big Fat Greek Wedding* for the tenth time."

"Only ten times?" His gray eyes flash with humor, and I'm momentarily struck silent with the realization that Nick and I have been talking for almost fifteen minutes and not *once* has our banter skated into dangerous territory. We're actually, might I say, *getting along*? *Hello, alternate universe*. "How about twenty, at least," he adds.

"I was trying to lowball it."

"Speaking of lowballing it, we're not doing that with your salon."

"But the plans—"

"Are awful," he interrupts, "and there's no shot in hell I'll ever put my company's name anywhere near them."

"Your ego is showing, Saint Nick." I sing-song the words, unable to keep myself from making fun of him. Just a little. "You better watch out before I start thinking all that good-guy niceness was only a façade."

Planting a hand on the wall to my right, he leans in, big body bending at the waist, lowering his face until we're nose to nose. Up close, his pewter eyes are as mercurial as ever, with flecks of blue and green. His gaze never wavers from mine, and then he lowers his voice, the gravel pitch slicking through my limbs like I've been dunked in molasses. "You do realize that you don't know everything about me, right?"

My breath constricts in my chest. "I think I know enough."

One shift of his large frame and then the toes of his work boots are kissing the tips of my flats. I catch his scent, that musky combo of male and sawdust and something woodsy that shouldn't be appealing given who he is—Effie's brother, my old, teenage crush—but nevertheless succeeds in sweeping around me like forbidden temptation.

Entrepreneurial spirit that I am, I'd bottle up that scent and sell it by the boatloads. I'd make a mint off it. Change the lives of millions of women and men because I'm not kidding when I say this: Nick Stamos smells *delicious*.

His warm breath wafts across my forehead, rustling the baby hairs that have escaped my top-knot. My knees pin together, unwelcome lust spiking at his nearness, and I shift my focus from the breadth of his chest to his too-handsome face.

Nothing in his expression speaks to the same arousal flaring to life within me.

As usual.

"We've known each other a heck of a long time, Mina, but make no mistake"—his gaze drops to my mouth, lingers, before lifting once more—"we've never been friends."

And welcome to that moment in my life when good reason disappears and need slips in. Licking my lips, I counter, "You're lying."

"Lying about what?"

"About us not being friends. We might not be besties"—he snorts derisively at that and I refrain from punching him in the solar plexus—"but I've known you my entire life. I know more than what Effie's told me over the years." I think back to the wooden sculptures in his office. Those took time and patience and an acute precision that most people lack. Not Nick, though.

"I know you're a details guy," I go on, refusing to step down and let him win this round. I would never consider him a close confidante—a frenemy, perhaps, more than anything—but to hear him dismiss our relationship riles me up in a way that leaves me feeling rattled. "I know that when you started Stamos Restoration, you lived off Ramen noodles for almost a year. You were twenty-three and full of dreams and Brynn hated that you put everything you had to give into a new business and not on dates and outings and the little trinkets she wanted."

Controlled as his expression is, I don't miss the flare of his nostrils. "I did it for her," he growls, drawing ever closer still, "for us, for our future."

"No." I angle my chin in silent challenge. "You worked all those hours for *you*. Because you spent years as a kid holed up in your room building anything and everything. You interned at an antiques place in high school, restoring furniture, long before Brynn entered the picture. So, maybe I'm not your *friend*, but let's not play it like I don't know you. I know plenty."

I'm breathing hard. *You revealed way too much*, my heart bemoans. I may as well have waved the *I-crushed-on-you-for-years* flag. A white flag, of course, for surrender and acceptance. Fact is, I spent my teenage years and early twenties collecting any and all anecdotes regarding Nick's life that I could. I know more than I should because I once *cared* more than I should.

Those old feelings may be long gone but that doesn't mean all the memories have dissipated along with them.

After my little rant that has nothing at all to do with the renovation project, I expect Nick to return to the topic of my salon and botched plans and new mock-ups and everything that is professional and orderly. Nick is, at the end of the day, a rule-follower.

Obsessively so.

But maybe he's trying to prove me wrong—to axe his saintly nickname once and for all—or maybe he's right and I've never known him the way I thought I did.

Because instead of wheeling around and leaving me alone in the hallway, he grinds his molars, jaw clenching, and then that hand on the wall is shifting over until it rests mere inches away from my head, invading my precious space. His sweatshirt-covered chest grazes mine with each labored contraction of his lungs. And those unreadable gray eyes blaze with emotion.

Too far. This time, I've pushed him *way* too far.

Abort. Abort the mission!

My feet refuse to move. They're rooted to the concrete flooring as my back collides with the wall and my fingers curl in at my sides.

"Nick?"

His full lips part and the words that spill out rock me to my core. "I know that you used to get bullied in high school because you collected Barbies. Some asshole saw you at Toys "R" Us when he was there with his little sister."

I blink, more than a little surprised by the admission. *Even if the admission is true.* Swallowing down my nerves, I find the need to defend myself a little, to make my younger self not seem quite so pathetic. "It wasn't like . . . I mean, it's not like I played with—"

Nick shakes his head, cutting off my tangent. "You practiced cutting hair on them. I remember, Ermione."

Between my difficulties in class and being that "weirdo with the Barbie fetish," high school was rough. Teenagers were assholes, and sometimes, when you were different—a little more *unique,* I liked to think—than your peers, your differences became an opportunity to be targeted. My learning disability, my Greek "otherness," my weirdness, all made me a prime target for getting shit on. Back then, I never had the self-esteem to hold my ground.

"I remember when he came in to school one day with a black eye and a busted lip." The memory pulls a soft, caustic laugh from me. "I wanted to feel bad, you know? I'm against violence, no matter if someone deserves it. Maybe the bully is being bullied at home—or maybe that's my brain making excuses for their inexcusable behavior. But after months of putting up with his asshole comments, I straight up walked around on cloud nine for days after seeing him like that."

"Weeks."

"What?"

Nick shifts his weight on his feet. "You walked around for weeks lookin' like you'd been hand-delivered a unicorn. And," he says, looking down the aristocratic slope of his nose at me, "I'd never felt so pleased with myself."

Pleased with—?

Oh. My. God.

"You didn't," I burst out, shock turning my heart rate into a rapid tattoo of disbelief. "*Did* you?"

Lips curling in a satisfied grin, he gives an ambivalent shrug. "How would you put it?" He pins me with a direct, daring look that I feel all the way down to my toes. "Oh, yeah . . . that Saint Nick doesn't gossip. Sounds about exactly what you'd say to me, nickname and all."

"If the shoe fits . . ."

His chin tucks in to his chest as he taps his work boot alongside my foot. "One of these days you'll see that being a good guy doesn't mean I can't be a little bad."

"Do you want to be bad?"

Another tap of his shoe against mine, and then, "*Óxi, Mina mou.*"

No, my Mina. My heart gives a little jolt at the teasing glint in his voice—and the Greek endearment that rarely anyone but my mother uses for me. It's not a possessive show of affection, as it sounds in English, but more of a . . . diminutive way to refer to someone. *Koukla mou,* my mom always calls me and Katya, *my doll.* I try not to imagine Nick whispering the words in my ear, his big body hovering above mine as those pillow-soft lips graze my neck and up to that sensitive place behind my ear.

You do not *like him anymore.*

I haven't in years. But that doesn't stop me from inhaling a little too often now that he's standing close, taking in that money-in-the-waiting scent of his that smells less like cologne and more just like *him*.

"Why be bad when being good is so rewarding?" he asks, and before I can digest that particular statement, he's stepping back and crouching down to pick up the Walgreens bag. Letting the plastic strap dangle from one finger, he ducks a hand inside, then pauses, as though thinking better of it.

"C'mere."

Nick has solidly knocked me off my axis this morning and I'm floundering, unable to move. "Why?"

He crooks a finger at me, then repeats, in Greek, "*Éla edó.*"

I go to him.

Wait with my heart in my throat as he peels the bag open wide and gestures for me to glance inside. Heart beating wildly against my ribcage, I do as he says—only to find the infamous yellow Domino's bag staring back at me.

Sugar.

The man brought me actual *sugar*.

My shoulder blades hit the wall as I tip my head back and laugh harder than I have in a good long while. It filters out of me, unweighted by the stress of life and *Agape* and my dwindling bank account, and echoes off the walls. Then deep, masculine laughter joins in, too. I can't believe he went out of his way to go to the store and pick it up, all for the purpose of proving *what*? That he can give a girl a little bit of sweetness? That he's not all rough edges and surly attitude?

I peer up at Nick, only to find him posted opposite me in the same position. But instead of cupping his hands over his mouth to stem off the laughter like I am, he's all smooth, male confidence with one hand buried in the pocket of his Blades sweatshirt and one boot planted on the wall behind him. He looks like he's got all the time in the world to stand there and change my perception of him.

"Funny thing," he says when he catches me studying him, "Saint Nick's got a weakness." He lifts the Walgreens bag and gives it a little shake. "Nice or not, good or bad, there's nothing I hate more than when people look at me and cast their judgments. It's one of the reasons this whole thing with the media and *Put A Ring On It* thing is driving me up a wall."

My fingers tap the wall at my sides. "Why?"

"What do you mean why?"

I kick my chin in his direction. "You went on the show, right? Anyone who's ever watched reality TV has to know that their character is about to be torn to shreds. Not even the good can survive."

He lets out a rough chuckle at my subtle sarcasm. "It's the sort of thing you don't notice much when you're out there. You're stuck in a house with twenty other guys, all vying for the hand of the same girl. The producers ask the same questions of everyone. *Do you love her? How's the chemistry? Are you mad you didn't get chosen for today's date?* They're there to do their job, and we were there to fall in love and wait, gavel at the ready, for our dreams to be crushed and decimated." Cocking his head to the side, as though giving my question deep consideration, he adds, "The judgment comes later, when it's all said and done and you're back home. When you check your email and scroll across multiple sites all having something to say about you. You become a one-note sensation, pre-determined by heavily edited scenes and your ability to stay true to yourself when you're thrown to the lions."

I swallow, hard, unable to tear my gaze away from his face. We've never talked about anything more important than *pass the tzatziki sauce* or *stop stealing my towel!* Even on his wedding night, conversation took a backseat to the numbing comfort of *I Love Lucy* and booze and room service. But, in this moment, I could stay here forever, listening to him philosophically analyze dating TV shows and the effect they have on the contestants' vision of self-identity. I wonder if seeing yourself in the headlines, on screen, changes the way you perceive yourself—or if it all just becomes white noise.

The idea captivates me, swirls around in my head, and demands to be explored further, but I push it aside for now and ask the one question that won't leave me alone: "What do they say about you?"

His Adam's apple bobs down. His gray eyes shift to the right, staring at the wall above my shoulder, before swinging back. Meeting my own, unapologetically direct. "That even a pretty face like mine can't convince a woman to stick by my side. Left once at the altar, and then during a proposal." His voice lowers to gravel, a sound so sexy and alluring that I could orgasm on the spot and die happy. "It makes me want to prove them wrong."

Even sexier than his voice is his confidence. "Yeah?"

He gives a curt nod. "*Naí.*" *Yes.*

Words fly to my tongue and stay in silence. Like an idiot, I repeat, "Yeah," because *clearly* that's a valid addition to our conversation right about now. Very riveting commentary. Honestly, how I don't win any conversational awards is beyond me.

Instead of walking away with the unofficial Most Likely

to Flunk Out of College award, my fellow high school peers did me an injustice. Obviously, I should have won Most Likely to Stand Silent When Faced With a Sexy Man Who Also Happens to Be My Best Friend's Brother.

Go me.

"You didn't ask me if I knew anything else about you."

Honestly, I'm not sure I can handle anymore revelations today. Not when he seems to have an arsenal at the ready to make me question everything I know about him. "Was I supposed to?"

He doesn't look away. "I think you should."

Heart beating rapidly, I tap the outside of my thighs. "All right." *Tap. Tap. Tap-tap-tap.* "If we're not friends, prove it and forever hold your peace. Unless there's something else you know about me."

Pushing off the wall, he slips past me but turns once he's another foot or two away. Walking backward, toward the main room of *Agape,* he flashes me a small, get-ready-for-it grin that lights me aflame. "I know that you liked me for years, Ermione. That, on the night of your prom, I crushed you when you realized I wasn't going to kiss you. It made me sick, thinking that, when all I wanted to do was to make you feel better, that I'd somehow made you feel worse instead."

Ringing.

A loud, ear-piercing ring is all I hear as his words sink in and the floor beneath my feet fails to heed my wishes and do me a solid.

By opening up and swallowing me whole.

"Nick," I whisper because, oh my God, I need to say *something.* Holy shit. Holy shit, I'm panicking. Straight up, freaking out as I stare at my best friend's older brother who apparently has known *for years* that I spent the majority of our youth wanting him the same way all the girls in my school wanted Nick from the Backstreet Boys. I'd wanted a different Nick, one less famous, and yet it might as well have been the same thing: neither me nor any of my classmates were going to get the Nick we wanted.

I swipe my tongue over my suddenly dry lips. I feel parched. On the verge of dehydration and a new illness called *fuck-me-sideways-this-can't-be-happening-itis.* The cure: currently unknown. "Nick—"

He watches me steadily, and there it is—the challenge in his gaze . . . proving me wrong. That I don't know him at all and have maybe *never* really known him.

"Tell me something," he says, turning on his heel as he moves toward the main room. He casts a quick glance over his shoulder, and I can't read him *again.* Embarrassment slinks into my veins and turns my limbs to liquid ice. "Tell me all about your dream salon and don't leave a damn thing out. I'm gonna bring it to life for you, just you wait and see."

The last thing I actually see before he turns the corner is his amazing ass in those dark jeans he's wearing.

This was supposed to be an exchange of services: he pulls a Chip and Joanna Gaines and rehabs my salon and I fake-date him until the paparazzi learn that Nick is the most boring lead who'll ever exist.

Except . . .

Nick apparently beat up the bully who made my life hell in high school.

And he knew how I felt about him on prom night when he danced with me in his arms, and I learned that even though I was finally eighteen and totally fair game, he'd fallen for someone else.

The woman who dumped him at the altar six years later.

10

MINA

"Welcome to our final stop of the night, Copp's Hill Burying Ground, where the tombstones are riddled with bullet holes and full-body apparitions are often spotted under the starry night sky."

Almost in unison, every member in the tour group holds up their cell phones and cameras and trains them on Effie, who's perched next to a tombstone and decked out in full eighteenth-century garb.

It's been a few months since I last joined my best friend on one of her tours, and since I've heard this particular ghost story at *least* as many times as I've watched *My Big Fat Greek Wedding,* I linger at the back of the group and keep my hands stuffed deep in the pockets of my wool coat.

The bite of the February wind cuts through my thick, fleece-lined leggings and I burrow deep in my scarf. It's cold, my nipples feel like frozen raisins in my bra, and I've spent the last two miles wondering why I opted for a dress tonight instead of jeans. Fashion over comfort was not the right decision, my friends.

I may have begged Effie for a girl's night—all the better to corner her and ask when the hell she told Nick how I'd crushed on him for years—but with the touring season slowing down for the next few months, I wasn't about to miss tonight for anything.

When you're best friends with someone, their successes become *your* successes and I make sure to hop on Effie's tours as often as possible. Tonight, she's got a few of the Boston Blades, and their significant others, along for a spooky walk through the city. It's a huge step for her career, and when she blurted out the news over the phone earlier today, excitement dogging every word, I knew my night would be spent tromping around graveyards and narrow, gaslit streets.

"And the bullets?" one of the hockey players calls out, his arm wrapped around a willowy redhead. "That's a real story?"

Effie tugs her shawl tighter around her shoulders, then lifts her lantern—all the better to cast a creepy shadow across her face. Her stained red lips part, and then she's giving the crowd her "tour guide" voice, deepening it to a raspy husk and stepping forward so that they're forced to clear a small circle for her.

"Legend has it that the British used this cemetery for target practice during the Revolutionary War. They ducked behind those gravestones you're standing next to"—she mimics the words themselves, her dress billowing out as she crouches, lantern still held at chin-level—"and prepared for the Battle of Bunker Hill. Boston was anti-loyalist at its heart, and the broken relationship between the colonialists and the Tories is still responsible, centuries later, for the ghost sightings spotted here."

One of the players—a huge, hulking guy with dark hair—creeps backward, feet silent on the grass and soil. He catches me watching, lifts a finger to his mouth to keep me quiet, and tiptoes in the way only a six-foot-plus giant can: like the Hulk prowling through the night.

"Orbs are the most common paranormal phenomena seen here, but a word for the wise," Effie says, "if you're taking photos, I suggest taking more than one consecutively. If something stays in one spot, it's likely just dust or—"

"Boom!"

The Hulk-slash-Blades player claps one of his teammates on the back, an arm circling his neck.

"Beaumont!" the unsuspecting dark-haired guy barks out. "You fucking asshole, man."

Beaumont releases him with a *there-there* pat that has everyone else laughing. "Aw, Cap," he says, "don't tell me you pissed yourself."

"Cap" turns to the blonde woman next to him. "I'm going to kill him," he says with an air of finality.

The blonde laughs and squeezes Cap's bicep. "Good news," she tells him, "if you're going to do it, now's the time. So many graves—what's one more?" She leans in and mock-whispers, "No one will ever have to know."

Cap releases a husky chuckle, and then calls out to Effie. "Sorry my teammates are buffoons. I try not to let them loose more than once a month."

My best friend grins. "Might I suggest a collar to wrangle them in?"

That has everyone rolling, and by the time she's wrapping up the tour fifteen minutes later, Jackson "Cap" Carter has promised Effie five rink-side tickets and a glowing five-star review online.

"Sarah's going to be beside herself," I murmur after the Blades and their other halves have descended the narrow, stone steps that lead down to the street from the elevated graveyard. "Free hockey tickets? The gods are shining down on us."

In the lantern's dim light, I catch Effie's eye roll before she flicks off the lamp and Copp's Hill is eclipsed by only the ambient light of the city. "I'm not even going to pretend that I'd win out over hockey." She raises one hand, palm flat and facing the sky, and tips the scale as she lifts the lantern a notch higher. "Me or hockey?" Her hands seesaw, up and down. "Me or hockey? Let's not fool ourselves here. Hockey wins every time."

"Those players did have very nice behinds." At Effie's deadpan stare, I shrug. "What? We can both appreciate a fine ass, no matter the gender. Like yours? Perfection. Feel free to give me some of the tightness factor, would you? I'm already developing the Pappas cellulite and I swear I'm too young for it."

My best friend nudges me forward with a hand to my shoulder. "Your ass is fine, Mina."

"It's big."

"Guys like big."

"Who cares about what guys like?" I tease, the soles of my ankle boots echoing over the stone steps. "My jeans are currently at my apartment and staging a revolt the likes of which hasn't been seen since the Revolutionary War. I'm scared the seams are on the verge of losing."

"On that note, how do you feel about Italian?"

I laugh lightly. Copp's Hill sits on the periphery of the North End, which is famous for its Italian heritage, its Italian restaurants, and the number of Italian flags spray-painted on the streets. Our dinner options quite literally consist of Italian pizza, Italian pasta, and Italian dessert—all of which will terrify my jeans even more. Thank God for skirts, though, and leggings.

"I'm in," I say, putting up a hand for a high-five.

Together, we buckle down against the nippy breeze whipping off the harbor just blocks away. At this time of night, the neighborhood is quiet as we meander toward the popular Hanover Street. Effie's wide hoop skirt bumps into me every other step, and I end up walking on the street while she takes up the width of the beyond-narrow sidewalk.

"Did Sarah want to come out for dinner?" Loosely, I wrap my hand around my hair to keep the strands from whipping me in the face. "Or is she still buckling down for that deadline?"

Effie lets out a little sigh. "I know she's stressed when I have to remind her to shower. Her boss is just such a jerk. You'd think they were working on a miracle life-saving drug the way they're all camped out at the office at all times of night."

Sarah works for one of the big investment firms in the city, but her latest project is centered around kids' toys. In particular, if one up and coming company should warrant any money from her firm.

Anytime I used to complain about a client at the salon giving me hell, I reminded myself that at least I wasn't sleeping at my desk at all hours of the night, only to wake up and do it all over again. Sarah is a beast, and though we share ambition, my dreams allow for showers.

You know, when I'm not wallowing in self-pity.

We cross the street as one, our arms linked the way we've done since we were kids, and hustle down a pedestrian-only walkway beside Old North Church. Smoothed cobblestones line the path with tall brick walls on either side of us.

I wait for Effie to spill her truth, knowing she's holding back, and it's only when we hear the music from Hanover that she finally relents. "I feel like I'm failing, you know? I love my tour company. I love storytelling and watching my guests light up when they hear a particular story that creeps them out, but . . ."

I elbow her in the faux-whalebone bodice. "But what?"

"It's not enough, you know? And I worry that adoption agencies are going to look at my choice of career and knock us down a peg."

It hurts my heart to hear Effie talk about herself like that—as though living her dream is somehow not enough.

It *is* enough. I have to believe that because otherwise I've been working toward something all my life, only to feel disappointed in the end.

"You can't think like that," I tell her firmly. "Between you and Sarah, you both bring in a great salary. You own your house and you've got a rooftop terrace and investments, and even though you're self-employed, you're putting money into a 401k." I nudge her again, wanting to see her smile and lose the stressed-out, *my-world-is-caving-in* look. "You're the most responsible person I know. Don't ever think you're not contributing enough when we both know you do just fine. Any adoption agency should feel *grateful* that you and Sarah want a kid of your own."

The beginnings of a grin curls her lips, and she taps my side with the lantern. "Yeah, you're right."

I straighten my back and give a little shimmy of my hips. "Of course I'm right. Now, which pizza place of all the pizza places is calling our name?"

WE END UP AT A RESTAURANT WITH THE SAME SLATE FLOORS I wanted in *Agape*, and rustic shiplap on the walls. Tapered candles sit in the center of every table and the air is a scented combination of pizza, garlic, and oven-baked bread.

It smells like a food orgasm—if food orgasms were a thing.

"Okay," Effie says after we've broken fast with a deep red wine that carries a hint of blackberry, "unload your burdens."

We tap wine glasses in a toast. "You told your brother about me."

She quirks a brow. "You need to be more specific than that. There are *many* things my brother knows about you. Including the fact that you've got an outie belly button."

Along with the precise shade of my nipples.

Those summers spent in Greece were a host of embarrassing moments, one after another, usually with me at the center of unwanted attention.

I swirl the wine in the bowl of the glass and let my shoulders droop. "He *knows*. About"—I lean forward after casting a quick glance over my shoulder—"the fact that I liked him. Back in high school."

Effie's mouth purses. "You're shaving off a few years there. Just in high school?"

"Oh, my God, do we need to go into timeline specifics here?"

"Hey, don't shoot the messenger." Her hands come up in mock-innocence. "All I'm saying is that you were still pining after him in your early twenties."

My ass slumps farther down on the wooden chair. "Okay, *yes*, I still—maybe—kinda liked him then too." Though I never once made a move because he was dating Brynn Whitehead. Slim, blonde Brynn, with her button nose and her narrow hips and her thighs that did not touch. "The specifics don't matter. What *matters* is the fact that he knows and I agreed to 'fake date'"—I throw up air quotations—"him while he deals with the press after that dating show you never mentioned to me."

Her shoulders hike up sheepishly. "It wasn't my story to tell."

"You tell me everything."

"Did you really want to hear about how my brother wants

to settle down with the whole nine yards? A wife and kids and the white picket fence?"

Probably not.

She knows me too well, dammit.

"Anyway," she goes on, "no one knew besides the immediate family. My *yiayia* was beside herself." She pauses, then winces. "We may have told her that he was going into an arranged marriage."

"An arranged marriage?" I down more wine because even the thought has me shaking with empathy. "Remember that time when my dad tried to pair me off with his single friend? *Ermione,* he said, *Stavros is the perfect, nice, Greek man. He goes to ecclesia. Father Valtaros loves him.*"

"Oh, the sign of every good future spouse," Effie drawls, lifting her glass in another toast, "a man who's in with the priest, has gray hair growing like a second mustache out of his nostrils, and doesn't speak a lick of English."

It's the last one that gets me.

If sitting in Algebra and English felt like punishment most days growing up, then trying to learn a new language felt damn near impossible. The number of hours I sat holed up in my bedroom, trying to memorize what letter matched to which sound was . . . my stomach sinks with the memory —the utter hopelessness I'd felt knowing I was a complete disappointment, somehow *less* Greek than my peers because the language remained a barrier I could never quite cross. Katya and Dimitri picked it up easily—born-naturals, I guess —and that felt like more salt in the wound.

Forget about the drastic age gap, marrying a man like Stavros would have been misery personified on the most basic, fundamental levels of communication. I shudder at the thought. "Your grandmother would be a better match for him."

"Oh my God, I know, right?" Effie's grin deepens. "But

let's get real, she's putting all the weight on Nick's shoulders. She's convinced he's her last hope for grandchildren."

"Is she still working under the crazy assumption that you and Sarah can't have kids?"

She rolls her eyes. "Interventions. We've literally sat down with her *multiple* times to tell her that yes, she will be getting a grandkid from us, but she's so old school—"

"It's the village in her speaking," I cut in, wanting to soothe my best friend's annoyance. "Not that it's an excuse, but hey, the woman still thinks your dad should have gone to school for business instead of opening a pizza joint, and he opened House of Stamos, what? Like twenty years ago? And, I mean, she *actually* thought Nick was entering an arranged marriage. Nick of all people—actually, no, I can see it." I tap my nose. "So orderly, so easy. How has this not happened already?"

That pulls Effie out of her funk. She laughs so hard that when the server comes around with our meat lovers' pizza, she nearly tips over her wineglass. "Forget that, how about the fact that my mom is having 'family' dinner this weekend all so she can introduce my big brother to yet another girl."

The cheese sticks to my molars as I swallow hastily. "Oh?"

"Yup." Effie plucks a piece of sausage off her pizza and pops it into her mouth, chewing. "How's that fake relationship working out for you two? Can you bust him out of family dinner? Also, I just want to point out how crazy cliché fake dating is. What? Are you practicing for a role in a Hallmark movie or something?"

I can't manage to withhold a snort. "Hey, don't look at me. It was all your brother's thinking."

"Figures. If it was up to me—"

"If it was up to you, I'd be married to your brother because you don't do anything in half measures. Why stop at dating when you could complete the cliché circle and get me to exchange rings?"

She points her pizza crust at me. "I've got your best interests at heart."

"My best interests or *yours*?"

"Well, mine, obviously. I've always wanted a sister. Nick doesn't cut it. Too hairy."

And, because Effie and I have known each other since before even puberty, I point at my freshly waxed upper lip. "We're *all* too hairy. It's the Greek blood."

"Mediterranean," she corrects, "the Italians and Lebanese are in the same boat as us."

I scratch my chin, pretending to think hard. "New idea. I'm bringing in an esthetician into the salon—it's a surefire way to guarantee I'll never go out of business."

Effie and I break out into laughter, and it's not until we're settling the bill and leaving the restaurant that she grabs my hand. When I meet her gaze, she squeezes my fingers. "You know I love you, right?"

I tilt my head to the side. "I mean, there were a few times over the years when I wasn't too sure—"

"Mina."

The joke dies on my tongue. "Yeah, Effie," I say, "I know. You're my best friend."

"Then, as your best friend, just hear me out." When I say nothing, she releases me and twines her fingers through her scarf. "I know you used to like Nick, but I . . ." Her dark eyes search my face. "I love you both, and you *know* I want to see you happy, but I don't think he's that guy for you. He's not the *one*."

My shoulders stiffen at her earnestness. Little pinpricks latch onto my heart, and I mentally pluck them off, one by one, until they're all figuratively gone. This is Effie, and I know she doesn't mean to upset me. "I'm not looking for the 'one.'" I throw up bunny quotes just to emphasize my point. "I'm focused on *Agape*, and *only* on *Agape*."

She doesn't look like she believes a word I'm saying. "I know you secretly love those romance audiobooks you listen to all day, but Nick's not one of your book boyfriends. He annoys you and you annoy him, and the two of you are just—"

"Opposites."

"Yes!" She snaps her fingers. "Total opposites. And that's not a bad thing, but you don't want to get married or have kids—you've always said so—and Nick . . . it's all he wants. All he's *ever* wanted. I love you both, but you've never once wavered with your opinion on marriage. It's not just that you two are opposites, it's that you have different dreams in life."

Marriage. Kids.

Even Effie doesn't know all the reasons why I've avoided the possibility of a quintessential familial unit, and the reasons extend far beyond my hair salon. Husband. Babies. A dog—although I wouldn't mind this one so much. It'd be nice not to feel so alone all the time. Yes, opening *Agape* is my sole focus, but I can multi-task with the best of them. If I want to date a guy *and* run a business, I know that I could—easily. When I want something, I make it work, no matter what.

But aside from youthful infatuations and uncomplicated flings, I've never craved anything more. Never craved longevity. Probably because my own parents have shown me that longevity doesn't always equate to trust, to true love, to loyalty. Growing up in the Pappas household taught me one lesson that I've never forgotten: love comes with conditions. And I've never been the sort of person to let anyone hold power over me, especially not a man. Hell, the only men I've truly trusted are George Pappas, Effie's dad, and my uncle on my father's side, who we visited in Greece each summer before he passed away.

Although I suppose Nick fits in that group, too.

The wind blows sharply around us, whipping the hem of my skirt against my legs, and I shove my shaking hands deep into the pockets of my coat. "I get it, I promise."

"I'm sorry—"

"Why be sorry?" I nudge her, as is our way, and then step to the right. We live in completely different areas with me in Harvard Square over in Cambridge, and her and Sarah living the glam life in Beacon Hill. "You're looking out for your brother, just like I look out for Katya or Dimitri. We're all good."

"Promise?"

Though ten feet or so separate us now, I hold up my pinky. "Promise. I'll call you tomorrow."

She offers a wave, then calls out, *"Filakia!" Kisses.*

I shout it back because it's a major red flag if I don't.

"Filakia," I whisper to myself, trying to emulate her exact pronunciation. Unfortunately, I still feel like a complete sham. And I don't suspect that feeling will be going away anytime soon.

11

NICK

"Hey, boss, you did say ten, right?"

Hands on my hips, I glance away from the front window of *Agape* to one of my guys, Bill, and give him a swift nod. "I did."

"You didn't get the key?"

I hold up the hot-pink key in question and promptly feel three pairs of eyes narrow on it. "Looks like Miss Pappas either forgot to get us the right one or—"

"I can pick a lock," offers one of my other workers, a guy named Mark who's done a round or two in the local penitentiary for misdemeanors. I took a chance on him when no one else would, and he's been one of the hardest-working employees I've ever had. At my raised brow, though, he backtracks with a cleared throat, his gaze flicking up to the sky. "Not that I *would* because, ya know, laws. And jail."

"And handcuffs," calls out Vince, my assistant GM and oldest friend. Standing next to Mark, Vince looks like a dark-haired mountain with an olive-toned complexion that matches mine. He's the Italian Stallion to my Greek Adonis—according to him, anyway. He punches Mark in the arm, nearly sending the shorter man sprawling to the pavement. "Don't forget the handcuffs."

"Furry handcuffs or that shit's not happening," Bill tells the group. As one, we all look his way, and he shrugs. "Listen, until you've done it, I don't want to hear any back talk."

Mark raises a hand. "Since I'm the only one who's done any time, I'd like to take a moment to point out that furry handcuffs aren't on the menu in jail."

"Neither are women," snickers Vince, and I choke back a laugh.

"On that note, ladies," I say dryly, "I'm going to give Mina a quick call and see if we can get ourselves inside and working sometime before I turn ninety."

Only, Mina doesn't pick up the phone.

Not the first time around.

Not the second time either.

By the time I'm listening to Beethoven's *Für Elise* for a third go-round, my patience is threadbare. Where the hell is she? Mina was the one to suggest today's meeting time, and the fact that she's over thirty minutes late doesn't make a lick of sense. My sister's best friend may be a lot of things, but she's never been forgetful. When she commits to something, she rarely turns tail and changes her mind. Her steadfast attitude is one thing I admire about her.

But admiration isn't the reason why I'm taking time out of my day to overhaul her dingy building.

Between the two of us, she's getting the better end of the bargain with this deal of ours. If I invoiced her a bill for the renovation, it'd number in the five-figures. My guys need to be paid, and if I do it all on my own, I'll be here for weeks—which means that their wages are coming out of my own pocket, and, unlike a normal contract, my palms aren't being greased beforehand. I let my guys think she's shelling out the money, mainly so they don't raise any brows and wonder why I'm bending over backward to help a woman who, for all intents and purposes, I'm known to not to get along with.

All so I can help her out.

And so I can help her to reach her dreams.

It was blatantly obvious how much it bothered her to come and ask for help—to *me* of all people, her old, high school crush. I'm not an idiot. Despite the fact that we both apparently know more about each other than either of us has ever previously let on, Mina and I have never been close, no matter the fact that she and my sister are practically insepa-rable. After that fateful prom night when she closed her eyes and swayed, ever so much, and I told her about Brynn, we've kept a wide birth from each other.

It felt safer that way. We stuck to our lines, to our roles as older brother and best friend, respectively, and continued on with life. Until she came to my rescue and had my back when I was spiraling.

Now she's the one spiraling. The "pro bono" renovation might as well be my form of repayment, though I have no illusions that she feels anything remotely "more" for me at this point.

Asking Mina to help keep the paps off my back keeps the playing field between us equal.

I scratch her back. She scratches mine, even if I highly doubt the media's interest in me will last longer than a few weeks. I'm not fooling myself: a construction guy in Boston isn't nearly as exciting as Dom, a former NFL tight end *and* a sports analyst on Sports 24/7. Poor bastard is already getting the brunt of the press, if our few phone calls are anything to go by.

But I wanted Mina to keep her pride, even when it's easy to see that her pride's already been scraped raw, and now . . .

Now she's fucking late, wasting time *and* money. Both of which are coming out of my pocket, not hers.

Impatience boils deep under my skin, and I shove my phone into the back pocket of my work jeans. She thinks I'm such a rule-follower? *Maybe it's time to change that.*

Turning on my heel, I move back to the guys. When I'm within earshot, I gesture toward Mark. "Pick the lock."

He makes a weird gurgling sound in his throat. Then, "Uh, boss?"

I kick my chin in the direction of the door. "Not gonna report you to the cops, Sheldon. Pick the lock, and let's get to work."

Vince steps up next to me. Like he's a mother checking for a fever, he plants the back of his hand against my forehead. When I move to bat it away, he jumps out of reach. "No temperature. If *you're* telling someone to pick a lock, it could be the end of the world as we know it."

"Is it wrong that I'm hoping for the zombie apocalypse?" Bill asks as he steps to the side to let Mark past him. "Like, there's something about *The Walking Dead* that's always called to me."

I glance over at him. "You got a fetish about becoming someone else's snack?"

His cheeks turn crimson. "Hey, if it was a zombie woman eating me—"

Vince claps him hard on the back. "There's help out there for people like you, Billy. 1-800-Got-Fetish. Press four on the menu and wait for the zombie specialists to come on. Rick's here to tell you to figure your life out before you end up like him, old as fuck and crying on every single episode."

Laughter reverberates in my chest, just as Mark pipes up, "Rick's a pansy. Everyone knows it. Also, we're in."

"We're in" sounds *way* too close to an actual B&E, so I shuffle the guys inside and break down today's objective. Tearing down the walls leading to the two backrooms is a hassle and a half, but the rooms are weirdly angled and useless as they are now. I'm envisioning an open floor plan, something expansive and elegant that captures a visitor's attention immediately upon entering the salon. A middle-sized backroom with sinks for the shampoo bowls will lead, through a set of antique parlor doors I've got in my warehouse, to a room that can be used for anything else Mina wants to incorporate into the salon's lineup. None of it, though, matches the plans I have for the main room's ceiling. A friend of a friend owes me a favor for the job I did on his house, and I didn't hesitate to call it in.

Annoyed as I am about her missing this morning's meet-up, I can't turn off the creator in me. I want to be the one to give Mina the salon she's always dreamed of.

I also want to know why in the world she hasn't come down to meet us.

"You guys got this, right?" I ask Vince once we've lugged in our tools from the company van parked outside on the curb. "I'm gonna head upstairs a sec and see if everything's all right with the queen bee."

The guys wave me off. Not even Vince sends me a second glance, and I wonder if it's because he would never think that Mina and I . . .

That Mina and I what?

Jaw clenching, I shove away the thought and head for the stairs that lead up to her apartment. I didn't have the chance to scope out the second floor when I was here earlier in the week, and now I can't help but note every creak and whine under my heavy work boots. The dark, wooden walls are splintered, too, with slivers of concrete peeking through. When I get to the top of the stairwell, there's no disguising the floorboards that sink an inch when I step over them.

Gamóto.

It's not just the salon downstairs that needs an entire

overhaul, but clearly the brownstone itself hasn't had its heyday in decades.

If ever.

Did Mina choose this place because it was all she could afford? Or did she see the beauty in the ruination and want to be the one to bring it back to life? My gut tells me it's the latter. Even when we were younger, she had a way of making a person feel *seen*, even appreciated. It makes sense that she'd bring that same attitude to a dilapidated building.

Standing in front of her door, I knock sharply. Once. Twice.

There's the distinct sound of shuffling inside, but then all I hear are the guys ribbing each other downstairs.

I knock again.

And again.

"Ermione!"

Another meeting of my fist on the pale blue door, and then it's swinging open and I'm glancing down and—

"Jesus," I grunt when I catch sight of her, "you look like hell."

She's wrapped up in a comforter, bundled tightly from neck to calf as though the heat's gone out in her apartment and she's on the verge of turning into Olaf from *Frozen*. Her cheeks burn a bright pink, the same color as the whites of her eyes. And her hair . . . her hair is a mess atop her head, piled high in a bun that's seconds away from coming undone.

She swipes her tongue over her bottom lip like she's parched for nourishment. "Nick," she whispers, her voice softer than I've ever heard it, "what are you . . . what're you doing here?"

Hell if I know.

Ten minutes ago, I was ready to chew her ass out for turning into a flighty mess and forgetting that we planned to meet.

And now . . .

Without an explanation, I nudge her back into the apartment, my hands closing in on her shoulders. Or, well, the comforter that's swallowing her frame. I grab a handful of fluff and polyester, but it's enough to fill my palms as I twirl her around. Kick the door shut behind me. "It was our first day on the job, remember?"

There's a minute pause and then her head droops forward in defeat. "Crap, crap, *crap*. I'm so sorry"—she licks her lips again, and I inhale sharply, tearing my gaze away—"I-I woke up this morning and . . ." She sways slightly, and before I can change my mind, I've got her hefted up and in my arms. "Nick. Nick, put me down."

As if she could make it another five seconds on her feet.

I lift my chin, giving her room to duck her face into the crook of my neck. I cradle her like I would a lover, one arm looped under her knees, fingers flirting dangerously with the curve of her ass—over the comforter, of course—and the other nestled behind her back. I guess it's a good thing we're exchanging favors nowadays: she *is* dating me, after all.

Somewhat.

In theory.

"Bed," I mutter under my breath, scanning the apartment's tiny layout. A small kitchen sits off to the right and the living room is nothing more than a loveseat and a TV perched on top of an ancient stand. There's nothing about the space that screams *Mina Pappas*. It lacks all of her creativity, all of her flair. "Is it the flu?"

She shakes her head, one of her arms coming up to hook around my neck. "Migraine. I get them . . . a lot."

Worry pierces me as I carry her down the short hallway, passing a bathroom on the right that doesn't look big enough for a shower, let alone a tub, and then to the only other door. Assuming it's her bedroom, I nudge it open with my shoulder and spot her bed. The sheets are in disarray, a pillow sits on the floor, abandoned, and the blinds are pulled shut over the window.

It feels like a prison.

After growing up in a tiny third-floor apartment in Cambridge with the smallest, most inconveniently sized windows, I'm a guy who needs natural light, and a lot of it. Within a month of buying my house, I knocked out the back wall and put in all glass. Mina's apartment reminds me of my childhood home—and that's not a compliment.

I set her down on the bed, then nab the pillow off the floor and stuff it behind her head, along with two others that are strewn in the far corner of the mattress.

Mina releases a soft moan at the sensation of me pulling the comforter out from around her body. She reaches for the blankets immediately, muttering about how cold she is, and I do my best to simply break her cocoon and lay the comforter flat across her without pulling it away from her skin.

"I hate them," she whispers, kicking her feet beneath the sheet.

Against my better judgment, I sit next to her. Plant one hand down next to her hip as I lean forward and press the back of my hand to her clammy forehead the way Vince did to me not even thirty minutes ago. "You hate the sheets?" I ask, trying to tease her. I should probably let her know that we picked her lock and technically broke in, but I figure it's best to leave that for later, when she's not looking like misery run over.

She burrows deeper in the blankets, turning her face away from my hand. "The headaches."

Ah. I pull back, curling my fingers into a fist that I dig into the mattress next to my ass. *Don't touch her.* It seems ironic that I need to remind myself of that, but I've never enjoyed seeing her sad. Not back when I taught that douchebag bully a lesson. Not on her prom night, when not a single guy had asked her to go, and she flipped the script to hide her hurt. She'd set up shop in my mother's living room, doing the hair of all the girls going to the dance. Effie acted as her bookie, collecting payment, while Mina curled hair and created up-dos and showed off her entrepreneurial spirit. But I'd seen the hurt in her eyes, the loneliness, and I would have done pretty much anything to make her smile.

Except kiss her when she clearly wanted it.

My knuckles crack as I shift my weight on the mattress. "I don't remember you getting headaches all that often as a kid."

Blearily, she peers up at me. Long, spiky lashes. Pink cheeks that speak to being ill and not a reaction to having me in her bedroom. It's been six years since we sat on a mattress together, and yet it strangely feels like no time at all. Finally, she edges out, "Older." She squeezes her eyes shut, then tries again. "They got bad in my twenties. Symptoms of dyslexia." The snort she lets out should sound sarcastic—I'm more than positive she meant it that way—but it strikes me as sad.

Resigned.

And then my brain rewinds her words and locks on only one: dyslexia.

I didn't even know she had dyslexia *at all,* although . . . it makes sense. All those years of listening to her struggle in Greek school, of her coming to our house on the weekends and quietly asking for my mom to help her with the words, and the writing, and the reading.

Why had she never asked her own mother?

The question slams into me, and I mentally drop it in a box and close the lid. It's none of my business.

"What can I do for you?" I watch her expression for any sign of discomfort, then question my own motives. Helping with the renovation does not extend to helping her *feel better.*

But I don't move away from the bed. If anything, I trail my gaze over the shape of her arm under the comforter. She's tapping her fingers even now, and her knuckles create tiny tents beneath the red fabric. I settle my hand over hers, squeezing her fingers. "Would caffeine help?"

She shuts her eyes but doesn't move her hand away. "Sometimes. Yeah."

"You got any coffee?"

A quick nod on her part, and I stand.

In the kitchen, I set about getting the miracle java going. As the coffee brews, I take a small tour of her main living area. Aside from the sofa and TV, she's got very little in the way of furniture or personal items. A picture of her and Effie sits on the little kitchen island that doubles as a table. Next to that one is another of her and her siblings at Katya's college graduation party from a few years back.

Mina's hair is still bright pink in the photo. Her smile is wide, her lips stained a dark plum that matches the shade of her dress and heels. She looks confident, edgy, and completely different than the woman currently huddled in her bedroom and hiding from the world.

I send a quick text to Vince that I'll be down in thirty, but that I'm handling a family emergency upstairs.

Pouring the coffee into a mug I found in one of the cabinets, I add milk and sugar, just the way she likes it. Quickly, I sponge down the spoon I used, and tuck it back into its drawer. I do the same with the bowl that's in the sink and a tall glass. The last thing she needs when this migraine bites the dust is a load of dishes that still need washing. I put them up, then head back to Mina's room. I knock once on the door, just to give her a head's up, then shoulder my way inside. The room's exactly as I left it—moody, dark, with walls painted a godawful green that would make even the Joker cringe—but Mina . . .

I slam to a halt, my heart crashing against my rib cage, and I draw in a sharp breath through my nose.

In the time that I left, she tossed the comforter to the side and sprawled out on her stomach. No pants, only panties.

A thong, if we're being specific about it.

Holy. Fuck.

Her T-shirt rides up her back, exposing her bare ass to me and to God and to anyone else who cares to take a look. And, in that moment, I care. A lot. More than I should. About the lush curve of her ass, the nip of her waist, the *tattoo* that covers her right butt cheek.

Holy. *Fuck.*

Mina's never made it a secret that she likes her ink. I've noticed the delicate tattoo on her inner wrist and the other one, on her rib cage, I recall from seeing a picture of her in a bikini on Facebook two summers ago. But this one . . . I blink slowly and feel heat stir low in my groin.

"Coffee?" she rasps from the bed, lifting her head just far enough so she's not talking into the pillow.

Eliminating the distance between us, when she's practically naked from the waist down, does *not* seem like a good idea.

No, it doesn't, Saint Nick.

Fuck the sainthood. I'm dying for a closer look.

What, exactly, does she have inked on her ass? And why *there* of all places?

I step close, gaze glued to bare, tan skin, and brush the backs of my fingers over her shoulder when I stand next to the bed. Her head is turned away from me, but the right half of the mattress is pressed flush with the wall, leaving me no room to stand over on that side, even if I wanted.

Unless I crawl onto the bed.

Get close to that tattoo and her warm skin and—

"Oh."

Every muscle in my body goes taut at the shocked vibration in her voice, and I fix my attention on her face. Only to find that *her* attention isn't on my face.

No, she's looking at my crotch.

At, specifically, the tent in my pants that shows no signs of going away anytime soon.

Gamóto.

Shit.

Dammit.

I clear my throat. "I brought you the coffee."

She hasn't looked away from my dick. In the dim lighting of the room, it's tough to tell if her cheeks are still pink but one thing's for sure: there's *no* denying the way she licks her lips.

Her throat is dry, maláka. *Give her the coffee!*

"Here," I grunt, because it's either that or ask for the little details I'm dying to know. All details that pertain to her ass and that tattoo. Now that she's on her side, butt facing the wall, I've got no chance of satisfying my . . . curiosity.

For my little sister's best friend.

I'm going straight to hell for this one—a one-way ticket for Saint Nick who isn't feeling saintly at all right now.

I set the mug down on the nightstand with a heavy clunk. "I've got to go."

"That wouldn't fit in my bikini bottoms anymore."

Obviously, she's delirious. Obviously, she's probably drugged up on over-the-counter medicine to counterattack her migraine. Obviously, I shouldn't say, "It barely fit when I was sixteen either."

But I do say it. Oh, fuck, do I.

The mattress creaks beneath her weight, her hand squishing the pillow as she leverages herself up onto her knees. She's eye level with my hard-on now, her mouth inches away from delivering me straight to perdition.

"Am I dreaming?"

Finally, she looks up at me with glassy eyes. "Nope," I croak out, "completely lucid."

Completely. Fucking. Lucid.

I want to sink my hand into that messy hair of hers and tug her close, until her lips are pressed to the zipper of my jeans. Until her fingers are popping open the brass button and my legs are threatening to mutiny and give out beneath me.

Until I'm so lost in her, that everything else fades to black.

The bed whines again beneath her, and I'm aware of her flopping back onto her ass, her knees bent and spread open wide as she blinks up at me, a crooked, medication-induced smile on her face. That thong . . . Jesus, it's barely a scrap of cloth, covering close to nothing, and I do what I should have done when I first walked in and saw her almost naked: I yank on her T-shirt and cover up the goods.

She swats at my hands, batting me away, laughing as if it's all a game.

"I remember when I saw you naked, your . . . *tsutsuli*"—here she waves at my dick, just shy of pointing—"when you were *ten*."

I choke on air, my lungs threatening to burst wide open. In my sternest voice, I warn, "Mina."

She only sways, wrapping her fingers up in the T-shirt's fabric, and stares at my erection that will *not* get the hint and go the fuck down. It perks up under her avid stare. *Jesus, take the wheel.*

"It was small then," she says, words slurring over each other. Whatever medication she took must be pulling its weight because she giggles and slaps her hand over her open mouth. "Oops! I'm not supposed to say that."

Someone kill me.

Voice pitched low, I mutter, "I can promise that all parts of me have grown proportionally."

As though the heavens have parted to shine down on me, I watch as her naturally olive cheeks flush with color. Her wide-eyed stare flicks from my face to my crotch and then back again. "*You're* not supposed to say that."

No, I'm not. But neither am I supposed to get *hard* when it comes to her: Mina, Effie's best friend, a girl I've known since I was eight. There are so many things wrong with this picture, starting with the fact that I need to get the hell out of here.

"I need to go."

She blinks, then snatches up the comforter to drag over her lap. *Thank God.* "Where?"

"Downstairs." Away. I need to go swing some hammers—and *not* the one in my pants that's offering to do the pounding. "With the guys."

"The guys?" A low, long breath falls from her lips, as though she's done too much strenuous activity. Like sit up and flash me, and stare at my erection. All in a day's work around here, I guess. "Did you use the key I gave you?" she asks.

Hello, Saint Nick is on vacation this week. Please leave your message after the beeeeep*!*

If only my life was as easy as a voicemail recording. I could excuse *all* sorts of not-so-nice-guy behavior. Like climbing onto the mattress, laying my body out over Mina's, and showing her all the ways I'd love to—

No, nope.

Time to go.

I step back. Then take another and another until my hand is fisting the doorknob and Mina's watching me like I've taken a hiatus from my life to join the loony bin.

"Nick?" she presses, brow furrowed. "The key?"

Oh, yeah. Not my finest moment for obeying the law. "We picked the lock."

Her eyes go wide, but I leave before she has the chance to say anything else. I make it to the hallway outside of her apartment, where I twist around and shove my back against the door. The heel of my palm goes straight to my cock, and I apply pressure, easing the ache.

The ache that *Mina* put there.

If it weren't so preposterous, I'd laugh. Except the laughter never comes, and it takes me a full five minutes to think of clowns, and my grandmother walking in on me naked, and bankruptcy, and Vince trying to hit on my sister way back when, for my cock to finally get the hint.

Mina is *not* on the menu.

Not now. Not ever.

12

To: Nick Stamos <nstamos@stamorsrestoration.com>
From: Mina Pappas <mina@agapehairsalon.com>
Subject: Dreaming of you

Okay, how's that for a subject line? Did it catch your attention? I'm practicing for when I start sending out newsletters for the salon. Did you know that the average open rate is 24.79%?? 24%!!! (According to Google, anyway, and we all know Google is the real deal). If your reading this, that means you fell in that 24% and I'm doing something right. YAY!

Anyway, back to the original purpose of this email: I dreamt you were in my apartment? I woke up to all the walls gone in the salon, a note from you on the receptionist's desk, and a cup of untouched coffee on my nightstand.

Were you my knight in shining armor? Am I going to have to report to *TMZ* that you're the best fake-boyfriend to ever exist?

Not-a-hug,

Mina

P.S., Thank you for emailing your plans for the salon last night. They're stunning and I feel a little teary-eyed that this is actually happening. Sometimes dreams really do come true.

To: Mina Pappas <mina@agapehairsalon.com>
From: Nick Stamos
<nstamos@stamosrestoration.com>
Re: Subject: Dreaming of you

Guess I'm in that 24.79% (that's an oddly specific number) because here I am responding. Although, can I give a little bit of advice? Looking out for your best interest, of course. But when you're creating the subject line, add in the personalization.

Dreaming of you

Dreaming of you, Nick

See the difference? Second one makes me think you want *me*.

Also, you aren't wrong. I was in your apartment (sorry for the B&E) but when you didn't come downstairs, I was concerned.

Not concerned enough for you to go to *TMZ,* though. I'm currently soaking up the fact that the press is wicked obsessed with Dom. He mentioned needing to get away and Boston all in the same sentence, and now I think the *maláka* is going to come here and bring the insanity to me.

If someone in my position were to change their number to avoid further contact . . . how bad would that be? On a scale of 1-100? Asking for a friend.

P.S., Someone once told me that dreams are temporary longings. You want one thing, and when you ultimately achieve it, your dream morphs into something new. Something bigger than anything else you've ever thought possible.

To: Nick Stamos <nstamos@stamosrestoration.com>
From: Mina Pappas <mina@agapehairsalon.com>
Subject: Dreaming of you, Nick

Tell your friend that if he's going to change his phone number, that's bad on a scale of 200-asshole-ratings. You don't ditch out on the people who need you. Ever. At least, that's my motto in life. Maybe ask if he'd like to visit for the weekend? We can treat him to a ghost tour via Effie, a haircut via me (by the way, I never cut your hair!!!), and a Blades hockey game. Not sure if you've talked to your sister, but she's got some tickets up for grabs. Yes, I'm inviting myself

P.S., Thank you for taking care of me in my time of need. You score a 10 on the scale of I'd-Like-To-Hug-You.

P.P.S., Tell me something, Nick. What's your temporary longing?

To: Mina Pappas <mina@agapehairsalon.com>
From: Nick Stamos
<nstamos@stamosrestoration.com>
Subject: Dreaming of you, Mina
STATUS: *DRAFT*

My temporary longing?

More like temporary insanity.

I've thought of nothing *but* you since carrying you to your bed.

Your pouty lips.

The slip of your waist.

That fucking tattoo that I want nothing more than to kiss,

to skim with my fingers while I learn the precise note of your moan, the way your body feels as you arch up against me while I fuck you.

To: Mina Pappas <mina@agapehairsalon.com>
From: Nick Stamos
<nstamos@stamosrestoration.com>
Re: Subject: Dreaming of you, Nick

I want you to come to family dinner this weekend. My mother would love to see you, and we both know she's your favorite person on the planet after Effie.

P.S., I aim to please. Always.

13

NICK

Even when we were filming *Put A Ring On It* over the fall into early winter, there was never any doubt that, next to Savannah Rose, Dominic DaSilva was man of the hour.

There wasn't a date he didn't score, a challenge he didn't win, a friend he didn't make. The other guys in the mansion swarmed to his side like locusts, and every one of them had something to offer to the former NFL player.

"You know," one of the guys said, "I got this badass bachelor's pad up in Manhattan. When we get out of here, you should totally come and hang out."

Another one, a doctor, praised Dom every chance he got: "Dude, if I had arms even *half* the size of yours, I never would have needed to come on this show. Talk about a chick magnet. Girls *love* arm porn."

There were only two of us who hadn't kissed Dom's ass and offered him our dicks *and* firstborns: a tattooed, bearded dude named Owen-something-or-other. He was sent home on the very first night, much to the delight of every other guy in the house. Never let it be said that men can't turn into catty assholes—not a single person was sad to see Owen go after the first ring ceremony.

And then there was me, the other non-ass-kisser.

"It can't be that bad, man," I tell America's favorite bachelor over the phone now, using my shoulder to keep the phone pressed to my ear as I sit on my mom's balcony, beer bottle clasped in one hand. It's February in Boston and my balls would be playing hibernation, if it weren't for the heating lamps I installed out here a few years back. One of the best decisions I made for the remodel of my parent's place. "Are they looking in your window, trying to get a free view of the goods?"

Dom snorts derisively in my ear. "You want to trade places?"

Beer bottle to my mouth, I take a long pull. Then, "You think they can handle that? One of us is well-hung, DaSilva, and it ain't you."

"Asshole," he grunts, even though I can hear his low chuckle. "Not all of us can be a pretty boy like you."

"And it's all natural, too. A gift from the gods." I lean back in the Adirondack chair, bottle resting on the armrest. Warmth toasts my scalp and shoulders. I would have had this conversation inside, but my mom is bustling around the house, preparing everything for the family dinner. Including for some girl she wants me to meet. As if I haven't gone on enough blind dates to last me a million years. "Don't be jealous."

"Only thing I'm jealous of is the fact that you're being left alone. One *TMZ* article and you're flying clear while I get the shit end of the stick."

"No one told you to catch balls for a living."

"Jesus, did you have to put it that way?" A low groan echoes over the phone, and I can practically see the guy banging his head on a wall. There's a clear-as-day *thunk* and I bite back a grin. "You think Savannah is getting it worse than us?"

Any worry that I'll feel like shit at him mentioning Savannah Rose disintegrates instantaneously. I made the right decision in letting her go, even if I ended up looking like the idiot on national television as a result. It was worth it, to make sure she came out unscathed. It's not her fault I didn't feel the chemistry between us.

But even though *I* didn't want to marry her, doesn't mean Dom didn't . . . or doesn't still want to, I'm not sure.

Knowing that he probably won't want to air his feelings but going for it anyway, I ask, "You good, man? I know you liked her a lot."

Silence greets me, and then I hear shuffling on the other end of the line. "Sometimes what we want and what happens aren't the same thing. Not the first time I wanted a girl who didn't want me back."

"Really?" Because I want to make him laugh, I go for sarcasm. "You mean this isn't the first time your heart's been broken?" I mock-gasp like an asshole. "Someone actually turned your arm-porn down?"

I get the result I'm looking for, and he barks out a sharp laugh. "Smartass. And, full confession here, because I think you're an okay guy who's not gonna sell me out, I haven't been turned down since high school."

"Welcome to the land of mortals. We're experiencing a cold front—hell hath frozen over now that the infamous Dominic DaSilva has joined us."

"I mean, at least I haven't been left at the altar like someone I know?"

Now it's my turn to laugh. "Savannah knew what she was doing when she turned you down. Total prick."

"Correction, *big* prick. Massive. The biggest one there is."

"And *now* it's clear why she said no. Sometimes there is a thing called too big."

"Says the guy with the micro-penis," Dom chimes in.

I roll my eyes, then take another pull of the beer. "Envy isn't a good look on you, *maláka*."

"Don't say sweet-nothings in my ear, Nicky. You'll just give me the wrong idea."

We both know that the Greek translation for *"maláka"* isn't, and will never be, classified as a sweet-nothing. Idiot. Fucker. The exact definition depends on the inflected tone, but even so, it's no "sweetheart," that's for sure.

Sitting up, I swing my legs down from the footrest to the old-paneled floorboards. I bought this house for my parents two years after starting Stamos Restoration. Neither my mom nor dad wanted it at first. They put up a fight, dug in their heels, but I didn't let up. They'd had me less than a year after immigrating to America, and though Dad finally opened his pizza place and Ma worked at a hair salon, the odds were stacked against them from the beginning. I was born, then *Yiayia* and my grandfather came to America, too. They moved in with us, and if the apartment wasn't tight enough already with five people, then came Effie. My parents deserve it all, and if I could give them the world, I would. Anything to make their lives easier, especially after everything they sacrificed and gave up for the sake of Effie and me.

"Come over to Boston."

Dom's shock practically radiates through the phone. "What?"

Thinking back on what Mina wrote to me in her email, I push to my feet. She was right, of course. Dom and I are friends—you don't go through three months of what we did, with TV crews in your face 24/7, and not come out on the other side feeling like brothers instead of strangers. Which means I'm gonna do for Dom what I'd do for Vince or Effie or my parents. *Or Mina.* My thumb slides heavily over the edge of the phone case. Yes, or for Mina, my little sister's best friend. "You want to get away from the rest of the world and nurse your broken heart, right? Well, no one's gonna expect to find you here. Not when you live out west."

"I . . ."

"You start crying on me, man, and I'll send you mini condoms for the rest of your life."

"Sorry." His voice is thick with emotion. "Yeah, yeah that could work. I'll book a room for a few days."

"As long as you need. I'd say you could stay with me, but I'll murder you within five minutes if I have to deal with your color-coordinating again."

"Hey," he protests, "did I or did I not do your laundry while we were holed up in that mansion for weeks on end?"

"You were a great TV-show wife, DaSilva. Maybe a little heavy-handed on the softener but—"

"I hate you."

I bark out a laugh. "Let me know what day you're coming in."

"Will do, man. And thanks."

ALEKA STAMOS IS A FORCE TO BE RECKONED WITH, BUT EVEN she can't compare to my father's mother, my *yiayia,* whose sole purpose in life is to see me married and popping out children while she's still drawing air into her lungs.

"This girl," she says to me in Greek when I walk into the kitchen after hanging up with Dom, "this girl, is she the one?" She's standing at the oven, vehemently whisking something in a black pot. The black pot matches her black sheath dress and the black sparkly slippers on her feet. She hasn't worn any other color since my grandfather died ten years ago.

Opening my mouth to tell her "probably not," I'm cut off by the sound of my sister's voice. "Of course she is, *Yiayia!*" Effie shoots me a saucy wink that might as well be synonymous with *fear me, older brother*. "What's her name again, Nick? Your one true love?"

I don't even know what this girl looks like, let alone her name. Hell, my mom didn't even mention that we were having company until this morning. Because that's the sort of low-ball chess game Aleka Stamos is into: she doesn't play fair, and she rarely plays with honor. Not when it comes to seeing her kids happily married. "Something with a *T*." I squint up at the ceiling. "I think. Maybe."

"No, *Niko mou*," the woman herself says as she sweeps into the kitchen, wearing a glittery dress that looks more at home on a mannequin in the department store than in this house. Who the hell is she inviting tonight? The queen of England? "Sophia. That's her name."

I narrow my eyes. "Sophia who?"

She spares me a side-glance that I don't trust. "Sophia," she repeats, bustling over to the counter where she pulls a wine opener from one of the drawers.

"Ma."

Her shoulders inch up closer to her ears like she knows I'm not going to appreciate her answer. "You went to Greek school with her."

Oh, fuck. *That* Sophia.

Effie bursts out laughing, and visions of sororicide start dancing in my head. "I can't," she whispers, clutching at her stomach as she collapses onto the closest chair, "I can't breathe."

I'm glad one of us finds this funny. "I'll keep Sarah in the living room so she can't resuscitate you."

I make the rookie mistake of not keeping my distance, and Effie promptly nails me in the shin with her pointy shoe. My sister is a lover not a fighter, but I've had permanent bruises on my body since opening Stamos Restoration and Co. eight years ago—her kick barely registers.

Ignoring my sister, I turn to my mother. "I invited Mina to dinner."

"Pappas?" she says, tugging at the cork in the bottle until I usher her out of the way and do it myself. "I love Mina! Do you think she remembers Sophia? How wonderful that we can all be together tonight."

Do I think Mina remembers Sophia? There weren't many of us kids at Greek school, which belonged to our local church. Maybe forty in total, throughout all the grades, which means that it's near-on impossible to *not* remember Sophia.

She used to cling to my arm. Sit next to me at every opportunity. Latch onto my hand whenever we lined up for our traditional Greek dancing lessons. And, always—always—she made sure to laugh at Mina's Greek accent.

Knowing what I do now, no matter that Mina probably didn't intend to let it slip about her learning disability, I can't help but get the feeling that Mina questioned herself more than she ever let on otherwise, thanks to judgmental people like Sophia.

The thought sits like acid in my stomach.

"Ma—"

The doorbell rings to the tune of *Zorba the Greek* playing throughout the house. I did it as a joke when I first bought the place for my parents. Only, the joke's on me—they thought it was the best thing ever and refused to let me rewire the doorbell to, you know, play something *normal.*

"*Niko mou*," Ma exclaims, "get the door, will you? Effie, bring the wine to the table. Where's Sarah?"

Something tells me that I won't just find Sophia on the other side of the front door, and sure enough, when I pull it open, I'm met with two pairs of eyes staring back at me.

Fuck my life.

14

MINA

You know you're officially an adult when you're standing next to the girl who made your life hell back in grade school—and all you want to do is offer to redo her hair because it looks like a Cheeto mated with Tony the Tiger and puked all over her head.

I clamp my hands behind my back, all the better to not pluck at her orange strands.

She stabs the doorbell for yet another time like the prospect of waiting with me is not something she particularly enjoys.

Right there with ya, lady.

Sophia's dark eyes narrow when a familiar tune erupts inside the house. "Please tell me that's not *Zorba the Greek* playing."

I avert my gaze and stifle a grin. "It's not *Zorba the Greek* playing." Except that it totally is, and I can't help but tap my shoe along to the beat as we wait, side by side. *Play nice, Ermione*. "How've you been?"

Sophia stiffens next to me. "Great. Totally great."

I bob my head in a quick nod, keeping my gaze locked on the door. "Divorce all finalized?"

"H-how?"

Tap, tap, tap-tap-tap. "Your husband used to come into the salon I worked at. I'm sorry that he was such an asshole to you." *Tap, tap*. "And that he did what he did."

"H-he didn't *do* anything."

Her ex-husband made it no secret that he was having an affair with a woman who worked in his office. He came in every Friday, as routinely regular as my period, to have his hair trimmed before he and his mistress (side piece? cheater-in-accomplice?) left town for the weekend. Sophia may have been my own personal Regina George from *Mean Girls* back in high school, but no one deserves the backstabbing assholery her husband put her through. On more than one occasion, I reached out to her over social media to broach the subject. On more than one occasion, she read my messages and never responded.

Zorba the Greek descends into silence, and then the front door pulls open and Nick is standing there. He looks . . . *yummy*, my brain happily supplies. Dark jeans, which seem to be his favorite; those amazingly soft leather shoes he wore for Toula's wedding; and a Red Sox T-shirt that lends him a casual vibe that I like more than I should.

His gaze visibly widens at the sight of us.

"Sophia," he greets roughly, and then his pewter eyes zero in on my face. Veer down the length of my body in a slow perusal before swinging back up again. "Ermione."

Ermione.

When he says it like that, all deep and masculine and confident, it sounds less mocking and more suggestive.

You do not like the suggestive! Remember what Effie said!

As though I can possibly forget. Plus, she's not wrong in her assessment: Nick and I want two very different lives.

Aside from that one, delicious moment earlier this week, he's made no move to make me think he wants anything more than a fake girlfriend to ward off the crazies.

I peek over at Sophia. Years ago, I would have labeled her as a crazy. The *queen* of the crazies, even. Now, though, she just looks worn down, a little defeated by love and life.

As much as I'd love to throw my arms around Nick's neck and play up the fake-relationship factor, it seems cruel to throw that in Sophia's face, given the circumstances. I mean, the girl has *orange* hair, for God's sake. Forget Tony the Tiger, it's like a traffic cone has taken up residence on her head. If that's not a cry for help then I don't know what is.

Without giving her the chance to leap out of the way, I loop my arm around hers, linking us together. Her muscles twitch under my touch, which I studiously pretend to ignore. "Sophia and I have *so* much to catch up on tonight." I blast her with a smile that I hope doesn't look deranged. Then I gesture to the man standing slack-jawed in front of me to get out of the way. "Scoot aside, Nick, before my nipples freeze off."

Ice crawls up my stockinged legs as I wait for him to move.

He stares at me, darts a glance to Sophia, then steps out onto the front porch. My high school nemesis wastes no time in rushing forward out of the cold. Before I have the chance to do the same, Nick shuts the door behind him and steps in front of me. Maybe it's the fact that I'm slightly hunched against the chill in the air, but he's got the whole human-mountain thing down pat. He looks massive as he blocks me from heading inside.

Voice pitched low, he says, "Let's take a walk."

My heart gives a little jolt of surprise. "It's cold out."

His thumbs sink into the front pockets of his jeans. "I run hot."

Oh, I just bet he does.

Standing on my tiptoes, I attempt to peer over his shoulder. Unfortunately, I'm a solid six inches too short to see much of anything. "Just because you're an aberration doesn't mean *I* run hot." I point to my outfit: suede, caramel skirt, with an emerald green blouse tucked into the waistband. My knee-high suede boots are warm enough, and flat enough, for a short walk, but that doesn't mean I'm keen on breathing out icicles for the next twenty minutes.

It's not even forty-degrees outside.

Nick closes the gap between us, his fingers going to the parted fleece collar of my coat. His breath is warm against my forehead as his fingers trail over the metal of my zipper, down past my breasts, down past my belly, down farther until my lungs are heaving and I'm welcoming short bursts of icy air into my body.

Then, swiftly, Nick zips my coat all the way up to the collar, locking in the heat he's so easily sparked to life.

"Feeling warmer yet?" he husks out by my ear.

He steps past me, tromping down the three front steps to the sidewalk.

I'm frozen for a heartbeat, maybe two, before I break into action and scurry after him. He slows his pace, no doubt hearing my shoes scrape over the gravel, until we're walking side by side, our elbows knocking together.

It's an instant reminder of all those days we walked home after school and I hoped with everything that I was for our hands to touch.

I shake off the memories and look at him out of the corner of my eye. The man is grinning like he's not even aware that it's freezing outside. *He's insane.* "You're crazy, you know that?" I pluck at the short sleeve of his T-shirt. "You're going to catch a cold."

With his hands shoved deep into his pockets, he tilts his

head. "Will you sit at my bedside in my time of need? Comply to my every whim and desire?"

"Every whim and desire?" Rolling my eyes, I pull my gloves from my coat pockets and put them on. And, yes, maybe I do it with a fair share of sass. He's lucky I never leave home unprepared for Boston's snowy winters. "What? Are you trying out for the role of Henry VIII?"

"Didn't he have nine wives?"

"Six," I tell him. "Divorced, beheaded, died, divorced, beheaded, lived."

"He loved the last one enough to let her live?"

The wind caresses my face with icy fingers, and I zip up my coat the final two inches. I should have opened up *Agape* somewhere warmer, like Florida or Hawaii. "Probably not. Or maybe he did, I don't know. He died; she became a widow. Thus, she lived."

"Huh." His bare elbow brushes my arm as he leads us down the winding street. "Where'd you learn all that?"

My cheeks flush with embarrassment. "*Jeopardy*."

For years, I spent hours watching the show, acquiring random facts the way some people collect baseball cards or rocks. Reading was hard, but my ears worked just fine, and TV became my saving grace. *Jeopardy*, the History Channel, PBS—I devoured them all. Let's put it this way: I wipe the floor with my opponent's tears on Trivia Night.

"I'm more of an HGTV guy myself," Nick drawls after a small pause. "Probably no surprise there."

"You mean, your favorite thing to do on a Friday night *doesn't* include watching paint dry?"

His deep laughter curls around me. "You've got the days mixed up. On Wednesdays, I watch paint dry. It's exhilarating."

"Oh, I bet."

At my sarcasm, his hip collides with mine and nearly

sends me stumbling off the sidewalk. Before I can fall to my doom, he catches me about the waist and hauls me upright. Correction—he tugs me right into him. My boobs smash against the hard planes of his chest. I fist his T-shirt; all the better to hold myself steady, I tell myself.

I've never been a very good liar.

Beneath my fingers and his Red Sox T, Nick's muscles are insanely firm. Nothing about his frame is soft, save for those lips of his which wreaked havoc on my fantasies for years. I used to picture them claiming mine, stealing away my breath the way I once convinced myself that he stole my heart. His mouth would dip lower, pressing kisses here, there, circling a nipple, before moving down, down, down to between my legs.

Unwanted arousal hits me square in the gut. *No, no, and oh, right,* hell no. Using his chest as leverage, I push out of his arms. "And on Mondays?" I ask, hating the way my voice tremors ever so slightly as I throw out a random day of the week. "If Wednesdays are for watching paint dry, then what are Mondays for?"

"Drilling."

Oh, my God.

He did *not* just say that.

"Picking out the right speed," he goes on blithely, seemingly clueless to the fact that I'm squeezing my knees together, not because it's cold out but because I'm turned on. Oh, the injustice of it all. "Slow . . . it's got its own merits. Precision, for one. Deliberate, for another. Or fast—gets the job done quickly. Instant gratification." He meets my gaze, a small smile flirting with the corner of his mouth. "Have a preference on how I put up the drywall in *Agape* this weekend?"

Agape.

He's talking about drilling in my hair salon, *not* drilling me.

I've never been so disappointed in my life.

Relieved, I shout at myself. *You mean that you are* relieved.

"Are you—" I clear my throat. "Are we already putting up the drywall?"

His nod is nothing more than a dip of his chin. "We'll be ready by Wednesday, probably, but I was trying to keep up the weekday game."

Because Nick Stamos is nothing if not a game player.

And I'm still crushing on him, Effie's older brother, like a loser.

My eyes squeeze shut. Haven't I been through this cycle enough times already? Liking someone—*him*—when the feeling isn't mutual? Ten years. I was into him for *ten* years before finally bottling up those lovesick emotions and throwing away the key. You'd think by now that I would have my shit wrangled together when it comes to Nick Stamos. You'd think, but clearly he's my kryptonite.

A cool, masculine palm cups my face, and it's so shocking, so *delicious,* that I don't dare move for fear that it'll end.

"Another migraine?" Nick asks softly, and then he kills me altogether by pressing his lips to my forehead. He lingers, and my pulse skyrockets. "No fever."

"I'm freezing."

"Are you?"

He voices the question like his mind is a million miles away instead of on this deserted strip of sidewalk, with the night sky a blanket to our secret desires—or mine, at least—and his family only a few houses away. Any moment, his *yiayia* will come storming down the street, soup ladle in one hand and her customary black slippers shuffling hastily over the cement. She'll demand to know what we're doing, firing off question after question, as is her way, and I'll stand here and announce: "I'm back in lust with your grandson again."

Not back in love, just lust.

Lust is a whole lot safer.

"C'mere." It's not Nick's *yiayia* saying that now, but Nick himself. *"Éla edó,"* he repeats again in Greek. Big, hammer-swinging arms wrap around my waist. They pull me in close, palms planting flat on my back, one between my shoulder blades and the other inches away from the curve of my ass.

And, just like that, Nick is holding me.

Hugging me.

Through the thin fabric of his T-shirt, I feel the heavy thud of his heart. It hammers away at a clip that matches the insistent beat of my own. Is he . . . is he as turned on as I am right now?

I whisper his name.

"I'm keeping you warm. Don't read into it," he mutters, and I recognize that tone. The surliness. The rigidity. Nick may have his arms wrapped around me, but his emotions aren't open for dissection.

Too bad. There's no way I'm letting him get out of being anything less than honest with me.

My hands snake around his solid form. "You're hugging me."

"I'm keeping you warm," he returns stiffly. "It's an exchange of body heat."

Sure it is. "Are you using me, Nick?" I palm his back, rubbing in small circles. His muscles leap under my touch, like each tendon is vying for attention.

"Ti?" The Greek word for *what* slips off his tongue.

I bite back a grin. "You bundled me all up, coat and all, and wanted to go on a walk. You're only in a T-shirt. I'm thinking you wanted an excuse to hug me. You could have just asked, you know. I wouldn't say no."

His hold on me tightens. "You're out of your mind."

"Am I?"

"Naí." Yes.

I plop my chin on his chest and look up at him. He's already staring down at me, his gray eyes wide, though they appear completely black in the evening light. "Then why did you want to take this walk?"

A tick bursts to life in his jaw. "I wanted to check on how you're feeling—after the migraine. I haven't seen you much this week."

His concern for me sparks warmth throughout my body, but it's not enough to put me off my intended course. We've exchanged emails all week. Platonic, simple emails—emails that never once indicated that I had his erection a hair's breadth away from my face.

That he got hard for *me*.

Talk about dirty dreams coming true. If I weren't so frustrated that he seems content to never mention it again, I'd feel like I won the lottery.

"Nick."

He draws in a sharp breath. "Yeah?"

"The migraine's gone. It never lasts longer than twenty-four hours."

A heartbeat of silence. "Glad to hear it."

I bury my nose in the hard planes of his chest. "Nick?"

"Ermione."

I'm prepared for this to blow up in my face. One hard dick does not take the fake out of our relationship. He's still overhauling my salon, and I'm still pretending—if he needs me—to love up on him when or if the media cares to pay him any attention.

But I have to know.

I *have* to know what the hell he was thinking about when

he stood next to my bed and got the hard-on to rival all hard-ons.

"Mina?" My name's a question on his lips, and it hangs there between us. Waiting for me to make a move.

So, I do.

"Earlier this week, when you came to my apartment . . ." Oh, God, here goes nothing. "You were hard."

Nick goes unnaturally still in my arms.

I squeeze my eyes shut and rip the proverbial bandage off. "I was drugged up on meds for the migraine, but I remember everything. I thought, maybe, you might bring it up this week. You never did." I hear him curse under his breath, and I shore up the last of my confidence. "You were hard, Nick, and I want to know why."

15

NICK

You were hard, Nick.

Thank God for below-freezing temperatures or I'd be facing the same predicament now.

Standing in the cold, wearing nothing but a T-shirt and jeans, it's Mina's warmth that chases the shivers away. Her nails digging into either side of my spine is the only sign that she might not be as confident as she'd have me believe.

The smart thing to do would be to haul ass back to the family dinner we're missing.

Except, for reasons I don't care to deliberate on, I can't find it in myself to walk away.

Obviously the chill in the air has turned my good sense into nothing but frozen blocks of *you're-an-idiot.* Something I confirm tenfold when I roughly mutter, "Don't knee me in the balls for this."

"Don't *what*? Nick—"

I cup her ass. Under her coat but over her soft skirt. I cup her ass like it belongs to me, like it's always belonged to me. Fingers pressing in, palms downright greedy. I block out every protest springing to life inside my head, starting with who she is and ending with I-don't-give-a-fuck because I've thought of nothing else but this for *days*.

"Your tattoo," I growl the words into the crook of her neck. "You want to know why I was hard? The ink you've got right here." I squeeze her right cheek, and my cock twitches at the moan she releases. Jesus, that sound. Feminine and throaty and so damn sexy. The latter isn't a word I'd have attributed to Mina Pappas in our youth. She'd been frustrating, always there, always pushing my restraint to the brink.

My restraint feels tangible now, ready to snap.

Distantly aware of the fact that we're standing in the middle of the sidewalk, I brush Mina's hair to the side and breathe life into the insane lust that's plagued me all week. "You in that thong"—my nose glides up along her throat, taking note of the quickening pulse just below her jawline —"is the thing of fantasies."

She arches her neck, giving me more room to play. "It's big," she whispers, squeezing my ass to let me know what she's referring to exactly.

"I like big."

"T-the women in my family . . . we call it the Pappas butt."

My lips graze her smooth cheek. "Passed down through the family?"

"Never skips a generation—*oh*, wow, that feels good."

I nip again at her earlobe, then soothe the sting with my tongue. She tastes sweet. Smells even sweeter, especially here near her hairline. Perfume, maybe? Or maybe it's her natural scent. Either way, it's addictive. Fingers tangling in her hair, I sweep the strands back from her face and pose the question that's nagged me for days: "Any other tattoos?"

"There," she says breathlessly, "behind my ear."

"Why?" I have two myself, both from my early twenties when I thought having tattoos made me somehow more of a man and less like a kid playing at being an adult. But getting ink didn't magically mature me—life took care of that all on its own. Most days I forget I have them until I see my reflection. Hearing about Mina's, though, feels like I'm uncovering something new about her. Like I'm opening a box that's long since sat on a shelf, the key poking out of the lock. Except that the key didn't belong to me, and I've never been one to push where I'm not wanted. Right now, right here, I feel wanted. It's a fucking heady sensation, and I pull back to meet her gaze. "It's my temporary longing," I rasp, "to know why you love tattoos so much."

Her laughter greets my ears. "I love when art takes shape. No one tattoo is the same as any other—they all take on the slightest deviation." She shrugs in my hold, stepping back. I miss her warmth immediately, but there's something in her expression that steals my attention away from the activity below my belt. Raw honesty lingers there, furrowing her brow as she rocks back on her heels. "Tattoos are like people. We're all unique. We all have our own temporary longings"—here, she flashes me a grin—"but whereas relationships can be fleeting, tattoos are an imprint of a memory marked in the skin. A snapshot of emotion or a moment forgotten to time and distance."

In twenty-four years, Mina has never opened up to me like this.

It's . . . humbling.

A wisp of black hair swoops across her forehead, and I itch to tuck it behind her ear. But the sexually-charged moment is gone, and it feels awkward—no, not awkward but inappropriate—to touch her. To *want* to touch her.

Temporary insanity.

This walk has been nothing but temporary insanity specifically designed to send my brain cells scattering like marbles on a downhill slope. Inevitable, perhaps, given how we've circled around each other for decades, but insanity nonetheless.

And yet I can't tear my gaze away from her.

"They're going to be wondering where we are," she says.

Let them wonder.

Squashing the thought into nothingness, I shove my hands into my jeans' pockets. "Your favorite one."

"What?"

I tilt my head toward my parent's house, then clarify, "Before we go back inside, I want to know your favorite tattoo." It's not my place, not my business, but I throw down the gauntlet anyway.

Seconds tick by as she watches me and I study her. We say nothing, allowing tonight's insanity to sweep away with the chilly night wind. Then, just when I expect her to bypass me, she steps in close. Her hand goes over my heart, her body angled parallel to mine, as though she's already prepared to run.

"To the surprise of no one," she says, humor lacing her tone, "it's not the ink on my butt that takes the number one spot."

I wait her out, not willing to say anything that might lead to a subject change. The need to know this piece of her is overwhelming, for a reason I refuse to look at too closely.

She huffs out a laugh under her breath. "You push a hard bargain, Stamos."

Mina doesn't even know the half of it. I haven't gotten to where I am today by sitting on my ass and letting the world run me over. If that was the case, then Stamos Restoration and Co. never would have gotten off the ground. My parents would still be living in that ancient, cramped apartment that I grew up in. Effie wouldn't have had the money to finish off her last year of college when I came damn near close to emptying my bank account to help my little sister walk across that graduation-day stage, diploma in hand.

Most days, I'm not pushing a hard bargain, I'm the one fucking dealing it.

Finally, Mina speaks—though it's not at all what I expected. "Patience," she murmurs, "written in script along the sole of my left foot."

If anyone else gave me that answer, I wouldn't think twice about it. But this is *Mina,* the woman who only just told me that tattoos are a camera reel of one's life, which means that inking a word like *patience* on her body carries significant weight. Particularly when Mina's the very opposite of patient. Impulsive. Reckless. Take-life-by-the-balls-and-go-for-it. That's her M.O.—always has been. And, like the opening of Pandora's Box, I'm desperate to discover more.

She slips around me.

I spin on my heel, gently clasping my hands on her arms, and stop her in her tracks. With her back to me and her wrists cuffed by my hands, she glances over her shoulder and quirks a brow.

"Why patience?" I ask.

That brow lifts higher, taunting me. "Why do you suddenly care? Because of one thong sighting?" She tugs on her wrists and I let her escape. For now. "Mine can't be the only behind you've seen, Nick."

She's not wrong. I've seen others.

For some reason, though, I can't bring any to mind—not even Brynn's.

"Tell me."

Her gaze never deviates from my face. "Because I've been waiting my entire life to feel as though I'm finally where I belong. You said that dreams are nothing more than temporary longings, one always leading into the next." Delicate shoulders square off, like she's going into battle instead of talking with me, a guy she's known her entire life. "But I've been dreaming of the same thing since I was a kid. So, patience. A constant reminder that no matter how many steps I take in life, no matter where I go, I still only want one thing: to belong."

My feet might as well be cemented to the sidewalk as Mina follows the curve of the street back up to my family's house. They're all probably wondering where we went, and it's safe to say that there's no chance of summarizing what happened out here into quaint, simplistic bullet points. No cliff notes that could possibly condense the magnitude of it all into digestible highlight reels.

I nearly kissed Mina.

For the first time in my life, I almost lost control with a woman I shouldn't even want in the first place. I've seen her sick. I've seen her cry. I've seen her casually flirt with guys at bars on the few times I've gone out with her, Effie, and Sarah.

But never, in all these years, have I seen the blatant *want* that was written in her expression tonight. It matched the need written in my soul, and though that should terrify the hell out of me, it doesn't.

Mina Pappas is the one woman I shouldn't crave.

Because I've been waiting my entire life to feel as though I'm finally where I belong.

Tonight, for a slip of a moment, a snapshot in time, she belonged with me.

16

MINA

It's official: Sophia is off her damn rocker.

I plunk my wineglass down on the dinner table. "No."

"Why not?" With careful, precise movements, she cuts a sliver of steak and pops it into her mouth. Bony elbow planted on the table, she stares at me, her fork dangling from loose fingers. "Do you know how much fun we could have?" Those tines swivel to point in my direction. "Think about it: a few days up on the ski slopes, wine, fires roasting, old friends you haven't seen in ages. What's there to say no to?"

A weekend trip to the middle-of-nowhere Maine with Sophia and the other kids from our graduating Greek school class is *not* my idea of fun. Picking out sinks for my salon? That's fun. Trimming off a client's dead ends? Shiver me timbers, someone hand me a pair of shears. Standing outside in the freezing temperatures, Nick Stamos's mouth inches from mine? Oh so tempting and the most fun I've had in ages. But a weekend trip with people I have little in common with aside from our mutual Greek-ness? No, thanks, I'm all good.

"I don't think so."

Sophia sets down her fork. "Think of it like a reunion." She turns to Effie's mom, determination etched into her expression. "*Kyria* Stamos, what do you think? This is such a great idea."

Aleka trades an inscrutable glance with her husband, George, who sits across from her. "*Well,*" she hedges, one hand coming up to pat her dyed-blonde bouffant, "My daughter is busy, yes?"

"Very busy," Effie confirms succinctly. She stabs a leafy green on her plate and gives it a swirl in a puddle of vinaigrette. "I've got tours all weekend. Man, just so many tours." With a free hand to her chest, she purses her lips. "If I could cancel them, I would in a second. But we're unfortunately rain or shine." A short, noncommittal shrug brings her shoulders up to her ears. "It breaks my heart to tell you that I can't—"

"Single people."

Um, what?

We all stare at Sophia, she with the crazy orange hair. I'm beginning to think the personality matches the bad decisions on her head.

Nick's gravel-pitched voice pierces the silence first. "I'm sorry, what did you say?"

"I thought that, you know, instead of inviting *everyone,* we could focus on those of us who are still single." She sends a *so-sorry* pout at my best friend, and then looks to Sarah, who's seated beside her wife and looking highly amused. "I mean, you're married, Effie. And"—Sophia takes a big breath —"since I'm recently divorced, I figured this could be a singles-only trip." She cuts her attention to me. "Though I didn't realize you'd be here tonight, Mina. I was actually planning to send you a message online." The smile she flashes me is so transparently fake that I almost call her on it.

Almost.

Unfortunately for her, she's now totally solidified my decision. A weekend trip with a bunch of single Greeks—it sounds like a naughty ballad, a bad Greek comedy, or the most epic of shit shows. Possibly all three, even. Since I'm already embroiled in a shit show of my own—*hello, Agape*—I don't have the time to consider adding another.

Plus, I'm more of a beach person anyway. If I want to sit in front of a fireplace, I can camp out at my parent's house on any given night. I'll be forced to stand vigil for one of my dad's lectures about my poor life decisions, but at least I can hop in my car and flee whenever I want.

The same can't be said for up in Maine, where I'll be hostage to Sophia's brand of crazy, endless mountains of snow, and shitty cell service.

I shiver at the thought.

"Aleka," snaps Nick and Effie's grandmother to her daughter-in-law. She's sitting diagonal from me, and altogether pretending I don't exist. In my defense, she rarely pays anyone attention but her grandchildren . . . and her old crony friends. She's predictable like that—same goes for her wardrobe. Dressed in mourning clothes, *Kyria* Stamos is a wrinkled, old thing, more bones than skin. Her tongue has always been rapier sharp, proving the old adage false. Her bark is *definitely* worse than her bite. I reach for my wine as she embarks on a verbal crusade in Greek.

She speaks too fast for me to translate on the fly, but I catch words here and there and piece them together like some mismatched puzzle. Something about Nick and Sophia and babies and disappointment.

Oh, Lord. Not back to this again.

Nick's natural olive complexion turns a little green. "*Óxi, Yiayia,*" he growls, his back ramrod straight as he pushes his plate forward and makes a desperate-looking grab for his beer bottle. "Let it go."

But his grandmother has never been one for letting anything go. See: finding me in her grandson's hotel room, completely clothed. She snaps back furiously, hands flying through the air and nearly smacking Effie in the face. My best friend ducks out of the way, eyes rolling toward the heavens, and downs the rest of her wine.

"Shoot me," she mouths in my direction.

I nod toward Sarah and make a show of tapping my bare ring finger. "Lucky bitches," I mouth back, and they both snicker and huddle their heads together, Sarah leaning over at the last moment to kiss her wife.

I'm not kidding. They really *are* lucky—to have found the *one*, their best friend, the single person they'd do anything to protect.

I return my attention to Nick, my fake boyfriend, who looks on the verge of losing his temper—which is *so* out of character for him that I'm tempted to see if Uber Eats will do a girl a favor and deliver a bowl of popcorn.

Nick shakes his head curtly at whatever his *yiayia* is tossing his way, then grimaces and looks toward Sophia. "Sorry," he mutters in English, "you're great, I'm sure, but I . . . I don't want to"—his jaw visibly flexes—"breed with you."

From the way his beautiful pewter eyes flick to *Kyria* Stamos, I'm guessing that was one of her grand ideas, repeated verbatim. If I know her at all, then I'm sure the "breeding" came in the same sentence as "before I die, *Niko*." Oh, the awkwardness. Screw the popcorn, it might be time to bust out the Tito's.

Or you can come to his rescue.

I could, but what was it he mentioned before? Oh, yeah, that his family would never believe it if we claimed to be dating. Effie knows my relationship with her brother is nothing but a sham, and I can almost guarantee that Sarah's in the loop too. Aleka and George wouldn't believe it either. Not because they don't like me, but because Nick has always had a solid type: women with "future wife material" written all over them. I don't know what Savannah Rose does for a living, but Brynn Whitehead is a kindergarten teacher and you don't get more "wifey" and "babymaker" vibes than that.

Except tonight he veered from the norm.

Tonight, he veered toward . . . *me*.

And there's one person at this table—the one causing Nick the ultimate level of grief—who would *absolutely* believe that I sank my claws into him . . . *Kyria* Stamos herself. If I were a lesser person, there would be no better satisfaction than playing my one trump card over the woman who made my life hell for months on end.

But there's no satisfaction thrumming through me right now, only nerves as I slap together the Greek words into a coherent sentence that she'll understand. I conjugate the verb for "dating" into the present plural, my mouth silently moving over the words as the wineglass in my right hand turns slippery from my clammy palm.

You can do this!

Si se puede!

Oops, wrong language.

Naí boreís!

That's better. Never let it be said that I'm not an overachiever.

The Stamos matriarch is still venting, rambling on about Nick's lack of babies and how disappointed she is that she won't have any grandchildren to spoil when she kicks the bucket—i.e. dies—and I clear my throat, set my wineglass down and move to stand up.

"*Kyría* Stamos—"

"Nick should come!"

My gaze flies to Sophia, who only clarifies, "To Maine." She leans across the table to settle her hand over his. "You should totally come with us to Maine."

The man looks positively terrified. "I wasn't in your grade."

"*And?*" Sophia visibly squeezes his hand. "We'll trade one Stamos for the other. You know, the married one for the *single* one."

Before I have the chance to throw out that Nick isn't single, not really, she's whipping around to *Kyría* Stamos and bursting into a fluent string of Greek. I envy her ease with the language, but that doesn't stop my gaze from volleying between the woman decked out in all black to the woman thirty years her younger, who's wearing so much pink, I'm worried Pepto-Bismol might come calling.

As much as I want to ask what's going on, that would be like admitting that I might as well be as non-Greek as Sarah. I search out my best friend's wife now, noticing the creases between her blonde brows as she struggles to wrangle the conversation into something coherent to an outsider.

You and me both, girl.

She catches my eye and cocks a brow, as though to say, *a little help over here!*

Unfortunately, she's all on her own. The words are moving way too fast for me to cling onto one of them, let alone all, and I inhale slowly to ease my frustration. Frustration with myself, not with the people at this table. It's not their fault that I'm me. Mina Pappas, my mother's daughter—and not my father's blood. Or rather, I'm the girl who's always wanted to belong, to feel like I fit in . . . and I've been reminded all my life that I don't. At school, I was the dumb girl with the Barbie fetish; at home, my dad never made it a secret that I'm nothing but the product of a short-lived affair with some random guy my mother met on a trip to America before they immigrated to the United States. A mistake my father *oh-so-kindly* overlooked for reasons they've never divulged.

But my half-Greek blood is something he's always made me aware of: that I'm not Greek enough, not Pappas enough, a little too wild, a little too *unlike him,* my adopted father. Growing up, I used to wonder how my father and my *Theio* Prodromos, his brother, could be so incredibly different. One thrived off anger and bitterness; the other wielded a smile like his personal weapon. I don't know if my uncle ever knew that I wasn't his brother's real daughter, but he never made me feel anything less than part of the family when we visited him. Those summers in Greece were my favorite times of the year—although that had to do with being near Nick 24/7 as well.

Still, my half-breed lineage definitely isn't something that's known outside my immediate family. Ahem. Rather, my mom's infidelity isn't known to anyone outside of my immediate family . . . although I did let the secret slip to Aleka Stamos way back when.

Because she was so nice and motherly and sweet and I was a kid in desperate need of comfort.

Because even then, when I was around twelve years old, I found every way to rebel against Yianni Pappas. It didn't matter that *he* didn't know that Aleka was in on the family scandal. *I* knew and Effie's mom knew, and whenever my dad started in on scrutinizing me for things I couldn't change —like, you know, his wife's infidelity—at least I had somewhere safe to retreat. With the Stamos family, I never felt anything less than supported.

Even tonight, Aleka's hug when I came inside soothed my frayed nerves, and George, who is my dad's opposite in every way, took the seat beside me so he could ask questions about *Agape. Do you need any help?* he asked. *I am proud of you, Mina,* he praised with a pat to my shoulder and a familiar twinkle in his eye.

Love. The Stamos family has it in spades, though, in many ways, Nick and my dad are a little too similar for comfort. Both men are uptight. Both men can be reserved, their true emotions shielded from everyone around them.

"I'm not fuck—" Nick clamps his mouth shut, biting off the curse before it can truly greet the world. He rubs a hand over the lower half of his face, his annoyance written in his expression.

Okay, maybe he's not *so* emotionally stunted. The man curses like a sailor, and in two languages at that.

Aleka jumps into the fray, casting a glance at Sophia like she hates having her mother-in-law lose her cool in front of people who aren't family. "Think about it, *Niko mou*," she says. "It could be fun, yes?"

"Like a root canal on the first day of my period."

Oops, that one was me.

Nick leans forward, elbows on the table, and turns his head toward me. He's two seats away, on the other side of his dad, but that doesn't stop him from announcing, "I'll go if Mina goes."

I open my mouth, then snap it shut. I do it again because I can't think of a damn thing to say that isn't *you're out of your flipping mind*. "I—"

Except now he's visibly warming up to the idea. With a little, self-satisfied grin he can't even hide, he plucks up his beer bottle from the table and drains the rest in one swallow. "Yeah," he says, voice all smooth and velvety and confident, "we'll go together. One car. A full weekend of skiing and—"

"I don't ski."

Nick doesn't cave to my stiff rebuttal. "Where in Maine are we going again?" he asks Sophia without taking his eyes off me.

"Bethel," offers up the instigator of this entire fiasco. "It's about three hours away. Maybe three and a half depending on how slow you drive."

Amused pewter eyes pin me in place. "Fast, then, just how Ermione likes it."

I'm going to murder him. Forget about kissing him, forget about doing anything *more* with him, I'm going to kill him and then do something horrible with his body. Like bury him in a 1970's home with awful wallpaper and shag carpeting in every room. Because *that's* the sort of godawful grave he deserves, the jerk.

I return his unblinking stare. "I'm going to be sick that weekend. I'm predicting the flu."

His mouth twitches. "All the better to let me take care of you for a full seventy-two hours. You'll never meet a better nurse than me."

"Your ego, Nick," I mutter, rolling my eyes, "seriously."

"A little birdie told me I needed more sugar in my life. Well, I'm ready to deliver."

With my gaze locked on his handsome face, I debate the meaning behind that. Is he . . . is he using *sugar* as a sexual euphemism? Something tells me he's only yanking my chain, but it doesn't stop me from shifting in my seat because, damn him, now I'm imagining him parting my knees and settling his big body between them. Does he have any tattoos of his own? Any snapshots in time that are forever marked on his body? It seems only fair that I find out, considering he got a full view of my rear end.

Finally, with the image of a naked Nick in my head, I drag the words out slowly like I'm being led to the gallows. "I'll . . . consider it."

Satisfaction curves his lips into a wide grin. "Glad to hear it. You need to remember to live, even when you're reachin' for those dreams of yours. Plus, I didn't want to break out the big guns."

"And those are?"

"Blackmail," he says with a wink. It's the second time he's done that tonight and my heart (and libido) don't know how to handle it. Looking altogether too pleased with himself, he nods toward Sophia. "Looks like you've got two more taga-longs. When's this shindig happening?"

It's only then I notice that Nick and I have caught the attention of every person at the table. In the midst of our banter, it was all too easy to forget that we aren't alone. Effie looks like she's swallowed her steak the wrong way. Aleka keeps staring at her husband, and I don't miss the way she checks out her mother-in-law.

Kyria Stamos, the one woman most likely to throw a fit at her grandson's new plans, sits perfectly quiet while she sips her *café*. Like me when the conversation was rolling in Greek, she's blissfully unaware of anything that's been said in English.

Sometimes, ignorance really is bliss.

"Two weekends from now," Sophia says, and, like Nick's grandmother, she doesn't seem at all perturbed by the fact that Nick just browbeat me into attending. Maybe she really does need a weekend away from Boston and her ex-husband? Or maybe she's got her eye on another attendee. Both seem like viable, *preferable* options. Way better than to think she's gunning for Nick. "Oh, this is going to be so much fun!"

Fun isn't the word I'd use.

But when I glance over at Nick, I amend that.

A weekend in snow-laden Maine sounds like hell, but with Nick there . . . well, maybe there's something to be said about body heat.

17

MINA

The next morning, I'm up early enough that I watch the sun hit the horizon from my salon's bay window. Its rays kiss the narrow, winding street, and the other brownstones that rise up like miniature towers and stretch toward the pink-and-orange sky. From a young age, I always loved coming to Harvard Square. It's a bustle of students and young professionals and creatives carving their place in the world.

Just as I am now.

Seated on the floor with paint swatches spread out before me, I lean forward and press my fingers to the cold glass. Snow fell last night, a good five or six inches that I shoveled at the crack of dawn this morning. Already there's a dusting of a new sheet of the fluffy stuff and I figure I have another hour or so before I need to bundle up and grab my shovel and boots for round two.

Shoveling snow isn't my thing. Although, to be fair, winter in Massachusetts isn't my thing, either. Maybe in five years or ten or twenty, I'll hire someone to plow the snow on my strip of sidewalk, but right now I'm enjoying the satisfaction of doing it myself. It took me a long time to get to this place in life, and I'm not ready to pass off even the most basic of responsibilities to anyone else.

Even if that means I need to get my butt out of bed at a ridiculous hour to ensure I'm not blocked in by a Nor'easter, I'll do it, no questions asked.

I shift my attention away from the quiet street and down to the myriad paint chips. It feels like I've waited years to pick out a paint color for the walls of *Agape*. Endless pictures on my Pinterest boards. Back further than that, I had binders stuffed full of cutouts from interior-design magazines. Each decision made for the salon is a win, a reminder that patience and hard work got me here, even when my own parents would have preferred me to choose the marriage route.

Except that marriage has never been in the cards for me. How can it be when my own mother, who claims to love my adopted father, cheated on her new husband? And with some random guy she met on a trip? Not that my dad is any better. He may have "taken me in" out of the kindness of his heart, but he took me to task in a way he never did with Katya and Dimitri. Expectations I would never meet were set out before me, and I tore through them all, knocking each one down.

Because unlike what most parents do for their children when they don't want to see them hurt, mine never hid that I was the outlier in the family. Not outside the house, of course, where they maintained their uppity, holier-than-thou act—but within our home, where both Katya and Dimitri were allowed to flourish and find their way, I was . . . controlled.

Picking a wall color feels like the greatest gift. A miracle that I still managed to find my path, despite being held back for so many years. A miracle that I refused to let my learning disability get the best of me, even when my father quietly, in that awful, reserved way of his, insinuated that the problem was all in my head and that I simply didn't apply myself hard enough.

Getting here, achieving the dream all on my own, is nothing short of a miracle.

Fate's tipping hand, even after being dealt bullshit card after bullshit card.

Quietly, I sort through the paint chips and hold them up, one by one, and try to imagine them on *Agape*'s walls. And, one by one, I narrow down the possibilities. Canary Yellow calls to my rebel soul but isn't the right fit. It goes in a pile with the other misfits. I pick up another, a muted gray, and slowly read over the printed name at the bottom of the chip: Reflection. Appropriately titled, maybe, but a little too morose for the salon of my dreams.

Beyond the window, the record store across from *Agape* floods with light and I spot the manager meandering through the aisles. I'm convinced it's the only remaining music store in the city, and, as I have every morning since moving in, I raise a hand and wave. The manager waves back, then goes on his way.

Happiness floods my chest. This right here, this is my life and it's *perfect*.

No, perfect was Nick Stamos almost kissing you last night.

My heart skips a beat.

That almost kiss, that tight embrace he wrapped me in, was better than any sex I've ever experienced. I'm not sure what that says about the men I've hooked up with, but it probably reflects more on me than it does on any of my casual flings.

I lift Reflection up once more, giving it a second thought, then add it to the pile with Canary Yellow.

Sifting through the paint chips, I come to a pretty one that straddles the line of gray and lavender. It's the perfect blend of elegant and feminine. With a darker accent wall to complement it, I can easily see this color painted throughout the salon. Plus, isn't lavender supposed to promote a calm atmosphere?

Pulling it closer to my face, I give myself a moment to study the letters. As a kid, reading of any kind sent me into a blind panic. The words blurred, they danced across my vision like a Whack-A-Mole evading the gavel; they gave me hell until frustration warred under my skin and in my soul, a constant battle of *maybe-you're-just-dumb*, and I gave up.

Like this salon, I've come a long way since then. Words no longer terrify me, and if someone has a problem that it takes me an extra moment to read the options on a menu or a long-winded text, then that's on them. Sorry, not sorry.

I sweep a cursory glance over the letters on the paint chip, absorbing them as a whole instead of individually as I once did, and whisper, "Elation."

Sounds like a winner to me.

Hell, I feel pretty elated about life right now.

Happy bequeaths happy—that's pretty much the mantra of my life.

I stick Elation in my binder of Wants for the salon, then check my phone. It's after eight now, and my ass is sore from sitting on the concrete floor for so many hours. I'd sit for another four if it means I can continue watching the world outside my window. *My* window. Man, I don't think I'll ever get over how good that feels.

My phone vibrates, and I glance down to see that Effie's texted me.

Oh, boy. Last night I fled the Stamos household before

she had the chance to have the come-to-Jesus talk I knew she so desperately wanted to have with me. She's obviously worried about Nick and me, and it's not that I'm slamming the door on her concerns. She's not wrong: her brother wants the whole shebang and I . . . well, I want what I have now. A quiet morning that belongs to me, watching the shops lining Bow Street come to life. I want to live on my own terms by my own rules without a heavy hand to ensure I comply with rules designed to hold me back.

But that doesn't mean I'm not attracted to Nick or that I haven't been attracted to him for years now. And I can't, no matter how much it would appease Effie's worries, ignore how insanely giddy I feel about the prospect that Nick may find me attractive too. I mean, talk about wishes cast on shooting stars *actually* coming true.

We're both adults. Assuming that last night wasn't a fluke, shouldn't a fling be a mutual decision between the two of us? I trust Nick to know his own mind, just as I know mine. I'm not going to be dick-tranced into changing my decision about a husband and kids.

Maybe you're getting ahead of yourself.

Sigh. Yeah, maybe that too.

We *almost* kissed, but we were also standing on a dark, empty street with no one to judge us or to question our motives. It's possible that he was only caught up in the sexually charged moment, but can't the same be said for me? I never would have been so bold if I hadn't—literally—seen his jean-covered erection only last week.

The way I look at it, Nick and I will have to talk at some point about what happened, and then we'll set down the rules. And, knowing him, he'll have a spreadsheet and approximately fourteen bullet points, all detailing the risks and potential hazards of a no-strings attached fling.

Call me ruthless, but I can't wait to see his expression

when I rip his precious list to shreds. He needs someone who'll yank him out of his shell, and I'm more than woman enough to do the job.

Tapping my phone awake, I pull open Effie's text, only to see that she messaged me a link to an article from a site called *Celebrity Tea*. I cringe, then cringe again when I spot the bolded byline: *Nick Stamos, America's Heartbroken Bachelor, finds Love with Unknown Woman.*

My stomach sinks.

Oh, crap.

I *tap-tap-tap* on the article, sending my phone into an apoplectic fit, and am visually assaulted by a blown-up image of myself in Nick's arms. As in, it's me, in the clothes I wore last night, hugging Nick in the clothes *he* wore last night. The Red Sox logo on his T-shirt is visible from the angle the photographer captured the picture. We're standing in the semi-dark, our arms wrapped around each other, our faces mostly shadowed by the street lamp overhead.

"Oh, fuck a goddamn duck."

I skim the article as quickly as I can, doing my best to keep my phone steady.

"*Put A Ring On It* contestant Nick Stamos (age 32) was spotted getting cozy late last night in his hometown of Cambridge, Massachusetts. According to one anonymous source linked to TV production, Stamos was a favorite from day one on the show's debut season. 'I really thought he'd walk away with the final ring, you know?' disclosed the source. 'Savannah Rose was absolutely smitten by him. There wasn't a date she didn't have Nick on, and anyone could clearly see that the two of them had *major* chemistry.'

And yet, major chemistry couldn't save Stamos—no relation to John Stamos, America's favorite uncle, by the way—from the last elimination round. A video of the

bachelorette turning down our Greek Adonis went viral just weeks ago, and now it seems Nick's already on the rebound with a new lady love. Who might she be? Time will only tell, but since the two lovebirds were spotted only a few blocks from his family's residence, it's easy to presume that a *My Big Fat Greek Wedding* may be in the making soon enough.

Let's raise a toast to leaked sources, shall we?

I'll be back soon with more details, dear reader. You know we at *Celebrity Tea* do our best at spilling the damn tea, 24/7."

Uh-oh. Grimacing, I fire off a quick text to Effie to smooth any ruffled feathers: *Looks like my unofficial role as fake girlfriend has begun.*

Immediately, three little dancing dots appear at the bottom left corner of the screen. I smooth my thumb over the glass and wait. Effie is not going to be pleased. Sure enough, I don't have to wait long.

Effie: *There were cameras near our house. Cameras neither of you knew were on the hunt. You were doing that crazy thing with your tongue when you want someone to kiss you!!!*

Me: *Crazy thing with my tongue??? I have no idea what you're talking about.*

Me: *Nick and I were just . . . having a conversation.*

Me: *About tattoos.*

Effie: *You're a shit liar.*

Me: *Tell me how you really feel.*

Effie: *Trust me, there are a lot of exclamation marks and four-letter words. You're gonna get hurt. He's gonna get hurt. This is going to be a disaster of epic proportions and I'm already foreseeing sending Tito's out of stock when I order everything they've got to keep you from going off the deep end.*

Me: *What makes you think I'll be the one who needs to be consoled?*

Effie: *Because you've been obsessed with my brother since the time you finally grew boobs.*

Me: *Obsessed is a strong word. I'm not a stalker, Ef.*

Effie: *And I repeat: obsessed.*

Me: *I know you don't want to hear this, seeing as you both came out of the same womb, but maybe Nick only wants a fling?*

Effie: *Maybe he does. And maybe you'll hook up with him and, for the first time in your life, realize that you want MORE. And he still only wants that fling. Let that settle in for a sec.*

I don't want to let it settle in, and thanks to the universe not being an asshole today, I don't have to.

The front door to my salon bursts open and Nick's workers spill inside from the cold with equipment cradled in their arms. Shaking snow from their hair, they stomp their boots on the two towels I laid out this morning after spotting the steady snowfall.

One last "let's not fight about this" text to Effie, and then I drop my phone onto the pile of paint chips and hop to my feet. Swipe my hands over my fleece-lined leggings. Unexpected butterflies erupt in my belly. Seeing Nick after last night . . . Well, it's moment-of-truth time. If he pretends nothing happened, I'll either knee him in the balls or shove his ass out into the snow to freeze.

Giving the group of three men a hasty scan, I note with disappointment that Nick isn't with them. Feigning a blasé tone, I ask, "Where's your hailed leader?"

The tallest of the bunch, a handsome guy named Vince, lets out a deep laugh. "He who payeth our checks wenteth to Dunkin's . . . eth."

"You been watching *Shakespeare in Love* again?" deadpans the redheaded, Rupert Grint lookalike, named Mark. He's built in a way that Vince isn't, with heaps of muscles on top of muscles that speak to hours spent in a gym. Height-wise, though, he might as well be Vince's little brother.

Vince flips him the bird with all the flare of a true Bostonian. "It's a great movie—a goddamn classic."

"Haven't seen it."

"You're un-American, Mark. You don't like the Fourth of July," Vince says, holding up one hand, his index finger extended. "You don't like *Shakespeare in Love*." His middle finger shoots up next. "You're squirrelly as fuck about cannoli, and I'm saying this for all to hear—if you don't like cannoli, you can't be trusted. It's in the Italian bible, right after *you-shall-always-listen-to-your-mother-or-risk-death-by-slipper.*"

Holding back a snort, I raise my hand. "I don't like cannoli." I don't touch the slipper comment—my mom never whipped out the *pandofla* herself, but that doesn't mean I haven't heard the horror stories from my peers. It's a Greek thing, too.

Vince slaps a hand over his heart and claws at his chest. Gasping, he pretends to collapse in a heap. "Blasphemer!"

"It's the texture that gets to me," I say with a lighthearted shrug.

That doesn't seem to make a difference. Vince side-eyes me with playful distrust. "Correction, Mina, cannoli is the texture of the gods."

Bill, the last one in the group, claps Vince on the back with a hearty *thwack*. "You say the same thing about your cum—"

Vince erupts into a coughing fit. The words "shut up" and "asshole" are meshed in, and I'm about to respond when I hear Nick's familiar voice behind me: "Keep that thing in your pants, man. No one needs to be scarred for life. And I speak from experience."

I turn, only to find Nick balancing a cardboard tray stuffed full of coffee cups from Dunkin's and a bag with what

I assume are donuts. At least, I hope they're donuts. I lift a brow. "Really?" I tease him. "From experience?"

Long-legged strides bring him to the receptionist's desk that we pushed into the corner of the room last week. He sets the coffees and donuts down before dragging off his damp coat and dropping it on the floor. "Gave me nightmares," he says, snagging one of the coffees from the tray. "You think you know a guy until you see his dick for the first time."

I grin. "Strangely, I can relate."

I watch as he moves toward me, and not for the first time, I can't help but admire his prowl. He walks with his hips, all loose, masculine fluidity that can turn a girl's brain to mush without a single bit of effort.

When he stops before me, I lift my chin and let my gaze climb up his sweatshirt-covered chest to the strong lines of his face. "Trust me," he murmurs, "Vince's a shocker down under."

"A shocker?"

He holds up his free hand, thumb and index finger barely separated by air. "Small, if you catch my drift. Vincent Miceli's been disappointing women around the world since circa 1986."

Nick's GM cuts loose a hearty laugh. "Bastard. The only shock happening is when your jaw hit the floor the first time you caught a gander of The Great One."

I lean toward Nick and drop my voice to a whisper. "Why do I get the feeling he's speaking about his penis *and* capitalizing the great one?"

Nick bends, bringing himself down to my level. The tip of his nose brushes the shell of my ear and my poor, needy body reacts all *oooh-that-feels-nice*. Goosebumps flare to life on my skin. "That's because his mama never taught him that lying to yourself might be good for morale but sets you up for a lifetime of anticlimactic moments. Poor guy's figuring it out the hard way, one small dick joke at a time."

Anticlimactic moments. Oh, puns, how I love you so.

Poor Vince.

My shoulders shake with barely leashed mirth. I don't want Vince to think I'm laughing at his expense—even though I'm sure Nick's only busting his balls as guys do—but, still, I'm *totally* laughing at his expense.

A firm hand connects with the small of my back, and the unexpected touch is enough to stem my laughter and clam me right up. I jerk my gaze up, only to find Nick already watching me with his full lips tugged up in a big grin. "*Yia sena*," he husks out. *For you.*

I glance down.

A little thrill zips through me when I see the coffee he's offering. Above the Dunkin's logo is my full name scrawled in black marker. Our fingers brush when I take it from him. "Thank you." I make a point to blow the steam away from the plastic lid and take a small sip in gratitude. "You didn't have to grab me anything."

His smile deepens, carving shallow dimples into each of his cheeks. "Couldn't leave you hanging this early in the morning." Briefly, so briefly I wonder if I imagine it, he applies pressure to my back before stepping away. "Coffee's up for grabs, guys. Same with the donuts."

Bill and Mark exchange a glance.

"He's trying to butter us up before dropping bad news," Bill grumbles with a middle finger rubbing along his hairline. Wicked subtle move, right there.

Nick only laughs. "The bad news is that one of you gets the *wicked* exclusive opportunity to come with me to check out the museum today."

"*What?*"

"Holy shit, dude. We got it?"

"Hell fucking yeah!" Vince calls out, rounding off the group's enthusiasm. "I knew we'd get the bid."

"What bid?"

My question echoes in the salon, and all four men turn to me in unison. In the soft, morning light, Nick's ears pinken. It's Vince who actually answers. He sidles up to his boss, throwing an arm around Nick's broad shoulders. "This guy right here"—he palms the side of Nick's face like a brother would—"just booked Stamos Restoration and Co. into the tightest race Boston's seen in light-years."

Bill lifts his gaze to the ceiling and lets out an aggrieved sigh. "First Shakespeare, now Star Wars. You're a goddamn pop-culture reference book, Miceli."

Vince ignores him completely, his dark eyes fixed on me. "There's a new history museum opening, a few blocks away, actually. It's all about the Victorian era in Boston, and Nick here landed us the deal to restore the building in prep for the curators to come in and doll the place up."

"Wow." I flick my attention to Nick, who looks mighty uncomfortable under all the praise. "That's amazing!"

He doesn't shrug, but the forced nonchalance in his expression does the shrugging for him. "It's a job like any other."

Except that it doesn't feel that way. I think of his miniature wooden structures in his office, all those hours spent perfecting the smallest, most intricate architectural details. Like me, Nick is a creator. An artist. Our chosen mediums may be different, but that doesn't mean he's not a complete badass. In the last few weeks, I've spent more nights wishing I could watch him work on finishing the church spire than I care to admit.

Sensing that he wants the subject to change pronto, I say, "And I bet you'll rock it like any other job."

The smile he gives me is one of relief. "Just like I need to rock *this* job." Pivoting on his heel, he crosses the room and grabs a donut from the container. Frosted chocolate, from the looks of it. He pops the small, round ball of chewy delight into his mouth, then sucks the glaze from his thumb.

Excuse me while I forget how to breathe.

No man has any right to look so sexy eating a donut. Seriously, no right at all.

Like a woman obsessed, my breath gets lodged somewhere in my throat when Nick opts for another and lifts it to his lips. He surveys *Agape* with a critical eye while he chews. "Drywall by Wednesday, guys. Today, let's put up the rest of the frames and start on the insulation." He gestures toward the receptionist's desk. "Hit up the coffee and then we'll get going."

Warm coffee cup in hand, I stare at the exposed wooden beams of the rearranged walls of the back rooms and hallway, unable to envision the end result—not the way I instinctively can when I'm cutting a client's hair or applying color.

"You look worried."

I twist at the waist toward the sound of Nick's voice. "I'm not."

"No?" He steps in close. Angles his body so that we're elbow to elbow. "What then?"

"Honestly?" My right shoulder hikes up in a shrug. "I'm admiring your work. I know 'amazing' is such a bland word nowadays. It's tossed around, used for every bit of praise, but I just . . ." I lift my free hand toward the restructured walls. "You see a room, a house, and you know exactly what to do to bring it to life. And that's—that's pretty amazing."

Silence is my only answer, and then he's clasping a hand around my elbow and encouraging me to follow him. Vince and Bill and Mark shoot the shit behind us, ribbing each other mercilessly about some fantasy football league they're all in, while Nick steers me toward his work bench.

Although perhaps calling it a work bench is a bit of a stretch.

It's more like a long board of plywood boosted up on stacked paint cans. I take a sip of the warm brew and watch as he sifts through large, illustrated mock-ups. I recognize most from the plans he emailed me last week, but my interest spikes when I spot a drawing that looks a lot like a mosaic. He flips past it, shuffling it in with the others, before stopping at a black-and-white sketch. Fingertip to the corner of the sheet, he spins it around for me to get a good look.

"After stalking your Pinterest board, I wanted your thoughts on this."

Anticipation spurs my feet forward. Closing the gap, I feel my heart give an extra thud of excitement when I realize what exactly he's showing me. At least, what I *think* he's showing me. I set the coffee down on the plywood, away from his sketches. "Is this—"

"Yeah, it is." Nick threads his fingers through his thick hair, then lets his hand fall to the plywood. Beneath the fabric of his nondescript gray T-shirt, his muscled arms bunch and tighten. "A hydrotherapy room? No way I could skip it after all those pictures you pinned. Here, let me show you."

He cuts around the work bench. I expect him to stand beside me and point out all the details my untrained eye has missed. He doesn't. Instead, he ambles up behind me, leaving no doubt in my mind that he's got zero regrets about what went down last night. My breath hitches when he nudges me forward, until my pelvis collides with the plywood and he's dropping his hands onto the bench on either side of me.

"You good with this?" he asks, leveling his profile alongside mine. And I swear I can feel the stubble of his jaw against my cheek. Holy-friggin-cannoli. Or, more appropriately, holy-friggin-baklava.

His thumbs skate over my pinkies, and my brain hollers, *don't forget to breathe if you want to live!* Living seems overrated when I've got a six-foot-plus Adonis plastered to my back. Blocked in as I am, I can't see Vince or the other guys behind us, and I can only imagine what they're thinking right now.

But maybe . . . maybe this is good, right? His family might not believe we're dating, but the same can't be said for his employees.

"Yeah," I whisper, "I'm all good."

Against my back, I feel his chest deflate as though he was holding his breath, too. "Good," he mutters, "that's good." His left hand lowers over mine, and then he's moving my fingers to trace the skeleton of the sketch, skirting along the periphery. "I know this wasn't in the initial plans I sent you, but I'm a firm believer in reaching for what you want."

"Achieving your temporary longing."

His fingers squeeze mine gently. "More like making it permanent." He pauses, and maybe it's my imagination but I hope he's as entranced by the sight of us holding hands as I am. Like a time capsule, it feels like we're teenagers again and experiencing lust for the first time. A handhold can be as exciting as a hot make-out session, if it's with the right person. Nick's thumb traces the outer line of my palm, dipping to the indentation of my wrist. "Anyway," he says, "I want you to have this, if it's what you want."

It *is* what I want, but that doesn't mean I have the extra funds to consider anything but the bare necessities. Floors, sinks, mirrors, hairdryers—those are the necessities. A hydrotherapy room, equipped with a massage table and a whirlpool, aren't even in the same galaxy here.

Mistaking my silence as the go-ahead, Nick scoots a little

to my left, all the better to point out the features marked on the blueprint. "I've been doing a shit ton of research over the last week, and with this . . . you'll leave your competition in the dust, Mina." He releases my hand to sift through his mock-ups for yet another. The second blueprint he lays over the first, and I realize the paper is nearly translucent. Between the two, his vision for the room crackles to life: Edison bulbs hanging from the ceiling, a Vichy shower set out in one corner of the room with a marble wall to keep it out of sight from the hydrotherapy tub. The floors are dark, and I eye his scribbles in the corner of the page: rosewood walls, slate floors, a periwinkle-painted ceiling.

It's . . . stunning.

And so out of my price point that I want to sob at the loss of it, even though it's nothing but a mere thought in his head. Except now it's in mine too, and I wish I could bring it to life with nothing but the snap of my fingers.

I turn to face him. "Nick . . ."

His head jerks up and those pewter eyes home in on me. "Is it too much?"

"No. No, it's perfect." If anything, it's almost *too* perfect. "But I can't afford this. You know I can't afford this."

"We'll figure it out."

"*We*?" I point to him, then stab my chest with the same finger. "Me, Nick. I need to figure this out, and I can't increase my budget. Maybe by a grand—I could scrape it together." Instead of dining out and hitting up the town like my peers, I'm scraping pennies together by feasting on Ramen noodles and taking cold-ass showers at the age of thirty. Forget the fact that I haven't even furnished my apartment more than is needed. All my money, every last dime, is in this hair salon. Shaking my head, I flatten my palm over Nick's beautifully etched draft, so I can't be tempted by what

I can't afford. "Nowhere in the budget do I have room for the sort of money we're talking about here."

He blows out a frustrated breath. "Any news on the asswipe who stole your cash?"

"I wish, but no." I purse my lips together, determined to hold my ground on this. "No extra money is coming my way, so although I love what you've done—and I'll be dreaming about it for years to come—we need to keep it simple."

"I'll take care of it."

I feel my nostrils flare. "No, you won't." I wave an arm at the rest of *Agape*. "You're doing enough already, don't you think? I'm not—I'm not a *charity* case."

The balls of his shoulders practically bulge as he plants his weight on his fists and leans forward. His chin juts forward when he growls, "No one said you're a charity case, Ermione. We have a deal, don't we?"

I think back to the *Celebrity Tea* article Effie sent me, and I wonder if he's seen it yet this morning. As much as I want to bring it up—and, better yet, discuss *us*—my stubborn streak boils to life, all to prove a point. At the end of the day, last night's private moment was captured and posted for the masses. It wasn't an orchestrated date, designed and premeditated to show Nick as someone moving on from the havoc of the show. No, we were *spotted* by a douchebag pap hiding out in a car or in the bushes, which means I effectively did nothing. He's got Vince and Bill and Mark out here working day-in and day-out to finish off my salon, and I'm . . . well, truth is, I'm getting a whole lot more out of this deal of ours than he is. I can't—I *won't*—allow him to throw anymore freebies my way.

My pride can't handle it.

And neither do I want to think of *Agape* and remember that it was built solely upon begged favors. It's an acidic, toxic thought, and my fingers launch into a *tap-tap-tap* rhythm, even as my gut twists.

Keeping my voice low, I meet Nick's gaze. "The deal is on, but there's no room for addendums. A hydrotherapy room is off the table. Not open for discussion."

A tick flares to life in his jaw. "We didn't sign a contract, Mina."

"An oversight, maybe, considering how much you love your rules."

He keeps talking, as though I didn't just hand deliver a jab. "No contract means we're not legally bound to keep to the terms of the same deal." His gaze falls to my mouth, and my core heats like he's directly wired my body to respond to him and him only. Chris Hemsworth could walk into *Agape* right now and I doubt I'd be as needy for him, a Hollywood A-lister, as I am for Nick. It's ridiculously unfair. "Adjustments," he adds, "can be applied as necessary."

No, they can't. I bite the words back and ask instead, "What sort of adjustments are we talking about here?"

My mouth practically tingles under his intense, steady stare. "I'm sure we can get creative."

Oh, my God.

He did *not* just insinuate that, that—

"I-I'm not going to *sleep* with you for a jacuzzi, you jerk." I push against his chest and fight an eye roll when he doesn't even a budge. "And, for the record, I *would* sleep with you. Actually, I've thought about sleeping with you for years, as you very well know because my best friend can't keep her lips sealed, but that doesn't mean I'm going to just . . . just open my legs like some eighteenth-century socialite all for a pretty room." I jab him in the chest again, right over the heart, and then proceed to emphasize every word with another finger-thrust. "End. Of. Discussion."

I twist away, not even acknowledging the wide-eyed

stares I'm getting from the guys, and head for the stairs up to my apartment. Nick Stamos may be my teenage crush, and he may be as hot as Hades, but I've got my pride. I've got my self-respect. And if he even thinks for one second that I'll jump in bed with him for a *massage room,* then he doesn't know me at all.

I don't have room in my life for asshole men.

Not even him.

18

NICK

"Goddamn, you *really* have a way with women, Stamos."

I barely take the time to flip Vince the bird before I'm storming after Mina.

"No, but for real, is this the sort of shit we can anticipate happening on that show you went on?" he shouts after me. "Your face was on *Us Weekly* this morning, by the way!"

Cutting a quick glare over my shoulder, I thrust a finger at my guys. "Lunch break. Take a fucking lunch break before—"

"He's cursin' in English," Bill says to Mark with a shoulder-nudge and a flat, open palm that he curls in a come-hither motion. "Give me my five bucks, man. I told you he'd crack before noon today. I just had that feeling, like when my bones ache before a bad storm."

"That's called arthritis, you moron."

I slam the door up to Mina's apartment closed, blocking out the ribbing of all three morons who call themselves my friends. And what the hell did they mean my face is on *Us Weekly*? Doesn't matter, I'll deal with that later.

I take the stairs two at a time. “Mina!” My voice bellows out like a foghorn and I’m surprised the walls don’t tremble in fear. I feel at loose ends, like I’m on the verge of coming undone and all because of a fucking jacuzzi. I thought she’d love the idea. I thought I could ruffle any flared feathers by telling her she could consider it as my thank-you for accompanying me to the crazy shit show that will be Maine in two weekends.

I thought—though all my thinking doesn’t seem to be doing me any damn good—that she’d see I spent more time than necessary studying every pin on her Pinterest board and doing everything in my power to make her dream a reality.

Because I remember being in her position. The worry that it all would come crumbling down around me, should I even blink a little too long. The fear that my good luck was running on a timer, and if I didn’t soak it up quickly enough, it’d all be gone before morning came around. The nightmares, the stress, the unrelenting anxiety of striking out on my own and having no one to fall back on.

But at least I had my parents and Effie to keep me steady and trucking forward.

Who does Mina have? Her parents who I haven’t seen in years? Her siblings? From what I understand, Katya is living somewhere down south, attending graduate school, and her brother, Dimitri, lives in New York City. Besides Effie, Mina has no one.

Except for me.

Because you’re forcing your way in.

Damn straight I am.

“Mina!” I call out again. “We’re gonna talk. In no way was I implying that you’d pay me with sex. Who do you think I am? Some asshole out of a romance novel?”

I palm the wall and prepare to make the short, tight turn

up to the next flight of stairs, only to have a dainty fist collide angrily with my shoulder. With fast reflexes, I catch Mina's wrist to keep her from pummeling me. "Jesus, are you crazy, *gynaíka?*"

Her honey eyes turn to slits. "I don't like that word."

I swear to God this woman is . . . *Gamóto.* Every time. Every time I think we're making headway, getting along, we revert right back to our perpetual role of frenemies. That's what the kids are calling it nowadays, right? Frenemies? Hell if I know.

Refusing to cut her loose in case she turns those flying fists on me again, I stand my ground. "You don't like the word for *woman*? Seriously?"

She tugs at her wrist to no avail. "It's condescending."

"How?" I pull her down to the stair rung I'm on, and yeah, maybe I do it because it gives me the advantage. I'm taller, broader, and, if I have to harbor a guess, I'm also the only one who's thinking rationally in this dark, dank stairwell. "Women call guys 'man' all the time. Everyone under the sun says 'dude,' and that's not even historically accurate because not all guys are cowboys."

"It's also a pimple on a cow's butt."

"*What?*"

"Dude," she mutters, her eyes never moving from the wall beside my head, "it's also another word for a pimple on a—"

"I heard you the first time." I scrub my free hand over my jaw, all the better to keep the sucker from hitting the floor in shock. "How do you even know this?"

"*Jeopardy.*"

Of course she knows it from *Jeopardy.*

When she pulls at her wrist again, I unleash my hold with a flex of my fingers. Her back collides with the wall behind her, and I can't even imagine how many splinters are baring their splintery teeth, ready to sink into her soft skin. *Don't touch her, and for the love of God, don't set her off again.* My hands ball into fists at my sides. "Back to the conversation, how exactly was I being condescending?"

Her arms fold over her small chest. "It's all in the tone. *Gynaíka,* fold the laundry. *Gynaíka,* is dinner done yet?" Her tone turns snide. "If I count the number of times my father has turned to my mom and said that word, I'll run out of the world's lamb population."

Trust it to Mina Pappas to make me want to laugh when she's chomping at the bit for a fight. I give in, just in the off chance I can make her smile. "That's a hell of a lot of lamb."

The fire in her honey eyes banks to a slow roast. "I'd save every one if I could. No more lamb on the spit for Easter or finding a head bobbing in a steaming pot in the kitchen."

"That happened to you too?" I ask, messing with her. Every Greek kid has been traumatized by smelling something amazing drifting from the stove, only to open the pot's lid and come face to face with . . . well, yeah. Like I said, traumatizing. "Also, probably not the wisest move to keep Greeks everywhere loving you."

Her nostrils flare at that, and she averts her gaze once again. "The Greeks aren't always the end-all-be-all."

"Don't let my grandmother hear you say that."

"Good thing I wouldn't say it in Greek for her to understand."

My lips twitch at her savagery. She's entertaining as all hell when she's spitting fire like this. "So, no *gynaíka* then." I give a curt chin dip. "That's fine with me. God knows I'm not trying to have you punch me again."

"The punch wasn't for that."

"Fully aware of that, *Ermione.*" I face her fully, balancing one foot on the rung above us. As much as I want to plant my hands on the wall behind her head, splinters be damned, I've got no interest in validating her assumption from downstairs. So I keep my hands down by my sides when I say, "Sex is not part of the deal. Not the original deal, not *any* deal." I duck my head, eclipsing some of the height difference, so I can look her in the eye. "You know me. I mean, your nickname for me is Saint—"

"Nick," she cuts in, her expression unreadable. "I know."

She won't meet my gaze, and for one of the first times in my life, I react on impulse.

Softly, I catch her chin between my thumb and forefinger, the lightest touch I've ever given to another person. "Look at me, *koukla*."

The words emerge raspy, the Greek endearment rolling off my tongue before I can even question its very existence—but it does the trick. Mina looks at me. Full-on. Zeroed in. And it rocks me to my fucking soul.

Honey rimmed with amber.

The smallest mole on the slope of her nose. Last night, it was too dark out for me to notice its existence but I do now. I take in my fill, studying every aspect of her face like I do a job site before I begin the restoration process. In my day-to-day life, I handle the finest antiques, the most fragile buildings that I bring back to life for another generation to enjoy.

I've never touched anything—or anyone—more important than I am right now.

Her chin trembles beneath the roughened pads of my fingers, and I finally give in by planting one hand above her head on the wall. This stairwell is cramped and not well-spaced—hardly any nineteenth-century brownstones are—and I breathe in her scent. Citrus. A hint of something sweet, like rose or lavender. Vulnerability.

The latter cloaks the air around us.

"I don't blame you for jumping the gun, but I wasn't thinking of sex when I offered to take on the hydrotherapy room at full cost."

Mina's tongue flicks out to touch her bottom lip. "You were staring at my mouth."

My cock, traitorous bastard that he is, perks up. I shift my hips back, away from temptation. It'd be all too easy to haul her up into my arms and grind my erection into her. But that defeats the purpose of this conversation in the first place.

Think of yiayia*! Count lambs, man! Just think of anything but her lips.*

Unfortunately, lying has never been one of my strong suits.

I stare down at her and hear the words of damnation echo in the stairwell: "I wanted to kiss you." When her brows shoot up in surprise, I hastily add, "Not that it matters. What *does* matter is that I wanted to do the room for *you*. Not as a favor, not in pity, but because I know how it feels to want something so badly you can taste it, and yet—because of circumstances out of your control—that fate no longer belongs to you."

She visibly swallows and maybe I'm absorbing some of her reckless habits because my fingers leave her chin to trace her jawline, then swoop down. The heel of my palm rests against her collarbone as my fingers curl around the nape of her neck. *More,* the new, reckless part of me begs, and I nurture the demand by pressing my forehead to hers.

Voice low, I urge, "Say something."

Another swallow, and this one I feel under my hand like a secondary pulse. "I appreciate the gesture, Nick."

"But?"

"It feels like a handout."

"Mina—"

"I know it's not one." Her hand scrapes over mine, her short nails dancing over my skin. "But thank you for the offer. And . . . and I'm sorry for lumping you in with a group where you don't belong. You were trying to help, and I jumped down your throat prematurely."

Her words wind my heart like a tightly strung coil. "Every person who's ever made you feel 'less than' is an asshole."

She meets my stare, and the slopes of our noses collide in a gentle bump. "The list is mighty."

"Ignore them."

"Already done."

"I'm not"—I skim my hand up, cupping her jaw—"I'm not like them, Mina."

"I know," she whispers.

Beneath my palm, her pulse flutters like a butterfly trapped in a mason jar. I study her features, tracing the lines of a face I thought I knew as well as my own. Twenty-four years, and yet it feels like I don't know her at all. Not the almond shape of her eyes or the sparse split of hair in her left eyebrow, near the tail. Not the tiny scar on her right cheek that's shades lighter than her olive skin or the slight widow's peak of her hairline.

Opening my mouth, I let the admission escape that could ruin us both: "I'm dying to know how you taste."

Her chest heaves and grazes mine.

Above her head, I curl my fingers inward. "I don't give a damn about the deal." My lips press to her forehead. "I don't give a damn about who owes who what." Down I travel, over the crooked bridge of her nose, purposely pausing over the bump. "I don't give a damn about what Effie might say or that I'm not supposed to want you." A lingering kiss to her cheek. "And I don't give a damn that I'm not the kind of guy who does flings and you're not the kind of girl who does long-term."

I move east, teasing, with my lips hovering over hers. I soak in her shuddering breath that wafts over my mouth, and

I fucking relish the way her nails bite into my skin, anchoring my hand to her jawline.

"I need to kiss you," I murmur, refusing to eliminate the final distance between us. I need her desperate like me, as stripped down to the bone as I feel. Nothing less will do. Purposefully, I press my weight into hers. And her throaty moan is a melody I could play on repeat for the rest of my life. *Goddamn perfection*. "Tell me no and we'll stop this right now. No one will ever know that we almost—"

"Stop talking and kiss me, Nick."

She doesn't need to tell me twice.

I crash my mouth down over hers and let myself freefall into possibly the worst decision of my life. But, hell, kissing her doesn't feel like a mistake. No, it feels like we've spent years working toward this one moment, dancing around each other, throwing barbs that carry more meaning than either of us have ever admitted.

It feels like fate.

My fingers bury themselves in her thick hair, winding those silky strands around my balled fist. And then I pull my hand back, sharp enough that a delicate gasp breaks from her mouth and she clutches my shoulders like I'm the only thing keeping her from tumbling down the flight of stairs.

I take full advantage.

I graze my tongue along the seam of her lips, demanding entry.

And she gives it with the neediest, sexiest whimper I've ever heard.

Oh, *fuck*.

The sound goes straight to my dick. It strains against the zipper of my jeans, hard and throbbing. I hear nothing but the whirring sound of blood thundering in my head. My lungs squeeze, and I think of nothing but the delicious hint of coffee on her breath and the way she's clasped one hand to the base of my neck. Reckless. Impulsive. Mina tugs me closer, as demanding as ever, and swirls her tongue with mine, playing, pushing me to give her more.

In this moment, she isn't Effie's best friend. She isn't the thorn in my side that she's been for over twenty years, always digging her way under my skin and spiking my temper at the slightest provocation.

If you had asked me ten years ago if I'd ever consider kissing Mina Pappas, I would have laughed in your face.

No, you wouldn't have.

As though to prove me wrong, my imagination takes me through a wheelhouse of memories. Memories of us in Greece with Mina in a bikini and me fighting the desperate need in my veins to look and keep on looking. Memories of us here in Boston, me walking Mina home after school, the way heat stirred low in my groin whenever our fingers accidentally brushed together.

Memories of her prom night, when I'd held her in my arms and her lids fluttered shut, and I thought, for one moment of temporary insanity, *if only*.

If only she wasn't my sister's best friend.

If only I hadn't started seeing Brynn.

If fucking only.

Mina wrenches her mouth from mine, gasping, "This is crazy."

And it's only about to get that much crazier.

Lust pounds through my limbs, and I let instinct take over.

My hands go to her ass, palms completely full, and I boost her up into the air. She defies gravity for only a second, eyes round with shock, before resettling into the cradle of my arms.

"Oh!"

"Wrap your legs around my waist," I growl, trailing my mouth over her jaw to the shell of her ear.

She does, and this time she whispers "oh" in a completely different tone. It's breathy and feminine and accompanied by a squeeze of her legs and a swivel of her hips. "You feel . . . you feel so *good*."

With her back pressed to the stairwell wall, I stabilize my weight on two rungs, one hand planted on the wall beside her and the other still clutching her ass to keep her steady. Her pouty mouth finds mine as I grind my erection into the fleece-lined apex of her thighs. Back and forth, a slow, sensuous glide directly over the seam of her leggings.

My control frays just a little more, and I force my hips to keep the smooth, easy rhythm instead of picking up tempo. *Slow. Easy.* I repeat the words like a mantra. *Slow. Easy.*

Mina arches her back, driving her hips against mine.

Slow. Easy.

She's killing me. Destroying any willpower I have left, decimating it into smithereens when she reaches between us and shoves my T-shirt up, exposing my stomach . . . and the crown of my cock trying to make an escape from my jeans.

I squeeze my eyes shut and drop my forehead to her shoulder. "You drive me fucking insane."

Avidly, I watch her fingertips trace the rigid lines of my abs. My breathing comes heavy and labored, and she takes no pity on me. Those fingers skate down, light as a feather, and tease the tip of my cock with a caress I feel to my soul.

"Fuck me."

She gives a throaty laugh. "I was so wrong about you."

I can't look away from her hand. It mesmerizes me with every torturous pass over my cock, never gripping me fully or pulling me completely from my jeans. But she circles her palm over the crown, spreading my pre-cum, and I'm powerless to the guttural groan that escapes me. "How?" I finally grunt, thrusting my hips upward.

Another swirl of her palm over my dick. "I thought you were rigid." She tightens her legs around me, and the very rigid part of me strains against the very soft part of her. "Cold," she adds softly. "But clearly I just need to listen for when you start cursing in English." Hooking a hand around the back of my neck, she drags me close and molds her mouth to mine for a hot-as-hell kiss. She pulls back only long enough to whisper, "It's your tell, how I know you're teetering on the edge of showing whatever you're really thinking."

I nip at her plump bottom lip. "Oh yeah?"

It's then I feel the button of my jeans come loose. The zipper inches down, far enough for Mina's slender hand to dive inside my briefs and circle my hard-on with a tight, confident fist.

Holy hell, she feels good wrapped around me. She pumps her hand once, twisting at the crown, and stars dance in front of my vision. Shit, "good" doesn't even cover it. This is . . . this is—my mouth parts as she glides up and down, up and down, never losing pace. She squeezes at the base, then allows her thumb to run along the vein on the underside of my dick on her next pass up my length. Another groan frees itself from my chest.

"That," she says, her honey eyes colliding with mine, "and I thought you'd be quiet in bed." Her lips curl flirtatiously. "Or maybe that was wishful thinking on my part, a way to make me feel better about not having you for myself."

A way to make me feel better about not having you for myself.

Her words only make my cock swell more. I've never thought about how I am in bed, aside from the basics: that I know exactly how to make a woman orgasm. But the particulars of how *I* am? Yeah, it's not something I dwell on. And it's not like anyone's ever called me out for being vocal in the sack—except for Mina.

The one woman who never fails to challenge me, no matter where we are, including an old and rickety stairwell, the location of our first kiss. It's a major contrast to my time on *Put A Ring On It,* when every date and every moment was orchestrated for a panoramic view and a drone flying high above us to catch an embrace from all angles.

I'd prefer the raw honesty of this moment with Mina any day of the week.

I lean down and whisper my lips over hers. Her fist circles my cock.

"You keep doing that and I'm gonna come." Without waiting for what I know will be a sassy comment, I hold her tightly against me and swivel away from the wall. I head up the stairs, ignoring the creaks and whines beneath my feet, and focus on the woman in my arms.

Except maybe I focus a little too much—on the soft skin of her neck and her full, kissable lips—because I fail to notice the wood groan on the third rung from the top of the stairwell. Not until my foot's already sinking down, down, down and Mina's crying out in panic and the rung gives out completely beneath me.

19

MINA

It's not every day that a first kiss with your lifelong crush ends with him thigh-deep in a stairwell.

I'm not sure which shocks me more: the kiss (God, that *kiss)* or the fact that Nick is seconds away from plummeting to his death. All right, so he probably *won't* die, but only because he's got the muscles of Ares and the self-discipline of the almighty Zeus.

In other words, Nick is a gravity-defying beast.

With his arms braced against the walls to balance his weight off his submerged leg, Nick's biceps strain with maximum, veiny effort. My gaze gleefully tracks the inverted triangle of his chest, and then lowers. His jeans are ripped at the thigh, torn through by jagged, splintering wood, and it's probably not the time to bring this up, but . . .

"Nick, your—"

He doesn't make eye contact. His cheeks do, however, flush with color. "Please, don't."

I swallow past the lump in my throat. "Is . . ." I lick my dry lips. "Is The Great One—"

Every line in his body sharpens. "Ermione. Please."

Wringing my hands in front of me, it's all I can do not to burst out laughing. Going from straight-up alpha, I'm-going-to-make-you-mine mode (not that I'm complaining) to wiping out from a weak plank of wood is something that *would* happen to Nick Stamos. Though I suppose we're both to blame since I was in his arms. His muscular, I-lift-things-for-a-living arms. *Hold me while I swoon.* Plus, now that I know he's not actually going to fall straight to his death, seeing Nick like this has me feeling like I've won the lottery.

All those years of me losing bikini tops and other, more humiliating moments, have culminated in this one moment where we've swapped places.

I'm secretly living for it.

"We can do this one of two ways," I tell him, purposely masking my tone of all amusement. *Do not laugh. Do* not *laugh.* The full-on dread in Nick's expression has me biting my lip. *Oh God, just don't make eye contact.* I seek strength by staring up at the wood-paneled walls. "Actually, there is a third way, but I doubt you want me hammering anywhere near your leg. Coordination really isn't my thing." My nose scrunches. "You'd also probably fall to your death."

He drops his head forward in defeat. "Death sounds pretty good right about now."

"Is that because your *tsutsuli*—"

"It's fine. *I'm* fine."

"You're the one who squealed as soon as it made contact."

"I didn't squeal."

Fingers suctioned to either wall like he's sprouted tentacles, Nick moves his free leg into a wide kneeling position to better distribute his weight. God, his abs must be *insane* to hold himself steady like that. Though his cheeks are rosy, he's yet to break out in a sweat. *Impressive.* Though not nearly as impressive as the size of his hard-on. The dick-print from my admittedly active teenage imagination was not misleading, thank you, Sweet Baby Jesus.

"And," Nick spits out, clearly desperate to defend his manhood—literally—"no man likes to have his junk flattened. It's like sitting on your balls—it happens all the time, but it still hurts like a bitch."

I consider him with a tilted head. "You say this like you've had previous experience."

"Mina." He mutters the two syllables of my name peevishly, in that way only a male whose pride has taken a beating can. "I've worked in construction for fifteen years. There's not one guy who hasn't been where I am now, but at least, usually, we don't have a witness."

"Aw, are you worried about what I think of you?"

He grumbles something unintelligible beneath his breath.

To fluff up his ego, I drop to my haunches and cup his stubbled jaw. Yup, his cheeks are *totally* flushed. It says something about the state of my mind that I think it's adorably cute. Dogs are cute. Babies are cute. Men like Nick are—

Pewter eyes flick up to my face. All train of thought careens to a standstill as I lean in and impulsively mold my lips to his, simply because I want another taste.

Delicious. Men like Nick are delicious.

He tastes better than in every one of my fantasies combined. For years, I've pictured him as the consummate gentle lover with a warm but unassuming embrace. Classical music might provide background noise to an otherwise romantic joining. He proved me wrong. Nick's kiss, his touch, the way his erection hardened unapologetically in my hand, was the very antithesis of unassuming. He took and he pushed and he bit and he sucked, and he almost had an orgasm knocking on my door without removing a stitch of fabric off me.

His body, tailored from years of hard, physical labor, left me breathless.

Leaves me breathless still, even as I fight to keep this kiss one of playful flirtation and not dirty hand jobs and dry-humping sessions against a wall. I kiss Nick long enough to distract him while I reach down and return The Great One to the confines of his briefs. Steel wrapped in velvet—all the authors of the romance novels I listen to would be pleased to know that Nick Stamos not only fits the description, he exceeds it.

I zip up his torn jeans and pat his ridged lower abdomen.

"We've got to keep him safe," I say with a grin.

Nick looks like he doesn't know whether to laugh or shove the rest of his body through the broken slat.

Taking the decision out of his hands, I pop a quick peck on his mouth and spy the staircase over his shoulder. Stairs that now taunt me like a deathtrap in the waiting. Ten minutes ago, my only concern was my condom-less apartment. A tragic ending to a hot, PG-13 groping session, but one easily solved with a run to the corner store down the block. Now these stairs are just one more thing to add to my never-ending list of Shit-That-Needs-Fixing around here. It's not as if my bank account can cry anymore at this point.

Carefully, I step over Nick's extended arm. "Hang tight, will you?"

"Mina."

"Too soon?" I deadpan, trying not to laugh at his expense. Clearly, the two of us together were too much for this old stairwell to handle. But I've gone up and down these flights tens of times on my own, and I'm confident they won't buckle under my weight alone. Hopefully. "I've got to get the guys."

"*Ermione*. No. Absolutely not." I glance over my shoulder in time to see him struggling to yank his leg out from the hole. He freezes within seconds. The broken wood is gnarly. One wrong move and it'll slice right through his skin. Something he must realize, too, because he blows out a long-suffering sigh. "I'm going to regret this."

ꝏ

IN THE END, NICK DOESN'T LIVE TO REGRET ANYTHING.

"No mean jokes," I warn the guys after I've filled them in downstairs.

Affronted, Vince plants a hand over his heart. "*Mean?* You've got the wrong guy, Mina. I've never been mean a day in my life."

I point a finger at him. "Or stupid jokes. Nothing that'll make Nick feel . . . embarrassed." Not that I don't think he can't handle any and all smack talk from his employees. I'm sure Nick can dish it with the best of them.

"Now you're just taking away my fun."

"You missed your opportunity," I say with a loose shrug. "The position has already been filled."

Vince's espresso-coffee eyes glimmer with humor. "Yeah? By who?"

"This girl." I flash him a quick grin, then circle my finger in the air in a *let's go* gesture. "Remember, no trash-talking of any kind. Bring me Mr. Stamos and not only will you three be eating more pizza than you can handle this week, but I'll also throw in a free haircut. You can thank me later when I make you look like the rock star you were born to be."

Bribery, my friends. It's a game-changer.

Bill slips me a proper side-eye. "All I want to know is if any of the pointy bits got stuck in his—"

Mark playfully swats him over the head. "Pizza, dude. Shut up and walk."

Holding back a laugh, I follow the trio to the stairwell

where we can hear Nick cursing loud enough for his mother to overhear from the other side of town. Four-letter words. Accented words. He gives them all his devout attention, and I holler, "Your rescuers have arrived!"

Vince leads the pack, Mark and Bill flanking him.

Within twenty minutes, after a fair bit of sawing and more than a handful of colorful phrases I'll never be able to bleach from my memory, Nick is extracted and doing a poor job of disguising a limp as he takes to the stairs.

When I stare a little too long at his roughed-up leg, he irritably grumbles, "I look worse than I feel."

I'm sure he's telling the truth. Even so, guilt sloshes around in my belly like I've downed one too many shots of Tito's as I touch a finger to his ripped jeans. They hang open from his right hip, exposing his navy briefs and the tiny scratches that are now etched into his muscled thigh. Most are pink but a few bleed red, and I force Nick to sit down while I rush out in the cold to the Stamos Restoration company van. It doesn't take me long to find the First Aid kit tucked away in the spare duffel bag he mentioned would be behind the driver's seat.

Back in *Agape,* I stomp the snow from my shoes and shake the flakes from my hair. After announcing, "You should go to the doctor," I drop the duffel at his feet. It hits the concrete flooring with a dull *thud.*

Nick spares me an inscrutable glance before unzipping the bag and riffling through its contents. "And you need to find somewhere else to stay while we fix that stairway to hell."

My lips purse at his unintended play on Led Zeppelin's infamous "Stairway to Heaven" song. *Focus, Mina.* Right, right. Under my breath, I can't help but hum along to the melody.

Pulling out a fresh pair of jeans from the duffel bag, Nick

drops them to the floor and flicks open the medical kit. Only when he's stripped off his tattered jeans does he say anything else—and, truth be told, I'm too busy admiring him in a pair of tight briefs to do anything but gawk.

The man is seriously blessed in more ways than one.

A masculine hand waves in front of my face. "Did you hear anything I just said?"

Cheeks flushing, I jerk my gaze up to safer territories. "Not a word."

I expect him to reprimand me the way he's always done, condescension coating each word. Instead, his mouth quirks up and he throws me a look like he doesn't know what to do with me. Under normal circumstances—you know, with him being surly and uncommunicative—that glance would leave me feeling chilled all over. Instead, I feel indescribably toasty which is insane considering I've still got snowflakes melting into my hair and clothes.

"Let me repeat from the top." Bending over, Nick grabs the medical wipes and proceeds to wipe away the beads of blood on his thigh. "You aren't staying here."

This time, I hear him perfectly. "Of course I am."

"Not a chance in hell."

Watching the rough way he deals with his injured skin, I bat his hands away and sink to my knees. "You would have gotten your point across better if you'd said, 'over my dead body.'" With the chill of the concrete flooring seeping through the thin layer of leggings, I crane my head back to look Nick in the face. "At least that would be reasonably appropriate given the situation."

He lifts one brow coolly. "Over my dead body."

"Great." I poke him in his uninjured shin. "Now lay down and play the part. You're bleeding all over the place."

"Better do what she says, boss," remarks Bill with a hearty chuckle. "She sounds like she means business."

Though I'm sure it grates on his nerves to play the part of damsel in distress, Nick maneuvers his big body onto the ground. While he doesn't lie back as ordered—and I don't blame him because this floor is filthy with sawdust and debris—he nevertheless reclines back on his palms and leaves his bare legs to my ministrations.

Even sitting, the muscles in his thighs are tight and incredibly firm. They clench when I hold a square piece of sterile gauze to the deepest gash. Pressing down with my thumb to stem the blood, I rearrange my legs so that I'm mostly seated on my butt. It's more comfortable this way, and I have a sneaking suspicion we'll be here for a while yet. No matter what he says, I can't just stay elsewhere until the stairs are restructured.

Hell, it's not even a matter of *can't* but a matter of *won't*.

"Let the guys go home for the day."

Tensing beneath my fingers, Nick shakes his head. "Can't. We need to stay on schedule. Drywall by Wednesday and floors put in by Friday. We keep this pace up, and you'll be ready to go by the middle of the following week."

I strip off another piece of gauze and apply it to one of his deeper wounds. Already the blood is drying. Growing up, First Aid kits weren't a thing in our house. My mom loved concocting creams and herbal remedies, allegedly all passed down through our family. One time, Dimitri sprained his ankle, and instead of painkillers and a set of crutches, my mom whipped up a poultice and slathered it all over his foot. My younger brother gagged from the noxious smell, and even I watched on with my fingers plugging my nose shut as my mom bandaged his ankle with plastic wrap from the kitchen.

Crazily enough, it worked.

Without my mom's magic, I settle for more hydrogen peroxide from the kit.

With a hasty look thrown over my shoulder, I spot the guys back at work. Rock music blares from the Bluetooth speakers as they nail another frame into place, and I find small comfort in all the noise. Hopefully it's loud enough they won't pay us any attention.

Nick's fingers brush my arm. "Get it off your chest," he murmurs, tracing those long, nimble fingers down to my wrist. "I can see the worry all over your face."

I keep my gaze on the task at hand, cleaning each scratch like it's a life or death situation. "I can't stay anywhere else."

"What about with Effie?"

Baby wisps of my hair fall into my face when I shake my head, and I shove them behind my ear with the back of my hand. "Not an option. She and Sarah are stressed enough without adding me as the unwanted third party to their twosome."

"You could stay with me."

He says it so simply, so matter-of-factly, that I laugh. Except —except that he doesn't laugh along with me. Lifting my chin, I meet his somber gaze and . . . oh. *Oh.* He was being serious. My heart performs a strange flip in my chest, like a beached whale moored on shore. "A fake relationship *and* moving into your house?" I press my tongue to the roof of my mouth to hold back a startled giggle. "What are we? The leads in a Hallmark movie?"

His broad shoulder lifts, even as his gray eyes shine with amusement. "You'd be helping the *I'm-over-Savannah* storyline. Consider it payment compensated for that hydrotherapy room."

"Now that's a shameless plug if I've ever heard one. We're not doing the hydrotherapy room."

"It's only shameless because you're considering it."

My hands pause over his leg. "Nick, I'm not—"

"Kidding," he says with one of his customary tight smiles,

"I'm kidding. Though it probably would help with the media."

"We don't need to move in together for that." It's only when he gives me nothing but a blank stare that I realize he doesn't know anything about *Celebrity Tea*. Oh, boy. Dating TV show or not, privacy is Nick's jam. And he has no idea someone followed us last night. Wishing I had some water to quench my suddenly dry throat, I motion between us. "Well, you know."

His lips press together. "No, I don't."

Ugh, great. Couldn't Effie have been the messenger for him too? "How do I even put this?" Struggling for the correct words, I drop the hydrogen peroxide bottle back in the kit and flip the lid closed. "You . . . *we* were tailed last night." Immediately his expression turns hard and I hastily add, "I mean, maybe not tailed. That might not be the right term. But obviously someone did their research and found out where your parents lived, so they—"

"Stalked me." His voice is pure grit. "They stalked me and caught us instead."

I fumble for the right thing to say. Words have never been my expertise. "Nick, this is . . . this is what you wanted, right? Out of the deal?" Pushing the kit to the side, I tuck my feet beneath me, sitting cross-legged. Wanting to calm his frayed nerves, I touch my fingers to his knee. "The gossip rags are reporting that you're seeing someone new, so it looks like we're in business."

The right thing to do would be to move into his house and uphold my end of the bargain. The right thing, maybe, but not the *smart* thing. I want to kiss Nick again. And, yeah, I want to strip him naked and let him return the favor. But I don't want to actually *sleep* with him, not together in one bed. That sort of proximity breeds closeness and deeper bonds, and the thought of baring more than just my body to Nick terrifies me.

It's one thing for him to look at me and feel like the attraction is lacking physically—another thing entirely for him to see into all the dark places in my soul and realize that my baggage, my insecurities, are not at all what he's looking for in a partner.

"It's not the same." Rising to the balls of his feet, Nick grabs his jeans and pulls them up his legs. Already I mourn the sight of all those muscles on display. He has the legs of a rugby player, and I can't help but wonder what sort of activities he does in his spare time because mortal men are *not* built like him. "It's not the same at all," he repeats roughly. "I figured we'd head into Boston, do something big and elaborate and public. Maybe post a picture on Instagram—even though that's against my contract with the show. Not"—he spears his fingers through his hair—"have someone camped outside of my parent's house on a Sunday night. Where's the common decency these days? Aren't there any goddamn boundaries? *Fuck*."

I drop my elbows to my knees. "So, I guess moving into your house is out of the equation then, right?"

Deep, husky laughter curls around me. "You're a piece of work, you know that?"

"I specifically remember you telling me that I get mouthier every year."

At my pointed stare, he only laughs again. "You're a woman of many talents, Ermione Pappas."

I throw him an exaggerated wink. "Just you wait and see, Saint Nick. Just you wait."

20

To: Mina Pappas <mina@agapehairsalon.com>
From: Nick Stamos
<nstamos@stamosrestoration.com>
Subject: question about flooring

What's your favorite food?

P.S., I shifted some things around in the budget and managed to work in your slate floors. And, yes, I promise that I ONLY shifted around the budget. Before I pick them up from the warehouse tomorrow, I want to know how you want them laid out? On your Pinterest boards, you've got everything under the sun. Square? Large and rectangular? Herringbone? Something else? Any preference before I get to work?

To: Nick Stamos <nstamos@stamosrestoration.com>
From: Mina Pappas <mina@agapehairsalon.com>
Re: Subject: question about flooring

How in the world did you work around the budget for *that*? Please tell me you didn't break a leg and donate it . . . although, that would be very gallant of you. (But, really, please tell me how??? Also, whatever you think looks best—and is the cheapest option.)

P.S., How are you feeling? I didn't make it into *Agape* the last two days now that I've been forced to evacuate the premises under someone's dictatorial orders. I won't name names to protect the guilty. (Good news: I booked a few clients and am doing house calls all week.)

P.P.S., Please tell Vince and Bill thank you for getting my stuff out of the apartment for me. I really appreciate their help. And yours.

P.P.P.S., I'm going to sound like a traitor of the highest order here, but . . . Italian food. Do I get to ask you a question now?

To: Mina Pappas <mina@agapehairsalon.com>
From: Nick Stamos
<nstamos@stamosrestoration.com>
Re: Re: Subject: question about flooring

Wow. Throw down the gauntlet and tear my heart out. *Italian*? You don't like cannoli so that can't be the draw. It's the pasta, isn't it?

And ask away.

P.S., I'm feeling all right. My pride is more bruised than my leg ever was. All's well over here.

P.P.S., We're happy to help, Ermione. I know it's not easy but we'll get you back in there soon enough, I promise. Trust me on this.

To: Nick Stamos <nstamos@stamosrestoration.com>
From: Mina Pappas <mina@agapehairsalon.com>
Re: Re: Re: Subject: question about flooring

Mr. Stamos, you didn't answer my question about the slate floors. Do a girl a favor and tell me you didn't axe something important . . . like a toilet.

P.S., Your pride can handle the fall. Your butt too—it's made of 100% steel, right?

P.P.S., It's totally the pasta. Carbs are my worst enemy (after you, of course) but also my fiercest lover. As for my question . . . are you a fan of *Lord of the Rings?*

To: Mina Pappas <mina@agapehairsalon.com>
From: Nick Stamos
<nstamos@stamosrestoration.com>
Re: Re: Re: Re: Subject: question about flooring

Toilet's out. Sorry to be the bearer of bad news. I've decided to dig a hole in the ground and buy one of those pop-squatter things from the store. Cheap and efficient, and you can admire your pretty slate floors as your clients throw fits about the lack of restrooms. You're welcome, Mina.

P.S., All steel, baby.

P.P.S., Two things. 1) Elijah Wood may have done a good job as Frodo, but that doesn't mean Frodo isn't the dumbest character on the face of the planet. STAY IN THE SHIRE, FRODO. 2) My precioussss.

P.P.P.S., In case you couldn't tell from above, the answer to your question is . . . yes.

To: Nick Stamos <nstamos@stamosrestoration.com>
From: Mina Pappas <mina@agapehairsalon.com>
Re: Re: Re: Re: Re: Subject: question about flooring

You never cease to surprise me.

P.S., I left you a gift on the receptionist's desk. Because I love to spoil surprises, here are the details: it's an empty box, fitted perfectly for the size of your heart if I learn you did away with my toilets or anything else important. You're welcome, Nick.

21

MINA

Returning home after the stairwell debacle wasn't my first choice.

To be honest, it wasn't my second choice either . . . or my third.

I wait for guilt to assail me for preferring to be *anywhere* but where my parents are, but it doesn't come. It rarely does.

Sitting on my old twin-sized bed, I cross my legs and prop my laptop against my shins. Plastered all over the walls are magazine cut-outs of models from various catwalks around the world, mostly dated to the late 90s and early 2000s. In the corner of the room, beneath the old, white desk I rarely used as a kid, is a tub stuffed to the brim with dolls. I remember needing to sit on the plastic lid while Katya helped me duct-tape it shut.

I feel a pinch in my heart that I studiously ignore by dropping my gaze to the voice-recorder app I've left open on my phone. Tapping the red, record button, I lean back on my childhood mattress and speak clearly for the microphone to pick up. "Date recorded: February seventh. Received invitation from local fashion show to participate as one of the hairstylists on recommendation from Tanya Banks, an old client and sister to model Chantelle Banks." Leaving the app to record, I reach for my glass of water off the bedside table and take a sip. "Must leave confirmation of participation by the twenty-fifth. Also, uploaded job posting for *Agape* interviews."

After another sip of water, I pause the app and save the voice memo to my drive, as well. I'll play it back later and make any notations in my calendar for cross-referencing, like the fashion-show gig. It's not the first time I've participated in large-scale shows, but this is the first time I'll be representing my own salon and my own brand. My stomach still flutters with giddiness whenever I think about the call I received early this morning.

But, good news or not, being back in this house and under my parent's roof, is a time warp I'd rather do without.

The mattress dips as I set aside my laptop and swing my legs over the side of the bed. The fuzzy carpet greets my bare feet as I crouch low and lift the old-fashioned skirt that my mom picked out years ago from some catalogue she obsessed over. I thrust a hand under the bed, patting around in the darkness for the slim box I know everyone but me has forgotten. My fingertips graze plastic, and I drag it out into the light.

Turning onto my butt, I pop off the box's lid and take a moment to breathe. I breathe in the old desperation to fit in with my family, with my Greek community, and breathe out a sixteen-year-old's identity crisis.

Finally, I peer into the box. Spiral-bound notebook after spiral-bound notebook greet me, my name written in my sloppy Greek script across the front of each one. *Ερμιόνη Παπάς*. The metal binding protests with a whine as I crack open the notebook sitting on top of them all. My sixth-grade handwriting is atrocious. "So bad," I whisper, flipping through the pages. But not as bad as all the eraser marks and crossed-out words in the columns of each page.

I toss that notebook to the carpet and reach in for another. Seventh grade. A small part of me hopes this one will be better and show some progression. I see my attempts to remember the proper way to conjugate the past perfect tense of the verb, to love. *Agape*—the noun, not the verb. I don't think I ever quite got the hang of it, but that didn't stop me from slapping it across my LLC and DBA and the sign I ordered offline that's sitting in my apartment.

One by one, I move through the grades until there are none left to review but one.

I don't know why I feel the need to look through them all. It's not anything I don't still know: I never would have passed any grades in Greek school if it weren't for the fact that kids flunking out didn't happen.

I passed on the sheer merit of pity from my teachers and some made-up rule by the priests of the church, who only cared to see kids in the *ecclesia* and learning the mother tongue. Kids like Nick and Effie, Katya and Dimitri, and, yes, even Sophia, earned their way through to our senior year. I faked it till I couldn't make it anymore, and then I kept faking it because to do otherwise would admit the truth: that I wasn't as Greek as them all, both by blood and otherwise.

My forearm rests on the plastic lip of the box as I hesitate over the final notebook. I drop my head back against the edge of the mattress. Why torture myself with yet another workbook memorializing my weaknesses? Why bother going through them at all? Self-punishment, maybe? Or a push to get me moving faster and turn the wheel of ambition once more?

A month ago, I would have messaged back the fashion show's director within seconds of receiving the email. And yet here I am instead, combing through decades-old school notebooks like they carry some mysterious piece of my soul.

"You're a *maláka*," I mutter, even as I snag the last notebook and prop it open on my knees. I've come this far. What's another ten minutes of feeling like the dirt on the bottom of my shoes?

Only, it's not another one of my workbooks.

Or, rather, it *is*—or was meant to be before I gave up completely, it seems, and used my time spent in Greek school penning my every thought down.

Well, damn. I totally forgot about this.

Even in English, my handwriting wasn't all that good by senior year. It still isn't, though I do my best to keep it neat and legible. I trace the heel of my palm over the penciled words. Then note the date at the top of the entry: September 4th, 2005.

Dear Greek School Notebook (because, let's face it, you're no diary),

Today is the first day of classes. I begged Mama to let me skip this year but she said no. I need to learn our culture, she said. No one else has any trouble but you, Baba told me. Why can't either of them see how hard this is for me? I'm not a brat. I can't remember the letters to the sounds and it's so FRUSTRATING.

No one talks in English, not even when we have a snack break. Even Effie, when we're here, sticks to Greek. I know she only wants a good grade. It has nothing to do with me. I wonder if this is what it's like for people who move to a new country where they don't know the language. Do they feel lonely like me? Do they feel like they don't belong?

In American school, I don't fit in because I'm weird and my parents immigrated to America, and I bring Greek food for lunch and my name is ERMIONE. No one can even spell it. Or say it. I see the panic on my teachers' faces when they get to it on the attendance sheet.

In Greek school, I don't fit in because I can't keep up with everyone else. It sucks. Big time.

See ya next time,

MINA

HEART HEAVY, I PALM THE PAGE, AS THOUGH THAT ALONE might connect me with my seventeen-year-old self. Anxiety pools low in my gut, but instead of putting the notebook to the side, I flip a few pages and find another entry, this one for December of the same year:

DEAR GSN,

Me again. As always, sitting in the back row and doodling. Doodling beats reciting my Christmas poem for the 100th time when I can't even memorize the first line. Effie offered to help but I think I'm going to fake the flu. Maybe a fever. Whatever illness is going around the third week of December, so I don't embarrass myself in front of everyone.

Including Nick.

Effie said he'll be there, and I'd rather stab myself with this pencil than mess up talking to him.

He's so fluent that the last time he came out to dinner with us, the waitress thought he just arrived off the boat. Or plane, ya know, because modern times. I wish I could impress him, but I'm like the ultimate Greek failure.

And Mama says Nick is going to marry a Greek girl, too, which means I'm SOL. I'm half-Greek. Other side of me: unknown. Sometimes I wonder if maybe that other half of me is stronger somehow. Like maybe I'm Brazilian? Or French-Canadian? Or Guatemalan? Maybe I could speak and read Portuguese or Span-

ish. Maybe I wouldn't just stand around, not saying a word because I'm so scared of saying it all wrong.

Then again, I'm pretty much failing Spanish class at American school. So maybe I should just hope I'm English or something, so I can stick to only sucking at two languages.

See ya next time,
MINA

IT'S A TRAIN WRECK: MY SPELLING, MY VERBAL DIARRHEA ON the page, and still I can't stop reading. Blood pounds away like an incessant drum in my head as I thumb some pages over, closer to the end of the notebook. I stop when I spot doodles across the headline of the page. March of 2006, two months before my graduation from both schools.

DEAR GSN,

Today, Mama got angry with me on the way to Greek school. I just wanted to know about my real dad, whoever he is. As I'm writing, everyone is standing up to do final presentations on our family histories. Athens. Thessaloniki. Sparta. Istanbul. The teacher made a face when Sophia admitted that her mom's side came from Turkey, before that bad war in the 1920s when her family had to leave.

I asked Mama about HIS ancestry. Maybe that would explain why my skin is darker than Katya and Dimitri's? Than Mama's, too? Or maybe why my hair is curlier and thicker than theirs? Everyone in my family has green eyes but me, even Baba, though I'm sure that's just a coincidence or whatever since Theio Prodromos has dark eyes. I used to wish that Baba's brother, my uncle, could be my dad. He's always so nice and encouraging and he never makes me feel like I'm not part of the family, even though he doesn't know I'm not actually a Pappas, but those were kid's wishes.

Now I just want to know WHY.

Who am I?

Can you be a part of a culture and still feel like an outsider? It's Greek this and Greek that and I don't look like my family and they don't look like me, and I'm going to get up in front of my classmates and stutter over my words and this stupid talk and lie about it all.

I can't wait to move. I'm going to go far away. I'll miss Effie but she can visit.

No more being stuck.

MINA

THIRTEEN YEARS LATER AND I STILL DON'T HAVE THE ANSWERS to any of the questions I asked myself then. Oh, I've thought about doing those ancestry tests and discovering the realities of my DNA. It'd be broken up by stats and color-coded charts and percentages that take a family's roots and segment them into a scientific hypothesis of one's genetic makeup.

Unfortunately, doing that feels incredibly less satisfying than learning the truth from my mom. If the prelude to my birth had been only a one-night stand, I wouldn't push. But she had an *affair* with my biological father, which means she knows a name.

And a name can tell a million stories all on its own.

But even the matter of DNAs and all that doesn't push away the clamping sensation on my heart—because *Theio* Prodromos . . . I rub a hand over my chest, as though the physical ache of his death is still pressing its weight down on me. For as bullish as my dad always was, my uncle was a gentle soul. A *kind* soul. The only reason we traveled to Greece every summer was to visit

Prodromos, my dad's younger brother. It was my *theio* who taught me to ride my bike the summer between kindergarten and first grade. It was my *theio* who woke Katya and Dimitri and me up in the middle of the night, sneaking us out of his house so he could buy us Nutella and strawberry crepes while we buried our feet in the sand and watched the waves crash onto the shore.

I longed for those summers spent in Greece, no matter how they often made me feel inadequate, because I always knew a friendly face waited on the other side.

And then there was Nick, of course.

"Mina," *Theio* Prodromos once said to me in his accented, stilted English, "if you stare at him any harder, the boy will disappear."

If only my uncle could see me now that I've kissed Nick *and* he didn't disappear.

I throw a quick glance at the clock perched on the nightstand. God, I've been reading for three hours. My parents will be home soon from dinner with friends, which means I'll need to make myself scarce before my dad can start in on me the way he's done since I returned to the birthing nest.

"One more."

The last one.

It's dated to the fifth of May, 2006. The day after prom. "Oh, girl," I mutter to myself, "don't even go there."

But like on prom night itself, I can't stop myself.

Dear GSN,

Why can't we pay to forget the bad memories? Why is it that we can rarely remember the good—like the time Yiayia *bought my very first audiobook tape, right before she passed away? I still have it and I'll never let it go. It showed me that I love books, even if I don't like to read. I had to stop and think about that for a second, to find that good memory. But the bad ones scar us forever . . . like*

Baba blaming me for Katya doing bad in her English class yesterday. He yelled a lot and he told me I was dumb and he thanked God that I wasn't really his.

I remember every second of standing there and trying not to cry. I remember when he said I'd be lucky if a man wanted to marry me because I'd probably have kids as stupid as I am.

He was angry and drinking and I'm sure he didn't mean it but . . . it hurt. A lot.

Probably didn't help that no one asked me to the dance. I thought, maybe, someone might. A few of the guys left notes in the girls' lockers asking them, and I checked mine every morning and every afternoon before I went home, but no notes.

Aleka told me boys my age are stupid, and I think she's right. So I went into business. Put up flyers all over the school that said I was doing girls' hair for the dance. I charged $15. Pretty good if you ask me, because I had TWELVE girls sign up!!! I went to Effie's house and even though it's not that big in there, she collected the money and I borrowed her mom's stuff. The girls and their moms came, and even though none of them are my friends, I'm glad I could make them feel beautiful. Everyone deserves to feel pretty. One day, I know I'll feel that way too.

But one of the boys came with his date, and I asked if he wanted me to style his hair. He flipped out. Said that I have a unibrow—I DON'T. I know because I shave it off because that's what happens when you're hairy. You shave every day. And then he said that I should just go back to my country. I LIVE IN AMERICA. And all because I said I'd do his hair. I hope it falls out and he goes bald and it all ends up coming out of his nostrils.

I cried.

I didn't want to cry but between Baba and that stupid boy, I cried. Nick found me like that. I wish I didn't like him so much. He's Effie's big brother and he's never looked at me as anything but a brat but then he asked me to dance, and he put on some Greek song and took me in his arms and I CRIED ALL OVER HIM.

He was just trying to be nice and I ruined the moment with snot. True romance right there.

The worst part is, I thought at one point he might kiss me . . . we were close, like almost nose to nose because I was standing on my tiptoes, and it could have happened. Maybe. I closed my eyes. That's what they all do in the movies. They close their eyes and lean in.

But Nick didn't lean in.

He told me he's dating this girl he really likes at school. Her name is Brynn and she's beautiful, he says, and he thinks it might be the real deal.

I thought HE was the real deal.

Stupid me.

So, yeah, bad memories, GSN. I'll pay to get rid of them. All of them.

I'll miss you, since today is our last day of Greek school FOREVER. Thank you for listening. It's nice to feel like someone understands me, even if you're only a notebook and I've probably ruined you with all my bad grammar and misspelled words.

Hugs,
MINA

I CLOSE THE NOTEBOOK AND TOSS IT BACK IN THE BIN. IT'S either stamp out the emotion or let it consume me, and crying gets a girl nowhere in life. *Patience,* like I have tattooed on the sole of my foot, gets me places. *Soaring,* like the set of wings I have inked behind my ear, reminds me to always keep moving, even if my steps are small and measured and frightened by the unknown lingering before me.

But I've lived my entire life with some unknown part of me taking up residence in my soul, and I've never been all that scared by the *what-ifs* of the world. *What-ifs* are useless wastes of time. Get out there, make the magic happen—no matter what—and learn as you go. It's the key to survival, and how I operate.

I could spend months lamenting Jake the IOU Asshole, but that would get me nowhere. Same with the damn stairs and my sudden move back to my childhood home. It is what it is, and so long as I give my dad a wide birth, I'm sure we can co-exist like normal people.

Shoving the bin back under the bed, I grasp the side of my laptop and haul it to the edge of the mattress. A few strokes of the keyboard later and I've officially accepted the invitation to participate in the fashion show.

"There," I say with an air of finality, "now move on to the next thing."

I smooth my thumb over the mouse pad. "Moving on to the next thing" reminds me of Nick and all his temporary longing theories. He's not wrong. Dreams change, they adjust and grow, and . . . I have no idea what in the world I'll start dreaming about after *Agape* opens. More clients, maybe, or more stints in hair shows and fashion shows or more followers on Instagram.

Or something.

I'm sure it'll come to me. It's not as though my ambition and drive will just roll over and die with the grand opening of a hair salon. That's not how this dream thing works.

I close my laptop and put it away, then putz around my room. Fiddle with old trinkets I haven't seen in years. Send Effie a text about grabbing dinner together later this week. Boredom clings to me like a second skin until I find myself stripping off my sweats and putting on a pair of high-waisted jeans and a crop-top sweater with bell sleeves. I grab a beanie hat and gloves and shove my feet into a pair of trendy snow boots.

I leave my face bare of any makeup, without even a trace of my trademark dark lipstick.

Being back in this house doesn't give me the warm fuzzies. No, it makes me want to run off into the night. Anxiety kicks boredom to the curb as I throw on a heavy wool coat, leaving it unbuttoned, and ignore looking in the full-sized mirror as I head out my bedroom door.

For the first time in years, I don't have a single destination in mind.

My nerves are on edge, all those long-buried emotions bubbling to the surface. I shouldn't have popped open Pandora's box. What good did it do for me, anyway? Add little pinpricks of hurt to my soul after years of carefully removing them all from my childhood?

I should have taken Nick up on his offer to stay at his house. "And here's another time when you ignored the obvious choice."

I'm making a bad habit of it, clearly.

The first floor is empty as I head for the front door. The lights are turned off, and my parents aren't the sort to leave a note on the fridge about their whereabouts—or to send a quick text to let me know when they might be home. More likely than not, they're at one of their mini-concerts down along the Charles River.

Sighing, I fist the doorknob and pull it open.

My heart flips over on itself at the familiar figure standing on the front stoop. "*Nick?*"

22

NICK

Mina looks like she's seen a ghost.

Or maybe it's that I'm seeing her without makeup for the first time in years. No spiky black lashes or lips painted the color of a deep, red wine. She looks . . . young, impressionable. A little worn down. No less beautiful, though.

And when did you start seeing Ermione Pappas as beautiful? I shake the thought away and give the woman in front of me my full attention, which is probably a good thing because her expression has *what-the-hell-are-you-doing-here?* written all over it, arched eyebrows and all.

"*Nick?*"

She says my name like I'm the last person she ever expected to see show up at her parents' house—she's not out of line to wonder. I came here on a whim because I . . . missed her. Rewind. Scratch the hell out of that. I didn't *miss* her exactly. More like, all day I wondered what it might be like to hang out with Mina Pappas. Grab some food for dinner or head to a bar for a cocktail. Engage in conversation that matters because I've got the craziest feeling that Mina and me, we're not so unlike as we've always thought.

Except that "hanging out" has never been our style.

Then again, up until three days ago, kissing wasn't our thing either.

Now look at me, standing on the Pappas' front stoop, hands buried in my pockets since I came empty-handed, wondering if the woman who claims she can never get a read on me can see that I'm wracked with nerves.

Clearly, I've stepped over the threshold into insanity.

I wasn't nervous about being "rejected" on national television. Hell, even on my wedding day while I waited for Brynn to walk down the aisle—before I realized that shit was about to implode and blow up in my face—I was completely calm. Meanwhile, my mom sat in the pews hyperventilating about her baby boy becoming a husband. My *yiayia*, as can be expected, sat knitting a baby blanket—as one does at a wedding.

The same can't be said for my state of being right now.

Oh, how the mighty have fallen.

Clearing my throat, I nod to Mina's getup, taking in the nondescript, gray beanie hat she's tugged down over her ears. "Heading out?"

She mumbles something under her breath, then steps out on the front stoop and tugs the door shut behind her. Louder, like she expects me to put up a fuss, she says, "I'm going on a walk."

A *walk*? To where, Antarctica? The ice rink? Granted, the latter is probably open but the last time I checked, Mina can't skate for shit. Her balance sucks, and she always throws her arms out wide like she thinks if she evenly distributes her weight, she might not face plant. It never did work for her. She's a beach girl, sandals optional.

Blocking her path to the frozen tundra, I stand my

ground and point to the slick frost coating the grass. "You don't do ice, Mina. Or snow. You're overestimating the right time for a walk by at least three months, maybe four if the snow gods want to play a sick joke on us."

"I can take care of myself, you know." As though determined to prove her point, she kicks out one foot, gesturing at her black snow boot like it's the miracle of all miracles. "I've got kicks."

Pressing my lips together, I pray for patience. Slowly, evenly, I mutter, "They have pom-poms."

She stands on her tiptoes and those furry, ridiculous pink pom-poms do a jig, bouncing this way and that. "They're stylish."

Because style really matters when you're wiping out on black ice and looking like an extra out of a horror movie. "Stylish," I draw out slowly, "is a nice leather shoe or a sleek-cut jacket, *not*—"

"Nick, you do realize you're getting wicked worked up over a piece of fake fur, right? You're practically frothing at the mouth."

"I—" My jaw clamps tight, back molars cracking together. Scrubbing one hand over my lower face, I remind myself that I didn't come here to battle it out with Mina on who can outwit the other. Although I'd be lying if I say that her feisty attitude and quick comebacks aren't part of her draw. "How 'bout we start over?"

"I'm not going back in the house, only to come out into the cold again. That's cruel."

"I'm not that much of a jerk, Ermione."

"Says the man who insulted my pom-poms."

Grimacing, I open my mouth and promptly dig my grave: "They look like something my grandmother would wear." At her furrowed brow, I hastily add, "*Not* that there's anything wrong with that. They're . . ."

"*Stylish.*"

"Right. Stylish." One curt nod that's so formal I might as well just salute her and snap my heels together like a cadet. I don't do either, and preemptively I keep my hands in my coat pockets before I can dig myself any deeper into dangerous territory. I do, however, give her my most charming smile before asking, "Do they come in men's sizes?"

Whatever she's got on her mind must be troubling her pretty bad; she doesn't laugh at my joke, though her expression does soften, and when she sidesteps me, it's with a squeeze of my forearm. I curse my coat for blocking the heat of her gloved hand on my skin.

"You're ridiculous," she tells me, already heading down the walkway to the sidewalk. "And I'm still going on that walk."

Stubborn. She's so damn stubborn and it makes me want to drive her to distraction some other way, with my mouth molding over hers until the only comebacks I hear are those sexy whimpers of hers.

"Mina, stop a sec."

Unexpectedly, she does, swiveling on the heels of her snow boots and crossing her arms over her chest. It's her *get on with it* stance, and I'm not interested in doing her bidding. So, I study her without reservation, taking in her tight jeans and the sliver of skin peeking out between the hem of her shirt and her waistband. I glance up at the wild, curly hair, tamed by only the hat pulled down to her ears—I haven't seen her hair natural like this since we were kids, long before she discovered the merits of a blow-dryer. I like it better this way, how it frames her face and hints at her rebel soul. Aside from the towering street lamp behind her, it's pitch-black outside. But there's enough ambient light for me to catch the fleeting expression on her face.

And what I see there twists my gut.

Restlessness.

It widens her gaze and tugs her full mouth into a straight, uncompromising line. Her brows, always her most expressive feature—the woman does love a taunting brow raise—are furrowed, the crease between them rooted deep.

Something's wrong.

Tilting my chin in the direction of where I parked, I rock onto the backs of my heels and force my voice to sound completely blasé. "How about a car ride instead?"

She casts a quick glance over her shoulder, deliberating on the offer, and I hear her speak before she's even turned back around. "I need to move, Nick."

Shit, the apartment.

Ambling toward her, I rub my hand against the outside of my thigh, trying to warm up. Boston in February is seriously no joke, and this winter seems chillier than most years. "I know you're wantin' to head back home," I tell her, deliberately pausing a foot away. Getting close but not *too* close, in case she needs space. "Vince and me, we've got you covered." I don't tell her that I brought in one of my temp guys to get the job done faster. Between overhauling the salon and taking care of my other clients, including the Victorian-museum demo, my hands are beyond full. They're straight-up overflowing. "You'll be back in by next week, at the latest."

"No, it's not that. I—" With a quick shake of her head and a single, furtive glance at my face, she blows out a hard breath. It's so cold that her breath immediately vaporizes. Damn. If she thinks I'm letting her walk in this weather—*alone*—she's out of her goddamn mind. The only thing she'll gain from wandering around tonight is frostbite. If she wants to "move," whatever the hell that means, then she's got a new partner-in-crime tonight. *Me*.

"In the car," I husk out, staring down at her upturned face. Fuck, I want to kiss her. Again. Until we either work this insane chemistry out of our systems or we . . . *What?* Date, for real this time? I squash the thought before it sprouts and takes roots like an unwanted weed. "You look like you're ready to jump out of your skin, and I'm all for hashing it out with the heat blasting in our faces."

"You wouldn't understand."

With a hand to the lush curve of her hip, I gently push her toward the car. "Then make me understand."

She must get the hint that I'm not budging on this, because she squares her shoulders and cuts around the hood of the car to wait by the passenger's side door. "No company van tonight?"

"Off the clock." I push the unlock button on the key fob, then motion for her to jump in. "The joys of making my own hours—though you may have heard about my needy-as-hell client. A recent acquisition for Stamos Restoration."

I slide into the driver's seat in time to hear her wry, "Needy, huh?"

"The neediest," I tell her after the heat's blasting hot air in our faces and my fingers have thawed. "She's got me working all hours of the day, kissin' her smart mouth when I should be focusing on the job . . ."

Mina huffs out a quiet laugh. "She sounds like a piece of work."

"More like trouble for my peace of mind."

Silence invades her side of the car. She reaches forward and twists the heat knob to the left, then plants her right hand on the dashboard. Her left arm she loops around the back of the headrest. "Nick, are you *flirting* with me?"

I match her stance, wrapping my right arm around the driver's headrest. My left elbow sits atop the steering wheel. Then, like I'm discussing the dreary weather outside, I drawl, "You got a problem with that?"

The corner of her mouth tugs upward in a half-smile. "Anyone ever tell you that you like to have the last word?"

Only every other day. "Anyone ever tell you that you're gorgeous in a beanie hat?" Her hand flies off the dashboard to palm the side of her head, and, because I'm enjoying the hell out of having the last word—and seeing the flush creep over her olive-toned cheeks—I add, "And I'm all for the no makeup for purely selfish reasons."

She visibly swallows. Meets my gaze head-on when she demands, "And those selfish reasons are?"

I don't even bother to smother my grin. Demanding or not, there's no missing the way her voice quivered when she spoke. Call me an ass, but I *like* that she's nervous around me. It's only fair, since she shakes me up like no other woman ever has. Mina might be all big talk, but she's not nearly as unaffected by my presence as she wants me to believe.

Check mate.

I lean in, redistributing my weight in the seat so that I'm half-leaning over the center console. I get as close as I can, given where we are, and press a soft, teasing kiss to the corner of her mouth. "I wanted to know the true color of your lips after all these years."

Her breath audibly catches. "And?" she whispers.

Another kiss, this one to the other corner of her mouth. What can I say? I'm an equal opportunist—can't leave one side hanging and risk it feeling jealous. "And what?"

"Are they"—she swallows again, and then her fingers grow bold as they gently rake through my hair—"satisfactory?"

In every single way.

I give her the only answer that matters: my lips on hers.

God, she tastes amazing. Like sunshine in the middle of winter and vanilla and something so sweet and uniquely *her.*

Her taste consumes me—and as balls-freezing cold as it is outside this car, there's nothing but combustible heat between us. It flames the fire and it arouses, and I graze my lips over hers, refusing to deepen the pressure. Not yet. Not until she's begging and needy and demanding more. With iron-clad will, I keep the pace slow, teasing, seductive. A brush of my lips over hers, a sensuous glide of my tongue at the seam of her lips before I retreat and relish the way she whimpers at the loss. And then I do it all over again, torturing us both.

My name falls from her mouth like a four-letter curse.

I hold my ground, kissing her, antagonizing her with a more thorough sweep of my tongue and my fingers pinching her chin, keeping her exactly where I want her. She squirms impatiently in her seat. Almost desperately, her gloved fingers follow the curve of my skull, sliding down to the nape of my neck. "More," comes her throaty demand, right before she yanks me closer. Her full lips nip at mine in a fight for dominance.

Gentleman that I am, I let her have it.

Right before I throw gasoline into the flames and slide my hand against that bare strip of skin. Cold against hot, she shivers at my touch and gasps into my mouth. *So damn responsive.* I shouldn't be surprised, not the way she's always baited me for a reaction. The nice-guy thing to do would be to keep my hand in neutral territory at the dip of her waist. It's what she expects, and I'm not above proving her wrong.

I gloss my knuckles up and over her ribs, never missing the way her breathing changes, hastens, as if she's a puppet strung to my every jerk of the master's string. I leave goose bumps in my wake, until the pad of my middle finger is dead center on her chest.

Meeting her gaze, I search for that bout of restlessness. It's still there, lingering in the furrow of her brows but over-shadowed by the same lust that's making my pulse race.

Pouty lips purse, then fall open on a harshly drawn breath. Heavy-lidded eyes stare back at me, not a hint of hesitation in their depths. The two of us, we've torn through every fenced boundary that may have existed. One hot, illicit kiss. One desperate, forbidden touch. And then all good reason came crumbling down.

I skim my finger up, tracing the cup of her bra. Thin lace, no padding. I bet if I were to look, the material would be transparent enough to show me the exact hue of her nipple. *Not that you've forgotten.* A dark, rosy brown imprinted in my memory from a sunny day in Greece when the waves stole her bikini top. It'd been a good, good day, but not as good as this one. Boldly, I trace the gentle swell of her breast.

"You won't," she whispers in a hushed dare.

I do.

I cup her breast, nothing but a scrap of fabric between us.

She moans against my lips.

And, fuck, that *sound.*

It's dirty and feminine and absolutely the fuel of fantasies. *My* fantasies, of mornings spent in bed, her body tucked under mine as I fit myself between her legs. Beneath my palm, it's like I predicted: a hard nipple that the thin material of her bra can't disguise. A groan reverberates in my chest, and when Mina shucks off her gloves and fists my hair, it's all I can do not to crank this hookup session up to a thousand and undo the button of her jeans.

This is a bad idea.

Maybe, probably, but it feels too damn good to stop.

I pluck at her nipple, then slip my hand over her back, right over her spine. And then I urge her even closer, until our chests are flush together and she's gripping my coat lapels and dropping her head back, exposing the slender column of her neck.

She's temptation like I've never known.

And in that moment, there's only one truth: this woman who I've known my entire life is going to be my ruin.

Get a grip, man.

Instead of following the yellow brick road straight to sexual paradise, I wrench away and plant my hands on the steering wheel. At ten and two, like a good ol', rule-abiding civilian. *Like Saint-fucking-Nick.* I draw in a sharp breath, trying my damned best to get a leash on my out-of-control lust. If we weren't a dozen feet from her parents' front door, I'd drag her over the center console and settle her pretty little ass right on my lap. I'd grind her down on me, until she either burst apart at the seams or started fumbling for my belt. Or both.

Jesus.

"I want to fuck you, Ermione."

Facing the windshield as I am, all I can do is imagine her eyes going wide at my confession. "Then why—"

"Because when I do, it's gonna be an all-night affair." The rubber of the steering wheel under my palms grows hot when I tighten my grip. *Keep your eyes on the street, Stamos.* The street's safe. Safer, at least, then how much I want to know exactly what it takes to make a woman like Mina come. I think of them all, shuffling through each option like a gluttonous man standing before a buffet. Me on my knees with my tongue playing with her clit. Me seated behind her, one curvy leg drawn up with her foot planted on my knee, exposing all of her to me as I thrust in, hard. Like my mouth has a mind of its own, I tack on, "Me, you, and that pussy of yours I want to devour."

She releases one of her trademarked whimpers, and out of the corner of my eye, I see her push her beanie cap back like she's too hot to keep it on. "I never took you for a dirty-talker in bed," she says, voice brimming with need.

I cast my gaze over her, a quick sweep that sends heat

straight to my hard-on. “Never have been,” I admit bluntly, “but every time I say something that makes those pretty lips of yours part in shock, it’s a win in my book.” It’s not only a win—it’s satisfaction like I’ve never known. I pause, collecting my thoughts before I give too much of myself away. “I like the way you gasp when I catch you off guard . . . more than I should.”

Silence greets me, hanging over my head like a guillotine of disapproval. But Mina only chuckles softly, as if she’s game to be surprised by me every day of the week. “Nick Stamos, the man who will go to any length to prove a person wrong.”

“Ermione Pappas,” I return in a voice carved from granite, my eyes locked on her flushed face, “a woman determined to bring chaos into my life. Careful, or I’ll get addicted.”

I watch her bite down on her bottom lip, and I know her well enough to recognize the tell; she’s doing all she can to stop from smiling. And then the tapping begins, a gentle drumming of her fingers on the center console.

“Do I want to know what you’re thinking?” I ask, slowly.

“Honestly? Probably not.”

I place my hand over hers, and the restless tapping eases into stillness. “Tell me anyway.”

23

MINA

"Do you ever just want to . . ." I drop my head back, trying to gather my thoughts. "I don't even know where to start."

"The beginning might be a good place."

At Nick's good-humored sarcasm, I feel another smile working its way onto my face. Which is *nuts*, honestly. There hasn't been a single time in years where I've smiled when thinking about my mom or dad, and definitely not right after a trip down memory lane. Except that since stepping onto my parents' front stoop, Nick has made me temporarily forget. First with the pom-poms and then with our hot-as-heck make-out session.

God, my sex clenches just *thinking* about it. His hand on my breast, his mouth ravaging mine with such slow, persistent thoroughness. The man is a walking sex machine. It's like he knows what I need before *I* even realize what I need. It's an alarming thought, and I immediately glance to where his hand swallows mine.

When was the last time I held a man's hand? I honestly can't remember, and I'm not sure what that says about me.

That I'm scared of commitment, probably. That I'm terrified of deep, complicated relationships, most definitely.

I think back to the last entry in my notebook and my sloppily written letters to GSN. I'm not completely clueless; I'm fully aware that my father's attitude toward me all my life completely impacted the way I react to men and to dating. I guess I just never realized quite how much—not until tonight, when I stared at my life through a seventeen-year-old's lens.

Nick's fingers ghost over the back of my hand, pulling back.

I grab them before he can retreat fully, catching us both off guard by my assertiveness. He quirks one brow but goes along with it. This time, he sets the back of his hand on the center console as my fingers intertwine with his.

Don't overthink it, I warn myself. After all, if I'm okay with letting him cup my breast, I can totally hold his hand.

Swallowing past the nerves lodged in my throat, I glance at the dashboard and breathe out through my nose. "Sometimes I feel like I'm drowning in my own skin. It's a weird way to put it, I guess. Maybe . . . maybe it's better to say that I feel like I'm trying to claw out of myself." I huff derisively. "That doesn't make sense either."

Nick squeezes my hand, and his deep, smoky voice swirls around with me like a ribbon of encouragement. "Try again, *koukla*."

There he goes again with that endearment. I hate that I love it. I hate even more how it makes my toes curl and my knees clench together in a silent plea of *yes, more*.

"I feel restless," I confess, barely above a whisper. "I feel restless in my skin, in my life. When I said I wanted to move, it's more that I need to get out, go somewhere, do something that makes me feel anything but the anxiety pulsing through me."

With his thumb caressing mine, Nick murmurs, "Being at your parents' makes you feel like this?"

He doesn't even know half of what he's asking. And the kicker is, I can't exactly tell him the truth about the unknown man. My sperm donor, if you will. Sure, I *can*—but what good does that do? I spent near-on ten years asking my mother for information she refused to give me. Re-hashing the details is like picking at an open scab I won't let be.

That's me in a nutshell: picking at scabs, watching the blood rise once more, and then hastily bandaging it up, never doing a good enough job for it to heal completely.

On habit, I start to tap my fingers—only for Nick's fingers to wrap around mine again.

"You don't need to be nervous with me, Ermione," he says, voice rumbling. "I've told you this before: there's nothing you can tell me that'll make me look at you any differently." He tugs on my hand, a silent command for me to look at him. So, I do. Full-on, with my emotions bleeding on my sleeve and this ridiculous sense of *hope* clawing its way up my chest. "Nothing," he repeats in that classic, no-nonsense way of his. "You got that?"

I meet his gaze. "It's when I get a tattoo." He pauses, and I see the confusion in his pewter eyes. "When I get like this"—I put a hand to my chest, over my coat—"this restless, on-edge feeling . . . it usually results in a new tattoo. Those snapshots I told you about, I wasn't all truthful about it. I mean, I *was* and I wasn't."

Releasing my hand, he leans forward, and, on instinct, I do too. His palm makes gentle contact with the side of my face, then delves deep into my crazy, untamed hair. I stare at him as his fingers graze the shell of my ear, and then my breath catches when he traces the sensitive skin behind my ear—right over my soaring-wings tattoo.

He remembers.

It's crazy how you can know a person your entire life and yet it's one moment, one sliver in time that tells you everything you need to know about their soul. And Nick's soul? I've never met anyone else with his quirky humor, his good nature, his damn *kindness* that radiates from every inch of him.

"I got all night," he husks.

I don't get addicted to men, not ever, but I could get addicted to Nick—so easily.

Tilting my head to give him more access, I curl my fingers into a fist when the need to start tapping kicks back in. "Each of my tattoos are always the opposite of what I'm feeling. When I got the one on my foot, I lived each day like I couldn't wait to get to the next big thing. I needed—"

"Patience."

I nod, feeling more exposed than I ever have in my life. "It was a reminder to cool my hungry ambition. You can't rush certain things. You can't make them happen just by *wanting* them to happen. Dreams need time to prosper and grow—and I firmly believe that they unfold when you can personally handle them manifesting, never before."

"And the one behind your ear?"

His fingers graze it now, and I fight the urge to nuzzle his hand. "A pair of wings," I tell him, "during a low point when everyday felt like a struggle, a constant stream of disappointment." I may not want to come clean about my mother's infidelity, but this I can tell. It's *my* story to tell. "I don't have the same outlook on marriage and kids as you because my parents just . . . I couldn't breathe. It was *stifling* living under their roof. They told Katya and Dimitri to reach for their dreams, but never said the same to me. I got the *you should be married by now* speech one day and the very next, they were telling me no one would ever want me because I'd accomplished nothing."

"Who said that? Your mom or your dad?"

I almost laugh. How can he read me so damn well?

"Mostly my dad."

"Your dad's an ass."

"You won't hear me tell you otherwise."

He gives a quick, teasing tug to my earlobe, and then pulls back. "You're one of the most accomplished, ambitious people I know. Don't listen to their bullshit."

My heart, traitorous, rebellious thing that it is, flutters to life. *Down, heart.* "No need to lay on the sugar, Nick." I pointedly look down at his crotch. "We both know you're just trying to get into my pants."

He grins wolfishly, and it's so surprising, so *unlike* him, that I audibly gulp—like the true, awkward person I am deep down inside.

"Later," he says before shifting the car into drive.

"Later?"

"Yup."

"But—" I cut off, completely befuddled. Men don't just ignore their erections for what, a random drive through town? *Most men aren't Nick-fucking-Stamos.* Too damn true. I'm sitting next to a guy with steel resolve. It's dreadfully unfair.

One palm on the steering wheel, the other on the gearshift, Nick glances over at me. *Damn him for looking so sexy like that.* He cocks a brow. "But what? Something wrong?"

He is *not* going to make me say it.

The car rolls to a stop at an intersection, and then his big hand is on my thigh and, oh, God, I love how it feels. If he moves his fingers up just a *little* higher . . .

"Out with it," he orders, and though I can hear a trace of his trademark surliness, I know better now. The man keeps his emotions on lockdown, yes, but he's got such a way of making me feel like I can open up and be myself with him.

So, I open up and tell him exactly what's on my mind: "I want you."

His hand tightens on my leg, fingers pressing in, all the while keeping his gaze locked on the road as he navigates the dark streets. "How bad?"

I smile, and then throw down the verbal gauntlet. "I'm wet." A small, deliberate pause on my part. "Does that answer your question?"

"*Fuck.*"

English profanity. God, I love it when his control slips. I can't be the only one riding the hot-mess express. A girl's got to have company, after all, and Nick . . . he's A-grade company.

"I know," I say, patting the hand he's still resting on my thigh, "an unfortunate predicament but one I'm sure you'd be happy to remedy."

"After." His voice sounds like he's swallowed a dozen nails, choked and ragged.

"After *what*?"

"Patience, Ermione. Find it."

FIFTEEN MINUTES LATER, WE PULL UP TO A STRIP OF STORES with neon signs and a narrow parking lot separating the storefronts from the street. One in particular catches my attention immediately.

My head juts forward, hand clapped on top of my beanie, as I crane my neck to look up at the glowing sign. "Downtown Tattoo?" I whip around to stare at the man in the driver's seat. "Are you serious?"

As if uncomfortable, Nick rubs the back of his head. "You

said this is what you do. Your outlet or whatever." His hand falls to clamp down on his thigh, and he gives me a look that I can't even begin to read. "I'll do it with you."

My mouth falls open.

He's back to rubbing his head, but not before swiftly averting his gaze. "Don't look so shocked, Mina."

Impossible.

This is *him* we're talking about. Rule-following Nick. *I-like-things-orderly* Nick.

I fling my arm toward the tattoo parlor. "Those are real tats." It's honorable he wants to get inked with me, but . . . "As in, the non-sticker variety. They don't wash off."

He barks out a sharp laugh. "You mean, they're not peal-and-press?" He slaps his leg with mocking gusto. "Well, damn, there goes that idea."

I scrunch my nose at him. "You're making fun of me."

"You're askin' for it, *koukla*." He dangles a wrist from the steering wheel, then makes a point to look me straight in the eye when he speaks. "Let me ruin whatever clean-cut image of me you're so determined to keep on that imaginary pedestal of yours." In the dark of the car, his gray eyes look positively black as he stares me down. I feel a shiver of want slip down my spine, heating me up—or maybe that's the butt warmers he turned on during the drive. "I can be shy," he growls, "and I can't stand small talk. I know how I come across, Mina. I'm not clueless as to how people look at me."

"I know you aren't."

"A guy can be nice without being weak," he tells me, and I hear the deep conviction in his voice. "I help people because at one time, no one could help *me*. Not the kids in school who made fun of me and Effie for our ratty hand-me-downs from Goodwill. Not your parents, who took us to Greece while my own parents worked themselves tirelessly to give us more than they had themselves. Although please know that I appreciate what yours did for me and my sister—trust me, I know I'm indebted to them for opening their doors to us for *years*.

"But it doesn't negate the fact that I still struggled. There wasn't anyone to help when I was working more jobs than I could handle, all because I was determined to open up Stamos Restoration on my own terms without investors having a say in my business." His molars crack together when he scrubs a hand over his face, exhaling roughly. "I'm not a walking rulebook, Ermione, ready to take you to task—unless it's to spank that gorgeous ass of yours. I love hard, but I promise you, I fuck even harder."

Oh. My. God.

I . . . I have no words.

For the first time in my life, I'm completely speechless. There are so many things I want to unpack about what he's just said—and, because there's nothing I love more than a philosophical debate about life and self-identity, I'm dying to know if anything he admitted correlates to his belief in dreams being just temporary longings.

I want to give voice to it all, but the parking lot of a tattoo shop isn't the right place. So, I crack a big smile, all teeth, and tease, "*I love hard and fuck even harder*. That's tattoo material right there."

I don't mention that I can't wait to find out the truth behind those words.

He says nothing, shoulders tense under his light coat. Gradually his expression eases, and I heft out a big sigh of relief. "Inside of my thigh," he says, patting his leg.

"With an arrow pointing straight to your crotch."

Nick snorts. "Nothing says classy quite like a dick tattoo."

"That's the spirit."

As one, we reach for the door handles to climb out of the car. I pause as I crank open my door, one foot planted on the cracked concrete. I look over my shoulder at the man who, in theory, should only be my best friend's older brother but who is quickly becoming so much more.

As though sensing my hesitation, Nick, already out of the car, drops down so he can peer through his open door at me. "What's wrong?"

"Let me choose yours." I say the words quickly, like I'm ripping off a thick bandage.

Nothing in his expression so much as twitches. "My tattoo?"

"Yes." Nervous, I lick my dry lips and then drag my clammy hands over my jean-clad thighs. "You choose mine and I choose yours. Trust, both ways."

He considers me silently with one of his unreadable looks. Just when I'm certain he's about to turn me down flat, he thumps his hand on the car's roof. "Don't make me regret this."

"Never," I vow.

24

MINA

Nick and I meet with two tattoo artists. We sit down separately, each detailing exactly what we want the other inked with, all while casting glances at each other from across the room. I'm careful to keep my voice low, except for when I boldly claim, "Yeah, we're gonna need a bigger arrow than that."

Nick jerks in my direction, those pillow-soft lips (now confirmed for softness!) pulling to the side in a sexy smirk. *Do it and die,* he mouths.

I toss him a kiss and turn back to the artist who'll be working on Nick. Carefully, I explain to him my thoughts, going so far as to head to Pinterest on my phone and scope out a specific example. It has to be perfect, something Nick will look at years from now and always remember this night.

Always remember *me.*

"There's a lot of detail work here," says the bearded artist, Zach. He has ear gauges big enough for me to stick my finger through and dark, messy hair combed over to the right. He looks like the quintessential tattoo artist, save for the fact that he has no visible ink.

I nod at his assessment. “I know. Do you think you can pull it off?”

His rugged features crease with a wicked grin. “’Course I can. So long as your boyfriend here doesn’t mind it on his arm or ribcage. I need a good canvas to work with.”

Boyfriend.

I guess, technically, we *are* dating. According to the online world, at least.

Still, the word elicits tingles I’d rather it not as I lean back on the rolling stool and shout at my *boyfriend*, “Any boundaries on your body off-limits?” When his gaze flashes with heat, I thrust a finger at him. “Anywhere else *besides* The Great One, I mean?”

Nick throws his head back with a deep, rumbling laugh. “I’ll leave that one to you, *koukla*. I’m at your expense.”

“Disposal.”

He stares at me blankly.

“The saying is ‘I’m at your disposal’ not ‘expense.’” I pause, then mutter, “You know what? Just add it to that book of yours.”

Turning back to Zach, I plant my elbows on the table. “The ribcage will do nicely, I think.”

NICK CHOOSES SCRIPT FOR ME.

After all my other tats, I recognize the familiar sensation of the needle treading back and forth in the shapes of letters. The more the machine buzzes, the less I feel much of anything, so I force myself to relax and loosen up.

Flat on my back on a cushioned table, I’m sprawled out, topless, with my hands covering my nipples. *Thank you for that one, Nick.*

The artist who's working on my ink drags a damp cloth over my bra line. "You doin' good?"

His Boston accent is so thick, he'd give Mark Wahlberg a run for his money. His name tag reads *Calvin*. To be honest, I expected more of a Matthew or a Sullivan to match his red hair. Calvin works just fine, though.

"All good," I tell him, dragging my gaze up to the ceiling. "How many words are we doing?"

Calvin laughs. "I'm under strict orders not to tell you anything."

Dammit. I think fast. "Well, what word are we on now?"

He makes a point of rolling his lips shut, then gets back to work. I'll give him another few minutes then make my next move.

Tipping my head to the left, I search out Nick on the far side of the room. He's posted up in a chair that's positioned to face me. Hugging the back, he sits still while Zach works diligently to bring my vision to life. As Calvin needles my skin, alternating between swiping the damp cloth and ink away, I focus on Effie's older brother.

His dark hair is in desperate need of a cut, and I vow to trim it soon. But it's not his hair that truly steals my focus—it's his naked torso . . . and the other tattoos I see marking his skin. There are only two, one gracing his pec—a quote, it looks like, that I spotted when he first removed his shirt—and another on the underside of his left ribcage.

I trace my memories with a heavy hand, trying to remember the last time I saw him shirtless. Back in high school, I think. And, boy, the years have made his already spectacular torso into a work of art.

Ropes of muscle clench as he sits under the needle, his eyes squeezed shut—leaving me full room to drool over him. His shoulders and arms are all bulging power, no doubt thanks to lifting things all day for Stamos Restoration and

Co. My face heats as I wonder what it would be like to be under all that bulky mass.

"Do you need some water?" Calvin asks me, snapping me out of my daze. "You're lookin' a little pink."

Quickly, I shake my head, muttering "no," and then return to my unbidden perusal.

Nick Stamos is a catch. Why in the world would that girl Savannah Rose turn him down? Seriously, who in the world could trump a guy with so much heart *and* sex appeal? It doesn't get better than him, that's for sure.

Flicking my eyes up to his chest, and then to his face, I startle when I realize he's staring right back. And my hands . . . my hands are cupping my naked breasts. The flush on my cheeks spreads down, warming my chest and then, yes, lower still. I cross my legs at my ankles, careful not to move too quickly.

He winks—*winks!*—and then mouths something that looks suspiciously like, *Like what you see?*

Turning my face back to front-and-center, I stare up the ceiling and fight the smile threatening to burst free.

Cocky, incorrigible man.

He's such a liar. He isn't shy *at all*. At least, he isn't with me.

I spend the next hour on the table. Then spend the following one flipping through a magazine in the main area of the parlor. When my phone vibrates, I pull it out of my coat pocket to see that Effie's texted me. Some of my happiness dims. She wouldn't approve of any of tonight's shenanigans, least of all our getting spur-of-the moment tattoos.

A permanent mark on our skin for a temporary, fake relationship.

I fidget in my chair. Hang my head in guilt. And then check my phone like any best friend ought to do.

Effie: *Good news!!!!!!*

Her enthusiasm is contagious as my fingers fly across the keyboard, not pausing to check for any possible typos before I shoot it off.

Me: *TELL ME. Did the Blades write that 5-star reveiw?*

Effie: *I think so? Maybe?*

Effie: *Actually, I think they did. Totally forgot to tell you about it. But that's not my news!!!*

Me: *Spill the tea, lady. I'm not getting any younger.*

Effie: *This is not a drill. I repeat, THIS.IS.NOT.A.DRILL.*

Me: *I just sprouted my first gray hair. Hurry it up!*

Effie: *Only the first? LOL*

Me: *Be glad I love you. Will you tell me already?*

Effie: . . . *we got the thumbs up! From the adoption agency! WE'RE GOING TO BE PARENTS!!!!!!!*

Oh, my God.

I jerk my gaze up from the phone, sending a wild glance around the parlor because, holy crap, I need to tell *someone*. My only option is a dude sprawled out on a bench across from me. He looks like he eats children for breakfast, then picks his teeth with their bones. The face tats really aren't doing him any favors.

"Hey!" I hiss at him, waving one hand when I notice he's wearing earbuds. "Hey, mister!"

He raises his head, eyes drowsily glancing over at me. "Sup?"

I don't even care about his lack of excitement. Holding up my phone, I thrust it toward him. "I'm going to be an *aunt!*"

He waits a beat. Pauses for yet another. And then tucks his earbud back in. "Does it look like I give a shit?" he grumbles.

Whatever. His loss, not mine. He has no idea how much of a badass aunt I'll be. The *best*. I turn back to my phone and send off another text to my best friend.

Me: *Who is it? A boy? A girl? How old is my nephew or niece? Who am I going to spoil???*

Effie: *LOL! We have no idea. All we know is that the adoption agency thinks we'll be a good fit for some child out there and oh, my heart is FULL with all the possibilities!! We need to celebrate.*

Me: *Yes. YES! This wknd? I'm so happy for you guys*

Effie: *Works for me. Love you!!*

Me: *Love you back. Give Sarah a hug for me!*

"That smile for me?"

My head snaps up at Nick's gravel-pitched voice. He's back in his T-shirt—another Stamos Restoration variation—with his coat tossed over one arm. He looks a little green around the edges, and I jump up from my seat to cross to his side.

"It can be," I tell him as I pull the coat from his grasp, "but"—I lean in, standing on my tiptoes to get my mouth close to his ear—"Effie just texted me. The agency told them *yes!*"

Nick's gray eyes widen. "Holy shit. For real?"

I grip his arm, my excitement bubbling over. "Yes!" And then, as though I have every right in the world, I hook a finger in the collar of his T-shirt and drag him down for a kiss. He stiffens under my touch for the briefest moment before squeezing my hip and nipping my lower lip.

"You two ready to pay?"

Oh. *Oh.*

Lowering to the soles of my feet, I laugh awkwardly. "Oops, sorry, Calvin."

"No need, you two lovebirds." He rolls his eyes, teasing us, before finishing up our joint transaction. Nick and I split the bill down the middle, and I do my best not to worry about the money. Sometimes you need to remember to live, to breathe. Plus, my stress levels feel nonexistent and I have zero urge to wander anymore tonight.

Some people take Xanax to calm down. I take a dosage of Nick Stamos.

Same results but the latter is a whole lot more fun.

"Anyway," Calvin goes on, "since you're both determined not to look at those tats while you're here, do me a favor and call in the morning. If there's something you don't like, we'll fix it up for you."

We take our self-care brochures, along with the ointment they force us to buy—even though I have two tubes at home—and then we're tromping outside to Nick's car. The cold stings my face as I slide into the passenger's seat.

"My place?" Nick asks quietly, one hand on the steering wheel.

I study his profile and feel myself nod. "I'd love to see where you live."

"Buckle up, then. One home tour on the way."

25

MINA

"This is the cutest neighborhood," I say when we pull up to a tree-lined street twenty minutes later. Nick lives in a quiet spot in Wayland. The small town is picturesque, even at 9 p.m., with two-story Colonial-era houses dotting the side of the road, wide-open pastureland tucked behind short, wooden fences, and curvy streets that might as well be trademarked to New England.

"I picked the house out right before I proposed."

Right. The proposal. I send him a forced grin he can't see in the dark. "The first time?"

"Smartass." He says it affectionately and without an inkling of heat. "Yeah, the first time. Figured I was heading right into marriage with children coming soon after, and I thought I needed something big and showy."

It makes me wonder how he felt stepping into that big and showy house alone after his failed wedding.

"I bet it's beautiful."

"It is." The car slows toward the end of the street, the headlights illuminating a gravel driveway that leads to a steep incline. As we head up to the house, Nick adds, "I did all the work on the house myself. Stripped out all the shitty shag carpet and brought in this amazing restored wood from an eighteenth-century mill that was being torn down over in Worcester. The back of the house overlooks a pretty big pond, and there was so much damage done to the wood that I actually put in—" He breaks off with a grumble deep in his chest. "Shit, sorry. You probably don't care to hear—"

Except that I do. "Don't stop," I tell him, and he doesn't.

I listen to him talk about some of the small details he incorporated—the parlor doors that separate the living room from the dining room he never uses; the six-burner stove he purchased from a restaurant in Somerville before they shut down; the beautiful, original trim work that he spent hours bringing back to life.

I can barely keep my mouth shut when he parks the car.

My nose presses to the window, and I fog it all up with my heavy breathing. "You live in a farmhouse!"

Nick chuckles. "Circa 1782. It's one of the oldest structures still standing in Wayland, though it's not a historical landmark. Probably for the best, since I axed the back wall and put in a glass window—this way I can look at the pond and woods whenever I want."

I follow him out of the car but can't quite bring myself to look away from the house. It's beyond stunning. A fairy tale come to life. "Woods and pond, huh? You're going to be a master at this Maine thing when we go."

He nudges me to the side when we step up to his front door, and he fits in a key before letting us in. "Lucky for you, I conduct training sessions for the uninitiated."

"Yeah? And what do these training sessions entail exactly?"

His smile is all wicked masculinity. "Orgasms."

I burst into laughter. "You're so full of shit."

One flick of a switch, and light floods the space. Immediately, I soak it all up.

The ceilings aren't particularly tall, maybe around seven and a half feet, but it's . . . *lovely*. Eighteenth-century meets rustic farmhouse. It's a style Nick has executed to perfection. Stonework takes up the lower half of the walls, painstakingly revealed during his renovations, I'm sure, whereas the upper halves are a solid plaster and painted the most exquisite Tiffany blue. Artwork hangs on the walls, featuring mostly landscapes and old architectural sketches.

I'm so busy taking it all in that I don't notice Nick toeing off his shoes. "Wine?" he asks.

I say yes just because I want an excuse to see the kitchen.

Trailing after him, I eye the rooms as we pass them by. Each has its own character and flair, some painted a light gray while one is a brighter yellow. Canary Yellow, maybe. The thought makes me grin. I so hope that once rehabbing *Agape* is over and done with, I'll feel the same amount of pride Nick does as he walks through the halls of his home.

The kitchen, not to be outdone by the rest of the house, is a stunner.

I feel a little blessed to be standing in here and I don't even like to cook.

"Nick," I murmur in awe, "this is just . . . *gorgeous*."

"Trust me, the rehab came with some headaches. Galvanized pipes were the least of my problems. Lead paint," he grumbles, sounding put out even though I know he probably lived for every challenge this house threw at him, "lead paint everywhere." He moves confidently over to a door nestled between the hallway and a stainless-steel refrigerator. "Red or white?"

"Where does that door lead?" I ask, ignoring his question because, *hello*, this house is like a treasure chest of secrets. I'm utterly enthralled with it already, although maybe that's because I can sense Nick's love for it. By default, my curiosity is at an all-time high.

"This one?" He braces a hand against the wooden door-knob. "It goes down to the wine cellar."

My eyes practically bulge. "You have a wine cellar?"

Flashing me a grin, he shimmies the knob. "On the scale of *I'd-like-to-hug-you*, what does a wine cellar get me?"

Stomach doing that weird flippy thing at our little joke, I boost myself up on one of the stools lining the island. "At least a nine-point-five."

"Not a solid ten?"

I shake my head. "I have the right to reserve perfect scores until I decide to dish them out. Also, you *do* realize we shouldn't be drinking, right? I mean, unless you're okay with thinning blood and a blotchy tattoo."

His fingers freeze, panic dashing across his handsome features. "Ah, *gamóto*. I didn't even think about that."

He is way too cute when he gets all worried. It makes me want to give him a perfect 10.0 and wrap my arms around him. "I'll take some water, if you have it on hand?"

Thankfully, he catches onto my joke immediately. "That was bad, *koukla*. Real bad. I've got all the water you could want. Except for sparkling—no self-respecting man drinks that."

I tap my chin, faking a put-out look. "Well, damn. Sparkling is my go-to."

He reads me in an instant. Disregarding the wine cellar, he crosses over to me and leans in close to drop a heady kiss onto my mouth. His fingers rip off my beanie hat and toss it on the granite island, and then they're in my hair, tugging on the strands in the same way he's tugged at my heart for years now.

God, yes.

His mouth moves roughly over mine, and it's so deliciously wicked that I push at his coat lapels until the heavy material is dropping to the floor at our feet. He wastes no time in returning the favor. My wool coat hits the marble flooring, and then he's planting his big hands on my knees, urging them apart. I spread them on command, reaching forward to hook my fingers through the belt loops of his jeans.

Nick needs no more encouragement than that.

He steps into the *V* of my legs, his mouth still molded to mine, our tongues dueling. "On the counter," he growls when he breaks away. "Now."

I like bossy Nick. A *lot*.

With a hand to his chest, I push him back with a flirty grin. His face is all rigid lines but his eyes . . . God, they set me on *fire*. More black than gray, they watch me steadily, never veering away. Wanting to provoke him—to see that tightly leashed veneer of his crack—I twist around, planting my hands on the wooden stool. I arch my back, sticking my butt out, rubbing up against the hard-on not even his jeans can hide.

He cuts loose a guttural groan, and I soak up the sound.

Step One to making Nick Stamos lose his ever-loving mind? Complete.

I pop the button of my jeans. Squeeze my eyes shut tightly. *Here goes nothing*. The only sound that echoes in the kitchen is the tab of my zipper inching down over each metal tooth. My fingers hook over the waistband, and I almost laugh at the way they tremble. Like this is my first time having sex—six years after everyone thought I ruined good, ol' Nick during his wedding night.

Broad fingers fold over mine. "Let me," comes Nick's rough timbre.

So, I do.

I hear his knees hit marble behind me. I feel the heat of

his hands graze my skin as he slowly, so slowly, inches the denim down over my hips. My sight is replaced by the sensation of touch, the way he kisses my exposed flesh like a man kneeling before an altar. It rocks me to my core, and I *feel* myself grow wet, there between my legs.

My jeans and underwear are tugged down to my knees—right before Nick's palm cups my butt cheek, right over my tattoo.

"You never fail to surprise me," he murmurs, brushing his thumb over the ink there: a wreath, the same one marked on Greece's Coat of Arms, encircling a phoenix, the national bird, rising from the ashes. It's no bigger than the palm of my hand, invisible to the eye when I wear underwear or bikini bottoms. It's for me . . . and now for Nick too. "Why this?" he asks, voice low.

Lids fluttering shut, I ball my hands into fists on the kitchen island. I don't want to lie to him, not about this, so I don't. Facing away from him, the admission slips out easily. "For all the times I've never felt Greek enough. Not speaking the language doesn't make me any less Greek—an *Ellenitha*. Not being able to read the words doesn't mean I'm not somehow connected to my heritage." I pause to beat back the tears that threaten to spill. "I *am* Greek."

He must hear the turmoil in my tone because he strips off my jeans completely, taking off my snow boots, too, and then rises to his full height. He towers over me, and I can feel his heat against my back when he brushes my hair over one shoulder and leans in. "One day," he says, "you'll trust me enough to tell me why this, of all things, turns your voice to fire."

A gasp rips from my soul as I feel his fingers delve between my legs. Oh, God. "Nick—"

His mouth rasps over my neck, and a shiver rakes down my spine. "One day," he goes on, just as reverently, "but not today." He turns his hand sideways, wordlessly ordering me to spread my legs. His free hand grips the lip of the granite island, his knuckles white with restraint. My mouth goes dry. "But I'm gonna tell you this once, Ermione. *You* are Greek. Your soul, your blood, your name that makes people stop in their tracks and ask for it again. You're an *Ellenitha, koukla,* and even if you weren't, I wouldn't give a damn."

And then, as if to prove a point, his finger collides with my clit and I *quiver*.

"Oh, my God."

My vision goes blurry around the edges as he rubs in small, little circles. My balled fists on the island go flat, as though I can ground my very being through my fingertips. Nick doesn't hasten the tempo of those circles. Like his kiss earlier in the car, he goes slow, every move measured and drawn out to make me beg for more.

And I beg, shamelessly.

In the way that I grind my hips down over those magic fingers, seeking more, seeking anything he can give me. He increases the pressure just enough for me to rise up on my toes. Electric. That's how his touch feels, like I've jabbed my finger into an outlet just for shits and giggles.

It twines through my limbs, and I'm keenly aware of my knees trembling.

I dart out one hand, clasping his that's still gripping the island, and I squeeze. A silent plea.

"Say it." His stubble scratches my throat as he drops his mouth to the place where my pulse pounds madly. "Tell me what you want, Ermione."

I've never been shy.

Insecure, yes.

But never shy.

Until now. Until a Greek Adonis finally looked my way

and hurled my carefully planned out life straight into the flickering flames of want, need, lust.

My lips part. "You." I swallow, thickly, then glance down. At the way he's anchored my ass to his groin with an arm wrapped around my hips. Those fingers play me like a finely tuned instrument . . . or a piece of wood he's molded and created into something beautiful. His fingers glisten with my wetness, and it's both the most obscene and sexiest thing I've ever seen. "Any way I can have you."

I cry out as he plunges that one finger deep inside me.

"You're gonna have me, *koukla*." Another finger enters me on the second thrust, and I'm so tight—it's been so damn long that I've thought about anything but *Agape*—that my head falls forward as I suck in a heavy breath. "My tongue on your clit," he edges out, his fingers curling to hit me just right, "my cock in your pussy." I feel myself tighten around his fingers, and a rough laugh rumbles deep in his chest. "You like that, huh? The visual or the way I'm fucking you with my fingers?"

"I'm not the only one around here with a smart mouth."

He curls his fingers again.

"Both," I whimper, giving him his answer. "Do it again. Please."

His fingers leave my sex, and I nearly whimper again at the loss. Except that he doesn't leave me hanging. He grabs the hem of my sweater and gently pulls it up and over my head, then does the same with his T-shirt. Immediately my eyes dart to the white bandage covering his new tattoo. His skin is still pink from the abrasion of the needle, and I'm sure the same can be said for mine.

Pink or not, though, there's no stopping me from looking at his gorgeous torso. Greek words are etched into skin—the quote I noticed earlier—and then I'm seeing nothing but hard pecs and even harder, finely ridged abdominal muscles.

A whole whopping eight because a man like Nick would never be satisfied with a measly six.

"I was right," I breathe out.

Big hands go to my ass, where he boosts me up onto the kitchen island. "About?"

"You look like a statue. One of those finely chiseled ones that stand sentry at every museum known to man." I'm naked, save for my pretty-much-useless bra, but not even that can keep me from running my gaze over his body and that drool-worthy *V* leading down into his jeans. God bless construction jobs.

He pops the brass button. "You talking about the ones with the appropriately placed leaves?"

I make a noise of agreement in the back of my throat. "The very ones."

Nick shucks his jeans, and his cock proudly bobs free. "I'm gonna need a big leaf."

Talk about the understatement of the year. I can't tear my gaze away. "Raphia regalis," I hear myself mutter.

"The *what?*"

I flick my attention up to his gorgeous face and all that messy, dark hair. "It's a species of palm tree. Biggest leaf in the world. I saw it on *Jeopardy.*"

His pewter eyes flicker with mirth. "Pick a category."

"What?"

"Humor me." He reaches around me to unclasp my bra. By my ear, he drops his voice to a low rumble. "Pick a category. I promise you'll enjoy every one."

Has he gone off his rocker? Given his firm constitution, probably not. Going along with his game, I say, "I don't know the categories."

"Animals. Westerns." He pauses, drawing his tongue along the front of teeth. "Planets."

I raise a brow. "Those are some interesting categories."

"Got a preference?"

"I'll take Animals for one-hundred, please."

His grin is positively blinding. "A woman after my own heart."

Before I can even decipher *that* particular statement, he's hauling me up into his arms. I bounce against his chest, careful not to disturb his bandage, as he cuts through the kitchen to a less formal room. A TV is strung up on one wall, and a sectional sofa takes up most of the space. But it's the wall-to-wall window that steals my breath. Lights flicker outside, and Nick, seeing my awe, murmurs, "Outdoor solar lights. It's cold out but there's still enough sunlight for them to do their job."

And do their job they do, twinkling like fairy lights leading into an enchanted forest.

Nick puts me down in front of the window. He grasps my hands and presses them flat against the cold glass. "I've thought about this," he tells me, reverent hands skimming my curves, "me fucking you from behind. You seeing our reflection and the outdoors all at once."

I feel the heat of his cock like a brand against my butt. It hits me, then, that this is actually going to happen. Me, Nick, sex. *Sex* with Nick Stamos. Pinch me, please, or at least don't make me wake up from the best dream of my life.

I turn my head, wanting his mouth on mine, and he gives it without question. His kiss, like the very essence of him, is hardness underlined with passion. Careful not to brush my bandages, he dips his fingers between my legs again, sinking two in deep.

"You're so wet," he grunts against my mouth. "Fuck, I can't wait to feel you come against my mouth." When I press my hips impatiently back into his, he chuckles. "Okay, after you come on my cock—better?"

And then, for reasons that I refuse to look at too deeply, I nip at his bottom lip and say, "I'm clean." More specifically, I've never had sex without a condom. Have never wanted to, until now. Until *him*. "And on the pill."

Nick's fingers pause. "You sure?"

So much yes. The vulnerability of the moment squeezes my heart like a vice. "Yeah. I mean, so long as you're . . ."

"Jesus, Mina." His eyes take on a wild bent, like he can't believe this is happening. "Yeah, I'm . . . right there with you. *Gamóto,* you drive me wild. I need this. I need *you*."

The same sense of urgency pulses through me as he lays a hand on my back and eases me forward, until my forehead comes close to kissing the glass window—and I feel the heavy crown of his cock slip through the wet folds of my sex.

This. Is. Happening.

After all these years, it's not Nick and someone else. It's Nick and *me,* his sister's best friend. His long-standing frenemy. The girl he's known since he was eight. But this thing between us is more than all that—it's unrelenting, combustible passion, something he proves when he mutters, "Hold on tight, *koukla*," and thrusts inside me.

My mouth parts in an *O*.

Big, so damn big.

His cock stretches me, my walls clinging to him tightly, and I hesitate on that fine line between pleasure and pain.

And then he moves, pulling back, pulling out, before slamming home, and the pleasure turns downright *euphoric*. He grips my hips, hard, yanking my ass onto his cock just as he drives forward.

"*Mina*." His smoky voice echoes in my ears, muddled with the rush of pressure in my head and the sound of how goddamn *wet* I am around him. I need to find it in myself to feel embarrassed, but I can't. Not when he growls my name again and *definitely* not when he groans, "You feel so good. Never—I've never—"

Me either.

Not like this. It's never felt like this.

"More," I urge him, craning my head to look over my shoulder at his powerful body. The veins in his chest and neck strain with each of his thrusts, his chest burns a ruddy red, and those wild pewter eyes are locked on his cock slipping in and out of my sex.

Heat curls through me, and I lose every inhibition.

I push back, greedy for the way he makes me feel. Sweat beads on my brow. My thighs cramp from the bent-over position he's folded me in. My breasts, unbound by a bra, small as they are, sway with the force of his hips.

It's divine.

Raw as hell.

And utterly perfect.

Throat tight, I cry out his name. "I'm so close. Please—"

My fingers dive between my legs, needing that direct bit of stimulation to throw me over the edge—but Nick bats my hand out of the way. I'm so wet that when he fingers the tight nub at the hood of my sex, they slip. His breathing audibly hitches as he goes back for more, circling, faster and faster, as his thrusts pick up speed.

I hear nothing but the slap of his hips meeting mine, the sound of our groans as we teeter on the verge of orgasm.

"Come all over my cock, *koukla*. Fuck, *yes* . . . just like that."

My inner walls clamp down on his hard-on. His fingers apply more pressure until I'm so fired up, so strung tight, that I have no choice but to do what he says. I come on a cry, my legs spasming as I struggle to keep up on my feet. It's a futile battle, one that Nick rectifies by bolstering me up with his arm banded around my stomach.

He plows forward, that big cock of his hitting me in all the right ways, until he gives me the slice of knowledge I've wanted to know since my teenage years when I used to slip my fingers under my panties and get off at the thought of him—with one, masculine groan, he disproves every hypothesis I ever had about him coming silently.

His hands sweep over my back, and he bends over far enough to kiss me right between my shoulder spines.

"I think I died," I whisper.

"That good, huh?" He's all smug masculinity when he playfully slaps my ass. "Tell me you saw the pearly gates of heaven the minute you came."

Laughter climbs my throat. "Your ego, Nick."

"It's almost as big as The Great One."

"You're ridiculous."

"Yeah, and you love it."

I don't, I tell myself. *I really, really don't.* Yeah, I don't believe myself either.

Nick gently pulls out of me, and with a casually asked, "Bathroom?" we both hurry for the half-bath just off the parlor. I shoo him out while I pee, and Nick doesn't even blush when he cleans himself off in front of me.

Men. No shame whatsoever.

Washing my hands, I watch as he leans a hip up against the bathroom counter. He studies me avidly, his gray eyes flitting over my legs and my hips and my breasts. "I don't regret any of tonight. I need you to know that."

My heart hiccups. "I don't either."

With a satisfied grin, he nods his chin toward my body. "Tattoo reveal time."

Nerves spring to life in my belly. "Yeah, okay." I hope he loves what I chose for him. Earlier tonight, I was so confident that he would, but now, standing here naked with him, I worry. If he hates it, it's going to be one heck of a painful removal process. I gulp audibly, and then reach for the clear tape binding the bandage to my chest.

"Let me," Nick says, interrupting my hands with his own. With his head ducked, a mask of concentration falls over his face. I stand, back straight, as he works to carefully remove each bandage from under my boobs. Already the soreness from the needle has worn off—for me, at least—and I hold my breath as one bandage lands on the counter. "We'll look at the same time. *Naí?*"

The second bandage lands on the floor, and we leave it there.

"Do me now."

I quirk my lips at the innuendo in his words but get to work unwrapping him. "Eyes on me, Stamos," I warn playfully.

"Trust me, *koukla,*" he murmurs with heat, "I'm not lookin' anywhere else unless I have to."

Goddamn him for making me want to swoon after he already had me orgasming on command! I laugh, because his good humor is contagious, and finally ease the bandage from his skin. The tattoo looks gorgeous against the ropes of muscles that work as the backdrop. As much as I want to trace the intricate black lines with my finger, I force myself to step back and give him space.

"Okay, we're doing this then?" I ask.

He grins. "You sound nervous. Need to hold my hand?"

I swat his arm. Draw in a deep breath, then face the mirror. Immediately I drop my gaze to my breasts—the high-peaked nipples standing at full attention, thanks to Nick's close proximity—and then lower, to the feminine cursive script. The words follow the natural, underside curve of my breasts, inked in delicate and thin font. It looks wispy, like if I breathe a little too roughly, the words might scatter away on a wild breeze.

"Without the night," Nick says, voice pitched low, "there are no stars."

I swallow, hard, hearing him repeat the words now etched into my skin even as I stare at them in the mirror for myself. My throat grows even tighter, and I press the back of my fist to my mouth. I don't want him to see my lips trembling, but there's no hiding the way I blink rapidly, chasing away the tears.

"It reminds me of you," he continues in a deep rasp. "No matter how bad it gets, no matter what you're trying to claw away from . . . just remember that you're *Mina* because of all those restless moments."

I don't stop to let myself think twice.

Twisting on my heel, I throw my arms around Nick's waist. He hisses out, "Shit, tattoo," and I immediately drop my right arm. One-armed hug it is, then.

"Thank you." I kiss his chest, as close as I can get to his mouth since I'm barefooted. "Thank you."

I feel him press his lips to the top of my head. Then, "My turn. Let's do this. No arrows, right?"

I ease back and hop up on the counter. "A huge arrow, like I promised. Look and see."

Slowly Nick turns toward the mirror, and I watch his expression, noting every change like I'm skimming through a flipbook. His brows rise first, and then his cheeks hollow out with a quick exhale. My own breathing kicks into overdrive, nerves eating away at me. Tentatively, he touches a finger to the top of the church spire.

"How . . .?"

Feeling a blush crest my cheeks, I bring my hands to my lap. "That first day I came to your office, I saw the miniature sculpture in the waiting area. It wasn't done, but I couldn't—*can't*—get the image out of my head of you working on it. The patience it would take. The acute attention to detail it requires. It could belong to anyone, but I saw it and I knew that it was yours."

His jaw works tightly. "I can't seem to finish it. It's the longest I've ever worked on a piece, but this one . . . I just can't get it right." He slides me a swift, searching glance that sparks goose bumps to life on my skin. "Maybe I will now."

"Do you like it?" I ask softly.

His gaze hitches back to his chest, to the geometric-inspired church window inked into the side of his ribs. The lines of the tattoo are intricately Gothic, almost haunting in their austerity.

He reaches for my hand, his thumb brushing over my skin. "You know me too well, *koukla*. It's perfect."

No, *this* feels perfect.

And it terrifies me how much I wish it all were real.

26

Celebrity Tea Presents:
Nick Stamos Spotted Getting Tattoos With New Girlfriend—And We Have A Name!

Readers, the headline says it all, but I'm here to spill the TEA. Take a seat, pour yourself a cup, and let's get down to business. You may remember recent reports of Put A Ring On It *contestant Nick Stamos stepping out with a mysterious woman. Well, a new source on Twitter claims that Stamos and his new girl (more on her in a minute) came into a tattoo parlor the source frequents. They picked tats out for each other, KISSED, and looked genuinely smitten.*

"I was just coming in when they were checking out," the source told Celebrity Tea, "and the moment I spotted Nick I remembered seeing your article! OMG, they were all over each other, and I secretly grabbed a video. By the way, he's even hotter in real life. She is one lucky girl."

Well, Dear Reader, we've done our homework (you're welcome) and this Mysterious Woman is none other than one Mina Pappas of Cambridge, Massachusetts. Her social media accounts are pretty sparse, but never fear! Looks like our girl Mina is opening a new hair salon—according to her Instagram bio link, anyway.

Did our boy Nick hammer his way into Mina's heart? Is Savannah Rose aware that her former beau has already moved on? So much to discuss, so little time. One thing's for certain, a little birdie told me that Put A Ring On It *will be airing sooner than expected, due to all the leaked footage. Grab some popcorn. Take a seat. It's going to be a wild ride and you KNOW I'm down to deliver the tea, 24/7.*

27

NICK

"Why is painting so satisfying?"

I stifle a laugh at Mina's question. We're camped out in *Agape,* painting the salon's walls a mellow mauve that she claimed she couldn't live without. Standing on the third-highest rung on a ladder, her hips sway back and forth to the tempo of a Greek song she's playing off her laptop.

"You laugh, but I'm not kidding." She dips her roller back into the paint. "It's calming."

"Said no one ever." At her *harrumph,* I drape one arm over my bent knee. Mina wanted the chance to paint the upper halves of the room, which means I agreed to do the bitch work: edging. I would have put Vince and the boys on it, but I need them over at the museum today doing some preliminary demo work. "Painting is tedious. Edging is tedious. I could live the rest of my life without picking up another brush and be a happy camper."

The roller *splats* against the white plaster as she goes back in for another round. She attacks it with such gusto I almost feel bad for the wall—it's beginning to look like an abstract mural. And not the good, expensive kind.

"Well, *I* like it." Mina's dark ponytail slips over one shoulder as she reaches her arm diagonal across her chest to paint a bare spot she missed. "It's a bit like coloring hair. So many stylists hate the process, but there's nothing more exciting than making someone feel beautiful through color. The brighter the better, if you ask me."

Everything about Ermione Pappas is bold: her personality, her laughter, the way she feels in my arms when she orgasms. *Anddd,* yup, there we go. Instant hard-on. If I had it my way, she'd skip staying with her parents and camp out at my place. I have a king-sized mattress, which beats the twin she's currently sleeping on. But Mina's stubborn, maybe even more stubborn than I am, and even though I've convinced her to come over for dinner, she's yet to leave her parents. Personally, I think she's holding out and hoping they'll come around and all sing Kumbaya together.

All I know is that I'm glad we have the salon to ourselves today.

Fixing my attention on that ponytail of hers that's swinging as much as her hips are, I ask, "You ever miss the pink?"

She touches her head with a gloved hand. "My hair, you mean?"

I nod. "Other than now, I can't remember the last time you went au natural. High school, maybe. Even then I remember walking into my mom's bathroom to find you and Effie covered in hair dye and scrubbing the floors before Ma saw it all. Purple back then, right?"

"You've got a good memory, Stamos."

"Attention to detail, Ermione." I tap my forehead. "As someone tells me frequently, I've got it in spades."

"No truer words have ever been spoken." Pausing with

her roller resting on the lip of the paint tray, Mina shrugs. "And I do miss it. The pink hair. I promised Toula I'd strip it for her wedding—you know how she is about pictures—and I honestly thought I would have already ditched the black, but . . ."

"You like it."

She nods, a small smile tugging at her lips. "Which one do you like more? The pink or the black?"

I hold my hands up. "You're not tricking me into answering that one, *koukla.* There's no right answer."

That small smile grows bigger. "It was worth a try." Another dip of the roller into the paint. "I'll probably go back to the pink soon enough. Clients like it when hairstylists are edgy and fashion-forward, y'know?"

I don't know a damn thing about cutting hair, but I love that *Mina* loves it—so I guess that's what matters.

"Plus, people are commenting on *Agape*'s Instagram page left and right since that article came out. They're loving any and all pictures of fun-colored hair inspos, so I guess I have my answer on that front. Colors of the rainbow, here I come."

I didn't have my second cup of coffee this morning, and I blame withdrawal for being slow on the uptake. Pushing up onto my knees, I drop the edger into the paint tray to my right. "Someone wrote an article about the salon? One of the local newspapers or something?"

Mina's painting draws to a stop. "Nick, you did see it, right?"

"The article about *Agape*?" And this is the part in every man's life that he fears. Mina and I may not be dating "for real"—yet—but that doesn't mean she won't do that woman thing where her eye twitches when faced with a guy fucking up. *Think fast, man!* "You know, I never really . . . read the newspaper. Much."

Or ever.

I get my news from the TV and the radio when I'm driving all over the goddamn state to various sites. Scratching behind my ear, I watch as she clambers down the ladder. "Send it to me and I'll read it. Promise."

She huffs out a laugh. "You're going to want to read this one—particularly since it's about *you*."

My stomach drops. "*Us Weekly* again?"

"Not them. At least, not yet." Dropping to her haunches by our pile of materials, she palms her phone, taps away, and then holds it out for me. When I eye it like it's a snake ready to attack, she rolls her eyes. "Someone saw us at Downtown Tattoo. There's a video of us kissing."

Well, damn.

Then again, this was the point of our entire deal, right? I overhaul the salon; she dates me in name only. Unfortunately, we've thrown the latter straight into the fire to burn to the ground. Hesitation slicks through me when I finally take the phone from her. I skim the article fast, and it feels like a damn miracle that it's not longer than a few paragraphs. I don't watch the video of us, mainly because I hate the idea of being filmed—again. What Mina and I have . . . it's not for mass consumption and gossip columns. "And these people commenting on your page—they're not being assholes?"

Her nose scrunches in confusion. "Why would they be assholes?"

There is seriously no good way to put this. I meet her gaze. Silently return her cell phone. "Because you're not Savannah Rose." When her shoulders jerk, I get my shit together real fast to explain what I mean. "These people"—I point at the phone she pockets in her jeans—"they're internet trolls, *koukla*."

"They seem like reasonably nice people," she tells me stiffly.

Ah, shit.

I climb to my feet. "And they *are* nice people. It's just that . . . how do I explain this?"

"From the beginning, maybe."

I give a low laugh. "Smartass."

She twiddles her fingers in the air, urging me on. "Keep going."

My girl pushes a hard bargain. Almost as hard as I do.

Heading for the mini fridge I installed as soon as my electrician did his thing, I pull out two bottles of water. "They prepped the two final contestants for the media right before it all went to shit. Might as well have been etiquette lessons for dummies—felt like it, anyway. And one thing they hammered home is that viewers grow loyalties just by watching us. Maybe one guy does something to hurt the bachelorette—viewers digest it as a personal attack. You hurt the person *they* were rooting for." Uncapping one of the bottles, I drain half. Then hand the full one over to Mina, who's watching me earnestly. "I may have been dumped, but now I'm worried they'll be out hunting for blood. Yours, now that I've dragged you into this with me. The internet is a world of trolls."

"But it was *your* idea for this fake relationship in the first place." She points the top of her bottle at me. "Did you think my identity wouldn't get out?"

Shifting my weight on my feet, I grumble, "I hoped it wouldn't. I didn't think . . . to be blunt, I didn't think anyone would care enough about me to be leaking shit to the press. I'm *me*."

"You're hot, Nick."

She says it so matter-of-factly that I can't help but laugh. When she doesn't join in, I toss the bottle from one hand to the other, buying myself time to think of something to say. Ultimately, I choose not to pussyfoot around the truth. "Mina, I work in *construction*. There's nothing sexy about that. Half the guys on the show were lawyers, investment bankers, actors . . . For fuck's sake, Dom played in the NFL."

Lifting one brow, Mina sips from her bottle. "You own a business, which means you're a CEO. Women love CEOs. Trust me, I listen to enough romance audiobooks to know. And, as if that's not enough, you're the CEO of a business that by all accounts is doing insanely well. You're kind and funny, and your arms are just—well, let's just say that I don't mind eating dessert at dinner because I know you'll be able to lift me up no matter what. You're a catch, Nick. Cream of the crop."

I try to smother my grin with a palm scrubbing over my mouth. Well, well, well, Mina Pappas thinks I'm a *catch*. A month ago, she was making fun of me for ordering two bags of popcorn on a date. Calling it like it is here: I should have kissed her years ago. Probably would have saved me from going on a show like *Put A Ring On It* in the first place—if I had a girl like Mina by my side, I never would have given the show a second thought.

As if on cue, I think back to her comment about dreams manifesting when they should and never before. Was I not ready for Mina all this time? Hell, am I ready for her *now?* I sure want to be, especially when faced with the thought of never having her again.

Oblivious to the dangerous direction of my thoughts, Mina says, "And in case you were wondering, everyone commenting on my pictures seems wicked nice. They're sending me DMs and asking me when *Agape* is opening. The thought that even a few of them might turn into clients is beyond exciting, particularly since I can now count all that I have on one hand. And—hold onto your panties, here—but they're *actually* commenting about how cute we are together."

Well, that's . . . surprising. The cute thing, I mean. Everyone should want Mina as their hairdresser—that goes without saying.

By leaving *Put A Ring On It* as I did, I expected some bumps and bruises after coming home to Boston. Once the footage leaked of Savannah Rose turning me down, those expectations metamorphosized into a very real reality of shit going south. Only, Mina and I have somehow managed to create our own narrative through no real effort on our part. Each moment that's been broadcasted to the press is all too real. That kiss in Downtown Tattoo, that raw moment of us standing outside my parents' house. What this *Celebrity Tea* site is capturing is a man falling in love.

Falling in love.

My eyes fly shut at the realization, just before I shove it in a lockbox and throw away the key. Mina's made no secret about being fearful of relationships and commitments—and I had sex with her knowing where she stands.

A fling.

This is only a fling.

The thought rings surprisingly hollow.

I guzzle the rest of my water, wishing I could just dump it all over my head instead. "Production is going to lose their shit over this."

"Do you really care? This Savannah girl turned you down. Not that she's not nice—I'm sure she is—but do you really care about what *production* thinks? They'll air the season when they air the season. Live your life the way you want to."

And I *am* living my life exactly how I want. Only . . . "She didn't turn me down."

I flick my gaze over to Mina in time to catch her jaw dropping open. "I'm sorry, but I thought you just said . . . I've seen that shot of you two on the beach when she told you no. *Everyone* has seen that shot. Everyone and their mother—except for your *yiayia*." She blinks, her honey gaze locked on my face. "That day in your office, you told me you weren't engaged."

God, this is going to be awkward.

I toss the water bottle into the open trash can near the ladder, then begin to pace. Dragging my palms over my face, I twist around and square off my hips. "For the record, I'm not engaged."

"I'd hope not," Mina says all prim and proper, "since I let you fuck me. Three times now."

Her *don't-fuck-with-me* tone brings a smile to my face. She's feisty as all hell and I love it. "Not engaged," I repeat more for her benefit than mine. "I went on the show because I wanted to find someone. I wanted someone to *love*, the way my mom loves my dad and Effie loves Sarah. By that point, Effie had forced me into all the usual outlets after everything with Brynn—online dating, blind dating, literally dragging me into a coffee shop and shoving me into a seat with the first random woman she saw."

"She was married, wasn't she?"

I bark out a laugh. "She sure as hell was. We ended up talking about the Patriots before I darted the hell out of there." Glancing at the half-painted wall to our left, I go on. "So Effie surprises me one day with this crazy, big news. Tells me all about how it's this huge opportunity that I can't pass up."

"She got you on the show . . . you said that before."

Nodding, I look back over to Mina. "She sent in my bio, some newspaper clippings of recognition Stamos Restoration has received over the last few years . . . and the video of Brynn telling me at the altar how she'd fallen in love with her boss."

Mina's hands come up to cover her mouth. "Oh, *Nick*."

My smile is a little weak this time around. "Yeah, I know. Awkward, right? Effie and I had a long chat and she knows if she ever pulls another stunt like it, I'll tell Sarah about how she used to wear her underwear over her head until she was eleven. But I guess the idea of a guy like me showing up on a show like *Put A Ring On It* was too hard for them to pass up. I was golden-boy material."

Mina's smile matches mine, turned down at the edges and completely somber. "Good, ol' Saint Nick."

"Yeah." God, how I hate that nickname. "So, I went on with high hopes. Or, at least, *reasonably* mediocre hopes because clearly I was having no luck on my own. The producers . . . well, they also pushed a hard bargain during the audition process. They told me all the things I wanted to hear—that they had done compatibility tests based on our personalities, and that Savannah and I were a perfect match. There was other stuff that I know now was bullshit, but yeah, they got me, hook, line, and sinker. I was tired of going on dates that led to nowhere, even more tired of my *yiayia* asking when I was giving her grandbabies, and I thought—stupidly, maybe—that letting someone else choose for me might be for the best."

"And you liked her?" Mina asks. "Savannah Rose?"

"I liked her, except that it never went further than that, not for me. I kept pushing at first because I know I'm not the most social guy. Maybe the chemistry wasn't there because I was—"

"Being surly?"

I let out a low chuckle. "Calling it like it is—I expect nothing less from you." When she opens her mouth to protest, I hold up a finger and cut her off. "But, yeah, surly. Rigid. However you want to put it. Savannah and I ended up getting along wicked well. We're more alike than I think either of us realized at the beginning of the show. Boston construction guy meets Southern, aristocratic socialite. The producers fucking loved the idea of it, and the thing with TV is, they manipulate shit all the time. For all I know, they could have been pressuring her to keep me on for the sake of ratings."

Mina's mouth purses. "I won't lie about the fact that I've watched every season of *The Bachelor,* but still . . . that seems wrong to me." And then, good soul that she is, Mina yanks off her gloves, puts her hands on her hips and says, "If that's the case, I feel bad for her. TV or not, no one should be forced into something they don't want. It's not right."

Her righteous sense of justice has me crossing over to her, clamping my hands down at her side, and lowering my mouth to hers. She exhales into me, and I swallow the breath to keep as my own. My cock twitches in anticipation, the greedy bastard.

"What was that for?" she whispers.

I brush another kiss over her mouth, this one lighter. "For being you." One more kiss because I can't help myself. "*But* you're right. It's wrong. There's only one time I can specifically recall Savannah putting her foot down and telling the producers to fuck off. It was the first night and we'd all just hauled ourselves out of the limo. What viewers don't realize is that process takes nearly six hours. It's brutal."

"It sounds awful."

"I never want to see the inside of another limo again—at least not when it's jampacked with eight other dudes." Narrowing my eyes, as though that'll bring me back to that moment when all I could smell was cologne, booze, and B.O., I press my tongue to the roof of my mouth. "There was this one guy. Owen. He was all tatted up—you could see the ink at the collar of his dress shirt and down to his fingers. We sat in that limo for long enough that I could start reciting the guys' family members by name, but he never said a single word."

Mina touches a finger to my loose T-shirt. "Maybe he was nervous."

"I think he was. I was already in the house by the time he met Savannah outside, but then shit hit the fan. I heard her talking to one of the producers in the bathroom. She was, ah"—I scratch my jaw—"demanding that he be sent home before the ring ceremony. She didn't want him there and she made it known."

"That's . . . uncomfortable."

It'd been the sort of TV drama producers only wish they could manufacture—and it'd been completely authentic. From the way Owen stood like a granite statue as Savannah asked him to go, to the way he'd reached for her, with a look on his face I'd understood instantly.

He'd looked at her the way I'd stared at Brynn, right after she dropped the bomb of all truth bombs.

I don't know how Savannah Rose and Owen knew each other, but it was clear that they did. And it was clear to me, even if not to anyone else, that she wouldn't change her mind about keeping him around. The sound of the door slamming shut behind Owen had reverberated through the house, shocking every contestant into silence.

I clear my throat. "Maybe, subconsciously, I realized that they had some sort of unfinished business. She kept me around, and I kept hoping that this was *it* and I'd wake up one morning and realize I loved her." Snorting derisively, I fold my arms over my chest. "That didn't happen. I demanded to talk to the producers, then the director. I wanted to tell Savannah, privately, that I wasn't the right guy for her. They wouldn't let me. We were in different housing complexes and they kept her in this . . . bubble, almost, where they plucked her out for dates and ceremonies and put her back when she wasn't needed. So I did what I had to do."

"Nick . . ."

I look her in the eye. "It seemed cruel to dump her on TV when I was meant to be proposing. So, I let her reject me."

Mina's expression shutters. "You shouldn't have done that."

"Because it makes me too *nice*?"

"No, you jerk, because you only made things worse for yourself. If people care about what's going on between us, what's going on with *you*, it's only because you gave them the ammunition. People love a good underdog story and you, right now, are the quintessential underdog."

The feeling of my phone vibrating in my back pocket has me cursing under my breath. "I got to take this," I mutter. "It might be one of the guys." I answer without screening the Caller ID. "Stamos."

"How do you feel about clam chowder? Goes well enough with your Greek palette? I just landed and I'm fuckin' starving."

Ah, *gamóto*.

America's other favorite underdog, Dominic DaSilva, has arrived.

"Meet me at that restaurant at the top of the Prudential? Say, thirty minutes?"

I glance over at Mina, then make a quick decision. "Yeah," I tell Dom, "I'll be there. And I'm bringing someone I want you to meet."

28

MINA

We meet Dominic DaSilva in the restaurant housed on the top floor of one of Boston's tallest skyscrapers—and let me be the first to say . . . he's a *total* hunk.

Dark hair styled like a woman's fingers have already run through it this morning. Dark, espresso eyes that exude warmth, but don't quite manage to conceal a cynicism I suspect runs deeper than he'll ever reveal. Unlike Nick, whose wholesome, model-good looks stop people in their tracks, the former NFL tight-end's appeal is rough around the edges. At six-foot-six, he's also a giant, standing even taller than Nick. And it doesn't help that the man clearly has a penchant for black: from the leather jacket encasing his broad shoulders to the unlaced combat boots on his feet, he's not wearing a single shade lighter than midnight.

Hello, Dominic DaSilva—Lucifer will see you now.

"And this," Nick says warmly, pressing a flat palm to the small of my back, "is Mina."

I grin up at him. "Dominic, nice to meet you. I've heard . . . well, *Celebrity Tea* likes you a lot."

His chuckle is low and raspy. "Not as much as they like my man Stamos over here." He claps Nick on the shoulder in brotherly camaraderie. "*Celebrity Tea*'s all up in your business the way *Entertainment Tonight* can't bother to show a single segment without flashing a shot of my mug." Dark eyes drop down to my face. "You can call me Dom, by the way. No one calls me Dominic unless I've fucked up."

"Well, we have that in common." I poke Nick in his rock-hard bicep. "No one calls me Ermione—my full name—except this guy."

Nick's fingers slip under the hem of my coat to graze my skin. "You like it when I do, *koukla*. No use denying it."

Dom arches a heavy brow, his gaze taking the both of us in. Then he breaks into a full-fledged grin. "Well, damn. So that prick at *Celebrity Tea* wasn't lying through his teeth for once." He points a finger, swiveling it between Nick and me. "You two together now?"

"Um . . ."

"About that—"

"DaSilva, party of three?"

Praise Sweet Baby Jesus. I whip around to face the host, who's holding black leather menus in the cradle of his arm. "Sure, we'd *love* to take our seat!"

The host doesn't even bat an eye. I can only imagine the sorts of shenanigans he sees working at a restaurant like this —a place for tourists and locals alike who want to feast on good New England clam chowder and even better views. We're led to a table positioned near the three-hundred-and-sixty-degree window. From every vantage point around the room, Boston is unveiled. Gorgeous Back Bay, the winding Charles River meandering through the city, the John Hancock building rivaling the Prudential's height.

Nick holds my chair for me—perfect Victorian gentleman, I'm telling you—before taking the seat next to mine.

Unlike Dom's all black getup, Nick's in his trademark work jeans and a Stamos Restoration T-shirt, this one a navy blue that plays off the gray of his eyes. He leans forward, elbows on the table. "How's the escape feeling so far?"

Leaning back, Dom throws one arm casually over the chair beside him. "Holdin' out the verdict on that for now." The corner of his mouth tugs down, and it hits me in the gut that Dominic DaSilva must be having a really rough time if he actually flew all the way out to Boston just to get away from it all.

I fiddle with the utensils before me. "Listen, Dom, if you want to talk to Nick about . . . whatever it is that's going on, you can. I'm not going to run to the media or to a friend with your laundry list of secrets."

Beside me, Nick stiffens. I only feel it because his knee presses against mine, and then he's relaxing, letting out a breath before draping an arm on the back of my chair. It's tough to tell if the touchy-feely bit is all an act, designed to keep up our ruse of fake dating. *I don't think it's an act.* I *hope* it's not an act.

Nick is a lot of things—reserved, stiff—but in the last few weeks he's let down his walls. Even now, his fingers softly tug on the strands of my hair, as though he does it absent-mindedly. That's not the mindset of a fake boyfriend. Right?

"You can trust her," he says, still playing with my loose ponytail. "I do."

I do.

Two little words with so much meaning behind them.

Our server comes around to take our drink and appetizer order. Once she leaves, Dom palms the edge of the table and exhales roughly. "Living in L.A. comes with its merits. Good weather, a quick ride to work. Except that means I'm in the cesspool of vultures." He drums his fingers on the table. "I went to see Savannah Rose after the show ended."

Nick curses beneath his breath.

I reach for my glass of water and pretend I don't exist.

"It was . . . a bad idea."

"DaSilva, man." Nick's free hand motions frantically through the air like he's trying to find the right words. "Why the hell would you go to her after she turned you down?"

"Because I liked her." He says it so simply, so easily, that I nod along with him, like I've known him for years and not just ten minutes. "I wanted to know why she rejected me, without all the cameras and shit in our faces. I'm not going to go into detail about what went down—clearly, I'm sure you can put two and two together—but someone caught me leaving her hotel room at almost four in the morning."

"*Gamóto.*"

I reach for Nick's thigh under the table. "There's good news!" I tilt my head toward the scenery out the window. "You're in Boston, which is great! And, oh yeah, no one's reported anything about you and Savannah being in some hotel. I've been"—I slide my gaze over to Nick—"checking the gossip sites daily after the first time we ended up on one."

Dom shifts his weight, elbows moving to the table so he can drop his head into his upturned hands. "I paid the asshole off," he mutters, so low that I almost can't hear him. Like honey, misery coats every syllable. "Ten-grand just to make sure he didn't go blabbing to his boss. Savannah didn't ask for me to go over there. I did it. And even though all we did was sit and talk, I couldn't let him run his smear campaign in the press."

I home in on his choice of words: *liked* not *loved.*

"Have either of you talked to her since?" I ask.

Both men shake their heads, Nick looking unperturbed by the thought, even as Dom grimaces in what I imagine is embarrassment for throwing his heart on the line and being rejected—twice.

"Jeez, reality TV sounds absolutely insane."

"You have *no* idea," Dom says, a trace of a smile finally ticking up one corner of his mouth. "There was this one night, the producers asked us all to come outside in nothing but our boxers. How many of us were there at that point, Stamos? Ten?"

"Thirteen, I think." Nick laughs. "It wasn't even raining, but they wanted to host a wet abs contest."

"They hooked up hoses to this tram type thing," Dom tells me, his hands referencing the build of it for me. "It was taller than all of us, and we stood beneath it, waiting for that moment where we *all* knew what was coming . . . dick shrinkage."

I can't stop myself from cringing, or from mumbling, "Oh, no."

"Oh, yes." Nick's arm leaves my back as he reaches for his glass. "We were wet. No one was packing any heat south of the equator, if you catch my drift. And then they brought out Savannah Rose and told her the challenge would be with her blindfolded. The first person she could correctly identify from their abs would win a date the next day."

"That's . . ." Two pairs of eyes fix on me. Oh, boy. "Is this where I plead the fifth?" When neither of them say anything, I place one hand down on the table, the other up, palm facing Dom, and open my mouth. "I solemnly swear that I would have correctly identified each one of you. No man would be left behind, and that's a promise."

Dom barely lasts a second before he's clutching his stomach and laughing hard enough that the glasses shimmy on the table.

I turn to Nick and mock-whisper, "I'm banking on the fact that you'd be first in the lineup."

His gray eyes glitter with laughter. "I was first that night too. Savannah did *not* match me correctly."

"Who did she think you were?"

It's Dom who answers, and he does so with a wry grin. "This body builder from Miami. But *nothing* beats this guy, Josh, an accountant from Idaho."

"An accountant. He sounds . . . sweet."

"Until it turned R-rated," Nick says, leaning back in his chair. "We were on full display, total shit storm in the making with fake rain pelting our backs, and Savannah went to touch his abs and miscalculated his height."

My shoulders hunch and I bracket my mouth with my hands because I already *know* where this is going. "Please," I whisper, trying not to laugh, "please tell me she didn't."

Nick nods sagely, offering a quick mark of the cross over his heart. "She did. Punched him right in the dick."

Lips parting, I gasp, "She *punched* him?"

"First-time offender. I think she went to, I don't know, feel him with her knuckles or something?" Dom lifts a shoulder, then drops his hand to his thigh. "Josh is six-eight. I played against him in college ball. Not a bad dude, except he always was a little handsy when it came to women. I like to think of this as . . . divine justice."

"Who was the winner?"

Slowly, as though he's savoring the moment and wanting it to last, Dom smirks. "You're sittin' with him." That smirk pulls just a little wider as he inclines his head with the grace of the victorious. "Not that I can blame her—I'm a pretty memorable guy."

Uh-huh. Cocky, is more like it. I open my mouth, prepared to deliver a stinging retort . . . except, wait. *I'm a pretty memorable guy*. Without reservation, I stare Dom down. Dark, edgy appeal mixed with a smooth confidence that lends toward humor and not total arrogance—oh, he's *perfect*.

Striving for nonchalance, I drop my chin onto my balled fist, elbow digging into the table. "What are you up to next weekend, *Dominic?*" There we go: perfect tone. Light, airy, unassuming.

"Next weekend?" Dom reiterates, cocking his head in curiosity. "I've got no plans."

"Ermione."

Oh, no. This is *not* something Nick will be able to talk me out of.

A familiar, masculine hand circles my bicep and tugs me in close. His breath coasts over my ear as he growls, *"Óxi."*

Actually, yes.

I pluck his fingers off my arm, one by one. "Dom, I'd love to extend an invitation to you, if you're still in town next weekend when we head up to Maine." Deliberately, I pause, prolonging the moment. "For a singles' retreat."

Should there have been a pin dropping, no one would know because Dom throws his head back with a sharp laugh. "A *singles'* retreat? Why the fuck would I want to go that? I just had my heart broken."

Ah, there we go. Liked versus loved—looks like Dominic DaSilva tipped the scale for the latter. "It's perfect, actually. That part of Maine? There's not much cell service, which means *you*, my friend, will have an entire weekend of your trip completely media-free."

"Jesus, you're laying it on thick."

I ignore Nick's grumbling. Men. They don't even see when someone is trying to help them. Swiveling my chin on my palm, I glance over to the man who rocked my world just two nights ago, who planned a tattoo for me that carries such beautiful weight and significance. "It's a singles' retreat. Think about it, Nick. What was the one thing both our parents tried to ship us off to back in high school?"

His grimace twists his handsome features. "Let's not talk about it, *naí?*"

No can do, Mr. Stamos. No. Can. Do. I didn't want to go

on this damn trip in the first place. "Dating camp for Greeks," I go on blithely, "also known as hell on earth."

"It sounds like a cult."

"Oh, no," I tell Dom, "it's definitely not that. Chaperones everywhere. Lots of awkward speed-dating rounds to try and find your perfect Greek match. Couple compatibility quizzes. *Loads* of fun, if you're into theoretical self-flagellation." I sip from my almost empty water glass, then scan the restaurant for our host. "I don't think we have anything to worry about with the Maine trip, but I'm pretty sure Sophia —who's putting it together—is on the hunt for another husband."

Dom's brows draw together. "And I would sign up for this willingly . . . *why*?"

"Because it's as far away from civilization as you can get on this side of Canada. No mention of Savannah Rose. Hanging out with your best bud, Nick. Possibly meeting a girl who *might* make you feel less like a stick in the mud— though, word for the wise, I'd leave Sophia alone." Carefully, I take note of his reactions. His features remain passive, but his eyes never lose that cynical gleam that's buried deep. "Plus, and I say this with total kindness, you look like you need to cut the cord to the public for a while. You can thank me after the trip when you feel like a new man."

Dom's attention shifts to my left. "Your girl should work in marketing. She's a bulldog."

Your girl. Nick's girl.

It's so wrong how very *right* that feels.

Nick lets out a choked laugh. "She's very *persuasive* when she wants to be." He says it like a compliment, and I fight the inane urge to preen under his praise. "Screw it. If we're doing this Maine trip, might as well live it up."

"Live it up" is not the catch-phrase of Bethel, Maine. Stunning, picturesque views? Yes. Gorgeous, little boutiques dotting the one major street the town has to offer? Absolutely. But when there's a will, there's a way—and I foresee more staring at the town's Things-To-Do website in my future, so long as I can keep Sophia from making a weekend adventure into some thirst trap for husbands.

29

MINA

"Biggest pet peeve about *Lord of the Rings*—go, don't think about your answer!" On my laptop, which is propped up on Nick's office desk, the rolling credits for *The Two Towers* start playing.

My head bobs along to the soundtrack. I've watched the trilogy more times than I can count since they released, but watching them with Nick on a Saturday night is a completely new experience. One that makes me feel positively giddy as I dig into the bowl of popcorn in my lap.

One bowl of popcorn, mind you.

To my left, Nick sits on a low stool, a sharp knife in hand as he carves a divot into the work-in-progress church spire. His dark, curly hair flops boyishly over his forehead, which he blows out of his eyes before answering. "Samwise not letting Frodo die."

I throw a popcorn kernel at him. "You can't just *kill* Frodo! He's a leading character."

Because Nick is Nick, he manages to catch the flying kernel in his mouth right before it would have bopped him in the cheek. "He's a *maláka, koukla*. He should have just stayed in the shire."

"You've said that before, and I'm here to play devil's advocate." Cupping the bowl with both hands, I swivel the office chair to face him head-on. "Frodo's character arc is by far the best in all three films. He's the heart of the fellowship, and the one forced to overcome the most obstacles while everyone and their mama wants his head on a pike."

"I thought the saying was 'head on a platter'?"

Maybe. Probably. "I'm going for the more violent option, considering that Frodo almost died twenty-two times."

Nick grins, slowly. "Is that an accurate count?"

I grin right back. "I've got no idea. I'm rounding up and hoping for the best."

He shakes his head, laughing, that curly hair flopping right back over again, and then hunches his shoulders to stare at the miniature sculpture, a mask of concentration pulling at his handsome features.

Deftly, I snag another popcorn kernel and pop it into my mouth. I spent the full three hours of *The Fellowship of the Ring* watching Nick instead of the movie. I watched as his nimble fingers, roughened from his daily job, skimmed the intricate lines of the half-completed spire. I watched as he sharpened the knife on a whetstone like some woodworker from days of yore. I finished half a bowl of popcorn, existing on the euphoria of seeing Nick in action and hearing my favorite movie play in the background.

Is this even real life?

I've gone right off the deep end.

"How did you get into this?" I ask.

Pewter eyes lift to my face. "The woodworking?"

"Yeah."

If I focus hard enough, I can hear the sharp-edged blade of the knife *swoosh* against the wood as Nick severs a stray knot he apparently doesn't like. "I took a class for it in college. One of the projects was creating a sculpture from a four-by-four block of Butternut, one of the easier woods to manipulate." The strokes of the blade are mesmerizing, making it hard to look away as he works. "Some people chose to carve animals, which is difficult in its own right. Feathers are tedious. Rounded limbs make me want to break out the scotch."

"I'm guessing carving birds isn't a favorite pastime of yours," I tease.

"Definitely not." His mouth curves upward, but his eyes remain focused on the task at hand. "I carved the Parthenon because it was always one of my favorite places we went to when we visited Greece, and it seemed only right that I have one in my own house."

A Greek carving only the most famous architectural feature in the country? I don't feel a lick of surprise. "How'd it turn out? Will I find any replicas in the gift shop on our next visit?"

Dark, smoky laughter drowns out the sound of Frodo begging loyal Sam to help him—again. "It was awful."

"*Your* brand of awful, which is still pretty perfect, or the rest of society's awful?"

"I got a D-plus, *koukla*." The stool beneath his butt creaks as he shifts it a few inches over, to reach another side of the sculpture. "I was too ambitious on my first go-round. But even though I came *this* close to failing, I didn't really care. I loved the way woodworking stole away my stress. I could work for hours and never feel my eyes start to strain or my fingers grow sore."

Earlier, when I asked if he wanted to hang out tonight—thus ruining any lies I've been telling myself about not wanting anything *more* from this fake relationship of ours—Nick suggested coming over to his office. He asked me to bring my laptop but that he'd cover everything else. And he had.

He was the one to bring the three *Lord of the Rings* movies, as though suspecting I might want to binge-watch them all. (I never turn down Orlando Bloom as Legolas—ever.) He brought the popcorn, going so far as to purchase a ticket at the movies just so he could hit up the concession stands for buttery, movie-theater popcorn. All before he confessed that woodworking was a solitude endeavor for him, something he did when no one else was around and the office was silent, save for the sound of the blade meeting the grain of the wood.

Except, for tonight, he made it into a date. Something we could enjoy together.

Nick Stamos, my best friend's older brother, is tearing down my life-long determination to keep my eyes on the dream—*Agape*—and leave dating and men and love to other people more cut out for relationships.

I want to hate him for it, but I'm having way too much fun to even consider pumping the breaks. He makes me feel *special,* and it should be noted that I've grown rather addicted to the way Greek peppers his English and when he *really* wants to turn me on, he knows that a kiss to the delicate skin at the base of my neck gets me revved up from one to one-hundred in no time at all.

"Can I try?" The question leaves me before I can talk myself out of it. Nerves flare in the pit of my belly, making my fingers dig into the cardboard popcorn container. *The worst he can say is no. Don't freak out.* Flexing my fingers to keep them from tapping, I tack on, "I mean, not on *that* one. The church spire. You've been working on it for years and God knows I'll—"

"*Éla édo,*" comes his low command. "I'll guide you."

Oh. *Oh.*

I practically throw the popcorn onto the desk in my excitement. "Wait, hold on—don't go anywhere!" Darting from the room, I head straight to the tiny bathroom tucked between Nick's office and the conference room at the far end of the hall. I don't bother to lock the door as I wash the butter and salt from my fingers, giving them a good scrub before I dry off and hurry back to where he's waiting. "Sorry," I tell him when I return, "I didn't want to ruin the wood with AMC's delicious butter."

Nick's mouth twitches. "Get over here, butter fingers. Let me show you how this is done."

He doesn't have to tell me twice, though I do roll my eyes at the silly nickname.

Spotting an extra footstool, I pull it over to where Nick sits. With the heels of his heavy boots, he scrapes his stool back, leaving me room to place mine closest to the spire. Threads of anticipation circle my heart, quickening its rhythm as I sit down and keep my knees wide to avoid touching the wood.

"Is this okay?" I ask.

Nick hums his approval, a throaty, masculine sound that twines the thread just a little tighter. "Perfect. Here, let me show you exactly what we're doing."

"You aren't worried I'll mess it up?"

"If you do, I'll fix it. The key is to make sure that you don't hack into the wood—that's an irreversible mistake." His bulky arms fold around me, and his chest gently collides with my back. I watch as he maneuvers the blade of the knife over the straight edge of the bell tower. "You always want to go with the grain of the wood," he husks out, his warm breath against my neck as he whittles the wood. "Go against it and the wood will peel or splinter. I don't work with an image. Never really have, which means it all comes down to instinct. A lot like when you work on a client's hair."

The comparison between our chosen mediums has never been lost on me. We work with our hands, day-in and day-out. We create beauty out of nothing, testing the boundaries, relying on the basics to guide our way: the grain of the wood or the texture of the hair, the softness or coarseness of them both.

I find myself leaning back into his chest, absorbing his warmth, my forearms resting on his muscular thighs as he shows me the correct technique to use. "The sharper the blade, the more the wood feels like butter," he tells me. "Here, want to try the detail work? I'll help you."

He hands me the knife, wood-handle first. It's light in my grip, lighter than I expected, to be honest. I eye the detail work he's already begun, along with the shallow groove that sits a few centimeters from the edge. Angling the blade as he showed me, I scoot forward on the stool and try to recreate the gentle motions he executed so naturally.

"A little harder," Nick encourages.

I try again, deepening the way I angle the blade down through the grain. The thinnest slice of wood curls free.

Excitement cuts right through me. "Look!"

"Ómorfi." Beautiful. Full lips find the space behind my ear, over my soaring wings. "Now let me show you how to make it look more Gothic."

We work together in companionable silence. *The Two Towers* exists as pure background noise as I carve the tiniest circles into the wood, using another one of Nick's whittling knives, this one for curves and rounded edges. He never moves from behind me, but his hands, when they aren't guiding mine, touch me instead.

His palm settles in the curve of my waist.

The other splays flat over my thigh, his fingers inches from my sex.

He holds me more possessively than he ever has, touching

me like we're in this together. Like *we're* together. And I can't deny that every time his chest lifts with an in-drawn breath, I feel myself breathe in time with him too.

Meanwhile, warm encouragements slip off his tongue.

"Yeah, just like that, *koukla*."

"Go a little deeper there, but otherwise it's perfect."

"Slowly . . . don't rush it."

Everything he says sounds downright sexual.

I refrain from squirming, even though the pressure between my legs is at an all-time high, and oh, God, how does he do this to me? *Focus, girl. Focus on the wood!*

Except that I want to be focusing on *his* wood. Pun so very much intended. Is he hard right now? Is he fighting the good fight, too, trying to keep the moment light and not steaming with *sex now please* vibes? I can't be the only one on the verge of losing the battle.

His palm, the one resting on my thigh, skims higher as he readjusts himself behind me.

Curious minds want to know *exactly* what he's readjusting.

The thought yanks a whimper from me.

Nick goes still, tension seeping into his hand and arms where there wasn't any before. I hear his breath hitch, then a deep pull in through his nose. The air fairly crackles with a time-old throw-down: who will make the first move?

Me.

I lower the knife, closing the switch blade, and deliberately place it on the floor at our feet.

The white flag of surrender. Throwing down the gauntlet. However you want to put it, I make it clear that the next move belongs to him.

He doesn't disappoint.

His lips wordlessly find my neck, in that spot I love so much. My skin flares with heat, and I allow my head to fall to the side in complete submission. *Yes, more of that.* His nose rasps up, up, up, until he's turning my head to the side and claiming my mouth with his. Whereas his hands were patient while whittling the wood, his kiss is not. It pulls me under like that long-ago wave crashing down over his head, and I go, willingly, moaning into his mouth.

One broad hand fits over my stomach, dragging me back until there's no space between us. His legs are splayed, his jean-covered cock thrusting against my back without a hint of shame, and I rock back and forth, trying to alleviate the pressure, my clit already pulsing.

"Keep your legs spread."

His rough timbre reverberates through me as his big hand moves between my legs, clasping me boldly through my fleece-lined leggings. As though I'm having an out-of-body experience, I watch, transfixed, as he rubs my clit through the material. He uses three fingers, the pressure he keeps relentlessly steady.

My head falls back on his chest. My hips rise, again and again, to meet the circling of those fingers. My eyes never once leave from ground zero.

"Nick," I pant, "that feels so good."

He chuckles against my back. Tears his fingers away, leaving me to protest with an attempt to grab his hand, before I realize he's aiming for exactly where I want him. He slides his hand under the band of my leggings. Under my underwear, too.

Yes, please.

Nick glides his fingers over my pubic bone, his other hand coming around me to hook a thumb under the waist-band to give him more room without the elastic snapping back into place. I feel the first touch of his fingertip to the hood of my sex like a junkie feels the first prick of the needle, my body jolting upward. His ankles hook around mine, keeping my legs from curling inward at the pleasure rioting through me.

We haven't even had sex more than a handful of times, and yet it's like he can already predict my every move.

Every need.

Every damn thought that enters my head.

Harsh breathing echoes alongside Gollum being Creepy Gollum on my laptop, and then I can't focus on anything else because Nick sinks two fingers into my pussy and steals every last thought that isn't *give me more of that.*

"C'mon, *koukla*," he grinds out roughly, "ride my fingers the way you ride my cock."

Dirty-talking Nick is my favorite Nick.

My hips swivel down, curling upward, before doing it all over again. He thrusts those fingers up, curling them on every pass. His thumb glosses over my clit, circling in time to the tempo of his magical fingers. Pleasure spikes through me like a ping-pong ball gone rogue. I strain against his legs, my fingers digging into his muscled, jean-clad thighs.

Those two fingers pull out of me, delving through my folds, leaving wetness in their path. And then they're pressing flat on my clit, rubbing and circling and driving me absolutely mad, and not the least bit concerned that it's Nick of all people seeing me come undone.

I cry out his name as the orgasm rips through me.

I'm aware of my legs quivering.

I'm aware of how he doesn't stop touching me until he's wrung out every drop that he can.

I'm aware of the hard-on against my spine, the way it twitches in Nick's jeans when I come.

I push Nick's hands away, then slip off the stool to my knees. Shoving my empty stool to the side, I don't waste time in reaching forward to the brass button separating me from Nick's very large bulge.

His hand lands on the back of my head. "Ermione, you don't need to—"

I pull his cock free from the confines of his jeans, zipper tugged down. One glance up at Nick's face shows me what he wants, what he needs, and I sink my fingers down to his base. His mercurial pewter eyes blaze with desire, and I don't look away as I lean forward, balancing my weight on his thigh, and then lick the crown of his dick.

"Oh, *fuck*."

English profanity—success strums through me.

I do it again, my tongue swirling over the head, before taking him fully into my mouth. That hand in my hair flexes as Nick emits a needy groan. *Again,* my heart whispers, *make him do that again.* I grip the root of him, bringing my hand up as I swallow him down. I work him in tandem, listening to every sound that leaves his mouth as guidance for exactly what he likes. Problem is, he likes it all.

Scratch that. It's totally not a problem.

His hips lift off the stool; his hand in my hair keeps me grounded in place as he thrusts upward. I relax my mouth, fisting his hard-on faster, tighter, until his hips are churning to match the very same rhythm I've set to drive him off the deep end.

"Shit, Mina." Flicking my gaze up, I watch the veins in his throat leap as he throws back his head. I wish I could see us together now: Nick losing control as he fucks my mouth, me on my knees, the root of all his pleasure.

I cup his balls with my free hand, tugging slightly.

But it's enough to—

He rips himself free from my mouth, his hands locking on my shoulders to haul me up to my feet. "Take off your pants or I'll tear them off," he growls, pushing his jeans down to his feet.

It's a tough decision to make. I have other leggings. I really don't need this pair.

But, ultimately, I strip them off myself because it's got to be quicker than the whole alpha-ripping-thing I've only heard about in my audiobooks. Without waiting for another order, I hop on his desk, legs dangling over the edge.

I fixate everything that I am on Nick.

He destroys the distance between us with three long-legged strides. Reaches behind me to close my laptop, leaving only the sounds of us breathing hard, and pushes it roughly aside. The popcorn scatters to the floor, victim to the cause, kernels flying every which way.

Nick grasps my right leg, drawing it up until my heel is planted on the desk and I'm completely exposed. Only, instead of slamming right into me, he drops to his haunches and flicks his tongue right over me without a single head's up.

My head drops back. "Oh, my God. Oh, my God."

"Correction," he drawls, voice thick with lust, "Saint Nick."

I want to laugh and I want to cry out and it only seems natural that I do a little bit of both when he clamps a hand down on my thigh and sweeps his tongue around my clit, spreading my wetness, adding his own. It's messy and raw and I've never, *never,* experienced such toe-curling pleasure in my life.

His fingers find me as he stands to his full height. He's still in his T-shirt, and I go with my gut, fisting the hem and silently ordering him to take it off. He does in one smooth move, then returns the favor.

"No bra," he husks out when my shirt meets the same fate as his and the popcorn.

"No bra," I whisper back, my fingers gliding over the ink.

Without the night there are no stars. I skim my hands up, cupping my breasts for him to see, tweaking my nipples.

It's all he needs to line his cock up with my entrance and plunge inside.

We moan together as my body adjusts to the length of him. Nick grabs my knee, holding me open, and pulls back—then thrusts even harder inside. I bite my lip and reach for the ball of his shoulder to keep myself in place.

Nick holds nothing back.

His thrusts are swift and powerful, short and precise. He never lets up the pace, and when I meet his gaze, I don't want him to slow down. Not now, not ever. He watches me like he can't look away, and when he finally does, it's only to stare at where we're joined. I'm spiraling, threads of anticipation turned into ropes of pleasure, wrapping me up, keeping me here with him when my soul has always run from the prospect of *more*.

"Fuck, Mina," he grunts, his features stark as he slams into me, "I'm gonna come. Touch yourself, *koukla*."

I slip my hand between our damp bodies. And then I do nothing but feel: the way Nick's hand trembles on my knee, the way he tilts his hips to make sure I cry out with every thrust, how I finger my clit sloppily, without precision, because I'm too far gone to do anything but beg for Nick to make me come.

Even though I want it, I'm not ready for the force of the orgasm that grips my limbs like anchors mooring me to a dock. I feel it up through my spine and down to my toes, and then I feel Nick release inside of me as he groans my name.

Better. How does it get so much better with him every single time?

Muscular arms draw me into his embrace, my cheek pressing against his sweaty, bare chest. I can't even find it in myself to care. "I like whittling wood," I mutter against his skin. "It might become my favorite hobby."

His fingers draw a random design on my back. "I'll never be able to look at the church spire without thinking of you."

"The one inked in your skin or the wooden one?"

I feel his wide smile against the top of my head. "Both. Definitely both."

30

NICK

"All right, boys, who's ready?"

I look up from where I'm installing one of the sleek, black styling chairs Mina spent a small fortune on. Standing next to the first one I put in this morning, Mina makes a *come-sit-down* gesture with her arms to Bill and Mark. Vince already went, the cheeky bastard jumping into the chair the moment Mina even offered to do a little trim.

Bill folds next. "Yup," he says, rubbing a hand over his messy hair, "I could definitely use a trim." He sets down the drill he used to screw the five-and-a-half foot tall, silver-embossed mirror into the floor. Six mirrors sit on either side of the room—officially the first furniture *Agape* welcomed within its walls. Mina spent the entire morning bouncing around, Windex in one hand and a rag in the other, spraying them all down until they shined to glossy perfection. Her excitement is contagious, and even though the boys and I should be heading over to the museum to finish off the rest of the work day, I couldn't resist getting started on the styling chairs.

After three weeks of putting in the time and sweat, *Agape* is finally beginning to look like a real salon.

"Come and take a seat!" Mina steps beside Bill and, with her palms on his back, she steers him toward one of the chairs. "What're we thinking today? Just a trim? Maybe bring down the sides and leave the top a little longer?"

Bill sends me a quick, panicked glance over his left shoulder.

I have no idea what he's looking at me for—I've spent my entire life dealing with hair that will not be tamed, no matter what I do with it.

"Shave it all," Vince shouts from the hallway. "If I can't see his head, it's not short enough!"

"Could be a good look," I muse out loud, one hand resting on my bent knee. "How's your head shaped, Billy? Oval? Triangle? Maybe a little penis-shaped?"

Bill's feet lock tight on the floor, unmoving. "Bald is not a good option for me."

Bless her hilarious humor, Mina does nothing but pick up a pair of shears and hold them up high like she's a doctor about to go in for heart surgery. "Take a seat, Billy." *Snip, snip.* "I have a vision and only *you* can help me bring it to life."

Bill's eyes pop open wide.

Mark, on the other hand, laughs so loud he drops his hands to his knees and nearly collapses. "Oh, man. If you ever decide to quit doing hair, I think you've got a future in horror movies ahead of you."

"Who says I'm just playing around?" Mina steps forward, shears still snipping threateningly at the air. Behind her back, she waves a hand to keep us quiet. And even though my guys don't know her well, we're all completely aware that she's full of shit—except for Bill, who looks ready to piss himself if that little dance-dance-dance-shuffle he's doing is any indication.

"Dude," Vince says to Bill, head sticking out from the hallway, "if you can't handle a woman with a pair of scissors, how the hell do you plan to survive the zombie apocalypse?"

"Valid point." I sink back on my heels, the drill lax in my hand. "Mina, give him your worst."

Her light laughter precedes her giving Bill a little nudge into the chair. He acquiesces, but only just barely. For the next twenty minutes, she spritzes his hair until it's damp—shampoo bowls aren't coming in till tomorrow—and then happily brings down his wild mane to a respectable cut that she claims shows off his features perfectly.

I don't know whether Bill's actually got himself some perfect features, but even I can admit the style she's gone for makes him look a few years younger.

While she blow-dries his hair, I return to installing the second-to-last chair. My time spent here in *Agape* is almost at an end. Besides the shampoo bowls, there's not much left to do—the bathroom is done and looking "chic and elegant," just as Mina wanted. The parlor doors, although a bitch to install, are also looking pretty. I went for a dark rosewood stain to complement the cream-colored walls Mina opted for in the two back rooms.

The last major task comes in the form of the mural I'm surprising her with. It's not ideal, having someone paint the ceiling when we've already put in the slate floors and furniture, but beggars can't be choosers. Before we leave for Maine this weekend, I'll be here with Vince, covering everything with sheets and tarps so that my buddy can come in and finish it all up before we get back on Sunday.

I hope Mina likes it.

Screw that, I hope she fucking loves it and thinks of me every time she looks up after a long day in the salon.

I nail the last chair down, flicking off the drill and setting it aside. Lifting my arm, I scrub the back of my gloved hand against my damp forehead. I'm not ready for this arrangement with Mina to end, and I've lost a lot of sleep this week trying to figure out how to broach the *R* word with her. A relationship, the one thing she avoids like the plague.

Except that, in the last few weeks, it certainly hasn't seemed like she's been avoiding it all that much. She suggests us getting together to hang out just as much as I do. We call each other throughout the day: between clients for her, who she sees at their houses, and jobsites for me. It feels . . . domesticated, almost, like we've been seeing each other romantically for years.

Forget the fact that I've *known* her for years or that she's my sister's best friend, this thing with Mina feels right. It feels *permanent*. And I can't help but think long-term: how she might look in a wedding gown, whether any kids we might have will inherit her honey eyes or my gray ones.

I'm hoping for honey rimmed with amber.

Rein it in, Stamos. Rein it the fuck in.

"Nick?" At my softly uttered name, I lift my chin and meet my favorite brand of honey. Mina motions to the empty chair. "How about I finally give you that trim I promised?"

"I thought you'd never ask."

I strip off my work gloves, dropping them next to the drill, which I unplug from the outlet before moving toward Mina. Today she's wearing a pair of gray sweatpants that gather at the ankle and another one of her sweater crop tops —this one is white and reveals a strip of tantalizing bare skin. She looks comfy and edgy and beautiful all at once, and it's no wonder that my hands have a mind of their own. The moment I step in close, I brace a hand against her hip and brush my lips over her forehead. "Don't turn me into Vin

Diesel," I tell her, giving us both a throwback to one of our very first emails that we exchanged.

The backs of her fingers gloss over my knuckles. "Or what?"

Gamóto, I love the challenge in her voice almost as much as I love verbally sparring with her. Pulling away, I drop my ass into the chair and swivel it around to stare her down. "Or you'll be lucky if you see any of The Great One on our trip to Maine this weekend."

Her face reveals nothing as she spins me back to face the mirror. "Men," she huffs playfully, "your entire sex gives *way* too much credit to your dicks. How many minutes do you think you spend thinking about it during the day? Asking for a friend."

"Percentage-wise?"

She nods, then reaches for one of the bottles sitting on her makeshift cart.

"Oh, I don't know." I pretend to think heavy on the topic while I watch her tip what looks like oil into the palm of her hand. "Maybe eighty percent?"

Rubbing her palms together, she meets my gaze in the full-length mirror positioned about a foot away from my feet. "And the other twenty percent?" she asks.

I offer a slow grin. "Spent thinkin' about you, Ermione."

Her cheeks grow rosy, and she pokes me in the shoulder with a knuckle, since her hands are all slick with oil. "Smooth, Stamos, so smooth."

And then she slips her fingers into my hair and I go straight to heaven.

"I thought you could use a little stress relief," she says, her attention fixated on my head while I watch her in the mirror. I've seen this woman naked, I've seen her orgasm so hard that her pupils dilate and her legs twitch, but to date, I can't say that I've seen her shy . . . until now. She doesn't look up as she massages my scalp, applying pressure with her fingertips. It's an act of self-control to keep from groaning out loud when she glides down to the nape of my neck and works to loosen the tense muscles there.

Voice rougher than I'd like to admit, I mutter, "You have unicorn fingers."

She laughs at that but doesn't stop her ministrations. "The old salon I worked at—we were expected to offer a short scalp massage before every haircut. If I have unicorn fingers, it's only because I learned the better the massage the higher the tip."

Makes sense. I feel like one lucky son of a gun right now. "You can have every tip I've got."

"Ah, I see we're firmly in the eighty-percent bracket right now."

"Don't forget the twenty, *koukla*. I'm thinking about you."

Briefly her fingers freeze, and my gut clenches with the worry I may have overstepped our casual boundaries. But then she continues, and it's the little smile gracing her mouth that has me relaxing again.

Once she's done making me almost come in my pants from her unicorn scalp massage, she starts in on the haircut itself. She spritzes my hair, using some shampoo that she says doesn't need to be washed out but will remove most of the oil she used on me. I understand approximately half of what she says, but I give her my undivided attention anyway, nodding and doing exactly as she tells me to do.

She spends more time on me than she did on my guys, and I like to think it's because she enjoys touching me as much as I enjoy being touched by her. She clips here and snips there, her fingers fluffing my hair, all while eyeing me with studious focus. Her teeth sink into her plump lower lip as she steps back to survey her handiwork.

"Satisfied?" I ask.

"I aim to please." She winks at me, then sets her shears down on the cart to her right. Picking up one of the smaller tubes with a glossy, blue coating, she squeezes product into her hand and rubs her palms together again. "I didn't want to go too short with these curls," she tells me, threading her fingers through my hair to evenly distribute the cream. "I like having something to hold onto when you're doing business."

Doing business. Now *that's* a euphemism I haven't heard before.

Cracking a grin, I shift my gaze from her face to my reflection. Call me a romantic or what have you, but I feel like I *look* different. It's not the hair. Mina's done a great job with the unruly mop on my head, for sure, but it's not what strikes me the most. No, it's the way *I* look younger—less surly, as she always tells me, less reserved. The grooves in my face appear softer, less deeply embedded, and I know I only have Mina to thank for the pep in my step.

I want this more than I should.

Me, her, and a fake relationship I desperately want to make real.

"Ermione, I—"

The sound of her ringtone cuts through the air and she flashes me an apologetic grimace before grabbing it from the cart. "It might be a client," she says, her honey eyes already fixed on the screen. "Hold that thought."

Keeping my gaze on her face, I listen as she answers the phone. "Hello, this is Mina." Her eyes go wide. "Oh! Yes, of course I remember you, Detective." She shoots a look my way, her honey eyes snapping with impatience. "You did? Oh, my God, that's awesome . . . I see." Mouth falling open, she plants a hand on my shoulder like she's searching for support, and I reach back, wrapping my hand around her wrist. "Well, damn. Sorry, not damn. I don't think I can curse

—oh, thanks for understanding. But, really, *French toast*? Company fraud all in exchange for . . . Yeah, I'll get myself a lawyer. Thanks for finding him, Detective. It's appreciated more than you'll ever know."

With a tap of her finger she ends the call and tosses the phone in the glossy black cart.

"That was the police officer in charge of my case with Jake Rhodan." She stares at the phone, then looks over to me. "The IOU man."

"Ah, the one who stole your check for—"

"A shit ton of money." She nods, pulling out of my grasp and planting her hands on her hips. "They caught him. He's at the station now."

"Well that's good."

"He bought some hockey player's French toast on eBay with my money."

I promptly choke on nothing but air. "I'm sorry"—I roll my hand, motioning for a repeat—"I'm going to need you to elaborate. Did you just say he spent thousands of dollars on *French toast*?"

"According to his transactions, I guess. His name popped up on their search list—the cops, I mean—and I can't even begin to explain how all of that sleuthing works but, yes, he spent *five-thousand* dollars on leftover French toast that some beefy player didn't manage to eat while he was on some morning show. The TV host auctioned off the breakfast on eBay as a joke. The rest of the cash he took from me . . . Well, hopefully he still has it." Her features pull tight. "I'm seconds away from tears and I don't know if they're laughing tears or oh-my-God-this-is-my-life tears."

I consider her features thoughtfully. It's a bad situation, but it's also hilarious—and completely unexpected. "I wonder if they auctioned it off sans maple syrup or if it was already drenched in it." Mina turns murderous eyes up on me, and I hold up my hands to ward her off. "It was a joke, *koukla*. Don't cry."

With an exhaled breath, her shoulders droop in defeat. "You suck, you know that? Now all *I* want to know is if he received soggy French toast in the mail." Her hands come up to shield her eyes. "Did he have to pick it up himself? Was it sent via UPS? Did this happen right before he was due to start on *Agape*, which is why he left the IOU? *Who buys French toast when they steal thousands of dollars?*"

There we go. The pinched look in her expression has turned more incredulous than sad, and I do her one better by pulling my phone out of my pocket and heading straight to the internet. I tap in the basics—*Hockey Player's French Toast Auctioned Off*—and wait for the search to load. When it does, I select the first article and read aloud, "An anonymous man from Revere, Massachusetts, breaks a previous record from 2000, when a 19-year-old bid on Justin Timberlake's half-eaten French toast. According to Blades Hockey player, Andre Beaumont, he was flabbergasted by the winning bid amount and is rumored to have said, 'Who the fuck does that? I feel like I at least owe the guy season tickets. Also, the money is going to charity—don't ask me which one yet. I'm still wrapping my head around a man spending five-thousand dollars to eat my leftovers.'"

"*I'll* eat his leftovers if someone gives me the money," Mina mutters, disgruntled.

I pocket my phone. "*Óxi*. You're gonna go down to the station, correctly identify him, and then you're going to let me take you out for dinner where we'll get some delicious—"

"Don't you *dare* say French toast, Nick, or I will—"

"—Pancakes." I grin down at her. "French toast's first cousin, twice removed."

"I'm going to kill you."

"Nah," I murmur smoothly, "you're going to let me feed you, and then you're going to let me do business." I lean down to brush my lips over her cheek. "Someone's got to do a test run on this new haircut, *koukla,* and that someone is you."

31

MINA

"I like Nick Stamos. A lot."

I repeat the words to my reflection in the mirror the night before our trip to Maine. I'm still holed up at my parents' house for the time being, while Nick and the guys put their full efforts into finishing off my salon, which means I have clothes strewn everywhere, leaving me little room to move around. There are choices to be made—what jeans and sweatshirts and knee-high socks to bring with me —but I can't stop re-reading the message he sent me via email. Sitting on the edge of my mattress, I swipe open my phone, and lucky me, his message was the last thing I looked at.

To: Mina Pappas <mina@agapehairsalon.com>
From: Nick Stamos
<stamos@stamosrestoration.com>
Subject: Can't wait

We haven't exchanged emails in a while. Just wanted to

send a reminder that I'll be by to pick you up around 8 a.m. We'll grab Dom on the way. Countdown to Epic Bad Decisions: T minus 12 hours. Let the shit show begin.

P.S., Already contacted the B&B we're staying at. I don't care what Sophia or anyone else on this damn "singles' retreat" says, me and you are staying in one room with one bed. Might have also snagged us a room with a fireplace—thought you might like it.

Hugs,
Nick

Hugs, Nick.

"He's killing me," I mutter, running my thumb along the edge of my phone case. It wasn't supposed to end up this way: Nick becoming the first person I think about when I wake up and the last person I talk to before conking out on my twin-sized mattress.

A fake relationship.

One overhaul of a salon.

I'm going to need to talk to Effie about my feelings for her brother. I know she warned me away. I know she was only looking out for both mine and Nick's best interests, respectively, but I think . . . I think I want to try out something more with him. Hell, we're practically dating anyway, and my life hasn't otherwise imploded. That's good news in my book.

Plus, I'm still *me*. Mina Pappas, hair-salon owner, lover of fantasy movies and bright, bold lipstick shades. Nothing has changed for the worse, only for the better. Somewhere along the way, Nick has become something so much more than just my best friend's older brother who I crushed on back in high school.

He's become *my* best friend. My partner-in-crime. The one person I know I can trust to get me, no matter what. If I could watch *The Lord of the Rings* with him every day of the week, just to listen to him bitch about Frodo, I would in a heartbeat. That's how far gone I am—Frodo is my favorite.

Besides Legolas, of course, because *yum*.

"You can do this," I tell myself.

"Can do what, *koritsi mou?"*

My head snaps up at the sound of my mother's voice, and at the Greek term of affection she's always used for me: *my daughter*. It's always felt a bit like a slight, if only because my dad never calls me that himself. It's always *Ermione*, or, if he's feeling particularly good-humored that day, *Mina*.

Standing in the doorway in her night robe, my mom's blonde-bouffant is tucked in pink hair rollers that are straight out of the 1980s. On her feet are the same *pandoflas* that Katya bought her for Christmas two years ago, and though they're a little tattered in the toe area, she refuses to get rid of them.

I toss my phone in the mess of clothes on my bed. "Just getting ready for that trip I told you about." I wonder what she might say if I confess that I'll be sharing a room with Nick all weekend. She'd probably be beside herself with joy —her eldest daughter *finally* dating a Greek man, the only thing she and my dad ever asked of me.

"Find yourself a nice boy, Ermione. A Greek boy. He'll take care of you." She's repeated the words so many times that I can repeat them verbatim, and though it rubs me a little raw to think I'm falling into their plans for my future—their narrow-minded, you're-only-good-for-one-thing plans—I want Nick way too much to consider sacrificing what we're building for the sake of sticking it to my parents where it hurts.

He doesn't deserve that. *I* don't deserve that.

My mom enters my room, her shoulders stiff as she looks around the space. "Of all my babies," she murmurs, "I knew you would come home, Ermione."

There's nothing remotely positive about her words, not with that disappointed look on her face. "It's not permanent, trust me." I give her my back, unwilling to let her see that *I* feel disappointed by her lack of faith in me. "I'll be out of your hair by next week." *If not, I'll be begging Effie to let me camp out on her couch.*

"You need to find a nice, Greek boy." She plucks at a sweater I was considering bringing with me and moves it over so she can perch at the head of the bed, near my pillows. "This hair business, *koritsi mou* . . . it's not going well." Her accent is thick and stained with disapproval. "You lose your money and then? Your stairs break and you come home." She clucks her tongue, then tips her head up in that classic, Greek head-nod I've seen from my family since birth. "*Óxi*, it's no good."

Age-old frustration grinds my molars together as I shove a pair of jeans into my small, weekend suitcase. "Katya is in graduate school for business management." *Calm,* I warn myself, *stay calm.* I force out a heavy breath before continuing. "You and *Baba* are paying her tuition."

My mom doesn't even look contrite at the mention of her and my father shelling out thousands of dollars for Katya's expenses. My sister is *not* a brat, and she never takes a thing for granted. She's all that's good in the world and has one of the best hearts I've ever met, but that doesn't help the pure hypocrisy in this house.

"Your sister is different."

This is a conversation we've hashed out hundreds of times before. Back when I had to stay home to babysit instead of joining sports teams or drama clubs or *anything* besides sit in this damn house all day long until my father came home from work and my mom decided to leave whatever friend she hung out with that day.

It wasn't that I was good at nothing, it was that between her and my dad, they trained me to only be good at one thing: being a parent.

I cooked dinner for Katya and Dimitri. *I* packed their lunches for school. *I* sat and supervised when they had friends over. *I* helped them with their homework when I didn't even have time to help myself. And maybe I would have done better in school if it weren't for the fact that responsibilities fell on my plate as a kid like rain falls from the sky during a storm.

There was no time to dream when all my hours were spent catering to the dreams of others.

My gut twists angrily, and I whip around before I can think better of it. "How?" The word explodes from my mouth like thunder piercing the sky. "How is Katya different than me? Go on, I'm *all* ears, Mama. You tell me why my sister can be studying for her MBA on *your* dime while I should be selling the business *I* own and marrying the first Greek man who asks me."

My mom sits with her shoulders straight and her mouth pursed and her fingers tangled in her lap. "*Koritsi mou,* Ermione, your sister—"

"Is? What?" I bite out the words, shoving my hair behind my ears.

"You are the oldest."

An incredulous laugh rips from my chest. "That's not an excuse."

I watch as she flounders for the correct English words, because unlike her two other children, I'm not fluent in the mother tongue. I have no doubt that she knows *exactly* what she wants to say but the language barrier, as it always has, remains a twenty-foot fence that could rival the Great Wall of China.

"You are . . . you are—"

"What?" I throw my arms up, completely at a loss. "I'm reckless? I'm impulsive? You think I need a man to *control* me?" Controlling the way my dad has acted toward her—the way he checks her phone routinely to see who she's talking to, how he scans her credit-card receipts and only gives her so much cash. My mom has never worked a day in her life. Twenty-something years of living in this country, never working outside the home, never doing much more than mingling with her Greek friends—it's no wonder she looks at the world through a non-inclusive lens that keeps everyone not fully part of her community *out*.

Including me, her own daughter.

My mom utters something in Greek, and I'm so sick of feeling *less than* in this world, in this culture that should belong to me but doesn't, that I snap, "In *English*!"

It's the first thing I say that shreds her proper posture. Her shoulders collapse and those tangling fingers rise up to press over her heart like I've wounded her. *Don't hug her. Don't you dare feel bad for finally saying what you mean.* My legs quiver and my hands turn clammy with guilt for being rude, and my stupid heart beats faster in a whisper of, *why can't you just love me as I am?*

Head dropping back, I stare up at the ceiling and seek patience. "Just say it," I grind out, hating the tremor in my voice that reminds me of my teenage years, "whatever you're thinking, just say it, Mama."

And then she shreds my heart in two: "Smart, Ermione. Katya is . . ."

I can't move.

She keeps talking, and I hear it all like I'm in a fog. Mentions of me failing classes in school and not being able to learn Greek the way my sister and brother did. She glosses over my pink hair and my revealing clothes like footnotes in a book titled Bad Girl Mina Pappas.

All while I stand here and try not to let the tears gathering fall and give her any amount of satisfaction. I'm not dumb or stupid or an idiot or any other word my peers once hurled my way.

I have trouble with *words,* no matter the language.

It doesn't make me incapable of learning. It doesn't mean that I absorb knowledge like a sieve, none of it sticking long enough to make a difference.

And even if I *was* that way, it shouldn't matter. My mom, my dad, they should still love me because I'm *theirs*.

The tears fall and I'm helpless to stop them.

"Ah, *Ermione*," my mom croons, coming to her feet and crossing over to me. Her arms wrap around my shoulders like she can make me feel better after tearing my soul in half. "It is okay—*naí*? *Baba* and I, we only want you to find a nice—"

"No!"

I shrug my way out of her hold, ducking under her arms before I can sink into their hypocritical, judgmental warmth.

"Ermione—"

With a hand slashing through the air, I cut my mother off. Her green eyes, so unlike my brown ones, stare back at me, completely bewildered. "I have dyslexia, Mama." I curl my arms around myself. "*Dyslexia*. It's not the plague. It does not mean that I'm incapable of taking care of myself!"

She falls back a step. "A husband—a *sýzygos*—will help you."

"Yeah? The same way *Baba* helps you?"

"Naí, koritsi mou," she says it so pleasantly that I want to scream.

Instead I do what I should have done thirty minutes ago. I point to the door behind her and swallow down every last bit of fight I have within me to rebel. There's no point. She's stuck in her ways, and I'm . . . *exhausted.* "I'm going to bed, Mama. We'll talk about this when I get back."

I hold myself ramrod still as she ambles over and kisses me on the forehead. *"Kali nichta, paidí mou." Good night, my child.*

I wait until the door shuts behind her before I fly into motion. I throw clothes and my blow dryer and shoes all into my suitcase. It all goes in, one by one, and on a random decision, I duck beneath my bed and dig through the bin of old notebooks until I find that stupid diary to GSN. I toss that one in, too, because Nick promised me a fireplace and it's time to see all those suffocating emotions go down in flames.

Only once I'm done, my suitcase bumping down the staircase behind me, do I call the one woman in the world who knows all that I am and still loves me anyway.

"Mina," Aleka Stamos greets when she picks up on the second ring, "it's late, *koukla mou*. What's wrong?"

"Can I stay with you tonight?"

Her answer is immediate. "Yes, of course. Come. I will wait up for you."

I manage to hold back all of my tears until I reach her house. It's not the same one I found refuge in while growing up, this one much bigger and nicer, but as soon as she sees me, it's like the time fades away. She pulls me into her embrace, and I catch her familiar scent of lemon. I don't know how long my best friend's mother hugs me. I don't know how long my tears last until I feel light-headed and she's pressing a glass of water into my hand and telling me to drink.

The last thing I do before I pass out in the spare bedroom is reach for my phone and call Nick. It's after 3 a.m. and I'm not surprised when I get his voicemail. "Pick me up at your mom's in the morning," I say, my voice thick and raspy from all the crying I've unleashed, "Good night, Nick. I . . . good night."

32

NICK

I let myself into my parents' house the morning of our road trip to Maine. Morning light streams in through the front windows of the parlor, and I follow the sound of voices to the kitchen.

Coming here this morning wasn't part of the plan, but neither was the choked voicemail I received from Mina in the dead of night. When I woke up and listened, it took everything in me to wait until eight, like we talked about yesterday.

Hearing her like that . . . I could almost hear her tears through the receiver, and the sound nearly broke me. And the worst of it is, I know the only people who would drive her to tears are the ones who birthed her. Much as I want to bang on my chest and break down doors and come to her rescue, I can't do any of that when it comes to *Kyrie* and *Kyria* Pappas.

Mina might not love her parents the way I adore mine, but that doesn't mean she wants me turning into the Hulk when it comes to them either. Not that I haven't been tempted more than once this morning.

No one messes with Mina on my watch. Not that asshole from back in high school. Not some prick on the street. No one.

The minute my feet hit the kitchen tiles, my mom and dad whip around. Identical grins lift their mouths, and even though I only saw them last weekend, they rush forward to hug me. Ma takes first priority, then my dad.

"Where's *Yiayia?*" I ask in Greek.

"In the sunroom messing with her plants." My dad rolls his shoulders. "You know how she is."

Yeah, we *all* do. I look toward the hallway, the need to see Mina and reassure myself she's okay pulsing through me.

"Nick." My mom loops her arm through mine. "She'll be fine. But don't . . . don't ask her to talk until she's ready, okay? Have a good weekend. Have some fun."

There's not a chance in hell I'm letting this die down. I want—I *need*—her to tell me herself that she's okay. And then I want to know why she came here of all places, not to Effie or even to me. *Especially to me.* The initial hurt from this morning resurfaces. I thought we were past keeping each other at arm's length, and it stings to know that while I'm all in with this sort-of relationship of ours, Mina might still be clinging to the idea that we're just a fling.

Just a fling.

Have Mina and I ever been "just" anything? Looking back on our interactions with each other over the years, I don't think so. Mina has always been *more* to me, even if I was desperate to prove to myself otherwise.

"*Niko mou,*" Ma says, drawing out each syllable patiently, like the mother she's been for the last thirty-two years. "Let it go."

I force the tension out of my limbs. "Working on it."

A small pause, and then she asks, "Is there something between you two?"

I could lie. They'd believe it. Mina and I have been at each other's throats for years, always circling, always pushing—but maybe they would see right through me. Mina and I have been at each other's throats, yes, but we've also shored up our differences when the other needed support.

When the other needed *love*.

My chest expands like I've swallowed a helium balloon.

I love her. Mina. I scratch at my heart, like that'll do something to appease the swell of emotion in my chest.

All these years, I've been looking for my other half, my Aleka to my George, my Sarah to my Effie. And she was right here all along. I almost laugh out of the pure ridiculousness of the situation.

Because how does a guy like me, who's always so careful with his emotions, not realize something as monumental as *loving* a woman like Ermione Pappas? I can't even say with certainty that it's a new thing. How can I, when I'm assaulted with memories of her in every aspect of my life? Her in that tiny bikini right before her top was washed away. Her in my arms on prom night, when I forced myself to do the responsible thing and put distance between us. Her in my goddamn bed on my wedding night, my own personal rock bottom, with *I Love Lucy* reruns playing and Mina—God, Mina—lending me a shoulder and a hug and an ear when I needed it.

And that night, rolling over and wanting to pull her in close.

This time the laugh comes, but it's thick with emotion and doesn't sound at all like me. Because, yes, even on my almost-wedding night to another woman, I caved to the desire Mina always sparked to life within me.

I didn't touch her. I didn't climb under the covers.

But I looked—oh, how I *looked*—at the way her brow furrowed in her sleep, how she quietly huffed and puffed while she snored. And my chest fucking ached at the way she slept on her side, facing me, and her fingers were stretched out, as though daring me to take them within mine.

Ermione Pappas has been a thorn in my side. She's driven me wild and made me want to haul her over my shoulder and spank her ass on more than one occasion, just to see her lips part in shock. But she snuck into my heart so many years ago that I don't know what it's like to live without her sewn into the fabric of my being.

Knowing that what I'm about to say is gonna shock the hell out of my parents, I square off my shoulders and add steel to my tone. "I love her. Mina, I love Mina."

I don't know what I'm expecting for a reaction but it's not the one I'm given. My dad claps me on the back with a *whoop!* and there's no hiding the tears that gather in my mom's eyes as she whispers, "Oh, *Niko,* finally."

That last word has my brows shooting up. *"Finally?"*

Sheepishly, she looks to my father. "Nick, you are not . . . you are not the best at pretending."

Pretending *what*? For me to get my shit together after all the years and realize I've had my head up my ass for just as long? "Ma," I start, "I don't know what you think—"

"Are we ready to go?"

At the sound of Mina's suitcase wheels rolling over the tiled floor, I move toward her instinctively. Taking the suitcase handle from her grip, I frame her face with my other hand and claim her mouth with mine. She jolts under my touch, eyes going momentarily wide.

"They know," I mutter under my breath when I pull back.

She glances around me to stare openly at my parents. "They do?"

Like they're welcoming her into the family—even though she's been one of us for decades—my mom and dad throw their arms around Mina, kissing her cheeks, pinching her chin. Poor Mina looks like she's seconds away from crumpling to the ground in embarrassment.

"All right, everyone. We'll see you when we get back." I manage to disentangle her, and, without giving my *yiayia* time to join the festivities and ruin it all, I usher Mina out the door to the car. I put her suitcase in the trunk along with mine, then climb into the driver's seat.

Mina plops down in the passenger's seat. "That was . . ."

"Fun."

The look she sends my way is all *are-you-kidding* incredulous. "I was going to say insane, but, sure, fun works too."

I keep an eye on the road as I pull away from the curb and steer the car down the street. I know my mom wanted me to cool it and let Mina come to me, but I feel like she needs to know that I'm here. If she needs me. *Fuck, I hope she does.* "Mina, I—"

Her fingers curl into a fist in her lap, and I hear the gentle exhale of her breath. "When we get back, Nick, I'll tell you whatever you want to know. But I just want to have fun—no stress, no real life for all of two-and-a-half days. Can we do that?"

I bite back the words begging to be released. Words like *I love you* and *please, take a chance on me, on* us. "Yeah, sure." I give a curt nod to show that all is well. "We can definitely do that."

Or we can try, at least, however good that'll be for us.

33

NICK

Bethel, Maine, is the quaintest, most picturesque New England town I've ever seen. There's not much more to it than one main street—appropriately named "Main Street"—with Victorian houses and shops lining each side of the narrow road. The town sits at the foothill of the White Mountains, and everywhere I look are fog-tipped mountains, iced-over streams, and pickup trucks.

Looking at all the snow outside, I'm predicting a lot of time spent on my ass this weekend. Skiing is gonna prove to be a battle of the wills, and I'm not sure I'll emerge victorious.

With Maine also comes Sophia.

Mina, Dom, and I haven't been in the bed-and-breakfast lobby for more than five minutes before I hear her squealing from the stairwell. "Eeep, you guys are *here!*"

"She's never sounded so excited to see me in her life," Mina mutters under her breath.

Whereas the three of us look like we've been traveling for hours, Sophia's decked out in a slim dress with a furred collar and the same furry trim at her wrists. She whizzes right past Mina to clamp her arms around my neck for a tight hug, which I barely return, before turning to Dom.

Her grin is lethal—and not the good, sexy kind.

He looks ready to run for the mountains—literally.

"And *who* do we have here?" she asks, sauntering close with a sway to her hips that all but says *you will be mine*. I've never been so thankful to be off a woman's radar in my life.

Dom's dark eyes shoot to mine, pleading.

I open my mouth. "This is—"

"My good friend, Don," Mina exclaims, leaving my side to stand by Dominic. She pats his chest like they're the best of friends. "He's gay. Right, *Don*?"

Oh, sweet Jesus.

Silence pervades our group of four, and I risk a glance at Dom to see him physically holding back his laughter. He's got a balled fist pressed to his mouth, and when he cracks out, "And ready to mingle," he nearly loses it.

Sophia looks from me to Dom—or *Don*—and then to Mina, like she's trying to figure out if she's being fooled. "Well," she finally drawls, "are you Greek?"

"Might be." Dom flashes her a grin. "I've got no idea."

That doesn't seem to appease her at all. She sniffs and folds her hands behind her back, which only manages to throw her chest out with sublime overconfidence. "*Endaxi*." *Fine*. Kicking her chin up, she stares at us with a little less pep than she had coming down the steps. "You'll find the weekend's schedule in your rooms. Don't be late to tonight's event." She turns to go, only to whirl back around and home in on me. "I was disappointed to learn that you booked a room with Mina for the weekend, Nick. Especially the room with the fireplace. That was *my* room."

She flounces off before I can get a word in.

"Don DaSilva," Dominic muses, rubbing his chin. "Can't say I've batted for the other team before, Mina, *but* I like the way you think quick on your feet." He nudges Mina in the shoulder, then grabs his duffel bag from where he dropped it on the settee to our left. "Meet you guys back down here in thirty? I'm game to explore the town if you are."

With a plan in mind, we go our separate ways, Dom tromping up the stairs while Mina and I head for the last room on the first floor. The wood floor creaks beneath our feet, and if I'm being honest, this place looks like my grandmother's wet dream.

Lace and crochet decorate every window. The wallpapers are a muted, paisley pink. As I unlock the door to our room, I can't help but feel like I'm walking into a Victorian dollhouse. It's unnerving as hell.

Glancing down at Mina, I mutter, "Let's hope for the best."

I let her go in first, only to realize I need to duck my head or risk smacking it on the frame. "*Gamóto.*" Hunching my shoulders, I step into our temporary room for the next two nights. I set my duffel bag and Mina's suitcase down by the door, noting its crooked frame. If that's any indication as to how this weekend is going to go, we're in for a doozy.

The rest of the room is decent enough. A full bathroom with more paisley wallpaper that should be thrown out or burned. A tiny kitchenette with floors that quite clearly slope. The bedroom itself is large, and the as-promised fireplace exists like the only beacon of hope.

Mina bounces on the bed with a sheet of paper clutched in her hand. "Our weekend schedule," she announces, shaking the paper. "You ready for this?"

I sit down beside her, and the mattress dips *deep* beneath my weight. Oh, this is gonna be fun. "As much as I can be."

Clearing her throat, she points to the first item on the list. "It seems the kind Sophia has given us a few hours this afternoon to do whatever we want, but tonight we have dinner at the Bethel Manor up the street for—and I repeat verbatim—dating games and dinner."

"That sounds terrifying."

"Which part?"

"Which one do you think?" I lean back, allowing my weight to fall onto the mattress. Right before I make contact, I hold my breath and pray the damn thing won't give out beneath me. I'm a big guy, but I've never worried about breaking beds before. Then again, I never thought I'd fall through a staircase either. "The last time I played any sort of dating game, I was fourteen and playing spin the bottle."

"Ah, a classic." Mina's face fills my vision as she braces her weight on her hand. "Who'd you have to kiss?"

I barely remember. "Some girl from homeroom, I think. No tongue. There was a parent chaperone."

"A *chaperone*?" She sounds absolutely aghast at the thought. "You're kidding, right?"

I chuckle, low. "Wish I was. It was more scarring than I'll ever admit, especially when one of the guys tried to get to second base and the dad—our chaperone—only turned on the TV and ignored the fact that his son was sticking his tongue down this girl's throat. What about you?"

Her honey eyes bore down on me, wide and unassuming. "You're funny, Nick."

I didn't think that was ever in question. Lifting one arm, I slip my fingers into her usual tamed and perfectly wavy hair. "Tell me what you mean."

She huffs out a breath. "I didn't have my first kiss until I was eighteen. No Seven Minutes of Heaven. No spin the bottle—though after hearing your story, I'm pretty sure that I'm the lucky one."

Eighteen . . . a year after her prom night. Angling my fingers at the base of her skull, I tug her down until she's inches away. "If there are any games tonight, just know that I'll be first in line to pop your cherry."

Her shocked laughter warms me inside out, and if it weren't for Dom calling to check on our ETA five minutes later, I would have been perfectly happy to never leave our rickety mattress.

WE SPEND MOST OF THE DAY CHECKING OUT THE BOUTIQUES along Main Street. The snow holds off long enough for the three of us to feast on fudge from a gas station, of all places, and to stop in an all-in-one type shop directly across from our B&B. With walls made of wood and the furnace burning hot, it's easy to imagine the two-story boutique as a log cabin in the middle of nowhere.

Then again, Bethel, Maine—beautiful as it is—isn't exactly the center of civilization.

"I'm gonna check out the winter apparel," Dom tells us when we step inside. "I'm hopin' they might have something thicker than what I've got."

I pluck at his rain jacket—fat lot of good that thing will do him tonight when it drops into the teens. "You're not in California anymore, Toto."

He flashes me the bird and heads off to the clothing section. "Asshole," he calls out over his shoulder.

Laughing, I turn back to Mina. "Anything you want to look for?"

She smiles up at me, and if it's not quite as bright as the ones she usually keeps in reserve for me, I try to keep the worry at the minimum. "How about we just browse around?" she says. "We've got time to kill anyway."

We wander through the various sections, my hand linked with hers. This store has everything a person could ever need, from paintings and artwork to even a mini-special-gems exhibit. They sparkle under the glass cases, drawing Mina's attention like a shooting star darting across the sky.

"Like them?" I nod toward the line of purple amethysts shining under the lamps.

"*Love* them." With a little shrug, she ducks down to look at them head-on. "I remember going to the Museum of Science as a kid for school. At one point they had a gem exhibit and it was just *amazing*. I mean, some of them stood nearly as tall as me."

I lean my ass against the case. "The dinosaurs got to me."

She doesn't bother to hide her chuckle. "Such a man," she says, a teasing note the only undercurrent to her voice. Maybe she's feeling better after whatever drove her to my parents' house? I can only hope. "Let me guess, you were enraptured by the T-Rex."

"*Pshh*." I wave my hand at her. "Overrated. The Allosaurus has my vote."

"Because it was bigger than the T-Rex?"

"Nah," I murmur with a wide grin, "but it was faster. More vicious. Shouldn't you know this, Miss *Jeopardy*?"

"Seems like I missed the dinosaur episode." She bumps her hip with mine, and I instinctively curl my arm around her. Our coats get in the way, so I slip my fingers into the back pocket of her jeans. "Please tell me you've seen *Jurassic Park*."

"Of course I have." She pauses, and then adds, "I mean, I've seen the Chris Pratt version. Because, Chris Pratt."

Mock-groaning, I drop my forehead to her shoulder. "Way to let a guy down, *koukla*. That *Jurassic Park* doesn't count. We're adding it to the list of movies to watch."

"Are we?"

"Yup." I let the *p* pop, squeezing her ass through her jeans before stepping away and drumming my fingers on the glass counter. "Now, asking for a friend, which one of these gems is your favorite?"

TURNS OUT, "DATING GAMES" IS AS MUCH OF A SHIT STORM AS we predicted.

The dinner plates have barely been swept away by the restaurant staff before Sophia launches up from her chair and proceeds to stand at the front of the room. "Thank you all for coming up to Maine!" Clapping her hands together, she does a little shimmy that coaxes some laughs out of this weekend's victims. "We're the last ones standing in our grade—single and ready to mingle!"

Mina elbows me in the side, hissing, "My nose is tingling. It's a bad omen."

I sling an arm around the back of her chair. "At least you know most of the people here. Dom and I are out of luck."

This weekend's shenanigans consist of twelve of us, including Dom. Although Mina seemed nervous when the others stopped by to say hello during dinner, she inevitably warmed up and relaxed. Or maybe it was the vodka talking. Either way, I'm two years older than everyone else—aside from Dominic—which means I may recognize faces but nothing more.

I'm going into this weekend completely blind, save for my partner-in-crime sitting beside me.

"I thought we could do a round of speed dating," Sophia goes on, "but then I thought . . . screw it, we're all adults! We should play a fun game."

Something tells me that my idea of a "fun" game and hers have very different definitions. Idly, my fingers play with Mina's dark strands.

"So! We're going to play Attached at the Hip! Does

anyone know what I'm talking about?" A few hands shoot up, but the majority of us do nothing but stare back at Sophia blankly. She counts all those who are in the know. "If you're clueless, never fear. Pretty much, we're all going to write down a body part on a slip of paper—I've got us covered—and pop it into a hat. We'll be paired into teams of two. Each of you will pick a piece of paper, and then you'll need to make sure those body parts are always touching."

"And if they don't?" calls out a guy with a man bun. "What happens then?"

Sophia's answering grin is downright diabolical. "You take a shot and you're out of the game! Easiest rules ever. Don't stop touching, *ever*. Not even between positions."

As though she has it all choreographed, the doors to the private room we're in swing open and two servers tromp in with shots perched on black trays.

"How well do you hold your liquor?" I whisper to Mina.

She makes the quintessential *oh, shit* face, and I figure that about sums up this night. "Not well enough," she grumbles, "especially if it's Tito's."

On my other side, Dom leans forward, elbow on the table. He points a finger at Mina, then says, "I don't know whether to love you or hate you for the Don bit. This is either going to be the worst night of my life or . . ."

"It's time to pick partners!" Sophia exclaims from the front of the room. "Oh, *Dooonnnn*! You're with me."

Dom's finger practically wilts. "When I purposely lose this game, be sure to carry me back to my room and lock the door." He pushes back his chair and strolls over to Sophia, looking like a dead man walking.

For a moment, Mina and I do nothing but mourn his bad luck.

Then we turn to each other in unison. "Partner?" we both ask.

"All right, let's do this." I toss back the rest of my wine and tap the base of Mina's. "Operation Never-Stop-Touching begins now."

As mandated by the rules, all of us write down a body part and toss it into the hat Sophia's procured from thin air. She shuffles them round, shaking the hat, then peers back up at us. "Do three more rounds of body parts, just in case we get 'leg' five times. Be creative!"

I toss my jacket on the back of my chair, then loosen the knot of my tie. One glance at Mina shows she's taking this seriously too. She's kicked off her high heels and put her hair up in a high ponytail. When she catches me staring, she offers a blinding grin. "Lucky for you, I wore trendy, fashion sweatpants." She plucks at the soft fabric before dropping to her haunches in what I think *she* thinks is a stretching pose. "I'm flexible and prepared to do anything it takes to win."

Biting down on my lip, I do what every other man does when faced with a sexy woman showing off how agile she is: I pull my button-down shirt out from the waistband of my slacks and hope it'll conceal the activity now happening south of the equator. There aren't many days that I prefer ditching my jeans and T-shirts for finer clothing—in this moment, with my erection threatening to announce itself to the world, I'm fucking thankful.

"Okay, partners! Stand together as a team." Sophia ushers one of the servers forward, and I almost feel bad for the utter horror he's about to witness tonight. "Sean here is going to come around with the hat. *Don't* look at what the paper says until I tell you."

Mina and I line up together. When Sean meets us, we each reach into the hat as one, our knuckles banging against each other's.

"Hand tango-ing," she says with a swift grin, "how good does it feel?"

"Better than expected." I meet her gaze. "Not as good as the horizontal tango, if you catch my drift, but it's good enough for now."

She rolls her eyes but I see the lightness there, and some of my concerns drift away. Once everyone has taken a turn with the hat, Sean calls out, "Okay! Go ahead and look now."

I peel open my slip of paper. "Right foot."

Mina glances over at my feet. "Back." Her nose scrunches. "Does that mean I need to lay on the floor? I mean, I will for the sake of competition, but this is *not* off to a good start."

"I'll do it." When her brows shoot up in question, I shrug. "Teamwork, right?"

All around us, couples are getting into position. I spot Dom looking pained as he gets down on one knee and Sophia perches herself atop it. He's going to wish he never came to Boston at this rate.

I lay down on my stomach, then feel Mina gently place her foot between my shoulder blades.

"Is this okay?" she asks. "I don't want to put too much weight on you."

Twisting my face so my left side is on the carpet, I try to twist my neck and catch her eye. "You're good, *koukla*. So long as we never mention tonight to Vince or the guys."

Sean comes around for round two. When he puts the hat at eye level for me, I'm convinced I've never seen a man look so close to pissing himself with laughter. I jam my hand in the hat, riffle around for the winning ticket, and pluck one out. Since I'm on the floor and practically out of sight from everyone else, I peek at my body part.

"Ah, fuck," says the dude to my left, and I shift my attention over to him. When he sees me looking, he mouths, "penis."

One guess as to who put that option in the hat. Starts with an *S* and ends with *ophia*.

Luckily for Mina and me, our choices are relatively simple this time around. She lowers onto all fours, so she can rest her right leg, from knee to foot, along my back, thus satisfying *right knee*. Me picking out "back" for this round feels like a miracle and a half, especially when Penis over to my left is stuck pressing his pelvis to his partner's ear.

"Oh, my God," I hear his partner cry out, "this is so humiliating."

Above me, Mina laughs so hard she snorts. "I can't," she gasps out, "oh, my God, Nick. You can't see Dom—*Don*—but . . ."

My ears perk up. "But what?"

"He has—He has his—"

Another peel of laughter escapes her, and I shake my back to get her attention. "He has his what on her *what?*"

"His teeth on her thigh!" More laughter that jumbles her words, and I only catch "looks like he's eating her" and "he's miserable" before Sean's back for round three.

The moment we scope out our next body parts, I curse under my breath. Obviously this is karma for laughing at Penis and Dom because I have zero idea how we're going to pull this off. With my "left knee" and her "right boob" it's almost impossible.

I attempt to bring my left leg up, so I'm sitting with my knee wide and bent at an angle. "You're gonna need to lay down," I say, "facing the opposite direction. Keep one leg touching me as you rotate or we've got nothing but shots in our future."

Mina huffs as she rotates her body. "Did I ever tell you how bad I am at yoga?"

"I thought you were flexible?"

"I am," she grunts out inelegantly, the top half of her body plunking forward. "I just don't have balance. It's a problem."

As though she jinxed herself, I feel her teeter, and I grind my teeth because, holy shit, she's got herself some bony shins.

"Are we good?" I ask when she's all settled in.

"Sure are." One hand squeezes my ass. "I have a pretty good view. You win the Buttocks of the Year Award."

Husky laughter escapes me. "Hey, we all got to be known for something in our lives."

Couples begin losing in the time it takes for Sean to come around again. I hear shot glasses being slammed down on the table and a few roughly uttered, "Jesus, I hate Ouzo."

"Can you see Dom?" I ask Mina.

"Not if you want to lose, Stamos. My boob is hereafter attached to your knee for the time being."

God bless his NFL-player body. I hope Sophia isn't scarring him right about now.

"Last round," Sean tells me when he comes back. "There's only three of you left standing . . . or, ya know, whatever it is you're doing right now."

Growing up, I never thought I'd find myself in a half-plank in a random manor restaurant at the age of thirty-two. Goes to show that life's just one grand adventure after another. I wonder if Sean, who can't be older than twenty, thinks we're absolutely insane. He's not wrong.

Mina wriggles above me. "Nick."

I hold in a large breath. "Ermione."

"I hate Sophia." She flings her piece of paper in my direction, and I catch it as it flutters to the ground. In feminine script, someone's written "chin." I open mine, and don't even bother to pretend this is going to work.

"I have Head," I tell her. Neither of us are contortionists. "We don't have time for you to remove three ribs, so unless you've got a master plan here, we're out."

"Dammit," comes her throaty reply. "I don't even know what the prize is and I'm feeling the loss of it already."

I curl my spine like a cat, tipping her off and onto the floor. She rolls easily over onto her back, a grin of contentment on her face. Aware of the people all around us, I grip her hands and pull her up onto her feet. "There's good news: now I know if I want to get creative in the bedroom, you'll be able to rise to the occasion."

Mina swats my ass. "Eighty-percent, Stamos. We're back in that eighty-percent margin again."

We are, but only because it's easier to make a joke about sex than it is to come clean: that there is no one else I could have laughed tonight off with other than her. This weekend I need to tell her how I feel, and I only hope she feels the same in return.

34

MINA

We spend most of Saturday outdoors.

While the group heads to the ski slopes, Dom, Nick, and I rent fat-tire bikes that are created specifically to ride through the forest's snow-dusted floor. With only the sound of our tires *swooshing* through the snow and the sounds of the whispering trees above us, the quiet hums in my veins.

Bethel feels like a thousand light-years away from Boston and *Agape* and *Put A Ring On It* and my parents. For the first time in years, it feels like I can breathe. In our little trio, Dom leads the pack while Nick pulls up the rear.

Last night at the Bethel Manor was pure insanity. Attached at the Hip was followed by a round of Sporkle, where we all had to pair up. When one person named a category, every person in the group had to name something that fit—like *Family Feud* but with drinking involved. Anytime I thought *this can't get any worse*, it did, but I guess Sophia knows the human psyche well enough because by the end of the night, couples began to pair off.

Dom, clinging to my excuse from our arrival, bowed out

when Sophia invited him to her guestroom for a nightcap. It was only after Nick and I climbed into bed, exhausted from the day's activities, that his phone vibrated with a text from Dominic that read, *If you hear a scream in the middle of the night, that's me calling for help because Sophia kicked down my door.*

We listened for approximately ten minutes and thirty seconds before rolling over and passing out cold.

"Taking a right up ahead!" Dom shouts back at us.

He swerves his bike, cutting around a sharp bend, and I follow next. Immediately I listen for the sound of Nick's tires making the same turn. My shoulders only loosen and relax when I hear him whoop out his excitement.

The trees grow sparser as we ride and soon we're treated to quick glimpses of the mountains through low limbs and thick trunks. My legs burn from the exercise, but I keep pedaling, enjoying the rush of the wind whipping my hair under my helmet. Every inhale is accompanied by the crisp scent of pine.

When we finally stop, it's at a clearing along the side of a bluff. Maybe fifty feet below is the iced-over Sunday River, one of Bethel's main attractions during the summertime months. One glance up at the horizon and the river is all but forgotten.

Rolling mountains span the width of my vision, and it's so beautiful, so awe-inspiring, that I can't help but clamber off my bike and let it fall into the snow. Two steps closer to the bluff's edge and I plop down in the snow, beyond grateful that Nick convinced me to purchase snow pants when we were at the outdoors store yesterday. He sits down next to me now, not touching me but still close enough that I can feel his body heat.

"This is beautiful," I exhale on a hushed breath, as though

fearful that if I raise my voice anymore, I'll disturb the tranquility.

Dom prowls close to the edge, peering over the side. "This view makes up for all the shit last night."

"You mean you didn't enjoy snacking on Sophia's leg?" I tease, to which he only smirks in my direction before sitting down on the other side of me.

"Unfortunately, she's neither my or Don's type." He packs the snow into an icy ball before tossing it from one hand to the other. "Not that she cares."

Although I'm not sure it's my story to tell, I snag the snowball during one of his throws and say, "She's going through a nasty divorce. Not that she should pressure you, by any means, but I know this weekend is her way of trying to have fun and forget all the nonsense."

He roughly releases a breath. "That makes us two peas in a pod, then."

Bending his knees, Nick drops his elbows on them. "It's only gonna get worse from here, DaSilva. They haven't even started airing the show yet." He digs his heels into the snow, pushing it into mini hills beneath the soles of his snow boots. "How long do you have before you have to go back to work?"

"Another week." Dom forms another snowball and, without even asking if I want it, he passes it over to me. I was right—beneath all those black clothes and bad-boy attitude is a man who is keenly aware of those around him. I take the snowball, hurl my arm back, and let it sail over the side of the bluff. "There's some shit going down with the Blades right now," he continues, already packing me another snowball. "It's a mess and Sports 24/7 is on it with this reality show the network is filming, *Getting Pucked*."

I think back to the Blades players who attended Effie's tour at the beginning of the month. "How big of a mess?"

"The captain's retiring—or, rather, he's flip-flopping on

the decision. I don't get involved in any of that, but if he *does* retire, the network wants to run a special on him exclusively. I'll be roped into it somehow."

Nick's rough timbre cuts through the silence of the mountains. "DaSilva, man. Can I be honest?"

Another snowball comes my way, and I can't help but wonder if it's a distraction for him: think about packing snow instead of whatever thoughts are running through his head.

Finally, he says, "Fuck it, go ahead."

"I think you need a permanent change of scenery," Nick says, right before he nails Dom in the shoulder with a snowball.

Caught in the crossfire, I dart out of the way and drop to my shins, quickly packing snowballs to launch one after the other. One smacks Dom in the middle of his back. Another I manage to aim at Nick's hip, but he's too limber on his feet and he dances out of the way—only to tackle me into the snow.

His sudden weight pumps the air right out of my lungs, and I come spluttering up. I hear Nick's deep laughter just as I feel his damn nose collide with mine, his cold lips kissing me on the mouth. Familiar heat spirals through me, shaking off the chill of the mountains and the snow. I wrap an arm around the back of his neck, keeping him close, and it's only when I pull back for air that I catch Dom off to the side.

He watches us with a somber expression, the rough edges that usually grace his aura now softened and sad. I recognize it all in a heartbeat—everything that he is was *me* before a crazy deal happened with the man sprawled on top of me.

"I PROMISED YOU A FIRE."

Lifting my chin from the bed, I fix my gaze on Nick kneeling before the fireplace, stoking the tiny flames. We opted against another night of shenanigans, and instead picked up dinner from the B&B's onsite restaurant and ate in our room.

Whether the food was any good is beyond me—I spent most of my time trying to win my hand at UNO against Nick, who does *not* play fair. No sooner would he drop a Draw Two on me before slapping me with a Draw Four. By the end of the game, I had two stacks of cards because I couldn't hold them all at once.

I prop my chin on top of my fist. "I'm glad we came this weekend."

"Couldn't have survived it without you, that's for sure."

His words make my pulse launch into a sprint even as they make my heart fill with dread—because under the teasing glint is a whole lot of hope, and I can't get my mom's words out of my head. They weigh me down like a sack of too-heavy barbells.

My parents' relationship has always been so one-sided, and hearing her tell me that I need a man to take care of me —to keep me propped up like some rag doll who can't handle her own business—sparks the restless panic within me. Are Nick and I lopsided? Are we balanced like Sarah and Effie or like his mom and dad? Or are we like my own parents, who, more often than not, are nothing but two souls coexisting in the same house?

Softly, I ask, "Do you think Dom will get over Savannah Rose?"

Lowering onto his butt, Nick uses the fire poker to shift around the logs. The light from the flames flickers across his face, casting his handsome features in a haunting, red shadow. "He will."

"How do you know?"

"Because it's what he's done his entire life." Nick puts the poker back in its wrought-iron stand. "He's a foster kid, Mina. Dom's spent his entire life bouncing from one safety net to another, and then when he was in the NFL, he exchanged foster homes for teams." He scrubs one hand over his jaw like he finds the words themselves distasteful. "One of the things they did on the show was force us to reveal one big, deep, dark secret, and that was his. It's a TV manipulation tactic, something I didn't really think about until they were forcing me to talk about Brynn."

"Oh. What did you . . . what did you tell them?"

With the fire crackling, I have to strain my ears to hear the low pitch of Nick's voice when he speaks next. "Maybe you should ask me what I didn't tell them."

I slip off the bed, down to my knees on the thin carpet. I keep my voice as soft as his. "What didn't you tell them?"

"That when I was laying in that bed with you, I felt nothing but relief."

My heart skips. "Relief that you didn't marry Brynn?"

Slowly, he shakes his head. "Relief that when I was at my lowest, I wasn't alone. You were there. I don't even know why you came to my room or how you knew that I needed you."

To open up now would bare my soul in a way that I never have before—not with anyone. And I hear the words escaping me, as though my heart and mind are on two separate wavelengths, one seeking to protect me and the other to expose me. "I was leaving the ceremony when I saw you dart up the stairs." Embarrassment clogs my throat, and I cough into a balled fist to clear it. *Here goes nothing*. "I followed you up to where the choir plays because I liked you. You called me out on it weeks ago, and I won't deny it. I followed because I cared more than I should have. You didn't cry but you looked so . . . broken." I stare down at my hands, unable to look him in the face. "I decided that I'd go to your room later. You needed a friend and I figured that, through my friendship with Effie, I was good enough to do the job."

A bent finger hooks under my chin and lifts, so that I have no choice but to meet Nick's gaze. "You were more than good enough for the job. I only wish that my grandmother hadn't busted in—I don't even know who she had to bribe to get the key—and turned shit completely backward for you."

I force a grin. "I'll have you know that I once thought about selling Bad Girl Mina T-shirts. I would have made a killing."

Nick groans, his arms reaching out to pull me against him. Burying his face in my neck, he heaves out a heavy breath. "All these years, I wasted my time lookin' elsewhere, *koukla*."

Like sludge, guilt thickens in my veins until it's hard to draw air into my lungs. Nick thinks he knows me, but the truth is I don't even know myself. *Do genetics really make a difference*? I've always thought so, but Nick brought up a good point. Dominic DaSilva was raised in foster care—does that make him any less of who *he* is? I see a confident man who's down for a good joke, even at his own expense. Yes, there's a sadness to him—but who doesn't have that?

I am who I am out of sheer will and determination to do more than what my parents ever expected of me. I've made mistakes, like the rest of the population, and I've celebrated triumphs and drowned my tears in cheap vodka. I'm no different, no worse off, than any other person combatting their own struggles.

"Can I show you something?" I voice the question into Nick's bulky shoulder, and I mentally pat myself on the back for not sounding timid and scared.

He lifts his head. "What is it?"

"My own deep, dark secret."

I clamber off his lap and crawl over to where I left my suitcase propped open. Sifting through my clothes, I search for my last-minute addition—my notebook from senior year of high school. I want to burn it, but I think, I need to show it to another person first.

35

NICK

"I'd like for you to read this." At my curious stare, Mina's honey eyes grow like saucers and she throws up a hand. "Not *all* of it, obviously. We don't have the time—okay, we do, but it's really not necessary. A lot of it is redundant, actually, though I guess that's like saying that *I'm* redundant, which honestly . . . I'm not putting any of this well. Sorry." She huffs out an awkward chuckle before mumbling, "I can point out the right dates to read. If you want."

I take the notebook from her grasp, letting my fingers purposely brush hers. Holding the book close to the fire, I watch as the words flicker across the lined page. "If this tells me anything about *you*, Ermione, then I want to read it. Trust me."

Her whispered, "I do," stokes the heat curling around my heart. This woman could tell me to put on a unicorn costume and dance in the middle of Copley Square and I wouldn't think twice. Or maybe I would, but only to make sure she's dressed as a unicorn right along with me.

Partners-in-crime and all that.

Lifting the notebook, I skim the edge with the pad of my thumb. “Tell me where to start.”

And she does.

Once I find the first entry, I angle the notebook to catch the moonlight filtering in through the window. I barely manage to read the first line before Mina’s voice diverts my attention. She speaks softly, like she’s uncertain if I’ll be willing to listen, and keeps her gaze rooted on her socked feet.

“I didn’t know that I was any different as a kid. I’m sure my teachers told my parents that I was a late bloomer or something, but at some point, the excuses wear thin.” Those honey eyes of hers flick up to stare into the crackling flames, with a look so heartbreakingly *lonely* etched in her features that it nearly destroys me. Muscles flexing at my need to *go, hug her, love her,* I gather every shred of discipline to sit my ass still and give her room to pour her heart out. “I was six when *Baba* let it slip that I wasn’t his. I didn’t understand, obviously—genetics aren’t something a six-year-old really gets. I sure didn’t. Mama was crying and apologizing to *him,* because he was angry and yelling at me, and somehow *her* infidelity was my fault. I stood in the center of the living room, still wearing my school uniform, and all I remember is feeling confused.”

The notebook’s pages crinkle in my grip.

I wasn’t his. I wasn’t his. I wasn’t his.

Mina’s words loop around like a broken record in my head. How did I miss it all these years? How did I not notice Yianni Pappas’s reluctance to show any hint of affection for his eldest daughter?

Except that Mina *isn’t* his eldest daughter.

Christ.

I study her features, the notebook all but forgotten in my hands, and mentally compare her to the Pappas clan. Warm brown eyes instead of cool seafoam green like her siblings. Darker sun-kissed skin than Yianni or Katya or Dimitri. Mina is downright beautiful, but it doesn't change the fact that—

"You see it now, don't you?"

At her pointed question, I hold her gaze, unwilling to sever the connection between us. The heat from the fireplace warms my skin to a feverish temperature. Or maybe it's the fact that I'm seconds away from losing my finally wrought control. And all because—"He's a fuckin' bastard." I bite out the words. Fast, sharp, completely unapologetic. "You didn't deserve learning about your mom like that. You don't deserve any of their bullshit at all—not for one second."

Her chin comes up. "But do you see it?"

What I see is a woman who's stolen my heart.

Knowing that she's waiting for an answer, I give her the bitter truth. "*Naí.*"

Yes. One simple word—and she visibly curls up in a ball.

Mina bends her knees, drawing them up to her chest. She wraps her arms around her shins, then settles her chin on her knees. She looks young, resigned, and God help me, but all I want to do is hold her.

"Once it was out in the open, there was no pretending otherwise." She licks her lips, but nothing about it is sexual. "*Baba* brought up Mama cheating all the time. He did it front of me, in front of Katya and Dimitri. He did it when we were out to dinner and she happened to look at another man a little too long. I realize now that it was classic manipulation and how he kept Mama in check. Back then, though, it felt like a thousand arrows landing in my already open wounds."

Squeezing her eyes shut, her shoulders draw up to her ears. "If I had been like Katya and Dimitri, maybe he would have let bygones be bygones. I was eight the first time he called me stupid. I didn't have a good grasp in many of my classes and we both know I struggled in Greek school. Every bad grade, every failed test, was like open season for him to belittle me."

Fury thrums through my veins. It's a miracle that I manage to keep my tone flat at all when I edge out, "You have dyslexia."

She shrugs stiffly. "I wasn't diagnosed until I was twenty. By then I was in hair school and determined to never go back home. I'm sure the counselors in grade school may have done something to help me, but I was always home, helping my siblings with whatever they needed. My dreams took a back seat."

Fuck it.

I drop the notebook to the threadbare carpet and crawl to her on my knees. Like we did when she helped me with the church spire, I assume the spot behind her. My legs spread wide, with her nestled in the V of my thighs. Fingers grazing the waistband of her leggings, I settle my hands on her hips. She shudders when I kiss that delicate spot she loves so much, right where her neck and shoulder meet. "Spill it all," I tell her, as she reclines back in my hold and my lips slip up to her soaring-wings tattoo. "I'm not goin' anywhere, *koukla.*"

Strong woman that she is, Mina does nothing but allow her chest to expand with a deep inhale. "Your parents want you to get married because they want to see you happy. Even your *yiayia* has good intentions." I feel, rather than hear, the angry hum that reverberates in her chest. "That's not my life. One day, my parents think I should let a man take care of me. The next, they're telling me that no one will ever want me—that I might pass on my dyslexia."

"So what if you do?" The words burst from my mouth like bullets discharging from a rifle. "So, *what*? It's not the plague."

"That's what I told my mom."

"Great minds think alike," I mutter, my frustration boiling

deep. "It's ridiculous. They roped you into their own mess instead of behaving like goddamn adults."

Like she's wanting to soothe *me*—because that's Mina to a T, always looking out for others—she trails her fingers gently over my arm. "I may have gotten the brunt of their crap, but I'm not the only one they messed up in the head. Katya's living in North Carolina and only comes home for the holidays. Dimitri is in Manhattan, and unless we go to him, he doesn't step foot back in Boston. The three of us all have our own issues, and I'm so tired—so incredibly tired—of being one of my parents' tried-and-true missiles to hurt each other."

No wonder she clung to Effie so tightly growing up. Our family may not have been well-off—we may not have had the newest toys for Christmas and we may not have taken a family vacation until Effie and I were well into our twenties—but there was never any doubt that we were *loved*.

"Did you and your mom get into it? Is that why you left?"

Mina gives a short nod that rustles her hair against my chin. "I had to get out of there. For as long as I can remember, your mom has always been there for me—more than mine ever has. I'm sorry if picking me up from there was uncomfortable for you."

It breaks my goddamn heart to hear her apologize for wanting something we should all expect from our families: comfort, love, acceptance. "Ermione, if you want to see my parents daily, I don't give a damn." I give her a gentle squeeze. "Not that I wouldn't mind having you come to me instead."

Her answer is lost to the crackle and pop of the firewood.

She shifts in my arms, turning around until she's resting on her knees and her hands are closing over my shoulders. My gaze moves north from her curvy thighs to the billowy T-shirt she borrowed from me. It's at least three sizes too large, and when she slowly lowers her hands to the hem to pull it over her head, it's finally the perfect size because it's gone, and all that's left is smooth, soft skin.

My cock hardens immediately. Perks up to full attention when Mina thumbs her nipple, rolling the peaked nub between her thumb and forefinger. *Gamóto,* but I've never seen a more beautiful sight.

She cups the weight of her breasts, squeezing softly, plucking at her nipple once more.

"I'm gonna need you to step aside and let me do business." My voice emerges deep and throaty, even to my own ears. I ignore the keening desperation for us to take it to the next level, to show her that when we fuck, we're really making love. But if she needs this physical connection right now after cutting open all those old wounds of hers, I'm more than willing to take up the task.

My hands glide from her hips to the small of her back, tracing up the line of her spine, until I'm palming her shoulder blades and encouraging her to thrust her chest out. She cries out the moment I graze my teeth over her hardened nipple. Her fingers sink into my hair, her nails dragging along my scalp, and the pain's as good as the pleasure.

I bury a grin when her lush hips push forward, seeking contact. One hand to her waist, I keep her in place as my tongue swirls over the rosy-brown nipple. Again and again, until she's writhing even as she kneels before me. She cups my jaw with the sweetness of a lover, feverishly rakes her nails down the back of my neck when I suck, hard.

This moment, this woman . . . There's no one else for me.

Now, my brain urges, *tell her that you love her* now.

Pulling back, my breath wafts over her breast and Mina shivers. *I love you.* I cup the back of her thighs, thumbs brushing the underside of her ass. She sways forward, naked from the waist up. *I love you.* Because I'm a goddamn sap, I press one palm to her chest and measure the heart rate speeding along.

It sprints like mine, tripping over itself as her breaths come shallow and quick.

I love you.

"I'm tired of feeling like I'm not good enough," Mina whispers with her lids squeezed shut and her heart pounding a mile a minute under my hand. "For the first time in my life, I feel like I'm doing the right thing. Not because I'm running from my parents and trying to play rebel to their every demand, but because it's what *I* want."

An unfamiliar edge to her tone raises the hair on arms. A sixth sense. A *spidey* sense, if you will, similar to the one I felt moments before I lifted Brynn's veil and found my ex-fiancée nibbling on her bottom lip and shooting harried glances at the pews.

Good news: I know Mina isn't about to marry someone else.

Bad news: the unease punching its way through my organs is not subsiding, not even a little and *especially* not when Mina begins to drum her fingers on the outside of her thigh.

I lean my back against the edge of the mattress, tearing my gaze from those tapping fingers to her naked tits and then up to her stark, *restless* expression. The question leaves me on a rough exhalation: "Why would you be playing rebel?"

"Because"—the tapping picks up speed—"they've always wanted me to find someone like *you*."

The heat dissipates just like that. "I'm gonna need more, Mina. What does *someone like me* entail?"

Her gaze falls to the carpet between us and her hands come up to cover her naked breasts, and I practically *feel* her retreat within herself. *Goddammit.* Under her breath, she mutters, "Someone good."

My fingers clench tight into fists at my sides. "Because *that's* a turn-off, having someone at your side who puts you first."

"Nick, it's not that—"

"Then tell me."

Her sharp intake of breath lifts her shoulders, and my gaze catches on the words I picked out for her. *Without the night there are no stars.* Ironic, because it feels like we're going straight into a period of darkness.

"You don't understand. You *can't* possibly understand when your parents have always stood by your side, no matter what." She scrambles to yank on the T-shirt, concealing her nakedness from me like she's closing me out from her vulnerability. It's not without a little dose of irony that the Stamos Restoration logo falls flat over her heart. She's wearing my shirt, and yet this is the first time since Toula's wedding and that damn elevator that I've felt like we're on two different planes, cruising in two different directions.

Mina pulls hard on the hem of the T-shirt as her voice cracks with barely suppressed emotion. "You wanted to date Brynn? Go right ahead, they told you. You want to go on a *dating show*? No one stopped you, Nick. *No one.* My entire life I've dreamt and celebrated my achievements on my own because—*newsflash*—nothing I did appeased my parents. But I could turn it all the way around and make them proud, for once, if I did just one thing: bring home a nice Greek boy."

Harsh laughter pushes its way up and out of me. "We're back to that again, huh?" I jump up to my feet, unable to just sit here. I need to move, I need to— I whirl around, anger sharpening my tone like a serrated blade as I loom over Mina. She drops her head back, unwilling to stand down, even though she's almost a foot shorter than me.

"So, I'm good enough to fuck but not good enough for more?" I've been there. I've stood at the altar, humiliated to my core when the woman I thought I loved turned out to love someone else. I'd rather take a punch to the gonads then go through the misery of that again. "And all because you're trying to stick it to your parents by not giving in?"

"I'm trying to tell you that I want you!"

My chin jerks back from the force of her shout.

With a hand pressed to her heart, Mina goes on, passion ripping through every word. "I want *you*, Nick, not because of your Greekness or how nice you are but because of how you make me *feel*. For once, I feel special. For once, I feel like I'm exactly where I belong. For once"—her features splinter right in front of me, and my heart shouts *go to her!* even as I force myself to stand completely still—"I feel as though I'm not seen as less than or the girl with the problems or Bad Girl Mina." She swipes angrily at her eyes, thumbs stroking along the damp tears at the crests of her cheeks, and my heart takes another heavy beating. *Fuck*. As much as I want to comfort her and kiss away her tears, I want to hear what she has to say even more.

"You enter a room and my body comes alive, my *soul* comes alive." Her shoulders square off like she's going into battle—against me? *Or against herself*. The thought comes out of left field but won't loosen its claws. "My entire life has been one great temporary longing. Get out of my parents' house. Open a hair salon. Be my own boss and create my own rules. And then shit hit the fan, and you threw all those temporary longings—all those dreams I'd harbored so close to my heart for so many years—straight into chaos until knowing what I want out of life isn't so clear-cut anymore."

"It's not an either-or situation," I grind out, feeling sick to my stomach. This conversation—this *anger* that's festering beneath her words—isn't even about us. It's about *her* and about the damage that existing in her parents' orbit wreaked on her. I feel like an idiot for not seeing it sooner. For not predicting that this fallout would be inevitable.

You can't accept love from someone else when you don't even love yourself, and Mina . . . God, listening to her now it's a wonder she doesn't hear the self-loathing in her own voice. I could bandage up her insecurities and self-doubt real nice, kiss them better, but at the end of the day, there'd be no hiding from the truth.

And the truth is that Mina is so caught up in proving her parents wrong that she can't even see that by loving me doesn't mean her own dreams need to take a backseat to the relationship.

I'm not her father. She isn't her mother. Can't she see that?

Chest hurting like I've taken a mallet to the heart, I step back, needing space. "I'm not the kind of guy—Greek or otherwise—who swoops in and strips you of everything that makes you *you*, Ermione. I wouldn't do that to a random stranger I just met, and I certainly wouldn't do it to the woman I love."

Mina blanches.

And the L-word hangs out in the open like a white, tattered flag of surrender. It hangs there, even when I don't take it back. And it sure as hell doesn't go anywhere while she tangles her fingers in the shirt I lent her and stumbles over her words.

"Nick, I—" She rubs her lips together, her gaze darting every which way but to me. "I-I don't know what to say."

Say that you love me.

I stare at her, waiting, hoping, and then she's staring back —and the divide between us grows.

I let my lids fall shut and tip my head back and do nothing to mask my expression. *This* right here, this moment of truth, is by far the worst pain I've ever felt. Worse than even standing at the altar as my bride sprinted from the church with her douchebag lover clutching the train of her lace dress.

Because what I feel for Mina eclipses anything I ever felt for Brynn or Savannah Rose or any of those blind dates I went on over the years.

I love her and *she doesn't know what to say back.*

Are you really that surprised? I shouldn't be. I'm the guy who does relationships and she's the girl who prefers no-strings-attached flings. In theory, there was no other path for us *but* this one.

My heart calls bullshit on that score.

I take a single step back, arms down by my sides. "I'm gonna sleep upstairs in Dom's room."

"No, please." Mina darts in front of me, blocking my exit. Her expression is nothing short of panic—but it's that ever-present restlessness that solidifies my decision, however much it kills me. She needs to figure her own shit out without me hovering over her shoulder. And if she can't do that, then I . . . Well, I'll figure it out. Because if there's one thing I know, it's that pushing her into accepting me—a nice, Greek boy—when doing so makes her feel like she's caving to her parent's demands, is only going to be the start of our troubles.

We can't move forward when she's stuck in the tangled web of her past.

When I move to the right, she mimics my step, her hands up and facing me as though she can stop me from leaving. "Nick, I like you so, so much. I don't know why I can't say the words back when I *feel* so damn much for you that it terrifies me."

"It's not the word that matters."

"Then why—"

"It's that you have that look on your face, the same one from the night I showed up at your parent's house and you were practically jumping out of your skin."

When we stepped into this room yesterday, I'd envisioned telling Mina I loved her a million different ways. All of them had a single thing in common: she threw her arms around me as soon as I said the words.

Stupid. Maláka. Fucking fanciful, romantic bullshit.

Voice gritty like gravel, I grunt, "You look like you want to *run*, Mina." Changing trajectories, I grab my duffel from the floor and stuff yesterday's clothes inside the top flap. "I can handle being the only one saying I love you, but I've been down this path before and I'm not gonna ignore the signs again that are telling me we're on a ticking clock."

"I'm not Brynn."

I meet her gaze and let it all out. "No, you're not." I hook the duffel bag's strap over my shoulder. "But I can't . . . I'm going to be blunt here, Mina. You think I looked broken when you found me after the wedding? How I felt in that moment would be unicorns and rainbows to how I'd be if *you* were the one to leave me at the altar. I'm not looking for a repeat situation. You need time to really think about what you want from me, from us, and I'm not gonna sit here and make you feel guilty for not sayin' the words back."

Her brows furrow together. "So you're doing the walking first this time? Is that how this is going to play out? You scurry off because you're worried that I'll do what Brynn did to you?"

"You already ran, Ermione. You might be standing right here in front of me but, mentally, you've checked out because you're scared." I stare down into her honey eyes. "You know I'm right."

She sucks in a harsh, reedy breath. "Please don't give up on me. I need to—I need to . . ."

Against my better judgment, I lean down and brush a soft kiss to her forehead. I soak up her scent, wishing that I could rewind tonight and hit PLAY with her shirtless in front of me and stars in her eyes. I feel her fingers grip the fabric of my shirt.

Give her space. Let her think.

This doesn't have to be the end—even if it sure as hell feels that way.

I skirt past her on my way to the door, where I glance over my shoulder to look back at her. "*S'agapo,* Ermione." *I love you.* "But I can't be the one to tell you why loving me back scares you; only you can figure that out. When you do . . . come find me. I'll wait. I'll always wait."

Fisting the knob, I pull open the door.

"I wish it didn't terrify me," she whispers raggedly from behind me.

My shoulders pull up. "*Kai ego, agape mou, kai ego.*" *Me too, my love, me too.*

Dom says nothing when I knock on his door two minutes later. He only looks from my bag hooked over my shoulder to my face, then backs up wordlessly to let me inside the room. His is smaller than the one I shared with Mina, and while he climbs back into bed, I sprawl out on the floor with a spare duvet and a pillow.

There's no fireplace to keep the space warm, and soon the chill of Mina's emotional mountains seep into my bones. The icy night keeps me company into the early morning while sleep proves completely elusive.

I never break hearts—but tonight I broke two.

36

NICK

"*Where is he?"*

Balancing the sledgehammer's wooden handle on my palm, I lean back from where I've been going to town on age-old drywall, and eye Vince, who's standing closest to the museum's front door. "Don't let her in."

He gives me a side-eye to rival all side-eyes, his hand already reaching out to the doorknob. "I don't have a death wish."

I chuckle, low. "Effie's not gonna kill you, Miceli."

"I'm going to kill you all if you don't open this door right now!"

Mark doesn't even bother to disguise his snicker. "She sounds pissed, boss man."

That's because Effie *is* pissed. After an awkwardly silent three-hour car ride back to Boston from Bethel, Mina asked for me to drop her off at my sister's house instead of at her parents'.

It took approximately twenty-three minutes after that for Effie to blow up my phone with texts that can be summed up by the following:

What are you, a MONSTER? Who walks away from a girl like Mina, huh?

I can't believe you left her high and dry.

Do I need to come over to your place and personally help you remove your head from your ass?

ANSWER ME, NICHOLAS, OR SO HELP ME GOD, I WILL PERSONALLY MAKE YOU CRY.

I haven't cried since I was seven years old when I somehow managed to crush my junk at my elementary school's jungle gym. For the record, tire swings are hell personified if not treated with care.

"Nick! Nick, you open this door right now!"

At the telltale sound of fists banging, Bill's left eyebrow starts to twitch. "Should we let her in?"

And have her berate me for ignoring her calls and texts for all of three days? Sure, why not. It's not like I'm not miserable enough already after everything that went down in Maine.

Ignoring the pinch in my heart, I jerk the head of the sledgehammer toward the door. "Go ahead."

Vince and Bill shove Mark forward with commentary about him having survived prison, so an angry woman should be no trouble at all. If they honestly think that, then they don't know Effie. But they praise Mark's boldness, gussying him up to the front door like a sacrifice to the gods, then promptly turn tail and shout at me that they're taking a lunch break.

When the door swings open, Effie spares Mark a once-over that could drop a man cold, then swings those dark eyes of hers over to me. She jabs a finger in my direction. "You," she growls.

"Me," I confirm with a nod.

"You—"

I cut my little sister off with a glance over to my employee. "Mark, get lunch with the guys."

He doesn't need to be told twice.

Scurrying from the room, he leaves me alone with Effie, to which she wastes no time in verbally sinking her talons into my flesh. "You're being the absolute *worst* right now," she snaps, hands on her hips as she swivels on her heels and takes in the renovation project. "I just want you to know that. Also, this place smells like shit."

It smells like sawdust, mold, and, yes, shit.

Gotta love the stray cat population in Cambridge.

I drop the sledgehammer on my makeshift work desk and get right to it. "I'm giving her time to think, Effie. There's nothing wrong with that."

She makes a buzzing sound with her tongue. "Incorrect, *Kyrie* Stamos."

Rolling my eyes, I cut the corner around the desk and lean my ass up against it, arms crossed over my chest. "Effie, do you remember that time Sarah dumped you after you were all up in arms about opening your tour business in Charleston of all places?"

My sister's mouth purses. "First, Charleston is known for its ghostly lore. Second"—her mouth flattens even more—"of course I remember. I was devastated."

Understatement of the year. For no less than a week straight, Effie had looked like a walking zombie. She didn't sleep. She didn't shower. All until she came to the lightbulb realization that the *only* reason she wanted Charleston as her home base was because Sarah had asked her to move in together and my sister had freaked out.

Not unlike Mina had done when I said that I loved her.

My stomach drops with the memory of Maine, and I ruthlessly shove the emotion aside. To my sister, I say, "Sarah gave you time to figure out what you wanted. She didn't pressure you. She didn't hound you for an answer. She let *you* come to your own decision." I swallow, hard. "I'm doing the same with Mina."

Effie narrows her eyes, lashes fluttering sharply enough to appear lethal. What the hell are women putting on those things nowadays? Miniature knives?

My sister turns her nose up at me. "You're being a chicken shit."

Even my ass clenches in indignation. "I'm not being—"

"You are." She sticks a finger toward me, wiggling it around like she's drawing abstract shapes in the air. "You think Mina's scared? How about the fact that the last time you went AWOL like this, it was because Brynn ditched you?" Effie meets my gaze, and I'm not at all surprised to find the love mingling with annoyance there. It's a natural emotional cocktail for the two us. "Mina isn't Brynn, Nick."

I groan loudly. "I know she's not Brynn. There's no comparison between the two." Because whereas my ex-fiancée thought of no one but herself, Mina is selfless, kind, and—I slam my eyes shut. The biggest difference of all is that Mina is my best friend and the one person I can't imagine living without.

Oblivious to my inner thoughts, my sister rants her heart out. "But you're worried she won't love you back, just like Brynn didn't love you back and Savannah Rose didn't—"

"I didn't love Savannah." Feeling uncomfortable under her astute assessment, I re-cross my arms and shift my weight. "And I can promise you, what I feel for Mina is . . ." I lift my arms, hands curving over the back of my skull in frustration. Blowing out a breath, I catch my sister's gaze and hope to make her understand. "Mina needs space to figure out what *she* wants without my presence making her feel guilty that she's done something wrong by not loving me back."

"She loves you back, *maláka*." Effie storms forward, her

purse flying open as she digs around inside. With her features pulled tight, she yanks out her cell phone and shoves it into my hand. "I'm betraying my best friend's confidence right now, I hope you know that. I told her . . . I told her that the two of you would never work out. I was wrong."

I blink down at her, all mock-innocence because there's not an older brother on the face of the planet who can hear those beautiful words and not give their little sister some grief. "I'm sorry," I say, leaning in with my hand curled around my ear, "what was that? I couldn't hear you."

"I. Was. Wrong." Her glare sings murder. "Happy now?" She waves a dismissive hand in the air. "Of course you are."

Glancing down, I run my thumb along the blacked-out screen. "Effie, I don't need to read your texts with Mina." Nothing about that screams, *good idea*. Their friendship is as sacred as mine is with Mina or mine with Effie. "I've got no interest in breaking your girl code or whatever."

I don't think I'm imagining the relief in my sister's eyes as she takes back her phone. "She loves you, Nick. Can't you see that?"

"What I see is that she needs time to process that being with me doesn't mean she needs to give up all that she's worked toward. I'm not her dad, Ef." Or her adoptive father, at any rate. "I'm not gonna be like that *maláka* who raised her to feel *less than* for following her own damn heart."

Silence permeates the museum's front entrance as Effie blinks up at me. Her mouth forms a little *O* and her brows knit together as she clamps her jaw shut. Open, closed. Open, closed. Whatever she's thinking about, she's thinking hard on it. Finally, she says in a voice so soft I need to lean in to hear it, "You love her, *adelphé.*"

She whispers the Greek word for "brother," and I dip my chin in a silent *yes*. "So much, Effie. And if she chooses to be with me, I want her to know that *she* came to that decision with a clear mind." I shove my hands in the front pockets of my paint-splattered work jeans. "I told her to come find me when she's ready. I'm gonna be patient. I've got all the patience in the world."

Patience.

Just like the script she has inked on the bottom of her foot. Just like the way she's lived her entire life, always taking measured steps to get where she needs to go, knowing all the while that when a dream is meant to come true it will. And never before she's ready.

My heart pounds erratically in my chest and my damn palms grow clammy.

Exactly how they were supposed to when getting ready to propose to Savannah Rose.

The irony isn't lost on me.

If Mina can spend thirty years practicing patience, then I've got more than enough in me to last a matter of weeks, months, or however long it takes for her to realize that she's stuck with me. For today. For tomorrow. For the rest of our lives.

"Effie?"

Her familiar dark eyes zero in on my face. "Yeah?"

"I'm glad Mina's had you by her side all these years."

Color flushes to her cheeks and she blinks rapidly up at the ceiling. "Stop it, *maláka*. You're gonna make me cry."

I shrug. "Just telling you the truth."

More blinking ensues. "My mascara is going to bleed—stop saying nice things."

"I'm a nice guy, Ef."

"Yeah, you are." Her lips pull up in a grin. "I'm glad Mina has a nice guy like you to love her."

She says it without heat, and I drag her into a hug, propping my chin on the top of her head. "*Kai ego,* Effie, me too."

37

To: Mina Pappas <mina@agapehairsalon.com>
From: Nick Stamos
<stamos@stamosrestoration.com>
Subject: who you are

Disclaimer: Don't respond to this email. I'm writing it because I wanted to get some thoughts off my chest. Thoughts about you. Thoughts about what I see when I look at you. This email is for you, Ermione, and not for us. I hope that makes sense.

All my life, I've always known two things about you:

1. You're a pain in my ass.
2. There is no kinder soul than you.

Every monumental event in my life has you written in the seams—and I'm not the only one who's experienced your friendship. The night of your prom, you spent hours dolling up the girls who made your life hell at school. When Effie and Sarah were on the rocks, you never picked sides even though Effie is your oldest friend. You listened to their heartache and celebrated when they got back together. When Katya moved down south for graduate school, you took time off with no pay so that you could help her make the trek . . . which *you* paid for. (And, yeah, this is one of those things I only know because Effie told me).

When your *Theio* Prodromos passed away in the car accident, it was you who hopped on the first flight to Greece to see him in the hospital before he died. It was you who helped your grandparents with the funeral arrangements. You did it without thought because someone you cared about was hurt.

What I'm trying to say—and maybe failing at—is that you deserve so much more than what your parents have given you. But what I'm also trying to say is, blood isn't everything and you are so much more than you see.

Not because of your Greekness or your "otherness" but because I've never met another person who can make someone feel like they belong—not the way you can.

You may be Bad Girl Mina Pappas.

You may be Barbie-Loving Mina.

But you are also Ermione Pappas, and to put it bluntly, there is no one else like you.

Hugs,

Nick

38

MINA

No one bats an eye when I speed-walk through the lobby of Effie's building looking like an absolute mess exactly one week post Bethel, Maine.

I'm wearing yesterday's sweatpants—honest to God sweats, not a cute pair of leggings—a Patriots sweatshirt that has a coffee stain over the mascot (which is unfortunately placed over my nipple), and two different sneakers.

The right is black and the left is gray and if that's not a metaphor for my life then I don't know what is.

"Slow it down, lady," one guy mutters in a thick Dorchester accent when we bump elbows near the elevator. "We're all goin' to the same place." His gaze falls to my feet, narrowing imperceptibly. "You mean to be wearin' two different shoes?"

No, I just decided to hell-with-it when I walked out of my apartment forty minutes ago. Of all the sarcastic retorts in my arsenal, I practice some award-winning self-restraint and only throw him a droll look. "It's a new trend, sir. All the kids are doing it nowadays."

He grumbles under his breath, and I've got no doubt that

it's highly uncomplimentary if his middle finger skating up alongside his temple is any indication.

Lucky for me, I only need to put up with his ba-humbug attitude for three floors. He gets off with another disgruntled look in my direction, and I jab a finger at the CLOSE DOORS button once again.

My mouth hitches up at the memory of blockading Nick in the elevator at Toula's wedding. And then I'm not just thinking about the elevator but the email I printed out and stuffed into my purse.

The email that Nick sent me just two hours ago.

Because the man is not content with only turning my life virtually upside down. He wants to worm his way into every breath, every crevice, and every single moment of my existence. I would hate him for it, if one week isn't already long enough to know that my days feel emptier without him.

In the week that we've been back in Boston, I've thrown my entire self into *Agape*. I finalized interviews and scheduled them for next week. I went to a local thrift shop to find original (albeit cheap) artwork to hang on the walls. I talked to the building inspector who gave me the thumbs-up—not only can I move back into my apartment and out of my childhood bedroom over the weekend, but *Agape* is ready to rock n' roll . . . even if I have only stepped inside for a matter of minutes on the day the inspector came to visit.

The salon reminds me of Nick. My lifelong dream—my *one* temporary longing—has the memory of Nick Stamos imprinted all over it.

So, I stayed away. Because Nick told me to figure my shit out and being in *Agape*—appropriately named "love" in Greek—only reminds me of him. Of *us*. And the fact that speaking the words "I love you" anywhere outside of my head leaves me feeling lightheaded.

Nick's email might not have explicitly said those three

little words but I heard them all the same. I heard their resonance in every comma, every letter, and for a girl who hates to read, I've poured over his email no less than twenty times since it hit my inbox.

He loves me. He loves me. He loves me.

It's the mantra of the week and I'm terrified—terrified for all the wrong reasons—and it's desperation that turns my hand into a fist as I bang on my best friend's door.

My knuckles thunder away as I knock, knock, knock, and then finally the door cracks open and I don't wait for Effie to welcome me in or kiss my cheeks or give me a hug. I burst through like a pebble springing from a sling shot.

"Are you wearing different-colored shoes?" she deadpans as I push past her.

"I'm having a moment."

Effie slides her gaze down over my outfit. "Understatement of the century, I think."

"It's your brother's fault."

"My brother made you come here looking like that? He's not heartless. And you should really burn that sweatshirt. The stain is unfortunate."

Ignoring her side commentary, I dig through my purse for Nick's email. Like it's a Wanted ad and I'm not sure I want to touch it, I pinch the corner between my thumb and forefinger. "Do you see this?"

My best friend looks from me to the paper and back to me again. "Do I need to get my glasses for this?"

"Yes."

Effie nods, then tilts her head to the side. "Should I bust out the Tito's too?"

"Might as well." I plunk down on her sofa, kicking off my mismatched sneakers, and smooth the email over my lap. The words stare back at me, all blurring together. For once, it's not my dyslexia playing tricks on me. Nope, that would be emotion bubbling its way up to the surface and threatening its presence with a possible tear. Or two. "Do you have tissues?"

"Are you planning to cry?" Effie asks, not sounding at all horrified by the prospect.

"I might, I don't know."

It's probably best that she doesn't know I've been a crying mess all week. Because what thirty-year-old woman can *feel* the most important words of her life inside her heart but can't find the strength to say them out loud?

As Effie trots off to grab our—*my*—supplies, I envision Nick as he uttered the words that tilted my world on its axis: *and I certainly wouldn't do it to the woman I love.* Since the age of six, I've seen my best friend's older brother impassive, I've seen him throw his head back in laughter, I've seen him so hot for me that I'm sure I'll combust at first contact. But I've never seen him like he was on our last night in Maine.

Resigned.

Like he'd already expected my response.

Only, words, as they always have, failed me when I needed to *tell* him—not show, as is my habit—that I care so damn much that I felt crippled when he walked out that door.

Rock bottom, you're a goddamn bitch.

"Here."

On cue, the bottle of Tito's appears before me. I take it from Effie with a pathetic sniff, twisting the top off and tossing it on the glass coffee table. "Please, read this." I slip the paper from my lap and place it down on the cushion to my right. "And then feel free to tell me how much of an idiot I am."

The sofa sinks with Effie's weight. Quietly, she picks up the email her brother sent me. She says nothing as she reads and I do nothing but stare at the label on the vodka bottle, unable to suck down any of the booze.

I don't want to wash away the pain.

That's been my lifelong M.O. Anytime the hurt and sadness and frustration has carved another notch in my flesh, I've shut it down and focused on *Agape* and on the dream. If Nick is my kryptonite, then my hair salon is my crutch.

Put all your love and hopes into the dream and nothing else can disappoint you. Not your parents or your peers who don't believe in you. Not anyone.

Until I disappointed myself by chasing Nick away.

My socked toes curl in as I lean forward and put the vodka on the table. "Your brother loves me, Ef," I say to my best friend, my voice hollow.

I hear the paper crinkle in her grasp. "I know."

"And I'm an asshole." I don't dab at my eyes or reach for a tissue, even when tears well up behind my eyes. "I'm that asshole who just *stood* there while he opened up. I wanted to say the words. They were there and they were ready and I-I couldn't say *anything*."

There have been many times over the years when the words wouldn't come and I stammered and clammed up. Visions of Greek school flit before me, one embarrassing moment after another of impatient faces and tapping feet. Other memories, too, of hearing my dad berate me for whatever it was that day, and yet me saying nothing at all.

From a young age, words—and, yes, sometime speech—have never been my friends.

But as I darted in front of Nick to beg him to stay, I have never felt so betrayed by my body as I did in that moment. He accused me of wanting to run, and he's not wrong. I *did*, I *do*, but only because I'm tired, so damn tired, of feeling like there's something so intrinsically wrong with me.

"First," Effie tells me, reaching out to poke me in the upper arm, "you're not an asshole."

"You say that because you love me."

"And that brings me to point number two." She holds up her index and middle fingers like two mocking bunny ears. "Answer me this, how many people have you ever said *I love you* to? Accurate count here, please."

"I don't know. That's a weird question."

"It's really not." Effie scoots in close to me, until our thighs are flush and she's flattening the email over our side-by-side knees. "You don't say the words often, Mina. Not to me, not to Sarah, not to your siblings."

Staring down at Nick's words, I suck my bottom lip in and try to sort through my chaotic thoughts. Do I really not tell the people I love how much I care about them? I know that I show them in other ways, but . . . "People lie, Ef."

My whole life has been a front. *Baba* wanted the world to believe that I was his and Mama wanted us all to pretend that she didn't sleep with some unknown American dude who acted as the prodigal sperm donor. One lie bleeds into the next, and promises, vows, and, yes, love, are the first to be sacrificed to preserve the façade.

I watched it firsthand with my parents.

And their lies continued and poisoned me, too. How many days did I walk into the house to hear them arguing about what to do with me? How many times did they lecture me about responsibility and taking care of my younger siblings while they couldn't even be bothered to come home before dark?

"Nick's not lying to you," Effie says, nudging me in the side. "Are you scared that he is?"

No. Maybe. I clear my throat. Drop my chin as I gather the right words to piece together. God, it's almost *painful* to reveal this corner of my soul. And when I speak, my voice emerges broken. "I'm scared that he'll wake up one day and realize he could have someone so much more."

"More than *what?*"

Harsh laughter rips from my chest. "More than *me,* Effie. Someone without dyslexia and daddy issues and insecurities running a mile deep and—"

A hand collides sharply with the middle of my back, knocking the wind right out of me. While I gasp for air, Effie points a threatening finger in my face. "I would have gone for your head but I'm not trying to leave visible damage." She pokes me right on the nose. "Do you hear yourself? You're talking like your parents. *More than.*" An aggrieved, disbelieving snort greets my ears. "My brother adores you. Look at the damn email he wrote after he *specifically* told me that he was going to give you space. And he couldn't even help himself! You stomped on his heart and he still wanted to comfort you."

Because Nick Stamos is the best kind of man.

Because he's as sexy as he is sweet.

Because he's so much more than a girl like me could ever hope to have by her side.

"Wipe that pitiful look right off your face, Ermione." Effie leaps from the couch, paces the room, then twirls back around before coming to stand directly in front of me. "Tell me one thing you like about my brother."

I blink up at her. "Is that a trick question?"

"Is that a—" She cuts herself off, seeking guidance from the popcorn-raised ceiling. Or maybe she's looking for strength. It's honestly tough to tell. "I'm not waiting around all day. One thing, Mina. Now."

Far be it from me to argue with my best friend when she's on a mission.

I answer off the cuff, completely on instinct. "I love the way he makes me laugh without even trying." Unconsciously, my thumb makes its way to my mouth, as though wanting to trace the smile threatening to peek through my week-long misery. "He says the most *ridiculous* things, you know? It's so out of character but I know he gets a kick out of surprising me. *Shocking me*, is how he puts it."

Effie folds her arms across her chest. "Give me another."

"His patience. Whether he's explaining something to Vince or Bill or Mark for the twentieth time or working on one of his sculptures, he's got the patience of a saint." *Oh, Saint Nick.* My heart pounds a little faster. "He balances me that way . . . the yin to my yang." I peer up at my best friend. "Is that cheesy?"

She gives me a lopsided smile. "No, Mina, it's not." A small pause. "Another."

The back of my throat itches as I shift on the sofa. "He makes me feel special—no, *adored*. He says this thing to me whenever I'm on the verge of blabbing something embarrassing." I lower my voice to mimic his deeper pitch. "*There's nothing you can say that'll make me look at you any differently.*" Oh, God, will the tears not *stop*? I'm like a freakin' sieve right now. I motion for the tissues and Effie plucks one from the box and pushes it into my hand. "It's more than feeling adored. With him, I feel respected, valued, like we're equals. Like what I have to say *matters.*"

The way my mother has never been on par with my father.

The realization sits with the weight of a stone in my belly. Briefly, I let my lids fall shut. Maybe Mama and *Baba* were true partners before she cheated on him. Maybe his insecurities and distrust clouded their entire relationship. Or maybe my dad really is just a controlling jerk who feels the need to keep everyone in their assigned seat.

But I've never remained sitting. I push back and challenge him and get tattoos when he hates them and date American boys when he curls his lip at the mere thought. I purchased a hair salon when he effectively told me to get married and retreat back to the household.

My adoptive father might view me as a threat to his perceived hierarchy but Nick . . . I glance down at his email one last time. My best friend's older brother challenges me, too, but he challenges me to take risks and be a better person and face my fears instead of running away.

I love him.

Truly, madly, deeply.

"One more, Mina," Effie pushes gently. "Give me one more, that's all."

"I love him." I exhale quietly, hands folded in my lap. "I think I loved him when I was seventeen and he danced me around your mom's living room. I think I loved him even on his wedding day because the relief I felt—" I break off with an uneasy laugh, but at Effie's patient expression, I let myself continue even as my cheeks burn with embarrassment. "We laid in that bed and all night I thought one thing: *maybe now*. Maybe now he would look at me as something more than his little sister's friend. Maybe now he would hold my hand instead of letting our fingers kiss, and nothing more. Maybe now . . . Maybe now he would *see* me and know, without a doubt, that I was always meant to be his and he was always meant to be mine."

"There's no doubt in my mind, *koukla*," says an oh-so-familiar voice from behind me, "I'm already yours."

39

NICK

Slowly, like she's in a horror movie and piss-her-pants terrified to see the axe-murderer standing behind her, Mina turns and spots me standing in the doorway leading into the kitchen. Her beautiful honey eyes are round in her makeup-free face, and those perfectly pink lips of hers part on an audible gasp.

"N-Nick! How, um, *lovely* to see you here!" She shoots a dirty glare over at my sister. Whatever communication she's trying to pass along via Eyebrow Code (the new and unimproved Morse Code) goes unreceived because Effie launches up from the sofa like it's caught fire.

"I have to pick up my laundry from the laundromat."

Mina's mouth gapes open. "Seriously? *That's* your getaway excuse? You have a washer and dryer down the hall!"

"It's broken."

"You're a liar."

"No, what I'm *trying* to do is give you and my older brother a chance to talk." Effie wriggles her fingers in the air at me. "Lucky for you, he was already here when you showed up. We were planning to go to dinner so he could spend the next three hours talking about how much he misses you."

I feel the rush of heat all the way from my chest to my face. "*Effie.*"

She rolls her eyes. "I'm leaving." Only, she doesn't make it more than halfway to the front door before she whirls around on her heels and stares me down. "Before I go, house rules—no sex."

Like I've had the wind knocked out of me, a hoarse cough gurgles to life and I pound a fist against my chest. *Gamóto.* I'm gonna kill her and enjoy burying her body. Out loud, I croak, "I have no idea why you're looking at me when you say that."

Her chin hikes up. "Because you're a man and all men are horny, and I refuse to have dried semen on my furniture."

Dried semen on her furniture . . .?

Christ, forget killing her. Someone just grab a knife and put me out of my misery. Huffing out a laugh, I scrub my hand over the side of my flushed face. "Please, say no more."

With her gaze narrowed on me, Effie clucks her tongue and then turns to Mina, completely dismissing me. "And you . . ." Her expression softens almost immediately. "I love you, *filinída.* No, I love you like a *sister* not just a friend. But him right there?" She gestures to me, not once looking away from Mina's face. "He loves you the way Sarah loves me. Best friend. Lover. Soulmate." With a small smile, she steps back. "Be brave and trust."

Silence invades the room as Effie lets herself out of her own condo with an undeniable pep to her step.

I give myself leave to soak in Mina's presence as she pushes to her feet and comes around the side of the sofa. Each step reveals more of her outfit: socks with holes in the toes, a pair of baggy sweatpants that give no indication that she's curvy in all the right places beneath all that fabric, a Pats sweatshirt with a stain . . .

As if noticing the direction of my attention, she clamps a hand over her breast and grins sheepishly. "I didn't expect to see you here."

A soft chuckle warms my chest. "You mean you would have worn shoes that matched, if you knew?"

She growls beneath her breath. The sound is cute as all hell and makes me want to smile. "You heard that too?" she asks, dread deepening her voice.

"It was hard not to." I jerk my thumb over my right shoulder, pointing toward the kitchen. "I was pouring myself some water when you came flying in here like a bat outta hell."

If possible, her cheeks turn an even pinker hue. "I didn't . . . I don't . . ." Her throat works with a hard swallow. "I wanted to get my thoughts in order before I saw you. I didn't want to lose the words."

I didn't want to lose the words.

God, this girl. She breaks me, challenges me, and in just a few sentences, cuts me right at the knees. *Patience, have some patience.* I told her that night in Maine that when she was ready to talk, I'd be here. I said nothing of the sort in the email I spent the last few days putting together, mainly because I wanted her to feel pressure-free.

But it's hard showcasing patience when all I want to do is push her back against the sofa and kiss her. One kiss for every day we've spent apart. Except not even that is enough.

Shoving my hands deep into the front pockets of my jeans, I try to make her smile. "Want me to wait outside while you think about it?" I cock my head to the side, pretending to give the idea considerable thought. "I can come back when you're ready."

"What? *No.*"

Heat seeps into my limbs, hope dogging its tail. "Just a suggestion, Ermione."

"I'm not a fan."

Taking a risk, I step forward. Half a foot at most, nothing more. A way to test the waters. I may have heard almost everything she said while I was camped out in the kitchen like a voyeur, but I'm not about to push my luck unless she gives me the go-ahead with blaring sirens and obnoxious confetti cannons.

I'm playing the long game here. Anything less won't do.

Cutting my gaze up from her stained sweatshirt to her face, I rest my weight on my left foot. "What are you a fan of, then?"

"*You,* Nick."

Well, damn.

I blink, then blink again, then do the very manly thing of coughing to keep from showing that I might—maybe—like that statement of hers a little too much.

She matches my step with one of her own, the hem of her sweats dragging along the hardwood floor. "I need to tell you something, and I need you to be patient with me . . . even if it takes me a few tries to get it out the way I want." She pauses, and the mask of pleasantry slips from her features to expose a desperation that matches mine. "Can you do that for me?"

Yes.

If this ends with her in my arms, I'll do anything she fucking wants.

"Go ahead." I tip my head in a small nod, my voice nothing more than grit and want. "I'm not going anywhere."

Her shoulders freefall with a relieved exhale that feels like a breeze kissing my skin. "This is . . . I want to—" She closes her lids, and I watch her mouth move to form the words, *You can do this*. Her silent encouragement to herself kicks my pulse into overdrive. "The first time I saw you, you were building a blanket fort in your old bedroom. I peeked inside when you were putting on the final touches. You asked if I wanted to join, and I remember how badly I wanted to say yes."

Mouth dry, I roll my lips together and regret leaving the water glass in the kitchen. I feel parched, but I've got a feeling that has more to do with the woman in front of me than actual dehydration. She turns me inside out. "You crept into my room once Effie fell asleep."

"Yeah, I did." She gives me a wobbly, tremulous grin. "We were in middle school when you started walking Effie and me home. Do you remember? The days when she stayed late for soccer practice were my favorite. We argued, as always, but I-I lived for those moments when I was *so* sure we were about to hold hands." Visibly swallowing, she moves closer. Only one step, but I feel the new proximity like a fiery brand to my skin. "But nothing compared to those summers in Greece. I—God, I can't believe I'm about to admit this."

Blood thunders in my head. I'm unaware of my feet moving, carrying me forward until my chest is inches away from hers. When she inhales sharply, I feel it, too. When her fingers curl in tightly, I put my hope on the map and slip my hand into hers. And then I repeat the words that she holds close to her heart: "Nothing you say will make me look at you any different."

Because I love you.

"Do you remember that day on the beach when I lost my bikini top?"

I give a low laugh. "How could I ever forget?" Against all better judgment, my dick had a different perspective view on the situation—particularly when I awoke each morning from wet dreams of a topless Mina and my hand gripping my dick like my only mission in life was to get off.

Mina tugs on the hem of her sweatshirt with her free

hand. "I was embarrassed, obviously, but more so because of how much I wished you had made a move."

"If I remember correctly," I drawl, "I almost died in the riptide."

"Your memory is faulty." She rolls her eyes—*there's* that sass of hers I love so much. "You came up for air within ten seconds."

"Longest ten seconds of my life when I was robbed of the opportunity to keep staring at your tits."

Mina throws her head back with a laugh. "After *that* comment, I feel better confessing how that was the first time I ever . . . *you know what*."

Fuck. Me.

Cheeks flushing, she presses her palms to the sides of her face. "Yup, okay I just said that. *Moving on*." I have no interest in moving on, now that I know Mina spent years playing with herself to fantasies about me, but she plows forward, clearly determined to air out all her deep, dark secrets. "The point of all of this is, I've always liked you, Nick. The night of your wedding, I felt so torn—stuck between wanting to do the *right* thing and offer only comfort and thinking maybe you'd finally realized that *I* was the girl for you all along."

"Mina, I—"

Severing our connection, her hands come up and she shakes her head. "But there's a difference between liking someone you think you know and loving someone who matches you in every way." She snaps her gaze up to mine. "*You* match me, Nick, like no one else. And I'm so sorry for letting lifelong insecurities get in the way of us. I let three little words, that have always come with conditions, influence my reaction. I'll never forgive myself for letting you think, even for one second, that I don't adore you. That I don't wake up every morning and wonder if I'll see you or if you'll make fun of me for having pom-poms on my snow boots."

"Koukla," I rasp, emotion clogging my throat, "I'm gonna be makin' fun of those pom-poms of yours until we're old and gray."

"I hope that's a promise."

For the first time in my life, words fail me. I stand there, mute, my heart on a platter—and she knows it.

"Hold on," she whispers, leaning over the back of the sofa to reach for something. My gaze unapologetically slips down to her heart-shaped ass in those baggy sweats before meandering north again in time to see her pulling an object out of her purse. If I'm not mistaken, it's antler bone. The frame is sleek, not bulky, and then she grazes her finger over the back end and a blade pops free. A small, shy smile curls her mouth. "I bought this at the outdoor store in Bethel when you went to the bathroom. The owner told me this one is the best for whittling wood, and I . . ." She snaps the blade shut. Then, with hesitation gripping her features, she hands me the pocketknife, handle first. "I wanted you to think of me while you worked."

Heart racing, I study the face I've known for years—this woman, my sister's best friend, who can obliterate every wall just by saying my name. I skim my thumb over the inlay of the whittling knife. It's a stunning piece of work with detailed carvings bordering each side of the silver blade. The fact that it was Mina who thought to get it for me? "I love it, *koukla*. Thank you." I squeeze it once, feeling the weight and texture of the bone, before slipping it into my jeans. "It's my turn now."

Her nod is clipped.

Christ, man, do not *cry.*

I summon up every bit of self-control that I've got in the reserves. "I'm gonna put this as eloquently as possible—I've never been one for pigeonholing people, Ermione. I don't give a fuck if you're all Greek or half-Greek, if you speak the language fluently or only know how to properly curse me out." Eliminating the last remaining inches between us, I spear my hands through her wild hair. I love that it's untamed and curly and impulsive today. Tipping her head back, my hands cupping the base of her skull, I meet her gaze. "Those things make up one small part of who you are, but they aren't what make me stop in my tracks and know that I'm one lucky son of a gun."

Closing my eyes, I brush my mouth over her forehead. "I love how you go for what you want at full-speed. I love that you've got dreams—big dreams—and you reach for them with all that you are." I kiss my way down to her cheek, then over to the shell of her ear, which I nip gently. "But, selfishly, I love that you make me feel *alive*. You challenge me. You push me to step out of my shell when I've spent years keepin' everyone at arm's length." My mouth glides to the right, to hover over hers, and I flick my gaze up to look her in the eye. "I'm done playing at temporary longings, *agape mou*. I want *you*, in my life, by my side, in my bed—and I'm gonna push a hard bargain, Mina, because I want you forever."

A fat tear rolls down her cheek that I catch with the pad of my thumb. "*S'agapo*," I confess roughly, "and you can take all the time you need to say it back—"

Mina hooks her hands at the base of my neck and yanks me down, my mouth colliding with hers. She kisses me the way she lives her life: bold, reckless, impulsive. Her tongue tangles with mine. Her fingers, rebels that they are, reach down to hook into the loops of my jeans. Her hold on me keeps her steady on her toes, especially when she tears away, panting heavily, and gifts me with the brightest smile I've ever seen. "I love you, too, Nick. And thank you."

My hands palm the curve of her ass. "For what?"

That smile of hers wavers, a show of sweet vulnerability, and then she whispers, "For making me feel like I'm finally home."

Ah, *gamóto*.

I crane my neck back, staring up at the ceiling, and do my fair share of blinking.

"Are you *crying?*" Mina demands, tugging on my shirt.

"*Óxi.*" *Fuck, man, make them disappear.* I squeeze my eyes shut, then press my tongue to the roof of my mouth—only for gentle hands to clasp either side of my face and make me look down, so that all I see is her.

"You're such a romantic, Nick." Though her tone is teasing, she uses the fabric of her sleeves to press to my closed lids. I feel her rise up on her tiptoes before soft lips kiss the underside of my jaw. "*S'agapo.* You can cry all you want and that's not gonna change. I know you're a man's man deep down inside."

I laugh, the sound gruff. She's busting my balls again, and I wouldn't change a damn thing about it. Hauling her up against me, my hands cupping her ass, I crash my mouth down over hers. The kiss is frantic, needy, and she gasps against my mouth as I stalk her backward until the backs of her thighs are colliding with the sofa and I'm lifting her up, propping her on top of it, and spreading her legs so I step in close. Her fingers push at my sweatshirt, tugging it off and —*fuck, yes.*

The fabric goes beneath her ass. "So Effie won't kill us if we get messy," I mutter, reining in laughter when Mina's eyes fly to meet mine.

"She'll kill us anyway."

"Payback," I mutter against the column of her throat, peppering her with light kisses. "For that one time I went to see Sarah at her office and found her and my sister hooking up."

Mina's throaty laughter sends a shiver curling down my spine. She hooks her legs around my waist, squeezing tightly. "Camping trip, 2015. I woke up in the same tent as them, only to hear noises that I would *kill* to forget."

"Sex noises?"

"Oh, yeah."

The heel of my palm gently collides with her shoulder, tipping her weight until she's falling onto the cushions themselves. She giggles—*giggles*—at my foul play as I hop over the back of the sofa, but it doesn't stop her hands from fumbling with the button of my jeans as soon as I crawl over her. Dipping low, I kiss the underside of her jaw. "It's only right that we break the house rules."

"Nick Stamos breaking rules?" Her hands come down to help me push my jeans down the length of my legs. "What's the world coming to?"

I drop to my haunches on the floor, then swiftly strip off her sweats. "I fell in love, Ermione." I kiss her inner thigh. Sweep my nose along the tendon leading to the apex of her legs. "And I'm only willing to break the rules with you."

Her choked laughter only precedes her gripping my hair, keeping my face between her legs. "We're totally going to be cleaning up the couch when we're done, aren't we?"

My thumb traces the elastic band of her underwear. They're pink, high-waisted, and not anywhere close to resembling sexy lingerie. But on the woman wearing them, they might as well be the hottest scrap of fabric I've ever seen. "Oh, yeah," I finally murmur back, boldly tracing my thumb over the damp spot not even the pink material can disguise. "Fabric cleaner. Putting the cushions through the wash. The whole nine yards." Her legs quiver, and I press a palm to her inner thigh to spread them wider. "She'll never have to know."

Mina's chuckle turns into a moan when I drop my head

and kiss her, right over where she needs me most. "I love you."

I glance up, staring past the line of her underwear, over her sweatshirt, and up to her beautiful face. "Say it again."

Her fingers curl into my hair, tugging hard on the strands. "I love you," she whispers, her hips churning upward, desire written in her every move. With glassy eyes, she lifts her head to meet my gaze. "I love you. I love you."

God, yes.

Hooking a finger under the fabric of her panties, I pull them to the side and inhale sharply. "You're mine, *koukla*," I growl, right before I press my tongue to her clit. Her whole body shudders, her knees clamping inward, her nails scraping my scalp. I don't ease up on the pressure, not once. Not when she begs for me to fuck her, not when she strains to lift her hips. I plant a forearm over her pelvis, keeping her locked into place, and then use two fingers to hold her folds open.

"*Nick*." Her body trembles as I suck on the hood of her sex. "*Please*." A low, keen moan rumbles in her chest as I plunge a finger deep in her pussy. I work her in tandem, my finger thrusting, my tongue flicking, until she's so far gone that I doubt she even realizes that she's crying out. "Oh, yes! I love you. Please, I need . . ."

Need claws at my body. The need to fuck her. The need to kiss her lips and then again, but this time right over that sensitive spot of hers, where her shoulder and neck meet. She writhes against my mouth, and still I don't let up. A second finger joins the first, and I curl them together, listening avidly for the hitch in her breath. She gives it, her hands leaving my head to grip the throw pillows behind her as her back bows and her mouth parts on one of her sexy whimpers. Desperation tugs low at my spine, and I pull back only long enough to grip my cock in my hand. Give it a slow pump, twisting at the crown. The second sweep up my length is faster, tighter. My fingers bite into Mina's thigh, and I know she'll have bruises tomorrow. But, still, I can't stop. Not my gaze from landing on her flushed face, not my hand from jerking my shaft like I'm some fifteen-year-old faced with his first *Playboy*.

"Are you touching yourself?"

At Mina's soft question, I let out a deep groan. "I'm so hot for you."

The cushions squeak as she sits up with her hands on my shoulders, her legs on either side of my torso as I continue to kneel on the floor. Under her watch, my hips move on their own accord, meeting my closed fist again and again.

Until it's me being pushed to my ass and Mina who's crawling up my body. She cups my balls, tugging gently, and kisses the crown of my cock. Her pink lips sink down, taking me inch by inch. Her cheeks hollow with each downward glide of her mouth, that wild, curly hair fanning around her face like a halo.

Having sex in my sister's condo isn't exactly the most appropriate or romantic of places, but I don't think she cares. I pull Mina's sweatshirt over her head, feeling a momentary bout of surprise that she's not wearing a bra. "I want to touch you," I say, raggedly, fisting her hair and tugging backward. It's either that or blow my load too early, and there's not a chance in hell that we're not finishing this together. Literally. "I want you to know that all of me is yours."

Her lips tremble, her hands finding my hips. She scrambles up to the sofa, then crooks a finger at me to join her. I do so with my chest feeling light even though I'm wound so tight I could burst on the spot.

Hands on either side of her hips, planted down on the cushions, I line up my cock with her entrance. I meet her gaze, see the heat and the love mingling there. "You were meant for me, Ermione."

And then I drive forward, pushing tight into her pussy, and her legs around my hips turn to steel and her lips part in a silent cry. She's so goddamn wet, so goddamn tight. My legs quiver, the one planted on the floor for leverage downright shaking. I'm already so close to coming.

"Hold on to me, *koukla*." My voice is pure grit.

So, she does. She clings to my shoulders as I thrust, nails biting into my skin and marking me as hers. Blood roars in my head, stripping the periphery of my vision until all I see is *her*. Her honey eyes blazing with passion. Her small, perky tits bouncing with the force of my hips slamming into hers. Her chest arching upward as I piston my hips forward.

In and out, in and out.

"I love you," I rasp in English.

"*S'agapo*," she whispers in Greek.

I drop my head, and—as she once put it so eloquently—do business. I change my angle, my hips moving faster, more urgently. I kiss that favorite spot of hers, my fingers gripping the armrest behind her head. Her palms find the expanse of my back, gliding down to curve over my ass. She meets me thrust for thrust, and heat builds at the base of my spine. Desperate to see her come before me, I lift my chest far enough to skate my hand between us. I circle her clit, pressure increasing, and—*fuck, yes*—her hips spasm as she cries out my name. Her walls tighten around my cock, and it's over right then and there. I follow her over the edge, hips pistoning fast and insistent as I spill myself inside her.

Only when I'm thinking somewhat clearly, my chest sticky against hers, do I ask, "Did you see the mural?"

Her voice breathless, Mina quirks a brow. "What mural?"

I hum a little in my chest, and thank God that somehow Mina, who always notices *everything*, failed to look up in her own salon. I like to think of it as divine intervention because for the last month since the thought occurred to me, I wanted to be there when she finally saw what I had painted for her.

"We're taking a little trip." Patting her hip, I pull out of her and reach for my shorts. "Bathroom, clean up so Effie doesn't murder us, and then we're going to *Agape*."

"To *Agape*?" she echoes.

But she does what I say anyway, no questions asked. Because she trusts me.

I smile during the entire ride over to Cambridge. We leave my car behind and take Mina's, and I playfully threaten that if she doesn't like what I have to show her, that she can't just leave me hanging with no way back to Effie's.

She quirks her lips and flashes that sultry smile and even though she has coffee on her sweatshirt and she's wearing two different-colored sneakers, I can't help but say, "You're gorgeous, *koukla*."

With a blush staining her cheeks, I pull her car into a parking spot. My heart goes fucking wild in my chest as Mina cracks open her door and steps outside. I follow behind her, content to let her lead. Throwing me a small smile over her shoulder, she unlocks the front door and crosses over the threshold.

After a month of renovations, *Agape* looks ready for business. Beautiful slate floors, that mauve color she loved so much coating the walls, silver-embossed mirrors seated at every work station. It's edgy and elegant and the physical manifestation of Mina's personality.

I pause just inside, shutting the door behind me. And then I wait.

I watch as Mina tips her head back to stare up at the painted sky now spanning the length of the room. I watch as she balls a fist and presses it to her lips. She turns in a small circle, her gaze locked up above, and I try to see the mural as she does now.

Closer to the door, the ceiling is dusted with white, fluffy clouds and baby blues. Farther down, toward the back end of *Agape*, the white becomes the pinks and reds and oranges of a sunset, until finally the dark, midnight blue of nighttime. Stars twinkle to life, but they don't remain isolated in just the night portion of the mural—they're painted throughout the entire piece, hidden within the clouds and scattered among the bright blue sky.

Without the night there are no stars.

Except that this mural proves that there are.

"When?" she whispers, her closed fist falling to her chest. "Did you . . .?"

"Paint this?" I laugh. "Nah, I wish I had this sort of talent. But I have a friend who might as well be a modern-day Picasso. I sketched out what I wanted, and he made it happen."

"And he did this while we were in Maine?"

"Yeah."

I hear her choked sob a second before she launches herself at my chest. Her arms loop around my back, and I don't mistake the kiss that she gives to my ribcage, right over my new tattoo. She squeezes me, hugging me tightly. "I'm in the mood for a dance."

My heart skips a beat. "*Naí?*"

"Yeah." She glances up, tears coating her dark lashes, happiness swimming in those honey eyes of hers. "A dance like on prom night—but this one can be under the stars."

My hands find the dip in her back, and I pull her flush against me. "I'm thinkin' this one should end on a kiss."

So, we dance. In the middle of her salon, in the middle of the day, underneath a painted mural of sunsets and stars that peek out through the clouds. I hold her tightly, spinning her around to the music no one else can hear. I catch our reflection in the mirrors.

My work jeans and messy, curly hair.

Her mismatched shoes and bare, beautiful face.

"Nick?"

My hands skim the curves of her body as I prop my chin on the top of her head. "Yeah, *agape mou?*"

She smiles up at me. "I was always yours."

I kiss her fully, then brush her hair to the side so I can trace a pair of soaring wings. It took me a trip to the altar and one stint on a bat-shit-crazy reality show to see it, but this I know to the bottom of my heart: "I'm hopelessly, recklessly, in love with you."

40

MINA

TWO WEEKS LATER

"I don't know if I can do this."

Beside me, my boyfriend—*boyfriend!*—leans forward to knock on the wooden door to my parents' house. "You can do this. Deep breaths, remember? I know you've got this."

My heart gives a swift, *I'm-so-lucky-to-have-this-man* kick in my chest. "You have such faith in me."

Nick gives a low, sultry laugh. "Always, *koukla*. I wouldn't let just anyone pick out ink for me, you know."

"You mean you weren't pleased that I strayed from the arrow pointing to your dick?"

A masculine hand circles my waist and squeezes me tight. "So long as you're the only one to know that it's there, I'd be fine with—"

The door swings open and I stifle the panic rising within me. It's not my mom who stands there but my dad—my *adoptive* father, anyway—and I don't miss the way he looks from me to Nick, curiosity furrowing his already craggy features.

For years, I've let this man ruin not only how I react to life but how I look at *myself*. I can't do that anymore. And I won't allow either him or my mom to drown me in their never-ending fight. If they want to hash it out with each other for the next sixty years, that's on them. But I want to *live,* and I'm tired of letting their shame hang over my head.

"Ermione," my dad grumbles, his expression neither pleased nor upset to see me back on his doorstep, considering I moved all my stuff out two weekends ago. I can't say that my apartment is homey, especially in comparison to Nick's humble abode, but it works for now. Until *Agape* is up and running, I want to stay close to the salon and put out the fires as they come. But I'm lucky—because Nick knows what it takes to kickstart a business, and rather than asking me to move in with him, he's effectively moved all of his stuff into my place instead. It's small and cramped, and every time he takes to the stairs, I know he sees his life flash before his eyes, but he never complains.

And, boy, do I love him for it.

Turning my attention back to Yianni Pappas, I note his impassive demeanor and the surly tilt to his mouth. I don't know how I ever managed to think he and Nick were ever alike, and the point is hammered home when *Baba* snaps, "What are you doing here?"

The words fire at me in Greek, and I tip my head back to meet his green eyes. "I need to have a little chat with you and Mama. Is she home?"

He steps back, begrudgingly inviting me in. "In the kitchen."

"Great!"

I storm past him, not bothering to pause and give him a hug. I learned many moons ago that hugging Yianni Pappas is like trying to hug a rattlesnake. He rejects affection the way my body rejects latex leggings; though I'll admit that, for the sake of fashion, I've stuffed myself in a pair or two over the years anyway.

Nick follows behind me, one hand rooted to the small of my back. He's the one who convinced me to come today. No matter how many times I tried to play devil's advocate and count all the ways confronting my parents was a bad idea, he quashed each one into the ground with the heel of his massive boot. He was right, of course. I can't move forward with us until I settle the past with them.

I throw a *thank-you* glance over my shoulder, to which he only mouths, *You can do this. I love you.*

Funny how the admission coming from his pillow-soft lips doesn't make me want to run—not anymore. He's my rock, my best friend, and I mouth back, *S'agapo.*

I square off my shoulders, then cut the corner into the kitchen. Immediately, I spot my mom standing near the kitchen island, a glass of champagne in hand while she flips through some magazine. She looks elegant and poised and I shove away the long-time hurt that she's so obsessed with the *image* of the perfect Greek family that she can't see that she's lost us all. Me, Katya, Dimitri.

"Ermione," she exclaims when she spots me. Her gaze tracks over to Nick, and though her smile falters at the sight of him, she's quick to recover. "And *Niko, agori mou,* how good to see you."

At the "my boy," Nick grumbles something beneath his breath. Not for a second do I think it's complimentary. He's not the biggest fan of *Kyrie* and *Kyria* Pappas. Then again, to be fair, it's tough to see the good in vultures when you've got Aleka and George Stamos in your corner. Even Nick's *yiayia* has softened toward me, though I know it's only because she wants grandbabies and lots of them.

Slowly, my dad moves to stand beside Mama. His hand on her shoulder, the way he curls his fingers in—that possessive incline to his chin that's so very *him.* "Do you need to come back home, Ermione?" he asks.

Never.

"*Óxi*." My voice is clear, succinct. "I came here to tell you that I'm done with your games." I turn to my mother. "I've spent years wondering who my real dad is." She gasps—no doubt shocked I'd mention any of this in front of Nick, a "stranger" to our home. She'll get over it, just as how I had to get over the prospect of ever waking up to discover that my parents are sweet, caring, *loving*. Our realities are much more cut and dry: *she* slept around on her husband and I'm the result. "I've spent years feeling chained to this idea of who I should be, because you and *Baba* force-fed me toxic ideologies since I was a kid."

"Ermione," my mom starts, finally putting down the champagne, "*mipos theloume—*"

"No. I don't *care* what you two only want—it matters what *I* want. And as my parents, you should encourage me. Boost me up. Take pride in the fact that your baby girl, your *daughter*, has her own salon, runs her own business, and she's done it all on her own." Nick's hand falls from my back as I step forward. Confidence kicks up my chin and clenches my hands into fists. "It is *not* okay for you two to make me feel stupid. Better yet, you shouldn't *tell* me I'm stupid either. It's not okay."

My dad barks out my name, like the drill sergeant he's never been. "You will not speak to us this way, Ermione."

Pity pushes aside the anger streaming through my veins. "Respect is earned, *Baba*, not given with blind loyalty—and neither of you deserve mine."

"Do you speak back because I will not say who your father is?" It's my mom who utters this, and I wish—oh, I wish—she looked anything more than frustrated right now. A hint of compassion would ease the burn. A show of affection to me, her eldest, would erase the need to be done with them both . . . or at least it would make me think again about severing all ties. "Is that what you want?" she demands, this time in Greek.

Ten years ago I would have said yes.

A month ago I would have said *yes*.

But as my heart races, I hear myself say, "It doesn't matter what I want, does it? You won't tell me and I'm tired of asking. It's your secret to keep but *I'm* tired of feeling like a secret too."

Mama's expression tightens, and her fingers begin to tap on the magazine. Her eyes dart to my father, and then fall to the kitchen island. Alarm bells sound off in my head at the tension I spot in the line of her trim frame. But it's those tapping fingers, exactly the same nervous twitch of my own, that hold my attention.

"Mama?" I ask, my hands down at my sides.

"Yianni, I need you to leave the room."

My father's face turns a blusterous red. "*Óxi.*"

It's all he says, and my mom physically shrinks into herself. Her shoulders round and her olive skin pales and the tapping increases speed. "Yianni, *now*."

It's the first time in my life I've ever seen her stand up to him, this man who isn't my biological father and doesn't even deserve the right to be my adoptive one either. He doesn't move a muscle, not until Nick steps forward.

They exchange words in Greek that I fail to interpret quickly enough, and then my dad is storming out of the kitchen. I don't expect him to leave, not completely, but either my mom doesn't care or she's itching to get whatever it is off her chest because her voice comes low and hurried.

"Prodromos."

One word. One word, and my knees buckle.

I expect to hit the floor but a pair of familiar, bulky arms catch me. They haul me upright, tugging me into a broad chest. I feel his heart hammering against my back. "Mama—"

"I will not say this all again, Ermione." Her face pinched, she casts a hasty glance toward the living room. "And he knows. I told him after Prodromos passed, and never once before. It was not . . . Your *theio*—your *father*—and I were, how do you say it? Together?" At my shallow nod, her lips flatten. "Only one time."

"But you said he was American!"

Her cheeks flush with color. "I lied, *koritsi mou*. Because I was ashamed of my cheating, and Yianni and I were only just married. We were . . . Prodromos was a kind man, Ermione. A gentle, funny man, and yet my parents picked his brother instead for me. You know that our marriage was arranged."

My breath comes fast and swift, and I'm thankful to Nick because without him, I'd be flat on my ass in shock. "Did *Theio*—did Prodromos know . . . about me?"

Shame chases its way across her features. "*Óxi*, no."

I swallow, and it hurts. God, it *hurts*. All these years, I saw him, my real dad, and neither of us ever knew. He taught me how to ride a bike. He sat with me while I braided his hair and used butterfly clips to hold the dark, curly strands in place. I was the last person, outside of my grandparents, to sit with him in the hospital just before he passed. A drunk-driving accident—and not his fault.

I'm desperate for the rage to come. I'm desperate for anger to sharpen my tongue and say spiteful things. In the end, I only ask the one question that matters most: "Did you love him?"

Mama bows her head and her shoulders rise with a sharp breath. "I loved the idea of him, and I wanted . . . *Koritsi mou*, it is all I wanted for you to meet someone nice, someone who will treat you well and love you, someone who reminds me of . . . someone who reminds me of Prodromos." Her gaze tracks from me to Nick, as though wondering if I've found the nice, Greek boy she's always wanted for me. "I have not shown you the best love."

But I tried.

I hear those three words even though she doesn't say them out loud.

That's the thing about secrets: they fester and they ooze with toxins and they infect every person around them.

I'm done being infected, even if that means removing myself from the inner Pappas circle. *Except that you really* are *a Pappas.* The news of my birth is shocking, and yet somehow not shocking at all. I've always seen *Baba*'s controlling nature. I'm not sure why today of all days my mom thought it fit to finally tell me who my real father is.

And that's okay. *It has to be okay,* I repeat to myself.

"No," I finally say, "you haven't." Because it's clear to me that my mom is fighting demons that only she can battle. No matter how I was conceived, I'm *hers*. Mother or not, blood ties or not, I can't go down in the flames alongside her. As for *Theio* Prodromos, I'll mourn his loss when I'm back in the safety of my home. "I want you to know, Mama, that I'm thankful—because if it weren't for you, I wouldn't be me, and I *love* me." I reach blindly behind me, seeking Nick's hand. Relief swallows the restlessness as soon as our palms kiss, his heat engulfing me. "I hope, one day, that you might be willing to share that best kind of love with me. I'm always here to talk, even if . . . even if it's about *Baba*. You can be happy, Mama. You can be so much happier than you are now. And if you need me, I'll always listen."

Because that's what true families do: they forgive and they learn and they adjust.

I hope, one day, that my parents will realize that they've driven everyone away. Deep down, I wish that my mom will see that an arranged marriage can be unarranged. She's already given herself three decades to a mean bastard, but that doesn't mean he's entitled to another thirty years of her time.

Quietly, I tug on Nick's hand, our signal that it's time to go.

"I love you," he murmurs to me, "and I'm proud of you."

"Proud enough that you'll let me convince you to stay home for the rest of the day and watch *Lord of the Rings* with me?"

"One bowl of popcorn or two?"

I wink at him, feeling the broken pieces of my heart mold back together—because of him. "Is that even a question? *Two,* of course. So we have backup after we demolish the first."

We almost make it to the front door when I hear my mom shout, "Ermione, are you and Nick . . . *together*?"

I raise my gaze to the man himself. His pewter eyes glitter with good humor and love, and I'm pretty sure I've never felt so lucky in my life. "*Naí, Mama*. You told me to find myself a good, nice Greek boy, so I did. Only, he's not always so good and he's not always so nice, which means . . . he's my perfect match."

EPILOGUE

ONE MONTH LATER

Celebrity Tea Presents:
Is that an ENGAGEMENT RING on Mina Pappas' finger?

Dear Reader, it should come as no surprise that the Put A Ring On It *franchise is in meltdown mode. With the show about to begin airing on TV late next month (ahead of schedule by THREE months, mind you), it only makes sense that they want their contestants on lockdown. There are a few problems with this, the first being that runner-up and resident Adonis, Nick Stamos, has flashed the network the middle finger by not only proposing to his girlfriend, Mina Pappas, but by broadcasting it on social media.*

We've seen the ring, and I'll be the first one to say . . . it's pretty but not as glittery and obnoxious as I'd hoped? Set in rose gold, the marquis stone is made of amethyst. Small diamonds decorate the intricate band.

The gem's creator, a man who would like to remain anonymous, but who can be found in Bethel, Maine, of all places, told Celebrity Tea, "I think I remember them coming in! But, honestly, the shop is so busy in February, that I can't be too sure. As for the *price of the gem, I can't specify but I can tell you that nothing goes for more than $200 in my shop. I like to keep our prices low for the guests."*

So, there you have it. Not only has Stamos put a ring on Mina Pappas, but second runner-up Dominic DaSilva has issued a restraining order on a certain member of the press—not I, *dear reader—and Savannah Rose, America's darling, has retreated from the limelight completely.*

The tea has been spilled, Dear Reader, and I know that I'm just dying to know what will happen next.

EPILOGUE

NICK

One Year and Four Days Later . . .

"She's here, right?"

"Jesus Christ, Stamos, ask me that one more time and I'm going to introduce your pretty boy face to my meaty fist."

I don't bother to look up at Vince from where I'm studying my reflection in the floor-length mirror. My clammy hands make it difficult to pin the damn boutonniere to the lapel of my wedding tux, forcing my best friend to swat my hands aside so he can do the honors himself.

"You're sweating like a whore in church," he grumbles.

"Technically we *are* in a church." It's the same Greek Orthodox church as the one Brynn stood me up in. I wanted to go for another one, but Mina put her foot down. It's within this building's walls that we attended Greek school together for years. We danced yearly at the festivals and reeked of *gyros* and *souvlaki* when it was our turn to serve the food. It's the church we attended every Sunday for mass, our families sitting beside each other, while Effie sandwiched herself between me and Mina so we wouldn't kill each other. It's our heritage, and our community, and I'll be honest—I'm not one to tell my fiancée no.

In about thirty minutes, she'll be your wife.

I swallow past the nerves and avert my chin so Vince can work without poking me with the pin.

"Stamos, man," Billy says, "do you need some water or something?"

The group of them hover like mama birds: Bill, Mark, Vince, and Dominic DaSilva.

But it's my sister's voice that pulls me out of the funk. "Your *nifi* looks beautiful, Nick."

Nifi. Wife.

I turn to my sister and clear my throat before I make an utter fool of myself. "Aren't you supposed to be with Mina right now? You didn't leave her alone, did you?"

Effie laughs, punching me in the shoulder before pulling me into a hug. "Lord, you're a nervous wreck. She's with Ma and Katya right now. *Kyria* Pappas—am I still supposed to call her that, now that she's getting divorced?" Her nose scrunches. "Anyway, she's gathering up the flower girls and putting everyone in their place. She keeps popping in to check on Mina, though, and I'm pretty sure I saw her stuffing a box of tissues into that big ol' purse of hers."

Mina's relationship with her mother in the past year has been a slow progression. Weeks' long stretches of silence turned into short chats on the phone, before becoming dinners and "family" nights where she regularly comes over for a movie and some popcorn. It's not perfect, but it's been better since her mother asked Yianni Pappas to move out of the house. When he caused a commotion and the neighbors called the cops, Mina and her siblings laid down the law: either their mom dropped her unhealthy marriage or they would drop her.

The ultimatum worked, even though it'll be a test of strength for me to avoid beating the man's face in when I see him today. Mina issued his invitation, but on the strict condition that if he even attempted to talk to his almost-ex-wife, he'd be forcibly removed.

By me, apparently.

I can't say the thought doesn't leave a giddy smile on my face. After years of him making Mina feel like crap, I'd be more than happy to return the favor. Tenfold.

The *papas,* or priest, pops his head into the room. "Time to get in your places. Effie, Ermione is waiting for you in the limo. Dimitri, you too."

My sister plants a quick kiss on my cheek, and then she and Mina's brother hightail it out of the room. My best man —Vince, because the bastard would let no one else have the title—claps me on the back and announces, "Let's do this thing."

The last time I stood at the altar waiting for my bride, I was blindsided. But Brynn wasn't the girl for me. No, the woman of my dreams had been sitting front and center in the pews. She rescued me that night. And I like to think that even then, I knew Mina Pappas, the girl I've known since I was eight years old, would be the one to piece me back together again.

As I walk down the aisle, my groomsmen at my back, I look at the people in the pews who have come out to see Mina and I get married. Old classmates, including Sophia and her new husband, wave to me. She called us after our engagement, taking responsibility for our relationship in the first place because love was in the air in Maine. Mina and I let her believe it because it made her happy. I spot my mom and dad chatting it up with one of their old friends, but the second they spot me, their faces light up with such joy that I feel a rush of gratitude.

Their affection for each other showed me the kind of love I wanted more than anything, the kind of love I found with Mina.

Beside them, Sarah sits with her and Effie's adopted daughter, Thalia. She's three-years-old, more adorable than any little girl has the right to be, and has completely stolen the hearts of every single one of us in the family. Seeing Mina hold Thalia does all sorts of things to *my* heart—namely, I can't wait to see our own child in her arms someday soon.

My gaze bounces over the guests until I spot a familiar brunette seated in the third pew from the front. I wondered if she would come, and I'm glad that she did. I stop beside her, dropping low enough to murmur, "Mina's gonna want to meet you later. She holds you singularly responsible for me coming to my senses and realizing she was the perfect girl for me."

Savannah Rose tips her head back to meet my gaze. "I wouldn't miss it for the world."

I nod to the dark-haired guy sitting next to her, reaching out a hand. "Good to see you, man. It's been a while."

His smile isn't as wide as Savannah's, but I don't miss the humor in his dark gaze. "Same to you, Stamos. Now get up there and get married so I can stop reading about this shit in *Celebrity Tea*."

I bark out a laugh. "Jealous I'm stealing the limelight away from you?"

The crow's feet at the corners of his eyes crinkle, and I slap him on the back before squeezing Savannah Rose's arm. "See you two later."

With sure steps, I move to stand in my spot. Vince falls into place behind me, and the rest of my guys sit in the first pew. Although we could have had them stand up with us, Mina and I decided that we wanted to keep the ceremony small and intimate with Effie by her side and Vince by mine.

I scrub my hands over my pants, and keep my gaze locked on the doors leading into the *ecclesia*. Any moment now, my *nifi* will walk through them. I wait, heart in my throat, as the guests take their seats and the music begins to play. I wait, even as the doors swing open and I spot Mina's mom walking down the aisle with the flower girls.

Her smile is hesitant, her shoulders not quite squared off, but she holds her chin up high as she keeps her gaze locked on me and the priest. The guests murmur to themselves as she passes them, and then their murmuring gains momentum when she doesn't take a seat in the pews but steps up to my side instead.

Surprise grounds my feet to the floor.

"Everything okay?" I ask, my gaze snapping to the front doors of the church. "Is Mina—"

"She's fine, *Niko*. She loves you." She fumbles with her purse, reaching inside. "I wanted to give you something."

Now? I bite back the question. "Of course."

I catch a flash of gold that she presses into my palm. Harsh edges cut into my flesh, and then Mina's mom is talking fast, in Greek. "The cross belonged to Prodromos. I've kept it all these years." She reaches forward and pats my chest, pulling at the lapels of my tux. Her lips slip into a watery smile. "You are everything I wanted for my daughter. Kind, honorable. A good, Greek boy who will cherish her. Thank you, *Niko*, for loving my Ermione."

My jaw tightens as I swallow. Every guest is looking our way, but I give Mina's mother my full attention when I kiss her cheek, then kiss her other, as is the Greek way. "You don't need to thank me for loving her, *Kyria*."

She nods succinctly, like she's on the verge of tears. With another pat of her hand on my chest, she murmurs, "Give her the cross when you give her the ring. So she knows her father is here with her."

"I will."

I make the promise as Mina steps inside the church, and then there's nothing on my mind but her. She has Katya on one arm and Dimitri at the other, and Effie behind her. My heart races inside my chest, and I lose all hope of keeping my hands dry when I drag my gaze over Mina's wedding dress. It's lace with a low neckline and no straps, and her pink hair —that hue that I remember so damn well—is down and braided, resting on her collarbone.

The veil shields her face from me but I know, deep in my soul, that she's the most beautiful thing I've ever seen.

The four of them walk down the aisle, and when they reach me, Katya and Dimitri kiss their sister and sit down together in the first pew with their mother. Effie hangs back, fluffing her best friend's train, before moving to the left.

And then it's me and Mina.

I don't wait for the *papas* to tell me to hold off or wait. Impulse guides my fingers to the gossamer veil, and I lift it up, revealing the jut of her chin, and the full, burgundy-painted lips, and the crooked nose, and those damn honey-rimmed-with-amber eyes that are my undoing. Around her neck is a copper penny hooked on a delicate rose-gold chain —a new lucky penny, given to her by my mother shortly after Jake Rhodan plead guilty in court. Only the love of my life would get more excited about a penny than the hydrotherapy room I finally put in for her a few months back.

I wouldn't change a thing, lucky penny or not.

"Hey, you," I murmur as I tuck the veil back.

Her mouth purses to keep from laughing out loud. "You weren't supposed to do that yet."

"I'm not supposed to do this either, but I'm willing to

break every single rule—for you." I hook my arms around her lower back, her father's cross clasped in one hand, and drop my mouth to hers for a heady kiss. The guests roar with applause, clapping and whistling, and I hear one deep voice holler, "Can't you do anything right, Stamos?" I know that last one is Vince, the asshole.

"I love you," I whisper by Mina's ear, "and I didn't want to wait until the end of the ceremony to tell you that."

Her smile wobbles, and her cheeks burn with color, and then she pulls me back down for one more lingering kiss. "*S'agapo*, and anytime you want to stop a wedding for a kiss, I don't see any point in protesting."

We exchange our vows, our crowns perched on our heads, as is Greek tradition, the strip of satin connecting the crowns together as a symbol that we're now united, and then I turn to my best friend, my lover, and my confidante, and, yes, my sister's best friend, and press her father's cross into her palm. At the question in her gaze, I murmur, "A wedding gift from your mother. It was your dad's."

Tears well in her eyes, and she sneaks a glance at the pews, no doubt looking for the woman who birthed her. She mouths something I can't quite read from my angle, and then she's glancing back up at me, her heart in her eyes and her dark-painted lips pulled wide.

"I love you," she tells me softly. "I love you so damn much."

She's not supposed to curse in the church, but I'll always be down to break the rules with her. Gently, with purpose, I slip a rose-gold band onto her finger, nestled next to her engagement ring.

Nifi. Wife.

Sýzygos. Husband.

My hands are clammy and my heart is racing and there's no use denying it: call me a romantic, a pussy, a believer in the unicorn of all emotions—true love—but I found the real deal in a woman with pink hair and a big heart and an even bigger smile, and I'm holding on with both hands.

I lean down to brush my lips with hers. "I love you, too, *koukla*. Now and forever."

Thank you so much for taking a chance on Nick & Mina's love story! Need more of our favorite Greek couple? Visit my website at www.marialuis.org/hold-me-today to read all about their big, fat Greek wedding.

What To Read Next?

***Kiss Me Tonight (Put A Ring On It, #2)* featuring the one and only Dominic DaSilva** is now available.

Swipe right past the Greek Glossary for an exclusive excerpt of this hot and hilarious single mom/enemies-to-lovers romance!

GLOSSARY OF GREEK TERMS

- **Gamóto:** *(Gah-moh-toh). Translates to: "fuck."*
- **Óxi:** *(Och-i). Translates to: "no."*
- **Kyria:** *(Ke-re-a). Translates to: "Mrs."*
- **Kyrie:** *(Ke-re-eh). Translates to: "Mr."*
- **Malàka:** *(Ma-la-ka). Translates to: "idiot."*
- **Koukla mou:** *(Ku-kla moo). Translates to: "my doll."* *Koukla,* used alone, is only "doll."
- **Éla edó:** *(Eh-la e-do). Translates to: "come here."*
- **Naí:** *(Neh). Translates to: "yes."*
- **Filakia:** *(Fe-la-kia). Translates to: "kisses."*
- **Naí boreís:** *(Neh bo-rees). Translates to: "you can do this."*
- **Gynaíka:** *(Gee-ne-ka). Translates to: "woman."*
- **Tsutsuli:** *(Tsu-tsu-le). Translates to: "penis."*
- **Ellenitha:** *(El-le-ne-tha). Translates to: "a Greek." Similar to "American."*
- **Ómorfi:** *(O-mor-fe). Translates to: "beautiful."*
- ***Koritsi mou:*** (Ko-ri-tsi mou). *Translates to: "my daughter."*
- **Pandofla:** *(Pan-do-fla). Translates to: "slipper."*

- **Sýzygos:** *(See-zee-gos). Translates to: "husband."*
- **Nifi:** *(Nee-fee). Translates to: "wife."*
- **S'agapo:** *(Sa-ga-po). Translates to: "I love you."*
- **Adelphé:** *(A-del-fe). Translates to: "brother."*
- **Filinída:** *(Fe-le-ne-da). Translates to: "friend."*
- **Mipos theloume:** *(Me-pos The-lu-me). Translates to: "we only want."*

KISS ME TONIGHT TEASER

Kiss Me Tonight is now available! This is an enemies-to-lovers romance you don't want to miss!

ASPEN

My spine snaps straight with awareness as the stranger gets comfortable beside me.

I don't even have to look at him to know that he's massive in a way most men aren't.

So tall that he can sit at ease with one foot planted on the floor and the other languidly parked on my stool's footrest. *Who needs personal space nowadays, anyway?* Not me, apparently. His bent knee is flush with my left thigh, and it can't all be in my head—tipsy brain or not—that I catch him angling his big body to face me.

Like he's possibly intrigued by what I have to say.

Even though I don't know him from a hole in the wall.

Out of the corner of my eye, I watch as he flattens one hand on his thigh. Casual. Confident. No jittering knees—

guilty—or any sign of flushed cheeks. Also guilty. Thanks to the candlelight—and, admittedly, the beer goggles I've donned since round two—he's nothing but olive skin revealed by rolled-up sleeves, a hard jawline dusted with dark scruff, and the crooked bridge of his nose.

The black baseball hat he's sporting unfairly obscures the upper half of his face.

After taking a moment to flag down Shawn and order a Bud Light, he props one forearm up on the bar. Then the distressed bill of his hat—not that store-bought frayed look, but honest-to-God tattered—swivels unerringly in my direction.

Oh, boy.

I blame the Guinness for the way my heart feels like it's trying out for *Fear Factor,* Adrenaline Edition.

Better to blame the beer than admit the truth: I don't remember the last time a man other than Rick paid me any attention.

Don't be weird. Act normal.

You can play it cool—

"Deserve what?" he asks again.

Here we go. I keep my gaze centered on the TV, where DaSilva is being carried off the field on a stretcher. "Having their tibia play peekaboo for the entire world to witness."

Shawn shoots me a reprimanding glance at the graphic visual I offer, then slicks the Bud Light across the bar with an indecipherable grumble.

Who's surprised when the stranger next to me catches the bottle with a cool flick of his wrist? Not me. He's got the confident vibes of an athlete—and the bulky size to match.

I turn a little.

Just in time to watch him grasp the glass neck with three fingers. Full lips, the bottom one plumper than the top. They wrap around the bottle's puckered mouth, then suck down the beer, his throat working smoothly.

Slow, precise movements.

For as Hulk-like as this guy is, he moves with a compelling grace.

Then he speaks again, and the idea of "grace" gets launched out the closest window.

"Happened to a guy I know. Hurt like a goddamn bitch." Another deceptively nonchalant draw from his beer. "Can't say anyone deserves a hit like that, asshole or not."

Rough around the edges.

Gravel-pitched voice.

Clearly, he's a fan of players like Dominic DaSilva, who retired from the league a few years ago. Much to Rick's delight.

My cheeks warm from the embarrassment of being overheard. "You say it like you're a hardcore fan."

His bottle hesitates midway down to his knee. "Of DaSilva?"

I nod.

"The guy's a goddamn legend." That full mouth of his ticks up in a lazy grin. "Asshole or not, he knows the game inside and out. You can't deny that."

Sure, I can't *deny* it. But knowing the game doesn't give him a free pass for everything he's done off the field. I mean, this is the same player who told my ex-husband that Rick could offer him all the pussy in the world, and DaSilva *still* wouldn't consider taking the Steelers up on their multi-million dollar offer.

I've read the email.

DaSilva didn't even bother to asterisk the heck out of the word pussy. Simply left it there—bold and brash and completely insolent. Just like him.

Feeling the Guinness-fueled adrenaline in my veins, I eagerly shift my weight to face the Hulk. Football has and will always be my kryptonite. Give me a chance to talk shop, and you'll be begging me to call it quits within the hour.

But this guy sat down next to me—his first mistake—and Topher *did* suggest I hang out with people my own age. My boy knows me too well. He also knows that his good-for-nothing dad preferred to pretend that his "dear wife" was way too busy to be included in Steelers business.

Oh, my wife? I can almost hear Rick say to any number of his peers. *Yeah, she couldn't make it out tonight. Too much on her plate, the dear thing. Now, how about we grab a drink at that strip club you mentioned last time I was in town?*

I'm not sure when Rick decided I was too much of a liability to bring around his fancy friends, but at this point in life, I don't give a damn. He can take his holier-than-thou attitude and shove it where the sun hasn't shined a day in his life, and I can . . .

Scrunching my nose, I survey the Hulk with a critical eye. Or as critical as it can be since I'm swaying ever so slightly and he's swaying right along with me. On second thought, pretty sure I'm actually the only one swaying. *Thank you, beer.* "How old are you?"

He barks out a startled laugh. "Legal." As if to prove it, he lifts the Bud Light and pointedly watches me as he takes a swig. "Does that count?"

Probably. As if I'm about to impart some big, crazy secret, I motion for him to meet me in the middle when I lean in close. "I told my son I'd come out tonight and get some adult conversation in. He thinks I need socializing."

Another slow pull of his beer, and like a moth to a flame, my attention drifts to the way his bottle reflects the TV's glowing screen. *Focus.* Nails scraping my pint glass, I look up at his face—or what's visible of it, at least.

Even though I can't see his eyes, I get the feeling that he's studying me shamelessly. Elbow planted on the bar, the bottle hovering millimeters away from his mouth. When the curve of his lips deepens into a smirk, like he can't help but find me amusing, I'm momentarily struck dumb.

"Socializing." He draws out the word on the cusp of a dry, masculine chuckle. "Well, in case you're concerned about corrupting a youngin', let me tell you a little secret . . ." Lowering the Bud Light to the bar, he shifts forward until his mouth brushes the sensitive shell of my ear and a shiver shimmies down my spine. "I don't have an innocent bone in my body."

My breath hitches. "Not even one?"

"You sound disappointed."

I blink. "Do I?"

"Nah, not even a little bit. But I don't regret lying." Warm lips graze my cheek. "You blush real pretty."

Oh. *Oh.*

I jerk back, nearly teetering off the bar stool. "Hold on." Tipsy me thinks it's a *grand* idea to lift my hands, palms up, despite the fact that I'm on the verge of going ass-down to the floor. "Are you *flirting* with me?"

As though he's used to putting up with the drunk and disorderly, he smoothly catches me with one of his mammoth-sized paws and hauls me upright. My naked bicep —thank you, universe, for creating tank tops—tingles at the warmth of his touch.

The physical connection lasts only seconds. One moment he's saving me from absolute humiliation and, in the next, he's sipping his beer again, cool as a cucumber. Slowly, he dips his chin.

Is he checking me out?

It certainly feels that way, especially when his chest inflates with a sudden intake of breath. In the year that I've officially re-entered singledom, I haven't given much thought to dating. I revel in going to bed and not worrying about slamming doors or living with a man who has no concept of kindness. I don't particularly miss sex, especially when my sex life with Rick dried up years ago.

He preferred the company of other women and, after the initial hurt of discovering my husband in bed with someone who was decidedly not me, I grew to treasure every moment that I didn't have to fake my orgasm for the sake of stroking his ego.

But I think . . . well, based on the way I'm squirming on my stool and sneaking peeks at this man's pouty mouth—to say nothing of the broad expanse of his shoulders or the hard pecs that stretch the fabric of his shirt—maybe I wouldn't mind flirting.

At least, I don't mind flirting with a guy like him. Whoever *he* is.

Finding a small seed of sexual confidence that has long lain dormant, I arch my brows and bait him for a response. *Is* he flirting with me? God, please let his answer be yes. "Well?" I ask boldly, going so far as to twirl a finger around a strand of my hair like the hot chick out of a romantic comedy instead of being, well, *me*.

"Old habits die hard."

Come again?

I'm blinking so fast, I'm half-convinced I've developed a sty in the five minutes since he sat down and interrupted my otherwise boring evening.

Quiet.

I meant my otherwise *quiet* evening.

Snapping my head to the side, I press my hand to my ear in disbelief. "I'm sorry. Did you just say *old habits die hard*?"

What. A. *Jerk*.

It's one thing to confess he's not attracted to me, and

another to go in for the *moment*—you know the one—the meaningful look, the throaty, sexy laughter that all but signals foreplay, orgasms, and expert make-out sessions—and play a game of takesy-backsies.

Takesy-backsies shouldn't even be *allowed* once you've spotted your first gray hair in your pubes. And I'm five in, ladies. *Five*. Maybe more. I wouldn't know, since I have my esthetician regularly wax the suckers out and call it a day.

Good*bye,* evil age reminders.

I reach for my clutch by my empty pint and pop it open. I'm fully prepared to drop cash on the bar for Shawn and get the hell out of dodge when the Hulk grunts out, "Look. Listen."

Hands clasped together, I turn to him, brows arched in expectation.

Unfortunately for him, I'm not in the habit of accepting casseroles in place of apologies like my mother.

I spent fourteen years kissing Rick's ass and I'll be damned if I do the same for a stranger. I don't care how muscular his arms are or that his chest is wide enough for me to curl up and take a nap alongside my nonexistent cat.

The Hulk hooks a finger in the collar of his black shirt. Then drops his hand to the bar, fingers closed in a fist. "Listen—"

"You said that already."

That tight fist unfurls until his fingers are digging into the mahogany bar, leaving me with the distinct impression that I'm poking a not-so-hibernating bear.

Bring it.

"You're cute," he says, like I should be grateful for the assessment. Like I'm not a woman closing in on forty with a teenage son and goddamn gray hairs threatening to sprout at any moment from my nether regions.

A puppy is cute.

A kid in kindergarten is cute.

I am *not*—

"Cute," he repeats with oblivious male arrogance, "but I'm not looking to pick anyone up tonight."

ꝏ

Buy or read Kiss Me Tonight via Kindle Unlimited now!

DEAR FABULOUS READER

Hi there! I so hope you enjoyed *Hold Me Today*, and if you are new to my books, welcome to the family!

In the back of all my books, I love to include a Dear Fabulous Reader section that talks about what locations from the book can be visited in real life or what sparked my inspiration for a particular plot point. (I like to think of it as the Extras on DVD's, LOL).

As always, we'll hit it up bullet-point style—enjoy!

- It seems only appropriate to first answer the question . . . why *Put A Ring On It*? I've been obsessed with *The Bachelor* franchise and its many spin-offs for years. Many amazing authors before me have centered their romances during the filming of the show, and I knew I wanted to focus on the "after." What happens when the contestants go home? What happens when footage gets leaked or someone falls in love while all of the world is watching—and expecting them to stay true to the "bachelor/bachelorette"? *That's* where all the juicy material really seemed to be, and naturally, I gravitated right to it! Expect many more shenanigans and *Celebrity Tea* reports ahead!

- Do you recall Mina's opening scene in the bathroom with Toula? Well, I'm here to disclose . . . that is from real life! When my god-sister got married, I was the one responsible for the dress holding, and I don't think I've ever laughed so hard in my life. There are pictures, but to protect the innocent (and to avoid her coming after me), it's best to keep those hidden. Even so, it was too funny to keep out of a book—so in it went!
- You may have noticed that this book is—ahem—very *Greek*. Many of my own experiences as a first-generation Greek-American bled into Mina's personality. Analyzing self-identity via a cultural lens has always fascinated me. My parents immigrated to the United States from Greece (my mom) and Portugal (my dad). Growing up, I may as well have been the poster-child for *My Big Fat Greek Wedding*. I learned Greek before I learned English, but I still remained out the "outside" with my peers, as I was, for a lack of a better term, a "mutt." Among the Greeks, I was the one with the Portuguese surname. Among the Portuguese (my dad did not enforce my brother and I learning the mother tongue), I was the one who couldn't speak the language. And among the Americans, I was that "other" one. You can quickly see how confusing, and impactful, this could all be to a kid's psyche! When writing *Hold Me Today*, I wanted to bring this cultural dissonance to light—but it's equally important to note that Mina's background is not

an experience isolated to Greeks. My hope was, and is, that we will all be able to see a little bit of ourselves in Ermione "Mina" Pappas, no matter your lineage or culture or upbringing. And hopefully you've learned a handful of Greek words to use, as well! (If someone asks how you know so many curse words, I plead innocent, LOL).

- Mina's dyslexia was inspired by a friend of mine who has dealt with it his entire life. Dyslexia comes in many levels and severities, but I chose to use his particular symptoms (strengths and weaknesses alike) as the foundation for Mina's. For me, her struggle with dyslexia is very much a physical manifestation/metaphor for the cultural clash she experiences within herself!
- Greek dating camp, anyone? Yes . . . this is *real*, at least it is where I grew up in Boston! My own lovely *yiayia* (grandmother) attempted to send me to it the summer before college. Was I still dating my high school (non-Greek) boyfriend at the time? Yes. Did I beg my mom to nip this plan in the bud? Oh, you better believe it! LOL. While my grandmother wanted me to find my very own "nice Greek boy" to marry, I put up the protest of my life and managed to escape a month-long summer camp guaranteed to find me a Greek spouse. When it came to writing *Hold Me Today*, there wasn't a chance in hell that I was leaving it out. Of course, I did put a fictional spin on it but I think Sophia approves. As for my grandmother, well, she's just holding out for grandbabies nowadays!
- If you visit Boston, you *must* take a small detour to the North End! This historical, Italian,

neighborhood is one of my favorite places in the city. The streets are narrow and winding, many lined with cobblestones. Copp's Hill (the stop on Effie's ghost tour) is an absolute must, as well! If you're in the mood for some Italian food, a ghost sighting or two, or just a jaunt around a beautiful area of town, then look no further!

- Oh, Bethel, Maine, how I adore you so. Like the North End, Bethel is another must-see place if you find yourself near the White Mountains in Maine. I visited over the fall of 2018 for my cousin's wedding, and many of the places there have been added to this book. It's as quaint, as New England, and as charming as portrayed in *Hold Me Today*. I loved it so much that (hint, hint) a future *Put A Ring On It* book will take place in Maine, as well. Can you guess who it might be? (Spoiler: he's an ex-football player!).
- Someone spending five-thousand dollars on French toast? While I was "researching" (I use this term loosely) for the craziest things people have ever spent their money on, you can imagine my surprise when I stumbled upon the treasure of all money-wasting treasures. You betcha—that mention of someone purchasing Justin Timberlake's eaten French toast off eBay? It's true! Naturally, I exaggerated the sum *just a little* (it's fiction, I had to!) and instead of a known celebrity I went with one of my Blades hockey boys. Either way, it's crazy, it's bonkers, and for that 19-year-old's sake, I sure hope the syrup was packaged on the side.

As always, there are many more but here is just a

sampling! If you're thinking . . . that seems rather fascinating and I want to know more, you are always so welcome to reach out! Pretty much, nothing makes me happier =)

Much love,

Maria

ACKNOWLEDGMENTS

I can't say thank you enough to everyone who helped make *Hold Me Today* what it is today. Of all my books, this one challenged me the most—and forced me to lean on my friends and team more than ever before!

Najla—you rock, girl! Thank you for not even batting an eye when I came (crawling) to you and asked that we recover the entire series before it had even released. I don't know what I did to deserve you, but you're stuck with me for life!

Kathy—Nick & Mina (and me) owe you everything. Thank you for pushing me to give this couple the HEA they truly deserved. Without you, *Hold Me Today* would not be the poignant romance I always envisioned it to be.

Brenda—I don't know what I would do without your friendship! Thank you—more than anything—for being my backbone when the doubts creep up.

Viper—no book could make it to editing without your eyes! I'm so glad to have met you, and I know that the latter half of this book thanks you *greatly* for your feedback!

Ratula—girl, I love you more than anything. Thank you

for reading and offering feedback as I wrote my heart out. Let's put it this way: Nick owes you his entire life, LOL.

Dawn and Tandy—you are the reason this book sparkles as it should!

Dani—I can't express how grateful I am that you took a chance on me. Thank you for believing in my work, and for giving me invaluable guidance! Nick and Mina thank you too =)

To my besties/family/awesome-sauce friends Tina, Sam, Terra, Jami, Amie, Jess, Joslyn, and to my girls in 30 Days to 60k and Indie AF, this author journey would be so much less exciting without you. Also, I'd probably never get anything done without you pushing me along.

To my VIPers and to all my friends in BBA, just know that every one of you has changed my life for the better. Also, without you, there's a good chance that the *Put A Ring On It* series would still be languishing away on my laptop! Thank you for wanting Owen's story, and thank you for still loving me when I decided to give you two other heroes before we get to Owen, LOL.

To my family, Greek and Portuguese, I adore each and everyone of you. And if you happen to see your name while reading this book, I plead the fifth in advance!

And, lastly, to you Dear Reader, for picking up this book and giving me a chance. Thank you for allowing me the chance to live my dream—my very own permanent longing —as a storyteller.

Much love,

Maria

ALSO BY MARIA LUIS

Nola Heart

Say You'll Be Mine

Take A Chance On Me

Dare You To Love Me

Tempt Me With Forever

Blades Hockey

Power Play

Sin Bin

Hat Trick

Body Check

Blood Duet

Sworn

Defied

Put A Ring On It

Hold Me Today

Kiss Me Tonight

Love Me Tomorrow

Broken Crown

Road To Fire

Sound of Madness

A New King

Freebies (available at www.marialuis.org)

Breathless (a Love Serial, #1)

Undeniable (a Love Serial, #2)

The First Fix

ABOUT THE AUTHOR

Maria Luis is the author of sexy contemporary romances.

Historian by day and romance novelist by night, Maria lives in New Orleans, and loves bringing the city's cultural flair into her books. When Maria isn't frantically typing with coffee in hand, she can be found binging on reality TV, going on adventures with her other half and two pups, or plotting her next flirty romance.

Stalk Maria in the Wild at the following!
Join Maria's Newsletter
Join Maria's Facebook Reader Group

Made in the USA
Columbia, SC
20 April 2022